The Cou...
Brid...

Dilly Court is the No. 1 *Sunday Times* bestselling author of over thirty-five novels. She grew up in North-East London and began her career in television, writing scripts for commercials. She is married with two grown-up children, four grandchildren and a beautiful great-granddaughter. Dilly now lives in Dorset on the Jurassic Coast with her husband.

To find out more about Dilly, please visit her website and her Facebook page:

www.dillycourt.com
 /DillyCourtAuthor

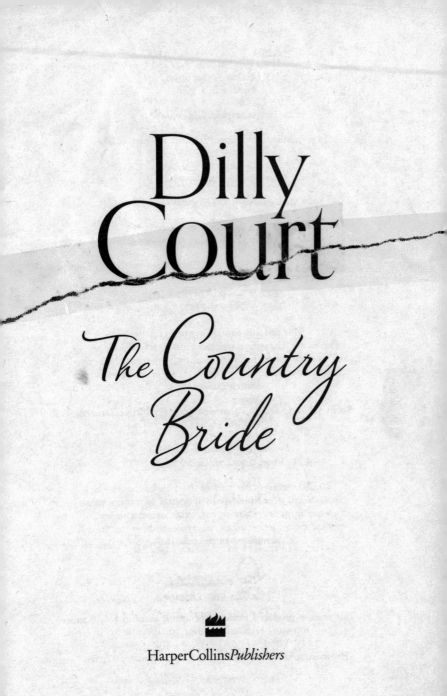

Dilly Court

The Country Bride

HarperCollins*Publishers*

HarperCollins*Publishers* Ltd
1 London Bridge Street,
London SE1 9GF

www.harpercollins.co.uk

First published by HarperCollins*Publishers* 2020
1

A catalogue record for this book is available from the British Library

ISBN: 978-0-00-828782-5 (HB)
ISBN: 978-0-00-828783-2 (B)

Set in Sabon Lt Std by Palimpsest Book Production Limited,
Falkirk, Stirlingshire

Printed and bound in the UK by
CPI Group (UK) Ltd, Croydon CR0 4YY

MIX
Paper from
responsible sources
FSC
www.fsc.org   FSC C007454

This book is produced from independently certified FSC™ paper
to ensure responsible forest management.

For more information visit: www.harpercollins.co.uk/green

For Ann Spivey

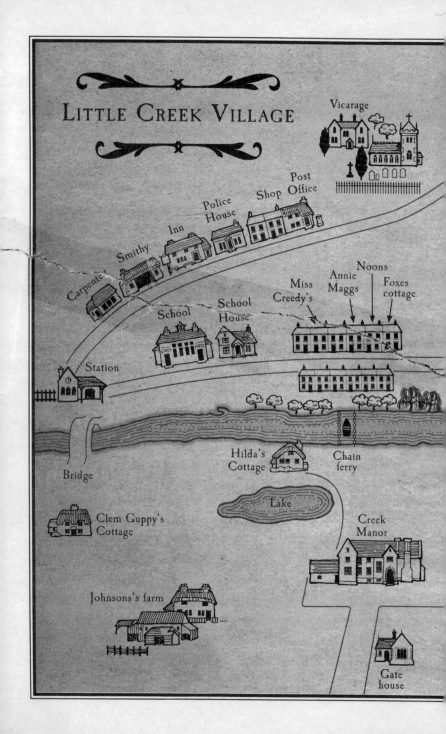

LITTLE CREEK VILLAGE

Vicarage

Post
Office

Shop

Police
House

Inn

Smithy

Carpenter

Noons

Annie
Maggs

Foxes
cottage

Miss
Creedy's

School

School
House

Station

Bridge

Hilda's
Cottage

Chain
ferry

Lake

Clem Guppy's
Cottage

Creek
Manor

Johnsons's farm

Gate
house

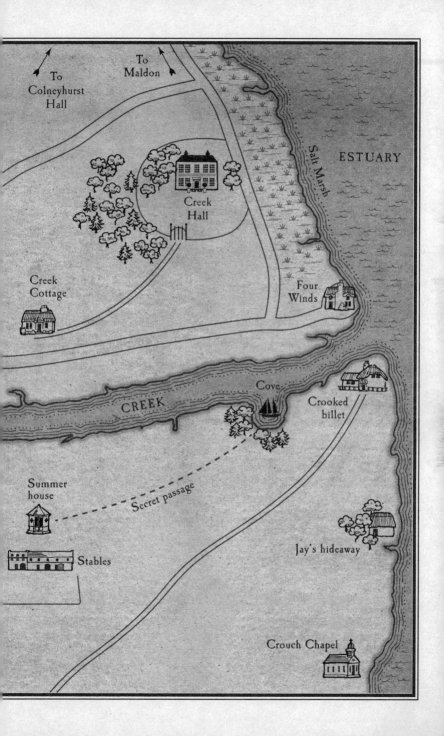

Chapter One

Creek Manor, Essex 1879

The old house seemed to have been awakened from a long sleep by the sound of children's laughter and the pitter-patter of scampering feet. Judy glanced anxiously at Mary Tattersall, who looked pale and tired as she sank down on the sofa, while the new parlour maid cleared up the debris left by Daisy Walters' boisterous young sons.

'Would you like me to make you a camomile tisane, Mrs Tattersall?' Judy asked gently.

Mary gave her a wan smile. 'No, thank you, Judy. I love Daisy's children, but they are exhausting. I'm always delighted to see them when she brings them over from Colneyhurst Hall, but it's a relief when she takes them home again.'

'They are very lively,' Judy conceded, smiling.

1

'To think that they might have been my grand-children.' Mary sighed and turned her head away. 'Jay not only cheated on Daisy and that other woman he married bigamously, he deceived me, his own mother, and that I find very hard to forgive.'

'Thank you, Lizzie.' Judy nodded to the maid, who had stacked a tray with the dirty crockery, half-eaten slices of bread and butter, and cake crumbs. 'That will be all for now.'

'Yes, Miss Begg.' Lizzie backed out of the door, narrowly missing collision with a young woman who rushed into the room, blonde curls falling loose to her shoulders, and her bonnet hanging over her arm.

'What have you forgotten, Molly?' Judy asked with a sigh. Her seventeen-year-old sister carried out her duties as nursemaid to Daisy Walters' children in a haphazard style all of her own. Scatterbrained and disorganised, Molly was disarmingly good-natured and extremely pretty – qualities that were guaranteed to make everyone forget her failings.

'I'm so sorry,' Molly said breathlessly. 'I forgot Master Henry's jacket.' She gazed round the room and her blue eyes lit up as she spotted the missing garment. 'There it is.' She pounced on it. 'I'd better hurry. They're waiting for me.' She left the room with a flurry of starched white petticoats.

'That girl gives me a headache,' Mary said feebly. 'She's exhausting.'

'She means well, ma'am.' Judy caught sight of herself in one of the gilt-framed mirrors that adorned the walls of the drawing room. The likeness between herself and her sister was striking, but Molly was the flighty one, who could get away with anything. Judy had always been the serious, responsible older sister. She raised her hand to smooth a stray curl that had dared to escape from the chignon at the back of her neck. 'I sometimes wish I was more like her.'

'You're fine as you are, my dear.' Mary fidgeted restlessly. 'I'm not very comfortable.'

Judy plumped up the cushions, and Mary leaned back, closing her eyes. 'Where's your mother, Judy?'

'She's in the study, ma'am. It's the end of the quarter and she's getting the household accounts ready for me to check before they go to Mrs Ralston.'

'I don't know what I'd do without her, or you, come to that, Judy. I've no head for figures and when Mrs Ralston finally retires, you will take over her position as housekeeper. That is, if you still wish to do so?'

Judy hesitated. To agree to such an offer at the age of twenty seemed like condemning herself to early middle age, but what alternative was there for a woman like herself? She could remember what life had been like in London when she was a small child. The smell of poverty, and the gnawing pangs of hunger were something she would never forget. Life had been so much better since Daisy, having witnessed the terrible street accident that had killed their father and crippled their mother, had brought Judy's small family to live at Creek Manor. They had nothing to complain about, although sometimes Judy found herself wondering what life would be like now if she returned to London. She had broadened her very basic education by reading as many of the books from the late squire's library as she could, and she had had the added bonus of sharing lessons with Mary's youngest son, Jack, who had been a somewhat unwilling student. They had been close friends since childhood, although she had seen little of him since he went away to the school that educated the sons of gentlemen and the ambitious middle classes. But that friendship had changed subtly last summer, and Jack's return to university had left Judy feeling bereft. She had been counting the days until his return. She came back to the present with a start, and realised that Mrs Tattersall was staring at her with a puzzled frown.

'You do want to stay on here, don't you, Judy?'

'Yes, of course, ma'am. This is my home and my family are here in Little Creek.'

'The position of housekeeper is a worthy occupation,' Mary insisted wearily. 'You could do a lot worse, and Ida Ralston is an excellent example.'

'Yes, ma'am.' Judy shifted from one foot to the other. They owed everything to the Tattersall family, but sometimes she longed to be free. There was a whole wide world out there, although her choices were limited, and she would either opt for a life in service, or marriage to one of the village boys she had known from childhood. Jack's friends Danny

Shipway and Alfie Green both vied for her attention on Sundays when everyone attended morning service, but she could never take them seriously. 'If that's all, ma'am, I'll go and check on the arrangements for Master Jack's return from university.'

Mary's face lit up with a smile. 'I can't wait to see him. I could never have imagined that my little Jackdaw would do me proud, and it's all thanks to Daisy's husband. I can never thank Marius enough for everything he's done for my son. Jack was born into poverty, but now he's a gentleman.'

'Yes, ma'am.' Judy had heard it all before, but she tried to look as if this was a revelation. 'May I be excused now, Mrs Tattersall?'

Mary raised herself to a more upright position. 'Not yet, Judy. I want a word with you before my son arrives. Sit down, please.'

Judy eyed her warily as she perched on the edge of a chair opposite the sofa. 'Have I done something wrong, ma'am?'

'No, of course not, my dear. It's just that things have changed since we first moved into Creek Manor. You were just a child then and we were all like one big family.'

'I'm sure we're very grateful for everything, ma'am.'

'I'm not asking for gratitude, Judy. But I'm neither blind nor insensitive. I know that you and Jack were always good companions, and I suspect that your friendship deepened into something more when he came home last summer.'

Judy felt the blood rush to her cheeks and she stared down at her clasped hands. 'Nothing untoward has ever occurred between us, madam.'

'I'm sure it hasn't, which is why I wanted to speak to you now. Jack will have to take over running the estate, because it's become too much for me, even with all the help I have had. Legally it all belongs to Jay, but I haven't heard from him since he left this house ten years ago, and I doubt if he'll ever return from Australia, so that means that to all intents and purposes Jack will be lord of the manor.'

'Yes, ma'am.'

'Do you understand what I'm saying, Judy?'

'Not exactly, ma'am.'

'This isn't easy because you're a sweet girl, and I'm fond of you, but Jack needs to marry a woman of good breeding, preferably someone with a decent dowry. The estate makes very little profit and the old house needs a good deal of renovation. Do I make myself clear?'

Judy bowed her head. Of course she knew all this to be true, and she should have been prepared for Mary's blunt statement of the facts, but facing the truth had hit her like a physical blow. 'I understand, ma'am.'

'I knew you would. Don't think this makes any difference to your position here, Judy. I value you more than you can imagine.'

Judy rose to her feet. 'I have work to do, if you'll excuse me, Mrs Tattersall.'

'Of course. What am I thinking of?' Mary sighed happily. 'I'll just rest my eyes for a few minutes before I go upstairs and change for dinner. We have to keep up the traditions of Creek Manor, after all, and with luck Jack will arrive soon.'

Judy left the room quietly. She had known all along that her position was tenuous, and her relationship with Jack was doomed from the start, but hearing it put into words had been the final blow. She stood for a moment, and took a deep breath before making her way to the study. One thing was certain: no one would ever know how deeply she had been hurt, although it was her own fault. She had allowed herself to dream, and that was fatal for a girl born in the East End slums.

She found her mother in the study, as expected, poring over an open ledger.

'Are you still at it, Ma?' Judy forced herself to sound normal, although her heart was still thudding away against her ribs and her knees felt weak.

'Nearly finished, dear. Has Daisy gone home?'

'Yes, and I'm not sorry. I love Daisy, but those boys of hers are tiny terrors. They've practically wrecked the drawing room and poor Mrs Tattersall is worn out.' Judy managed somehow to sound normal, knowing that her mother would spot the slightest tremor in her voice or a fleeting look of sadness.

'They're full of life, and Daisy adores them. I always knew she would be a good mother.'

'Yes, but she has Nanny Cummings and Molly to

look after the children. I had to take care of Molly, Pip and Nate when we were little because you and Pa had to go to work. I was left in charge when I was just a child, and it was hard.'

Hilda closed the ledger and turned to give her daughter a sympathetic smile. 'I know, dear. But things are different now. One day you'll have children of your own and you will give them a better life than we gave you.'

'I didn't mean that,' Daisy said hastily. 'It's just that Mrs Tattersall is convinced that I'm going to take over from Mrs Ralston when she retires. I'm young, Ma. I don't want to spend the rest of my life waiting on other people.'

'You're an extremely pretty girl, love. With your looks and charm you won't end up on the shelf.' Hilda put her head on one side, smiling. 'Danny and Alfie are always making excuses to see you, and that new young curate went out of his way to speak to you last Sunday. If he decides to stay in Little Creek I've no doubt he'll take over from Mr Peabody one day, and you could be the vicar's wife.'

The idea of taking over from Grace Peabody, who thought she was queen of Little Creek, made Judy smile. 'Thank you, Ma, but I don't think so.'

Hilda rose awkwardly to her feet. Although she managed well with the wooden leg, crafted for her by the village carpenter, the stump left after the amputation became inflamed if she put too much pressure on it, forcing her to rest.

'Don't look so worried, Judy. I did too much gardening yesterday and I'm paying for it today, but it will wear off.'

'You ought not to work so hard, Ma.' Judy knew only too well that her mother did not want sympathy, but sometimes it was necessary to remind her that she should take care of herself. Hilda Begg was a hard worker by anyone's standards, and the small cottage that Daisy had given them when she had run the estate was kept spotlessly clean. The garden produced enough fruit and vegetables to keep them going all year round, even allowing for the huge appetites that Pip and Nate brought home from the stables, where they were now employed. Jack had also worked there for a time, but that was before it was known that Mary's illegitimate elder son, Jay Tattersall, had married Daisy bigamously. Judy had only been ten at the time, but she remembered the hurt it had caused and the ensuing scandal, which had rocked the village. All these ghosts from the past had been resurrected by Mary's blunt words, and the names and faces whirled around in Judy's mind, shattering her hopes and dreams.

'Are you all right, dear?' Hilda asked anxiously. 'You're very pale.'

The sound of horses' hoofs and the grinding of carriage wheels on the gravel brought Judy abruptly back to the present.

'I'm fine, Ma.'

'That sounds as if Jack has come home. You'd better go and see if he needs anything, Judy.'

'Yes, Ma.' Judy made an effort to walk slowly, but her feet did not seem to be linked to her brain and she ran to the front entrance.

Jack Fox leaped down from the carriage, exchanging a cheerful greeting with James, the footman, who had been with the family for as long as Judy could remember. She stood at the top of the stone steps, smiling despite the pain in her heart.

'Judy, you're looking well.' Jack was at her side before she had a chance to back into the shadows of the great hall, and he was even taller and better-looking than when she had seen him in the summer. Was it her imagination or did his blue eyes dance with pleasure when he looked at her? Was he even more handsome than the pictures she carried of him in her heart? She lowered her gaze.

'Welcome home, sir.'

'Since when did you become so proper, Judy Begg?'

She met his amused gaze with a determined look. 'We aren't children now. You're the master of Creek Manor and I'm one of your servants.'

'That's nonsense and you know it. Nothing's changed, Judy. We're both older, and I hope a bit wiser than we used to be, but we're more than just good friends. I intend to marry you one day, but not yet.' Jack moved to one side as James came puffing up the steps carrying heavy luggage.

'You're wrong, Jack,' Judy said in a low voice. 'We can never be married.'

'Why not?' Jack caught her by the wrist as she was about to walk away. 'What's this all about?'

She gazed down at his slim fingers as they circled her slender arm like a band of steel. 'Let me go, please.'

'For heaven's sake!' Jack released her with an exclamation of annoyance. 'What sort of welcome home is this?'

'Your mother is coming.' The conversation with Mary was still fresh in her mind, and Judy prepared for flight.

'Thank you, Judy,' Mary said firmly. 'I hope you paid attention to what I said earlier.'

'Yes, ma'am.' Judy bobbed a curtsey and hurried off in the direction of the servants' quarters. She could hear Jack demanding an explanation, but she knew in her heart that his mother was right. A girl from her background could never aspire to mixing with the gentry, and although Jack had not been born to the position, in his brother's absence he would inherit the manor house and the estate together with all the responsibilities. Judy remembered only too well the struggle it had been for Daisy when Jay disappeared on their wedding day, and had left her to drag the estate back into profit after years of neglect by the old squire. There had been enough heartache and unhappiness in this house, and Judy was determined to avoid being caught up in the curse of Creek Manor.

She made her way to the kitchen to give Cook the good news that Master Jack had returned and there would be one more for dinner that evening. Nell Pearce had been Judy's friend since she was a child, and Nell had taught her how to make bread, cakes and tarts, as well as the basics of roasting meat and making savoury stews. The delicious aroma of cooking and the warmth from the great range had always made the kitchen a welcoming place. Nell was always patient, even when Judy had burned the meat pies, or when she had put salt in the gooseberry tart instead of sugar.

'What's up, love?' Nell eyed her curiously. 'Have you been crying?'

'No,' Judy said too quickly to sound convincing. 'I had something in my eye.'

'Sit down and I'll pour you a cup of tea. It's freshly made.' Nell bustled about fetching a cup from the dresser and filling it with the hot brew. 'Now then, the girls are too busy to pay any attention to what you're saying, so out with it, my duck.'

'It's nothing really, Nell.' Judy sipped her tea, giving herself time to think.

'Lizzie said that Madam was angry with you? Is that true, or did the silly girl get it wrong?'

'She wasn't angry. It was more of a warning. Mrs Tattersall thinks there is something going on between Master Jack and myself.'

Nell leaned her elbows on the table, giving Judy a searching look. 'And is there?'

'I'm fond of him, of course. We were friends when we were younger, but I know my place, Nell. He isn't for me.'

'But does he know that, love? I've known you both since you were nippers, and there was always something special between you two.'

'Maybe, but it has to end now and I've told him so.'

'Unless he's changed while he's been at university, the Jack Fox I know will do as he pleases, and the devil take the hindmost.'

'I know,' Judy said with a reluctant smile. 'That's why I think I should go away from here.'

'Oh, no, dear. Surely you don't have to run away? Master Jack might not remain at home for very long. He's young and he'll want to see a bit of the world before he settles down.'

'I suppose so,' Judy said doubtfully. 'Don't tell anyone what I've just said, Nell. I'm only thinking about leaving here if things become too difficult.'

'Then let's hope the young master listens to you, dear. Because, if he does, it will be the first time in his life he's taken notice of anything anyone's said to him.'

Later that evening, when Judy had finished work for the day, she set off through the park, heading towards the cottage that had been her home for the last ten years. It had been a squash in the old days when she had had to share a room with her mother and Molly, but now Molly lived in at Colneyhurst

Hall, and the boys had accommodation above the stables. For the first time in her life Judy had a room of her own, but that in itself was a source of worry. If she left Little Creek it would mean that her mother had to live alone, and although Hilda was perfectly capable of coping with her disability, it was always in the back of Judy's mind that Ma might take a tumble and lie helpless until someone missed her at the big house. She knew that her mother would laugh if she brought up the subject, and she would tell her not to be so silly, but still it was a concern, and one that bothered Judy.

The evenings were drawing out and the air was sweet and fresh with the scents of spring. It was a time of year that Judy had always loved, when everything was coming back to life after a long hard winter. She was listening to the birdsong and inhaling the scent of bluebells from the nearby woods, when she heard footsteps behind her and she came to a halt outside the cottage gate. She turned her head, although she knew instinctively who was following her.

'Judy, I must talk to you.' Jack was at her side in two long strides.

'There's nothing to say. Your mother made it very plain that you will look higher for a wife than a mere servant, and I know she's right.'

'I don't care what she says. I want to be with you always, Judy. I want us to be as we were last summer.'

She smiled, lifting her hand to touch his cheek. 'We were playing a game then. It wasn't real, Jack.'

He grabbed her hand and held it. 'I was serious.'

'There's no future for us.'

'You don't believe that and neither do I.'

'What do you want from me, Jack?'

He hesitated, frowning. 'What do you mean?'

'That's my point,' Judy said sadly. 'You want me to continue to be the companion I was when we were younger, with a little flirtation for added spice, with the prospect of marriage in the distant future. Well, it won't work. I have feelings, too. I can't turn them on and off to suit you.'

'I wouldn't do anything to hurt you, Judy. You know that.'

'Not deliberately,' she said, sighing. 'But you go your own way, and you always have. One day you'll have to face the fact that you're responsible for all this, and you'll need a wife who was born and bred to the life of the squire's lady, and preferably one with a generous dowry.'

'This is ridiculous. I haven't even considered marriage to an heiress. I need you, Judy. You're part of all this.' Jack encompassed the estate with a sweep of his arms. 'You're part of everything that's good – you're part of me.'

'You haven't listened to a word I've said.' Judy shivered as a cold wind whipped in from the east. 'It's getting late and I've had a long day. I'll see you in the morning.'

'I do care about you,' Jack said angrily. 'I'm not playing games.'

Judy stood on tiptoe to kiss him on the cheek. 'Good night, Jack.' The gate creaked on rusty hinges as she opened it and closed it behind her. She walked resolutely up the path and let herself into the cottage, but she did not look back. If she did, and saw Jack looking like a despondent schoolboy, she knew she would weaken. She had always been the first to give in after a quarrel, but not this time. She slammed the front door and leaned against it, closing her eyes in an attempt to blot out the vision of Jack's bewildered expression.

'Is that you, Judy?'

The sound of her mother's voice brought Judy back to her senses and she hurried into the kitchen. 'Yes, Ma.'

'I wasn't expecting you until later.'

'I'd done everything that needed doing, so I decided to finish early.'

'I've saved you some supper, Judy.'

'Thanks, but I'm not hungry.' The moment the words left her lips, Judy knew she had made a tactical error. Her mother's eyebrows shot up and her smile faded into a worried frown.

'Are you sickening for something? I'd better make you up a tonic.'

'No, thank you. I'm just tired, but I'll be fine in the morning.' Judy gave her mother a hug. 'I love you, Ma. Good night.'

* * *

For the next few days Judy was kept busy. Ida Ralston was still in charge of the household, but she had allowed Judy to take over some of her duties, which included organising the linen cupboard and making sure that the servants' uniforms were laundered and kept in pristine order. It was a peaceful task and Judy was painstaking in her attempts to list each and every item, and to ensure that mending was sent to the sewing room, where sheets were turned sides to middle if they had worn thin, and any garment that was torn was either darned or patched, as necessary. Mrs Ralston clearly intended that Judy would take over from her when she retired, but Judy was having ever more serious doubts as to her position in the house. Her relationship with Jack had been doomed from the start, even though it had begun innocently a year ago, but they were adults now and Jack seemed to think that they could simply carry on as before. Judy had managed to avoid him so far, and he had been kept busy with the constant flow of family visitors. His sister Dove, who was married to Dr Neville, brought her three children, two rowdy boys and her much quieter four-year-old daughter, to see their uncle. His other sister, Linnet, and her husband, Elliot Massey, the village schoolmaster, arrived with their eight-year-old son and their newborn baby girl, but Judy kept herself to herself and avoided close contact with the family.

*   *   *

It was late afternoon, a week after Jack's return home, and Judy was on her way to the sewing room with a pile of mending. Having climbed the stairs from the basement, she decided to take a shortcut through the great hall in order to use the servants' staircase on the far side of the house. It had been a particularly quiet day and there was no one about, not even James. Mrs Tattersall and Jack had left soon after breakfast when Fuller brought the carriage to the front entrance, and they set off for Colneyhurst to celebrate Daisy's eldest son's eighth birthday. They were not expected back until late evening, and with no family meals to prepare there had been a holiday atmosphere in the kitchen and servants' hall. Judy suspected that James had taken the opportunity to visit his current ladylove, who worked in the laundry room, and she smiled to herself. Tall and good-looking, and well aware of his physical attributes, James was a heartbreaker. Mrs Ralston warned each new female servant from the outset, but few of them took notice, and it never ended happily. Judy was of the opinion that it was James who ought to be sacked, but he was very clever at talking himself out of a difficult situation, and Mrs Tattersall was not immune to his charm.

Judy crossed the hall but the sound of horses' hoofs on the drive made her run to the window and she saw the carriage come to a halt outside. With her arms full of linen and no sign of the footman, she was at a loss until Molesworth appeared suddenly at her side.

'Put that down and be ready to take Madam's cape and bonnet. I'll have words with James when I find the lazy layabout.' Molesworth went to open the door and Judy placed the linen on a nearby chair.

Mary Tattersall was first to enter and she was clearly upset. She allowed Judy to take her outdoor things without seeming to notice that her footman and housemaid were not on duty.

'Poor little Timmy has gone down with chicken-pox. We stayed long enough to cut the birthday cake, but the boys were all out of sorts, so I decided it would be best if we came home.' Mary shrugged off her cape and handed it to Judy. 'You must tell Cook that there are two for dinner this evening, Judy. I'm going to the drawing room for a rest. It's been a very trying day.'

'Yes, madam.' Judy was about to do as she was asked when Jack strode into the hall.

'Judy. Where've you been hiding? I've been looking for you.'

She glanced anxiously at Molesworth, but he was otherwise occupied. 'You've been busy, sir.'

Jack caught her by the arm. 'Stop calling me "sir". I won't allow this offhand treatment to continue a minute longer. Put my mother's things down and come into the morning parlour. We'll sort this out for once and all.'

'Really, Jack! Why won't you listen to me?' Judy protested as he closed the parlour door with unneces-sary force.

'Because you're talking nonsense. I refuse to allow my mother to rule my life. I need you and I always have. We're cut from the same cloth, Judy.'

She shook her head. 'Oh, Jack! You know that's not true. You've managed without me all the time you were at boarding school and university, and I doubt if you missed me at all.'

He grasped both her hands. 'That's not true. Your letters brightened up the most miserable days when I was first sent away and homesick, even if you can't spell.'

'That's not fair. I was just a child,' she said, chuckling. Jack always had the power to make her laugh, and it weakened her defences.

'That's better. That's the Judy I know and love.'

She met his gaze with a startled gasp. 'You're fond of me. It's not love.'

'How do you know? Can you read my mind?'

'I used to, especially when you were planning some mischief with Alfie and Danny.'

'Don't push me away. I can't stand it.'

'Your mother won't allow us to be together in any way, friends or not. If I get the sack my mother will lose her cottage, and the boys will have to leave, too. I can't put their future in jeopardy. You must understand that.'

Jack gazed into her eyes, and then he pulled her roughly into his arms and kissed her long and hard on the lips. 'What's your answer now, Judy? I'm not joking. I want you with me always.'

Chapter Two

Judy moved away, giving herself time to think. The embrace had left her shaken, but wanting more, and that was even more disturbing.

'Answer me, please.' There was a note of desperation in Jack's voice, quite alien to his normal tone.

'I don't know what you want of me.' Judy met his intense gaze with a searching look.

'What is there to know, other than the fact that we were always together. I want that to continue. I'm not the type of man to be lord of the manor, any more than my brother, Jay. I won't renege on my responsibilities, but I need you to help me through all this.'

'Are you asking me to marry you?'

'Marriage? Of course I want that, but not just now. In a few years, maybe.'

'Oh, Jack. You know that's not good enough. I

don't want you to feel obliged to do anything. You either want us to be together always, or you don't.'

'That's exactly what I'm saying. I want you here with me.'

Judy shook her head. 'It wouldn't work. Life isn't a game of chance, Jack. You should listen to your mother. She has plenty to say on the subject, and I hate to admit it, but I think she's right.'

'What does my mother know about how I feel?' Jack demanded angrily. 'She has no right to interfere.'

'She loves you,' Judy said simply. 'From what I was told, your mother suffered greatly at the hands of the old squire, and her marriage to your father wasn't a particularly happy one.'

'That has nothing to do with us. I want things to be as they were.'

'That's not possible, and you know it.'

'I'm not asking anything of you other than to be here for me. I need you to keep me from doing stupid things, and I want to hear you laugh again.'

He looked so downcast that Judy was deeply touched and she moved closer, taking his hands in a warm grasp. 'You were always impatient.'

Jack drew her closer, but the door flew open and Hilda burst into the room. 'What's going on?'

'Nothing,' Judy said firmly. 'We were just talking.'

'Your mother wants a word with you, Master Jack.'

'Stop calling me that,' Jack said crossly. 'It makes me sound like a ten-year-old. Who told you we were in here, anyway?'

'It was Molesworth, if you must know. I was sent to fetch you and that's what I'm doing.' Hilda gave Judy a warning look. 'We'll talk about this later, my girl.'

'We've done nothing wrong,' Judy said tiredly.

Hilda turned to Jack and he held up his hands. 'All right, Hilda. I'll go and placate my mother, but only if you promise to leave Judy alone. This was my fault, not hers.'

Hilda opened her mouth to answer, but Judy laid her hand on her mother's arm. 'No, Ma. That's enough.' She sent Jack a warning glance and with obvious reluctance he left the room.

'You'll find yourself in trouble if you go on this way,' Hilda said warily. 'I don't want to interfere, Judy, but someone must tell you how things are.'

'What are you trying to say, Ma?'

'Remember what happened to Mary at the hands of the old squire,' Hilda said darkly. 'Times haven't changed that much. Jack is a man now, with a man's needs, and you are a servant in his house. Do you understand?'

'I think you insult both of us.' Judy walked to the door and opened it. 'I have things to do, but you can tell Mrs Tattersall that she need not worry about us. I won't fall into the same trap that she did.'

Her mother's words echoed in Judy's head as she went about her daily tasks, and when she went to bed that night she found it impossible to sleep.

Eventually, having tossed and turned for more than an hour, she went downstairs to make herself a cup of cocoa, using the remaining heat from the range to warm a pan of milk. As she sat at the kitchen table, sipping the comforting drink, Judy came to the inevitable conclusion: the time had come for her to leave Creek Manor. It would break her heart to be parted from all those she loved, especially Jack, but she could see no future for herself if she stayed at the manor house. It had been different when Jack was away at university, and she had looked forward eagerly to his return at the end of each term, but he had come home to take up his responsibilities as lord of the manor, he was now at home for good and the relationship he wanted would prove difficult, if not impossible.

Judy finished the cocoa and washed the cup and saucer before returning to her room. Her thoughts had clarified and she knew now what she must do.

At first light Judy was on the road to Colneyhurst and in less than an hour she was seated in the breakfast parlour, drinking coffee with Daisy, who was still wearing a silk wrapper over her lacy nightgown.

'So you see my problem,' Judy said, sighing. 'I love Jack, and I suppose I always have. I think he loves me, but there's no question of marriage and I don't trust myself to stay strong, if you know what I mean.'

Daisy nodded and her dark curls flopped over her

brow, only to be brushed away with an impatient hand. 'Of course I do. I think anyone who has ever been in love would understand, but I'm sure Jack wouldn't do anything to hurt you.'

'Not intentionally, but his mother wants him to marry someone much more suitable than I. No matter how much Jack pretends it's of no matter, he is the lord of the manor in his brother's absence.'

'If you're worried that Jack is like his half-brother, then don't be. Jay takes after the old squire and Jack's father was a good man at heart, even if he was a bully. Jack wouldn't chase after other women if you and he were to wed.'

'He doesn't want to commit himself to something so permanent, but if I stay at Creek Manor under his terms I would be living on a knife edge. Mrs Tattersall would sack me instantly if she discovered we were having a secret liaison.'

Daisy was silent for a moment as if considering the situation. 'Then you have no alternative,' she said slowly. 'I think you're right, Judy. You need to go away for a while. It will give you both time to think.'

'I was wondering if your brother, Dr Marshall, might need a servant,' Judy said hopefully. 'He was always so nice to me whenever I saw him, and so was his wife.'

'Minnie is the kindest person I know, and with boisterous five-year-old twins she might very well need help.' Daisy frowned thoughtfully. 'I tell you what, Judy. I'll write a letter to my brother and sister-in-law, and even if they don't need anyone, I'm sure they will help you find a suitable position. It's not as if you are a stranger to London. You were born there, after all.'

'And I lived there until I was nine,' Judy added, smiling ruefully. 'Although I wouldn't want to go back to Green Dragon Yard.'

'There's no question of that. I have a much better idea. I'll send a telegram to say that you're coming, and I'll write a note to Minnie, asking her to help you to find accommodation in London.' Daisy rose from her seat and went over to the sideboard where she took pen and paper from one of the drawers. She sat back at the table and began to write, while Judy sipped her coffee, feeling more positive than she had done since Jack's return home. She knew now what she must do, even though leaving Creek Manor and those she loved would break her heart.

Sidney Square was close to the London Hospital and not far from Mrs Wood's boarding house in Fieldgate Street. Daisy had told her amusing stories of the time she lodged there, although these were not uppermost in Judy's mind as she stepped down from the hansom cab outside the Marshalls' residence. She paid the cabby, picked up her carpet bag and crossed the pavement to knock on the door.

It was opened by a young maidservant, who stared at her blankly.

'Mrs Marshall is expecting me,' Judy said firmly.

The maid, who could not have been a day older than twelve, blinked, nodded and closed the door. Judy was left standing on the step, not knowing whether to knock again or to wait, but a couple of minutes later the door opened and Minnie Marshall greeted her with a smile.

'Come in, Judy. I'm sorry about that, but you'll have to forgive Sukey as she's only been with us for a few days.' Minnie stepped aside and ushered Judy into the narrow hallway. 'Come into the parlour and Sukey will bring us some refreshments. That's if she doesn't trip over the mat and drop the tray as she did earlier this morning.'

Judy placed her bag at the foot of the stairs, not knowing what else to do. The house was much smaller than she had imagined it to be, and she could hear children's voice coming from a room upstairs, followed by the deeper tones of their nanny.

'I hope I'm not inconveniencing you, Mrs Marshall,' Judy said anxiously.

'Not at all, my dear.' Minnie opened a door to her right and led the way into a small, but well-proportioned living room, which was furnished for comfort rather than elegance. Minnie sat down in a chair by the empty hearth, motioning Judy to follow suit. 'Daisy's telegram said you would be arriving today, and that you needed help to find a suitable position in London.'

Judy retrieved a wooden doll from the chair before taking a seat. She clutched it in her hands, holding on to it like a good luck charm. 'I'm afraid it was very short notice, but I had to get away. It was a rather difficult situation. Mrs Walters has written you a note.' Judy put the doll down and took the sealed letter from her reticule. She handed it to Minnie, who opened it and studied it intently.

'I understand, Judy. I expect we've all experienced times like that at one point or another in our lives. Would this have anything to do with Jack's return from university?'

Judy stared at her open-mouthed. 'How did you know that?'

'I didn't, but from the urgency of your departure I guessed it must be something of the sort, and it was always obvious that you two were close. Anyone could see that, even when you were just children.'

'I suppose I should have stayed where I was, but I couldn't make him understand my position.'

Minnie smiled and nodded. 'He's a man, my dear. They believe what they want to believe, and I suppose Jack wants to keep his freedom, but he needs you to be there for him every step of the way.'

'Yes, that's about it, Mrs Marshall. I had to come away or who knows what might have happened? Jack is master of the house now, and I'm just a servant, or rather I was.'

'And you didn't tell him you were leaving?'

'I couldn't,' Judy said simply. 'He would have persuaded me to stay.'

'Then I think you did the right thing, and I would

28

employ you if it were possible, but, as you can see, this is a very small house. We'll be moving to a much larger residence in the near future, but that doesn't help you now.'

'I was just hoping you might know of someone who would employ me. I can cook and Mrs Ralston has taught me household management. I'm honest and hard working.'

'I know all that, Judy. Mrs Tattersall was always singing your praises when we visited the manor house.' Minnie jumped to her feet at the sound of crockery rattling together in the hallway. She wrenched the door open in time to rescue the tea tray as Sukey tripped over her feet and stumbled. 'Thank you, Sukey. That will be all for now.'

Sukey gazed up at her with red-rimmed eyes. 'You won't tell Cook, will you, miss?'

'It's "madam" or "Mrs Marshall", Sukey. I won't say a word.'

'Ta, ever so, miss. I mean, madam.' Sukey scuttled off towards the back stairs and Minnie closed the door before placing the tray on a table in the window. 'If only you'd arrived two weeks ago I could have taken you on with pleasure, but I haven't the heart to send young Sukey back to the orphanage.'

'No, of course not,' Judy said earnestly. 'I wouldn't want that either.'

Minnie poured the tea and handed a cup to Judy. 'Would you like a slice of cake?'

'Thank you, Mrs Marshall.'

'What will you do now? I'm afraid I don't know of anyone looking for servants at the present.'

'Daisy – I mean, Mrs Walters – gave me the address of the boarding house where you both lived when you were younger. I thought I might try there.'

'Did she also tell you that Mrs Wood is a tyrant and that her daughter, Gladys, is a spiteful cat? Although I believe she is married now and lives above the saddler's shop in Whitechapel, which oddly enough was where my husband and Daisy grew up. Gladys married the man who took over from Mr Marshall senior.'

'Would that be Jonah Sawkins?' Judy accepted a large slice of chocolate cake, and bit into it hungrily.

'Yes. How did you know that?'

'Daisy used to tell us stories about her time in London when Molly and I were much younger.'

'Well, yes. Jonah was always hanging around Daisy, no matter how many times she snubbed him. Our friend Ivy, who later married Clem Guppy, went out with Jonah until she realised what sort of man he was, but Gladys didn't seem to see his faults. They say that love is blind.' Minnie helped herself to cake and returned to her seat. 'On a more practical level, Judy, have you got enough money to support yourself until you find a suitable position?'

Judy nodded, chewed and swallowed, licking the delicious crumbs from her lips. 'Yes, I have. Mrs Tattersall was very generous. She gave me enough money to pay rent for a week or two, if I choose somewhere cheap. I think she was glad to see the back of me.'

'I'm sure that's not true, but I expect she was concerned. She might have been afraid that Jack would take after Jay, who, like his namesake, flew away, or should I say he sailed away to the Antipodes? Anyway, I'm sure that Jack isn't like his brother in that respect.'

'No, he isn't,' Judy said firmly. 'Jack is an excellent person and I . . .' she hesitated, 'I am truly fond of him, but he needs to marry a well-bred lady with a sizeable dowry.'

'I don't think those are your words, Judy. It sounds more like Mary Tattersall speaking.' Minnie leaned forward, lowering her voice. 'Let me tell you that what Jack wants, and what his mother wants for him are almost certainly two different things. Do you understand me?'

Judy's throat ached with unshed tears. Minnie's kindness was disarming, and she obviously understood. It was a relief, and yet it made the pain in Judy's heart even more acute. She inclined her head. 'Yes, ma'am.'

Minnie leaned over to pat Judy's hand. 'I'll come with you to Fieldgate Street and introduce you to Mrs Wood as a prospective tenant. I wouldn't want you to work for her, but if you stay there it's reasonably cheap and quite central, and you can look for a position elsewhere. What do you say?'

'Thank you. I'd be very grateful.'

Minnie pulled a face. 'I can't say that she runs the best lodging house in the East End, but at least it's clean and respectable. You'll be safe there.'

'Thank you, Mrs Marshall.' Judy tried to smile, but she felt as though she was about to jump off the top of a cliff into the swirling sea of the unknown. London seemed so much bigger, noisier and dirtier than she remembered, and Little Creek was a haven of peace and tranquillity in comparison. Her first instinct was to rush back to the station and catch the next train home, but she knew that she must be strong and face whatever the city had in store for her.

Minnie rose to her feet. 'I'll go and fetch my bonnet and shawl and we'll set off.'

The maid who let them into the house ushered them into Mrs Wood's parlour.

'Thank you, Aggie,' Minnie said, smiling.

The maid bobbed a curtsey and backed out of the room. Judy eyed Mrs Wood warily – her first impressions were not favourable. Years of bullying servants and lodgers alike had left a network of lines on Mrs Wood's face. Twin furrows between her brows gave her a permanent frown and her mouth was dragged down at the corners, stamping an expression of disapproval on her face, which lingered even as she attempted to smile.

'Mrs Marshall, how nice to see you again.'

'And you, Mrs Wood. You're looking well.'

'I might look good, my dear, but my rheumatics play me up something awful, particularly in winter. A life of hard work and service to others has told on my poor aching body.'

Judy shot a sideways glance at Minnie, who remained outwardly calm and smiling.

'Your lodging house has always been deemed one of the best, Mrs Wood,' Minnie said with a persuasive smile. 'And for that reason I've brought my friend Miss Begg to see you. She's in need of accommodation while she looks for work.'

Mrs Wood looked Judy up and down with a critical eye. 'And what line of work is that, may I ask?'

'I'm trained in all household matters,' Judy said with a determined lift of her chin. 'I was assistant housekeeper in my last position.'

'So you're looking for a job in service?'

Judy nodded. 'Yes, ma'am.'

'Might I ask why you left your previous employer?' Mrs Wood's eyes narrowed and her lips tightened. 'I have to ask these questions, you must understand. I can't afford to take in tenants who have left under a cloud, if you get my meaning.'

'I can vouch for Miss Begg,' Minnie said firmly. 'I've known her since she was a child, and she is above reproach.'

'It so happens that I have a small attic room vacant at the moment, but I want a week's rent in advance.'

'I'll take it.' Judy opened her reticule and took out her purse. 'I'd like to move in right away.'

'Like that, is it?' Mrs Wood held out her hand. 'Two and tuppence, but if you want meals it's ninepence a day.'

Judy counted out two shillings and two pennies and laid them in Mrs Wood's palm. 'I'm not sure about meals, ma'am.'

Minnie laid her hand on Judy's arm. 'You must dine with us tonight, dear. I want to catch up on all the news from home.' She turned to Mrs Wood. 'I seem to remember that we used to have a choice of dining in or out, depending upon the demands of the workplace.'

'Of course.' Mrs Wood rang the bell on her desk. 'Aggie will show you to your room. Now, if you'll excuse me, Mrs Marshall, I have work to do.'

Minnie was about to answer when Aggie burst into the parlour so precipitously that it seemed to Judy that the maidservant must have been listening at the keyhole.

'Show Miss Begg to the gable-end room, Aggie.'

'Yes'm.' Aggie held the door open for Minnie and Judy, closing it after them. 'Follow me, if you please.'

Minnie came to a halt at the foot of the stairs. 'I'll wait here, Judy. I know what the rooms are like, and I don't suppose they've changed much since I was last here.'

Judy followed the maid up three flights of stairs, which grew steeper and narrower as they reached the top floor. A narrow landing led between the attic rooms, one of which Aggie pointed out as being where she slept, and the furthest and biggest was Cook's domain. Two of the smaller rooms were filled with discarded or broken furniture and items that might be of use if kept for long enough. The third was quite literally under the eaves, with a small dormer window throwing light on the bare floor-boards, and a narrow iron bedstead set against one wall. There was a deal chest of drawers, a wooden chair and a washstand, complete with a jug and basin, both of which were slightly chipped. A candle stub in a chamber candlestick and a box of matches must have been left by the previous occupant, and the lingering smell of body odour remained like a ghost of the same person. As the jug was empty and the basin covered in a thin layer of dust, Judy supposed that the last woman to rent the room had not bothered to trail down to the kitchen to fetch water for washing. She could tell from Aggie's tight-lipped expression that she was not prepared to wait on the lodgers.

'I comes up here once a month to change the bedding,' Aggie said as if reading Judy's mind. 'And I don't drag up here with jugs of water, nor do I empty the chamber pot. You have to bring that downstairs yourself. You have to keep the room clean, unless you're willing to pay extra, in which case you deal with me direct. D'you understand?'

'Perfectly.' Judy made for the door. 'I've seen

enough, thank you.' She turned to Aggie as she was about to leave the room. 'There's no key.'

'We don't lock doors in this establishment. Mrs Wood is the only one who has a key, but take a tip from me and don't leave anything valuable lying around. Things have a habit of disappearing.' Aggie brushed past her and headed for the stairs. 'You'll soon learn,' she added darkly.

Judy followed her downstairs. It was impossible not to feel downhearted and depressed by her new surroundings, but at least she had a roof over her head for the foreseeable future, and it was up to her to make the best of things. She was, after all, a born Londoner, and she would have to call upon the lessons she had learned when very young to cope with life in the metropolis. Even so, Judy had a sudden longing for the sweet scent of fresh air, and the tang of the saltwater from the marshes, untainted by city smells. Even in Sidney Square, with the neat garden at its heart, she had missed the sound of birdsong. The pigeons cooed and the sparrows hopped around chirruping incessantly, but there were no song thrushes or skylarks to fill the sooty air with their musical warbling.

'Don't tell me.' Minnie looked up as Judy descended the last flight of stairs. 'I've only been up there once, but I doubt if it's changed.'

'It will be fine,' Judy said bravely. 'I've seen worse, and it's temporary. I'm sure I'll find something soon.'

'I do hope so, for your sake. Come with me now

36

and Toby will see you back here after dinner tonight. By the way,' Minnie added when they stepped outside onto the pavement, 'if you want your bedding changed or if you need clean towels, you'll get what you need much faster if you tip Aggie. It's always been that way, I'm afraid.'

'What happens if I do it myself? I'm used to managing the linen cupboard as well as making beds.'

'I wouldn't advise it, my dear. Servants can make your life a misery if they choose to do so, and you won't get any support from Mrs Wood. She doesn't care what goes on as long as she gets her money each week. Anyway, don't dwell on that. I'm sure you'll find a suitable position soon. Maybe my husband knows of someone looking for a trustworthy servant.' Minnie linked arms with Judy as they set off in the direction of Sidney Square. 'Might you even consider returning to Creek Manor, Judy? Perhaps your absence will shake Jack out of his complacent attitude.'

'If he really cared he would have followed me,' Judy said sadly. 'He thinks I'll weaken and go home, but that's not going to happen. I am stronger than he imagines and I won't give up so easily.'

That night in her chilly attic room, Judy tossed and turned on the lumpy mattress. It was obvious that Aggie had not changed the bedding, as the last occupant's odour was imprinted on the cotton sheets and pillowcases. The rustlings beneath the eaves might have been nesting sparrows, but more likely they were rats and mice, and Cook's snoring echoed down the narrowing landing. The sounds from the street filtered up to the top of the house. The rumble of wooden wheels on cobblestones, the clip-clop of horses' hoofs, and the loud voices of drunks weaving their way back to their homes seemed to go on for hours. Judy longed for the comfort of her bed in the cottage, and the silence of the country, interrupted only by a distant bark of a dog fox or the hoot of a barn owl. Her pillow was wet with tears as she drifted off to sleep eventually, worn out by the events of the day and crippling homesickness.

She awakened next morning wondering why her whole body was aching, and for a moment she could not think where she was. Then the reality of her situation hit her with the force of a physical blow. But giving way to despair was not in her nature, and she was even more determined to prove that she could make a life for herself away from home. She dressed quickly and made her way downstairs, carrying the chamber pot very carefully, with the ewer tucked under one arm. The pump and the privy were situated in the back yard, and as it was still early Judy had the facilities to herself. She used the privy and washed in ice-cold water, sticking her head under the pump to rinse the dust and soot from her hair, wringing out her long locks and tying them back with a ribbon.

On her way back to her room with the clean chamber pot and the ewer filled with fresh water, Judy almost bumped into Aggie. A few coins changed hands and Aggie unlocked the linen cupboard, giving Judy a towel, but she stood back when she was asked for clean bedlinen. More coins landed on Aggie's outstretched palm, and somewhat reluctantly she gave Judy two sheets and a clean pillowcase. With these hitched over her shoulder and a much lighter purse, Judy made her way back to her room.

The smell of hot toast and coffee wafted up the stairs, making Judy's stomach rumble with hunger. It was many hours since she had enjoyed the delicious dinner in Sidney Square, but now she must face the real world, and that meant a choice between handing out yet more money for breakfast at the lodging house, and going without food until the evening. She had not yet worked out where or what she would eat, but she vaguely remembered stalls selling coffee and tea, baked potatoes and rolls filled with ham or cheese.

'Ah, Miss Begg. I see you're dressed and ready for the off.' Mrs Wood appeared suddenly at her side. 'It's not good to go without breakfast, which is still being served in the dining room.'

'Thank you, Mrs Wood, but I'm not hungry. I need to find work and that's what I'm about to do.'

'Oh, well, I suppose you know best, but this evening there's Cook's speciality for dinner. Boiled beef and carrots. I urge you to take advantage of our meals, Miss Begg. You won't find such delicacies at such a good price anywhere else in London.'

'Thank you, ma'am. I'll think about it.' Judy made her escape and rushed out into the street. She stood on the pavement, looking this way and that, but she had no idea which direction to take. Jack would have tossed a coin – the memory of him brought a smile to her lips and a lump to her throat. 'Follow your nose,' her mother would have said. Judy turned to the left and walked to the end of Fieldgate Street, finding herself in the busy thoroughfare of Whitechapel Road. Slowly memories of childhood began to emerge and she recognised places she had frequented. The street was chaotic with horse-drawn traffic of all types from omnibuses to brewers' drays, removal carts, hansom cabs and growlers. It all came flooding back now: the dreadful poverty of Green Dragon Yard and, despite her parents' best efforts, the hand-to-mouth existence they had endured before the accident that had changed their lives for ever.

A wave of nausea made her gasp and suddenly the world seemed to spin around her in concentric circles. Judy clutched at nothing but thin air and felt herself falling . . .

Chapter Three

'Oy! Look where you're going, you silly mare.'

The irate voice brought Judy back from the realms of semi-consciousness and she realised that she was clinging to a woman's arm.

'I'm so sorry. I felt a bit faint.'

'Probably drunk,' the woman's partner said angrily. 'At this time in the morning, too. Shame on you, miss.'

Judy staggered to the nearest shopfront and leaned against the door. Was everyone in London rude and mean? If that had occurred in Little Creek, someone would have helped her and taken her into their home. She would have been offered tea and something to eat, even if they had very little themselves. The hunger pangs were another reminder of her childhood. She had roamed these streets looking for farthings or halfpennies that might have been dropped by more affluent people, and she had snatched up bruised fruit that had fallen off costermongers' barrows to take home for Molly and the boys. Those days were far behind her now, but an empty stomach felt the same whatever her age.

The scent of hot tea and coffee floated past on a gentle breeze, blotting out the less pleasant smells of the city, and as her mother had always said, Judy followed her nose. The stall was set up in a narrow alleyway and she bought a ham roll and a mug of coffee laced with sugar. The vendor had taken pity on her and had given her a broken biscuit as well, and she gobbled the food in a way that would have earned her a sharp rebuke from her mother or from Cook at Creek Manor, but she was too hungry to care. The hot, sweet coffee went down well and she handed the empty mug back and thanked the stall-holder for his generosity.

'You're welcome, miss,' he said, grinning. 'You was half-starved by the look of you.'

She smiled. 'I used to live near here, but I've been away in the country for a long time.'

'Looking for work, are you, love?'

'Yes, how did you guess?'

'I see many like you every day. Folk come up from the country thinking that the streets are paved with gold, like in the storybook, but they ain't. You ought to go back to the country and settle for what you had, miss.'

'I do need work, but I don't know how to set about it.'

'You could look in shop windows. Sometimes people put cards in, advertising vacancies, but you need to be careful what you go for. Or you could look in the posh newspaper.' He leaned over and picked up a tattered copy of *The Times* that someone had carelessly discarded. 'Take a look in the "Situations Vacant" column. You seem like a well-spoken young lady. Maybe you'll find something there.'

'Thank you,' Judy said eagerly. 'I'll read it and return it to you.'

He chuckled. 'Don't bother, love. I never learned to read proper. I can write me name, and that's about it. You keep it and good luck to you.'

Judy folded the newspaper and tucked it under her arm. She remembered the churchyard of St Mary Matfelon, where she used to play hide-and-seek with Molly, although at seven years old, Molly had always given herself away by giggling, and it was there that Judy headed. At least it was quiet and peaceful in the graveyard. She sat down on a low wall to read the advertisements in *The Times,* but there was nothing remotely suitable, so she resumed her walk, gazing in shop windows to see if there was anything for her.

At the end of the afternoon Judy had walked so far that her heels were blistered and sore, and her limbs ached so that each step was torture. She managed to get back to Fieldgate Street, but she had not eaten since the ham roll and coffee that morning, and she was ravenous. Aggie let her in, but as luck would have it Judy almost cannoned into Mrs Wood at the foot of the stairs.

'Well, you look as if you've had a hard day, Miss Begg.' Mrs Wood did not sound sympathetic. 'It's not as easy as you would think, is it?'

'No, ma'am.' Judy was not in the mood to argue.

'Do I take it that you will be having your evening meal in the dining room?'

'Thank you.' Judy was tempted to refuse, but she was too tired to go out again, and it had started to rain. 'I will.'

'Excellent.' Mrs Wood beamed at her. 'I'll put it on your bill. I expect payment first thing each Saturday morning.'

'But I've already given you a week in advance.'

'That will be returned to you when you leave this establishment. I have to do that, Miss Begg. You'd be surprised how many people are prepared to walk away without settling their debts.'

Judy nodded. There was no point in protesting and she started up the staircase, holding on to the banister rail.

'Dinner is at half past six on the dot,' Mrs Wood called after her. 'Latecomers do not get served. I have to have rules or people would take advantage of my good nature.'

'I'll be on time,' Judy said wearily as she trudged up the stairs, heading towards the cheerless room that was now her home.

At six thirty on the dot, Judy walked into the dining room. She had kept her bedroom door ajar in order to listen for the booming strikes of the grandfather clock in the hall indicating the passing hours, and the chimes that announced the quarters. The other diners were already seated at a table in the centre of the room, except for two much older women who shared a small table in the window. Judy hesitated, not wanting to take anyone's place.

A thin woman in her thirties patted the empty chair beside her. 'This one's free, love. Miss Wentworth left yesterday and she won't be coming back. I'm Phyllis Dean, by the way.'

Judy smiled. 'Judy Begg.'

'Wentworth is the lucky one. She's found a man to marry her.' A younger woman with mousy hair and freckles gave Judy a weak smile. 'I'm Mabel Field. You're new here, Judy.'

'I arrived yesterday.' Judy sat down beside Phyllis. 'I'm looking for work.'

'It's not easy to find a job where the boss doesn't expect you to stay after hours, if you get my meaning.' A strikingly pretty girl snatched up a bread roll and tore it into small pieces, shoving them into her mouth one after the other. 'I'm blooming starving. Where's the damn food?'

'Don't take any notice of Fanny,' Mabel said, giggling. 'She don't mean half of what she says.'

Before Fanny could respond, which would have been difficult anyway, considering the amount of bread she had stuffed into her mouth, the door opened and Aggie staggered in carrying a large tureen, which she placed in the centre of the table. She picked up a pile of soup bowls from the dresser and put them in front of Phyllis.

'Help yourselves.' Aggie left the room, slamming the door behind her.

Fanny chewed and swallowed the last mouthful of bread roll. 'That person needs to learn some manners.'

'Have a heart, Fanny.' Mabel reached for a plate. 'I wouldn't like to work for Mrs Wood. I'm sure she bullies poor Aggie.'

'Never mind her. I could eat the carpet I'm so damn hungry.' Fanny elbowed her out of the way, grabbed a bowl and helped herself to the thick slices of boiled beef and chunks of carrot in a thin gravy. 'I hope this tastes better than it smells. I think the ox died of shame.'

Phyllis stood up, filled two bowls and took them to the two older ladies, who were chatting to each other in low voices. 'There you are ladies. Enjoy your meal.' She returned to her seat. 'Best help yourself, Judy. These gannets will devour the lot while you're sitting there being polite.' She passed a bowl to Judy before serving herself. 'Take a roll before they all go, too.'

Judy concentrated on her food. It was not good, but at least it was edible and she was too hungry to be fussy. There was silence while everyone demolished their meal, and it seemed to Judy that she was not the only one who was starving.

Phyllis piled up the empty bowls and rang the bell for Aggie, who cleared the table and they had to wait until she returned with a treacle pudding and a jug of custard.

'It's not bad for ninepence,' Phyllis said as she finished her portion. 'I've tasted better, but at least it's filling.'

'Yes, I agree with that.' Judy stared at the two older women. She lowered her voice to a whisper. 'Who are those ladies, Phyllis? And why do they sit on their own?'

'They've been residents here for years, and they're quite nice when you get to know them, but they keep themselves to themselves, and that's fine with me.'

'Have you lived here long?' Judy asked in a low voice.

Phyllis gave her a pitying look. 'I'm thirty-five – well and truly on the shelf. What choice do I have?'

'I'm sorry, I didn't mean to pry.'

Mabel stood up and stretched. 'I reckon I'll go for a walk. I can't face a whole evening in that dreary front parlour. Are you coming, Phyllis?'

'No, love. I've got a pile of books to mark. My pupils keep me so busy that I don't have time to do it in school.'

'Where do you teach?' Judy's interest was aroused. Maybe she could help in the school, if they were willing to pay her a wage.

'It's the ragged school in George Yard,' Phyllis said, sighing. 'Poor little devils, half of them turn up barefoot, even in the winter. If I can teach them to read and write and add up, I'm doing well, but most of them are put to work by their parents, if they have any. It's time the Government stepped in and made education compulsory, at least for those under the age of ten. It's heartbreaking to see little ones on the street selling matches or bootlaces.'

'Or, even worse, ending up picking pockets,' Mabel added, shaking her head. 'I've seen mothers selling their little daughters to old men for their pleasure. You learn to be thankful for what you've got.'

Fanny pulled a face. 'I'm tired of being grateful for everything. I want to marry a rich man who'll pamper me and shower me with gifts, and I'll never have to work in that bakery again.'

'At least you get free cake,' Mabel said, patting her flat belly. 'I'd be fat as a pig if I was let loose amongst the pies and pastries.'

'We get the sack if we so much as lick our fingers.' Fanny tossed her head. 'No chance of getting podgy when you work for old Sour Puss. Anyway, I'm meeting Ronnie in ten minutes so I'd better go upstairs and make myself presentable.' She hurried from the room, leaving a waft of lavender cologne in her wake.

'Let's hope Ronnie comes up to scratch,' Mabel said, pursing her lips. 'Poor Fanny has been let down too many times in the past.'

'She'll bounce back; she always does.' Phyllis headed for the door. 'Must go and get those books marked. Good night, Judy. I'll see you at breakfast.'

'Maybe,' Judy said doubtfully. The cost of the meals did not sound much if said quickly, but added up over a month it would come to a tidy sum, and unless she could find work she might be forced to return home.

'It's always hard at first, love.' Mabel reached out to give Judy's back a gentle pat.

She stood aside as the two older women made for the door. One of them gave Judy a nod, but her friend walked on without acknowledging either Judy or Mabel.

'Don't take no notice of them.' Mabel shook her head, clicking her tongue against her teeth. 'They don't take kindly to strangers, but they'll get used to you. It was the same for all of us.'

'I thought I must have offended them.'

'They were like that with me, but now I get the occasional smile. The poor old dears have been here for so long they think they own the place. Anyway, I've got to go. I've got a night shift at the hospital.'

'Are you a nurse?'

Mabel threw her head back and laughed. 'No, love. I clean the wards. I'll look on the notice board and see if there are any jobs going. I suppose you don't mind what you do.'

'No, not really. I need to start earning money or I'll be forced to go home.'

'I'll see what I can do.'

Judy found herself alone in the oak-panelled dining room, and she struggled with a sudden wave of homesickness and assailed by doubts as to the wisdom of running away. It had seemed like the right thing to do at the time, but she had not given a thought to the difficulties she might face, or the heartache she would suffer. This was the end of her second day away from Creek Manor and Jack had not come after her. If his feelings for her were genuine, surely he would have made the effort to travel up to London, if only to make sure that she was all right? She left the dreary dining room and made her way slowly up the stairs to her lonely bedchamber. Raindrops were running down the windowpanes like tears and there was a chill in the room that made her shiver. She lay down on the bed still fully dressed and pulled the thin coverlet up to her chin. Perhaps things would be better tomorrow. She closed her eyes and drifted off to sleep.

At the end of the first week Judy still had not found employment, although she had been for several interviews. However, she soon discovered that she was not the sort of person that middle-class wives considered suitable as live-in housemaids. When Judy said that she had been assistant housekeeper at Creek Manor it seemed that the shutters went down. One woman even admitted that she would not consider employing an attractive-looking housemaid, as it always caused trouble with other servants. Others thought that she was over-qualified for positions as lowly as scrub women, who came in daily to do the hard work in their houses. Shopkeepers thought that Judy spoke too much like a lady to serve customers, who might think that they were being mimicked. No matter what job Judy tried for there was always a reason for rejecting her. Even worse, she had not had a word from Jack. He had not written and her mother's letter made no mention of him at all.

The final straw was the fact that her money was running out. She could not exist on one meal a day, and she had been forced to buy a second-hand pair of boots as hers were worn beyond repair. Her fellow sufferers at the hands of Mrs Wood, whose strict rules governed every waking moment they spent under her roof, were sympathetic at first, but Judy realised that they were all desperate to escape the drudgery and loneliness of their lives. Perhaps the only people who were content with their lot were the two older ladies, who lived in their own little world. Judy found herself envying them.

With just a few coins left in her purse, Judy went to seek Minnie's help and advice.

'I haven't come to borrow money,' Judy said hastily when Minnie automatically reached for her reticule.

'I can lend you enough for next week's rent.'

Judy shook her head vehemently. 'No, Mrs Marshall. Thank you, but I want to find work and I was hoping you might have heard of something. I'll do anything.'

Minnie looked up at the sound of the door opening and her husband strolled into the parlour. 'Judy is finding it almost impossible to find work, Toby. Can you help her?'

Dr Toby Marshall bore a striking resemblance to his sister, Daisy. It was a likeness that Judy had not noticed before, but it was something about the eyes and the kindly smile that reminded her of Daisy, and of home. She felt tears threatening to overcome her and she took a deep breath.

'I'll do anything within reason, Dr Marshall. I'm a good worker, but I can't seem to convince anyone to give me a chance to prove myself.'

Toby went to sit beside his wife on the sofa. 'Have you tried the hospital, Judy? They're always looking for domestics. Or would that be too menial?'

'No, sir. Of course not. I have to support myself.'

Toby exchanged worried glances with his wife. 'Jack Fox has a lot to answer for,' he said gruffly. 'You should be with your family in Essex. Never mind what Jack told you.'

'It is difficult, dear,' Minnie said quickly. 'You probably can't remember what it was like when we first knew each other, but it's a delicate balance.'

Toby shrugged. 'The fellow has been leading you

on, Judy. I'm fond of Jack, but he's too much like his brother, and we all know that Jay behaved abominably towards Daisy.'

Judy lowered her gaze. She was not in a position to argue with someone so closely involved in the old family scandal, and she held her tongue, although she wanted desperately to leap to Jack's defence.

'That's not helping, Toby,' Minnie said, frowning. 'I think you ought to take Judy to the hospital and put her forward for a position. With a good reference from you, I'm sure they will snap her up.'

'Why not? I'm going there now, Judy. Would you like to come with me?'

'Yes, please, Dr Marshall. If I don't find work in the next day or so I'll have to go home, and I'd rather not do that. Not yet, anyway.'

'I like to see enthusiasm in my staff.' Toby rose to his feet. 'Best foot forward, as Aunt Eleanora used to say.' He leaned over to kiss his wife on the cheek. 'I'll see you at dinner, darling.'

Minnie smiled up at him. 'Try to get home before the twins' bedtime, Toby. They always want their papa to kiss them good night.'

'I will, but you know how things are. I'll try my best. Come along, Judy. Let's see what we can offer you at the London.'

When Judy entered the hospital she was struck forcibly by the strong smell of carbolic and the subdued babble of voices. The waiting area was crowded, but Toby walked on purposefully, stopping briefly to acknowledge a younger man.

'I see you've drawn the short straw today, Ben.'

'Henson went down with a fever, so I volunteered to take his shift. At least I feel I'm doing something useful with these poor souls who can't afford to pay for private treatment.'

'We'd all starve if we followed that rule,' Toby said, chuckling. 'I'm late for my ward round, but I'll probably see you later.'

'Most probably.'

Judy had to hurry to keep up with Toby. 'Who was that?'

'He's a really brilliant man, but he'd rather work with the sick and needy than set up a lucrative practice in Harley Street. I'm afraid I'm not as dedicated as Dr Godfrey. It's no wonder the patients call him Dr God.'

Judy glanced over her shoulder. Even in such a short time she had been impressed by the young doctor, who was not classically good-looking, but he had a pleasant, open countenance and she could see why his patients thought so much of him. His brown eyes sparkled with good humour, and if the warmth of his smile was anything to go by Dr God had a kind heart. Judy felt suddenly more optimistic. If Dr God represented the rest of the staff, maybe working in the hospital would be a good thing after all.

*　　*　　*

Judy returned to the lodging house with a smile on her face. She had a job at last, although she knew that it was going to be hard work. Cleaning hospital wards was not the most glamorous occupation, but as Matron had explained, it was a vital part of keeping infection at bay. The hours were long – from seven in the morning until nine o'clock at night – but the wages would pay for her room, and meals were provided while on duty.

It was not until she was in the privacy of her tiny bedchamber that the irony of the situation occurred to her: she would be working in the hospital that had saved her mother's life. Judy took off her shawl and bonnet and laid them on her bed before going downstairs to the communal parlour. She knew from experience that it was usually deserted at this time of day, and she went to sit at the small desk situated beneath the window. Mrs Wood supplied headed paper on the understanding that her lodgers only used one sheet at a time, and that they did not include adverse remarks about their accommodation.

Judy sat down to write a letter to her mother, keeping the lines as close together as possible and using both sides of the rather inferior quality paper. At last she had something positive to pass on, and she would not have to return home a failure. If cleaning wards was not a glamorous job, at least it was worthwhile, and she would be starting work tomorrow. She could hardly wait.

*　　*　　*

At seven o'clock next morning Judy waited for the sister in charge to give her instructions. She had arrived early and was eager to start work, despite the gloomy predictions of her fellow lodgers in Fieldgate Street. Mabel had not yet returned from her shift when Judy made her announcement that she had found a position at the London Hospital, and the news had been met with exclamations of horror and much shuddering. Fanny had been the only one among them who had seen the possibilities of working with handsome young doctors, and she had teased Judy mercilessly when she blushed. Now, in the cold light of morning, as she waited outside the sluice room, Judy could not help wondering if perhaps her friends at the lodging house had been right. Then the sound of footsteps made her turn her head and the sight of Dr Godfrey's beaming smile banished all her worries.

'Good morning. I'm afraid I don't know your name. My friend Toby Marshall was in too much of a hurry to introduce us.'

'Yes, sir,' Judy said shyly. 'I know who you are.'

'Then you have the advantage of me, Miss er . . .'

'Judy Begg, sir.'

'I'm Ben Godfrey, and this is one of my wards,' he said, smiling. 'I hope you enjoy working here, Judy.'

'Thank you, Doctor.' Judy glanced over his shoulder and saw the ward sister bearing down on them.

Ben looked round. 'Good morning, Sister.'

'Good morning, Dr Godfrey. I'm sure you have

better things to do than to waste time chatting. We most certainly have.'

Judy stared at her in amazement. Sister Harris was an older woman, but to speak to a doctor in such a tone must surely earn her a sharp set-down.

'Indeed I do,' Dr Godfrey said, smiling urbanely. 'Thank you for reminding me.' He strolled into a ward, leaving Judy open-mouthed.

'It's not polite to stare, Miss Begg.' Sister Harris glared at the ward maid, who came hurrying towards them. 'You're late again, Wallace. If this happens once more you'll face disciplinary proceedings and possible dismissal.'

The young woman flushed uncomfortably and bowed her head. 'I'm sorry, Sister. My mother was taken poorly in the night and—'

'I don't need excuses, Wallace. Get on with your work. I want you to take Begg with you today so that she knows the layout of the hospital and what's required of her, but first I want you to show her where to get her pinafore and cap.'

'Yes, Sister.' Wallace shot a wary glance in Judy's direction. 'You'd best come with me, Begg.'

'Thank you.' Judy followed her to the linen room where they were both given caps and voluminous cotton aprons. 'I can't call you Wallace. I'm Judy.'

'Gertie,' Wallace said reluctantly. 'Just do as I tell you and we won't fall out.'

'Of course. I'm here to learn, and I want to do well.'

Gertie gave her a searching look. 'You'll get over that soon enough. We do just enough to get by and no more. It's a thankless bloody task. You get no gratitude for all the hard work and you go home stinking of carbolic.'

By the end of the morning every muscle in Judy's body ached and her hands were reddened and raw from dipping them in the hot water laced strongly with disinfectant. She scrubbed floors and washed down tiled walls, following Gertie's directions, although she soon realised that Gertie was taking it easy and allowing her to do the bulk of the work.

They were allowed half an hour for their midday meal, which was taken in the staff dining hall, where the differences in the hierarchy were even more notice-able. The menial workers were relegated to the back of the room, whereas the nurses sat in order of seniority at the tables nearest the serving hatch. There was no sign of the doctors, but Judy assumed they must have a separate room. She did not like to admit it, even to herself, but she was rather taken with Dr Godfrey, and that had come as something of a shock. Her heart belonged to Jack, of course, and she had never looked twice at another man, but there was something about 'Dr God' that she found very appealing, and she could understand why the patients hero-worshipped him. Even Gertie, who said very little at the best of times, had blushed and simpered when Dr Godfrey happened to come upon them as they scrubbed the floor of the women's surgical ward. He had greeted them both with a smile, but his gaze had lingered on Judy, as Gertie had been quick to point out when he had walked away. She brought it up again as they sat down to eat their meal.

'Does Dr Godfrey fancy you, Judy Begg? I saw the way he looked at you this morning.'

'Of course he doesn't,' Judy said hastily. 'I met him for the first time yesterday and that was in passing. I can't think what put that into your head.'

'Don't act so innocent, miss. You was smiling all sweet and coy, and he lapped it up.'

'I was not.' Judy bent her head over her meal. 'Don't talk daft, Gertie. It's all in your imagination.'

'Is it? All I can say is that you'd better watch out. Nothing good can come of it, that's for certain, and if Sister Harris finds out you'll be in double trouble.'

'Why?' Judy demanded angrily. 'What has it to do with her?'

Gertie opened her mouth to reply, but closed it again as she looked up at the person who had walked up to their table.

The young probationer nurse gazed at Judy with barely concealed glee. 'Are you Miss Begg?'

Judy swallowed a mouthful of dry bread. 'I am.'

'You're wanted in Matron's office. I'd hurry if I was you. She don't like to be kept waiting.'

'What did I tell you?' Gertie said triumphantly. 'You've only been here five minutes and you're already in trouble. You're for it now, Judy.'

Chapter Four

The probationer led the way to Matron's office and knocked on the door. 'It looks like you're in trouble, Begg. I bet she's going to give you the sack.' She waited for a few seconds before thrusting it open.

Judy entered the office and came to a halt when she saw Minnie Marshall, who sprang up from the chair in front of Matron's desk. 'Judy, my dear, I'm afraid I've got some bad news for you.'

'What's happened?' Judy demanded anxiously.

'There's been an accident at the manor house.'

'I think it best if you sit down, Miss Begg,' Matron said firmly.

It was not an invitation to refuse and Judy sank onto the nearest chair. 'Who was it? Please tell me.'

'It's Jack. He was thrown from his horse and he sustained serious injuries. He's been asking for you, dear.'

Judy took a few seconds to assimilate such terrible news. Jack was a good horseman and he had always seemed indestructible. 'How bad is it?' Her voice sounded hoarse to her own ears.

'It's early days yet, but I would imagine that Dr Neville will consult a specialist who deals with such injuries. We'll know more then.'

'What sort of injuries?' Judy demanded dazedly.

'He hurt his back,' Minnie said evasively. 'He's confined to his bed.'

'Can he move?'

Minnie shook her head. 'Not very much.'

Judy covered her face with her hands. She was too numb to cry, but the mere thought of Jack being crippled for life was appalling. Jack was too full of energy and love of life to exist as an invalid. 'It can't be true.'

'We have to be strong for Jack,' Minnie said earnestly. 'He wants you to go home. Mary sent the telegram to us, and even in a few words I could feel a mother's agony. He needs you, Judy.'

'I'll be sorry to lose you, Miss Begg.' Matron opened a drawer in her desk and took out a cash box, which she unlocked. 'I can pay you for one morning's work, which will help towards your fare home.' She took out a few coins and laid them on the desk.

'Thank you, Matron.' Minnie picked up the money and pressed it into Judy's limp hand. 'Come along, dear. I'll help you pack your bag and we'll take a cab to Bishopsgate Station.'

Judy shook her head. 'It's kind of you, Mrs Marshall, but I don't want you to go to all that trouble. I'll do as you suggest, but I can manage on my own.'

'Nonsense,' Minnie said with a wry smile. 'I lodged in Mrs Wood's house for several years and I know how difficult the woman can be. She might try to squeeze a few more shillings out of you, and that would never do. I'm up to her tricks.' Minnie rose to her feet. 'Come along, Judy. Together we'll vanquish the old dragon.' She turned to Matron with a charming smile. 'Thank you, Matron.' Minnie left the office and Judy followed blindly. All she could think about was Jack, lying broken and probably crippled for life, and she had been thinking badly of him. If she had not run away he might still be the same energetic, fun-loving young man. It was her fault and she would never forgive herself.

'You mustn't take it so hard, Judy.' Minnie's gentle voice interrupted Judy's agonised thinking. 'It was an accident, and it could have happened to anyone. I don't know the details, but from what I remember of Jack Fox, he was always a daredevil.'

The description was so apt that it brought a reluctant smile to Judy's face. 'That's so true.'

They had reached the main reception area and Minnie hesitated, gazing round expectantly. 'I was hoping to see Ben Godfrey. I want him to give Toby a message, just in case he goes home and finds me gone. I left a message with Sukey, but I expect she'll forget to pass it on.' Minnie edged her way between the patients, some of whom were blocking the aisles while others wandered aimlessly, and were chivvied along by the busy nurses. Minnie came to a halt when she spotted Dr Godfrey, who was talking to the sister in charge. He broke away, and came towards them, smiling.

'Minnie, this is an unexpected pleasure, and Miss Begg.' His smile faded when he looked at Judy. 'Is something wrong?'

Minnie placed her arm protectively around Judy's shoulders. 'I'm afraid Judy has just been given bad news. She's going home to Little Creek.'

'I'm sorry to hear that, Miss Begg. Is there anything I can do to help?'

Judy shot him a sideways glance. 'No, Doctor. But thank you for asking.'

'We have to leave now, Ben. Judy has to collect her belongings and I'm taking her to Bishopsgate Station. Will you tell Toby that, if you see him in the staff room?'

'Of course I will, and once again, I'm sorry we're going to lose you, Miss Begg.'

'Thank you.' At any other time Judy would have been pleased and flattered to receive such attention, but her thoughts were firmly fixed on getting home as quickly as possible. Jack had sent for her – he wanted her – and that was good enough. She needed no more encouragement to go home.

* * *

It was not far from Little Creek Station to the chain ferry, and when it reached the far side of the river Judy walked the last mile home. It was late afternoon when she arrived at Creek Manor and she was eager to see Jack, but fearful of what she might find. The feelings of guilt had plagued her during the journey home, and she was trembling as she waited for someone to open the heavy oak door.

James let her in and took her valise. His normally impassive countenance was troubled. 'Glad you came home, miss.'

'How is the master?' Judy asked anxiously.

'They say in the servants' hall that he'll never walk again, but I can't tell you that's a fact because I don't know, and I don't think no one else does neither.'

It was hardly an encouraging start, but Judy braced herself to face the worst. 'Where is Mrs Tattersall?'

'She's in the drawing room now, but she's spent most of the time at the master's bedside. Your ma was with her not so long ago. She might still be there.'

'Thank you, James.' Judy hurried through the great hall and the familiar oak-panelled passages to the drawing room. She hesitated outside the door, taking a deep breath before she knocked and entered.

Mary was lying on the sofa with a cold compress on her forehead, while Hilda poured tea.

'Judy, love.' Hilda placed the pot back on the tray and leaped to her feet. In an unusual show of emotion she gave her daughter a hug, and then released her. 'Thank goodness you've come home. We're all at sixes and sevens.'

Judy glanced over her mother's shoulder. 'How is Mrs Tattersall?'

'Not good, dear. It's been a terrible shock.'

'How did it happen, Ma?'

'I only know that Will Johnson came across Jack's horse running loose, and he found Jack unconscious in ten-acre field. The workers brought him home on a hurdle, and Dr Neville came to see him, but he's going to send for a specialist from London because he doesn't know enough about spinal injuries to be certain of the outcome.'

'He must have some idea. Does he think that Jack will be crippled for life?'

'Hush, dear. Keep your voice down. We're trying to keep it from Mrs Tattersall.'

'Where is Jack now? I want to see him.'

'The workers brought him home on a hurdle and carried him upstairs to his room. He's been there ever since.'

'I'll go and see him now.'

'He's done nothing but ask for you since he regained consciousness. For two days he just lay there like a stone, and when he opened his eyes he spoke your name.' Hilda buried her face in her apron. 'I've tried to be brave for Mrs Tattersall's sake, but I'm so glad you've come home, Judy. Please don't go away again.'

Judy laid a hand on her mother's shoulder. 'Don't worry, Ma. I'll stay as long as I'm needed.' She glanced at Mary, who was lying inert on the sofa. 'Is she all right?'

'Not really. Dr Neville gave her a strong dose of laudanum, but she'll be pleased to see you when she comes to herself.'

Upstairs in the master bedroom, Jack was flat on his back and at first Judy thought he was asleep, but as she approached the bed he seemed to sense her presence and opened his eyes.

'Judy. I knew you'd come.'

She perched on the edge of the bed and reached out to grasp his hand as it rested on the coverlet. 'I can't leave you for five minutes without you getting into bother,' she said, forcing a smile although she felt more like crying.

'I don't remember how it happened,' Jack said angrily. 'One minute I was on horseback, and the next thing I remember is waking up in my bed.'

'Are you in much pain now?'

'I can't feel a thing, and that's what frightens me most. I can't move my legs, Judy. I'm a cripple.'

She squeezed his fingers. 'Don't say that. It's early days yet, and I'll make sure you get the best medical attention possible. You'll be up and about before you know it.'

Jack curled his fingers tightly around her hand. 'Do you really believe that?'

She met his anxious gaze with a straight look. 'We must believe it, Jack.'

'You won't leave me again, will you?'

She raised his hand to her cheek. 'No, of course not.'

'I want you to promise.'

'I do – cross my heart and hope to die.'

A faint smile creased his pale face. 'I've hardly slept since the accident. Will you hold my hand until I fall asleep?'

She edged carefully onto the bed and lay down beside him, clutching his hand in hers. 'Of course I will.'

Judy waited until she was certain that she would not wake Jack by getting up. She leaned over the bed to drop a kiss on his unruly curls; he looked so young and defenceless while he slept, and her heart went out to him. Biting back tears, she went downstairs to the drawing room where she found Mary deep in conversation with Dr Neville. He looked up and his expression was serious.

'I'm glad you came home, Judy. You're just what Jack needs.'

Mary nodded. 'Yes, indeed. Hilda told me you were here, Judy. I've been so worried about Jack, but I know you'll do him a power of good. I want you to forget what I said to you before. I didn't want you to leave us like that, and Jack was furious with me.'

'We will all do our best for Jack,' Dr Neville said earnestly. 'I've sent for a specialist from London.'

'I don't care what it costs,' Mary said feebly. 'I'd sell my soul to make my boy well again.'

'Of course you would, Mrs Tattersall,' Dr Neville said gently. 'My knowledge of spinal injuries is limited, but Toby recommended a young doctor who trained at the City Orthopaedic Hospital in Hatton Garden. I've met Ben Godfrey and he's a decent fellow, who won't charge you a full consultant's fee.'

Judy stared at him in surprise. 'Dr Godfrey? I met him in the London Hospital. He's very nice.'

'He's a very presentable fellow,' Dr Neville said, smiling. 'But he's also a very good doctor.'

'When is he due to arrive, Doctor?' Mary asked urgently.

'He'll be here in a day or two, but you mustn't expect miracles, Mrs Tattersall. Jack damaged his spine when he was thrown from his horse. It's too early to tell if it will be permanent, but there is the possibility that he won't walk again.'

Mary reached for her hanky. 'Oh, no! I can't bear to think about it.'

'He will recover fully,' Judy said firmly. 'I won't let him give up.'

Dr Neville gave her an encouraging smile. 'That's the right attitude, Judy. If anyone can keep his spirits up, it's you.' He turned to Mary, covering her hand with his. 'I'm sure that Daisy would be happy to give you a hand, should you need help. She was an excellent nurse.'

'You always had a soft spot for Daisy,' Mary said

with a ghost of a smile. 'I know she's happy now with Marius, but Jay should be here to manage the estate instead of running away to the other side of the world. He's let us all down.'

'Have you heard from him since he went to Australia? It's hard to imagine that he would abandon his family so completely.'

'No, Doctor. Not a word, and it's been ten years since he left us. He probably thinks he'll go to prison for bigamy if he comes home, so I doubt if I'll ever see him again.'

'I'm sorry, it must be very hard for you.' Dr Neville patted her hand before rising to his feet. 'I'll go upstairs and see my patient. There's no need to accompany me, Mrs Tattersall. You need to rest and take care of yourself.'

'I'll try, Doctor.'

He paused by the doorway. 'Might I have a word with you, Judy?'

She jumped up and hurried after him as he stepped outside into the corridor. 'What is it, Doctor?'

'Jack won't be able to do anything much in the way of running things for quite some time, and Mrs Tattersall isn't a young woman. Your mother and Mrs Ralston are quite capable of dealing with household affairs and, as far as I can tell, Clem Guppy is a good estate manager, but they need someone to take charge. Someone they can turn to if they need help or advice.'

'I don't think I'm the right person, if that's what you're thinking,' Judy said hastily. 'I'm not family.'

'It was Jack who brought the matter up, Judy. He begged me to send for you and he has enormous faith in you.'

'I know Mrs Tattersall wanted me to take over as housekeeper when Mrs Ralston retires, but running the entire estate is not the same thing, Doctor.'

'I understand, and I have spoken to Mrs Tattersall about it. She's desperate to keep the estate together, and she had to admit that there is no one else who is as close to the family as you are, Judy.'

'Yes, but I have no authority when it comes to making decisions about the estate.'

'Jack trusts you implicitly and, if the truth were told, you probably know a great deal more about day-to-day matters than he does. He's willing to back up any decisions you make, should you decide to accept the responsibility. It's just a temporary measure, until he's recovered sufficiently to take the reins again but, speaking as his doctor, I think that, above all, he needs complete rest and peace of mind.'

'I really wouldn't know where to start, Doctor.'

'Then may I suggest that you visit Colneyhurst and have a word with Daisy? I'm sure she would be only too happy to help you, considering the fact that she ran this place single-handed after Jay deserted her. She had to make it pay for itself and she did a splendid job.'

Judy met his earnest gaze. 'I'm not entirely

convinced, but I'll go and see Daisy first thing in the morning.'

He patted her on the shoulder. 'I have faith in you, Judy. I'm going to see Jack now, so I'd like you to come with me. I'll tell him about Dr Godfrey, and you can calm any doubts he might have.'

After eating her supper in the servants' hall Judy went upstairs to sit with Jack while he picked at his food. 'If you don't eat up I'll have to spoon-feed you as if you were a baby.'

Jack pulled a face. 'You would, too.'

'Yes, indeed, and I want to see a clean plate. You won't get better unless you get your strength back.'

He managed to eat a few more mouthfuls. 'What's this London doctor like?'

'I only met him briefly, but he seemed quite nice. Apparently his patients call him Dr God – his name is Dr Godfrey, if you remember what Dr Neville told you earlier.'

'My brain works very well, thank you, Judy. It's my legs that were affected by the fall.'

She smiled. 'I'm glad to see you haven't lost your sense of humour.' She leaned over to take the tray from him. 'You'll walk again, I know it.'

'I don't think I could go on if I were a cripple.'

She placed the tray on a side table and went to sit on the edge of the bed, taking both his hands in hers.

'I won't allow that sort of talk, Jack. I'm with you now and for always, if you need me.'

'I've no claim on you, Judy.' His eyes brimmed with tears and he turned his head away. 'If I can't walk again I'll only be half a man.'

'Absolute nonsense. You are the same Jack Fox I've always known and loved.'

He turned to face her. 'You love me?'

'Of course I do, silly. I've always loved you, and nothing will ever alter that, so when you start talking like a lunatic, just remember the people who care deeply for you.' She put her arms around him and gave him a long, but gentle hug.

'That's half the trouble.' Jack sank back against the pillows, smiling ruefully. 'My family are driving me mad. Dove and Linnet have been here every day, sometimes with their children. I love them all, but I don't know what to say to them. Ma keeps crying and kissing me, which she never did before. Keep them away from me, Judy. Please.'

She pulled the covers up to his chin. 'I will. Now try to sleep.'

'Did the doctor speak to you about taking care of things while I'm laid up?'

'Yes, he did, but don't worry about that now.'

He grasped her hand. 'I want you to manage the estate for me. You're the only person I really trust.'

'Let's not talk about that just yet. You must rest.'

'I won't sleep until you promise you'll stay and do what you can to keep things together. Promise, Judy.'

She raised his hand to her lips. 'All right, I promise I'll do everything I can.'

'Thank you.' Jack closed his eyes and then opened them, staring at her in alarm. 'You're not going back to the cottage, are you?'

'Yes, of course. It's where I live.'

'No,' he cried childishly. 'I don't want you to go so far away. You must sleep in the room next to mine. It was Daisy's bedchamber until she married Marius. Please don't go.'

She clasped his hand. 'All right. I'll do as you ask, but I have to let Ma know, or she'll think something awful has happened to me.'

'You'll come back and say good night.'

'Of course I will. Stop worrying. I'm here and I'm never going to leave you again.'

He closed his eyes again and a smile curved his lips.

Judy tiptoed from the room and went to find her mother. She had expected to be bombarded with objections when she told her mother that she was going to move to the manor house, but Hilda merely smiled.

'If that's what makes Jack happy, then that's what you must do. The poor boy has been in a terrible state since you left.'

'I thought I was doing the right thing by going away, Ma.'

Hilda patted her on the shoulder. 'We do what we can in this world, dear. Now I must go. Mr Faulkner is waiting for me.'

Judy was suddenly alert. She had detected a subtle

change in her mother even before she left for London, but she had been too immersed in her own problems to question her. Now she was suspicious. 'Why would he do that?'

'He's been very considerate since Jack's accident. Being the head groom and all that, I think he felt responsible for the way the horse bolted, but of course it had nothing to do with him. Anyway, he's taken to walking me home after dark. He says there are poachers in the woods, so I'm glad of a bit of protection.'

'I see.' Judy stifled a giggle. It seemed that Ma and the head groom were walking out together, although of course Ma would never admit to such a thing.

'I know you're laughing at me, Judy Begg. You can wipe that smirk off your face.'

Judy leaned over to kiss her mother's lined cheek. 'I'm not laughing at you, Ma. If you enjoy Mr Faulkner's company, that's fine by me.'

'He's very patient with your brothers,' Hilda said stiffly. 'He says that Pip and Nate both have a way with horses.'

'I'm sure he's a good influence on them. It's hard for boys to grow up without their father. I don't think either of them remember Pa, but I do. He was kind and funny.'

'I'm not trying to replace your father, Judy.' Hilda's face flushed rosily. 'I'm too old for all that, and no man would want a woman with half a limb missing.'

'Ma, you're only thirty-nine. You're not old, and

if Mr Faulkner really likes you he wouldn't care about your injury.'

Hilda tossed her head. 'I don't know why we're even talking about this, Judy. Wilfred and I are just friends.'

'Wilfred?' Judy chuckled. 'Oh, Ma! I'm delighted that you have a gentleman friend. You are much too attractive and nice to spend the rest of your life as a widow.'

'You're talking nonsense, as usual. I'm going home.'

'You mustn't keep Wilfred waiting,' Judy said, smiling.

'It's a pity you're too big to put over my knee.' Hilda stalked off with her head held high and Judy dissolved into a fit of giggles. Suddenly she felt better, and she went to the linen cupboard to fetch sheets and pillowcases for the bed in Daisy's old room.

Dr Godfrey arrived next day and was met at the station by Dr Neville. Judy was halfway down the grand staircase when they arrived. She reached the foot of the stairs in time to greet the new arrivals.

'It's so good of you both to come all this way.'

Dr Godfrey bowed over her extended hand with old-fashioned gallantry, which she found rather touching. 'Not at all, Miss Begg. I've always been interested in spinal injuries, and Dr Neville has explained the nature of the accident.'

'Would you like to see Mrs Tattersall before you

75

examine Jack?' Judy asked cautiously. 'I expect she had many questions to put to you.'

'Of course.' Dr Godfrey gave her a smile that seemed to light up the great hall even though it was raining outside.

'That's a good idea,' Dr Neville added. 'Dr Godfrey will be able to give her much more up-to-date information than I could.'

Judy led the way to the morning parlour where Mary spent much of her time these days. It was a relatively small room, furnished with comfortable, well-worn chairs and a tea table set in front of a tall window, which overlooked the parterre garden in all its spring glory. Mary was seated by the fire, which she insisted on being lit even though it was reasonably warm. She put her embroidery hoop down.

'Yes, Judy? What is it?'

'Dr Neville is here with the specialist from London, Dr Godfrey.'

'Oh dear. I'm not sure I'm ready for this. What will I do if he says there's no hope of Jack ever walking again?'

'He might say the very opposite, Mrs Tattersall. Dr Godfrey is the expert.'

'Show them in, and then you'd better go upstairs and warn Jack to expect them.'

'Yes, of course.' Judy opened the door and beckoned. 'Mrs Tattersall will see you now.' She ushered them into the room and closed the door. Taking a deep breath she headed back through the great hall and, picking up her skirts, she raced upstairs, arriving in Jack's room slightly breathless.

He was propped up on a mound of pillows. 'Why the hurry?' he demanded peevishly. 'Your hair is all over the place.'

She went to the dressing table and smoothed a stray lock of fair hair back from her forehead. 'Your mother sent me to tell you that the specialist is here. Dr Godfrey is particularly interested in spinal injuries.'

Jack turned his face to the wall. 'I feel like an exhibit in a freak show.'

'Nonsense, Jack. Stop being so melodramatic. The doctor is here to help you.' A sharp rap had Judy hurrying across the room to open the door. She let the two doctors in and rather reluctantly left them to carry out whatever examinations they thought necessary. She made her way slowly downstairs, where she found Mary pacing the floor in the great hall.

'Are you all right, ma'am?' Judy asked anxiously.

Mary shook her head. 'I can't carry on like this, Judy. I know I should be stronger and more capable, but I really can't continue to manage the estate as I did when Jack was away at university. Jack spoke to me about you and I agree with him. There is no one that either of us would trust to take over while he's in this state, other than yourself. Will you forget everything I said in the past, Judy? Will you take over from me and keep the estate from going bankrupt?'

Chapter Five

It was almost an hour later when Dr Neville and Dr Godfrey returned to the morning parlour. Judy had managed to calm some of Mary's fears by promising to do everything in her power to keep things running until Jack made a full recovery. She had kept her amused with descriptions of Mrs Wood's lodging house and the people who lived there, but she was rapidly running out of stories.

'Well?' Mary demanded, rising to her feet. 'What is the likely outcome, Dr Godfrey? There's no need to mince words. I'm prepared for the worst.'

'I've examined your son to the best of my ability and, apart from the obvious bruising, it's difficult to ascertain whether or not there is more serious damage to his spine.'

'So you can't give me a definite diagnosis,' Mary said slowly. 'I thought you were an expert.'

'I understand your concern, Mrs Tattersall, but in a case such as this we have to wait and see. It's going to be a slow process, but I would very much like to come again in a couple of weeks' time, and perhaps by then I'll be able to make a more accurate prognosis.' Dr Godfrey looked from Mary's downcast face to Judy's equally sad expression. 'However, I am very hopeful. Jack is young and strong, and I know he will have the best of care.'

Mary sank back onto her seat. 'Send your bill and I'll make sure it is settled quickly.'

'There will be no charge for this initial visit, Mrs Tattersall. I'm happy to be of service but I will return in a fortnight's time, if that's acceptable to you.'

'I'll call again tomorrow,' Dr Neville said hurriedly.

'I'll see you out.' Judy hesitated in the doorway, glancing anxiously at Mary, who was deathly pale.

'All this is too much.' Mary leaned back in her chair, closing her eyes. 'My poor boy.'

'I'll be back in a minute.' Judy hurried after the doctors and she caught up with them as they were preparing to leave the house. 'Are you really hopeful, Dr Godfrey,' she asked anxiously, 'or were you trying to keep up our spirits?'

'A bit of both, I suppose. As I said, it's a difficult one to predict, but time will tell.'

'Mrs Tattersall is naturally very concerned,' Judy insisted. 'Could you be more specific? Will Jack ever be as he was before the accident?'

Dr Godfrey patted her on the shoulder. 'I'll do

everything I can for him, but I can't promise anything. However, I can see that he has an excellent nurse, and it's just a matter of time before we know anything for certain. In the meantime, try to keep him calm and don't allow him to worry.'

Judy dropped her gaze. She could feel the colour rising to her cheeks as it had done when she first met Dr Godfrey. 'Thank you, Dr Godfrey.'

'I'll drive you to the station, Ben,' Dr Neville said cheerfully. 'Unless of course you'd like to stay on for a day or two.'

'I'd love to, but I have patients to see at the London, although I might take you up on that offer when I return. Little Creek seems such a charming village and a pleasant change after the hurly-burly of the East End.'

'The station it is then.' Dr Neville gave Judy an encouraging smile as he left the house. 'Try not to worry, Judy. We'll do our best for Jack.'

'Yes, Doctor. I know you will.'

Judy stood in the doorway, watching them as they climbed into the chaise and drove away. She knew that they would do what they could for Jack, but she had hoped for more encouraging words from both doctors, and she struggled with feelings of disappointment and frustration. Jack might be laid up for weeks, months or, heaven forbid, even years, and what would happen to the estate? It would not run itself and she had made a solemn promise to do what she could to avert disaster. The servants would do their very best and Clem Guppy was capable of dealing with the day-to-day problems that arose on the estate, but it was clear that Mary Tattersall was close to breaking point. Judy had never before considered how hard it must be for a woman on her own to take charge of a large household as well as the demands of a working estate, but it was becoming clear to her now. Suddenly the divide between mistress and servant had narrowed. Judy knew that she owed it to Jack to do whatever she could to ensure that things ran smoothly until he was well enough to take over.

She turned to James, who was standing behind her waiting to close the door.

'James, will you send a message to the stables, please? I'd like a horse saddled and ready to leave for Colneyhurst in twenty minutes.'

'Yes, miss. I'll see to that myself.' James hesitated, clearing his throat, and it was obvious that he had something to say.

'What is it, James?'

'We're wondering if things will go on the same now, miss. I mean with the master laid up for goodness knows how long, will there still be a place for the likes of me and some of the other servants?'

'Of course there will,' Judy said firmly.

'Begging your pardon, but can you say that for certain? I'll be honest with you, miss. There's talk of bankruptcy in the servants' hall. They say that Madam has allowed the estate to run into debt.'

'I'm sure that's untrue, James.' Judy was shocked, but she tried to sound positive. 'But it does look as though the master might be laid up for a while. You can tell them in the servants' hall that I have matters in hand. We will keep going until the master is well again. Have no doubt about that.'

'Thank you, miss. I hope you don't mind me asking.'

'Please send the message to the stables. If anyone asks, I'll be back in time for dinner.' Judy headed for the grand staircase, taking the steps two at a time as she made her way to Jack's room. She burst in without knocking.

'Well? What did you think of Dr Godfrey?'

'He prodded me about as if I were a lump of meat.'

'He had to examine you, Jack.'

'He tried to sound hopeful, but I still can't feel my legs. I think it will always be like this.'

Judy hurried to his bedside and sat down, holding his hand. 'I want you to stop talking like that. The doctor was much more hopeful when he was talking to your mother and me. We have to be positive, Jack. You're not to give up; I won't let you.'

He raised her hand to his cheek with a wan smile on his lips. 'You're a bully, Judy Begg.'

'I most certainly am, when need be, and I'll be very cross if I hear you talking like that again.'

'All right, I'll try to be positive, but it doesn't stop me worrying about what's going on downstairs. I feel so cut off up here.'

'I know you do. It's miserable for someone like you to be confined to one room, but I'm sure it won't be for much longer.'

'I was shocked to see Mama looking so pale and wan. I don't think she's been coping very well, Judy. Running the estate is too much for her; I should have left university sooner.'

'She's tired and she's worried about you. I'll do everything I can to make life easier for her.'

'I can't expect you to manage things on your own, Judy. It's my job, but there's very little I can do, laid up like this.'

'You have to concentrate of getting well again, and I'm going to ride over to Colneyhurst and ask Daisy for advice. She knows more about running the Creek Manor estate than anyone.' She leaned over to brush his tangled hair back from his brow. 'It's only temporary, Jack. You'll be back in charge in no time.'

'That's the trouble, Judy. I never expected to be the lord of the manor, but now I'd give anything to be able to take back the responsibilities that irked me so much.'

'And you will again.' She rose to her feet. 'I'm leaving now, but I'll be back in no time at all and I'll tell you all about it.'

'Don't jump any fences. That's how I came a cropper.'

'I'm not as adventurous as you, Jack Fox.' She left him with a cheery wave, but she was worried. Despite the doctors' attempts to sound hopeful, she was far from certain, and trying to convince Jack that he would recover fully was exhausting. She went to her room to change into her riding habit, which fortunately had been in the valise containing her clothes that James had collected from the cottage that morning. It was only when Judy saw her garments lying on the rich damask coverlet that she realised how shabby and old-fashioned they were. Most of them had been darned or patched, and even though the mending was neatly done, it was obvious that this apparel belonged to a menial. The riding habit was perhaps the best of the collection and that was a hand-me-down from Daisy.

Judy went to the mirror to pin the smart little hat in place. 'You're a fraud,' she said out loud. 'And everyone will know it. You are Judy Begg from Green Dragon Yard. You're a servant, and no one will take you seriously.'

An hour later, seated in Daisy's elegant drawing room, Judy struggled to put her fears into words. 'I was a child when you brought us to Creek Manor, and I grew up working in the kitchen. How can I expect the rest of the servants to take orders from me?'

Daisy shook her head, smiling gently. 'I started out in service, Judy. I was governess to a small boy in a grand London house. You know the story, as does everyone in Little Creek, but when I had to take over the running of the estate I had to put all that behind me. It's not *what* you are, but *who* you are that counts. You must have faith in yourself, and the confidence to put yourself forward. It's harder for a woman than for a man, but you can do it. You have to decide what you think is best when it comes to running the estate and the household, and then stick to your guns.'

'What do you suggest? Where would I start?'

Daisy was silent for a moment, a frown marring her smooth forehead. 'If I remember rightly, the first thing I did was to ride around the estate and make myself known to all the tenant farmers. They are always willing to express their views and they'll probably hand out advice, whether you want it or not. You still have Clem Guppy to manage the day-to-day affairs, so you just need to assure everyone that there is someone in overall charge.'

'That sounds like a good idea. What did you do when it came to running the house?'

'Well, I had a chat with Mrs Ralston and we went over the household accounts. I gave her free rein to manage the house servants as she saw fit, and then I had a long talk with Cook, giving her the same responsibilities for the kitchen staff.'

'What about Molesworth?'

'Ask him about the cellar. That's his favourite place, and he looks after the wines as if they were his children. He also has charge of the male indoor servants.'

'What about the outdoor staff? I don't know anything about gardening or the stables.'

'You need to talk to Clem about that. He's been

a good estate manager for ten years and he's reliable, especially with all those mouths to feed. I believe he and Ivy have seven children now.'

'Will you come to the manor house and back me up? They'll listen to you.'

Daisy shook her head. 'No, Judy. You must do this on your own if you want them to respect you, but I'm here if you need me, and of course I'll ride over to see Jack. Poor fellow, how is he?'

'You know him as well as I do. He hates being laid up in bed, and neither Dr Neville nor Dr Godfrey can give us a definite diagnosis.'

'Dr Godfrey? Who is he? I don't know the name.'

'He's a doctor at the London Hospital, but I believe he trained at the City Orthopaedic Hospital. He came down from London especially to see Jack.'

Daisy smiled. 'That will be my brother's doing. Well, let's hope Dr Godfrey can work miracles, because I fear that's what it will need to make Jack walk again.'

'I dare not think like that. I have to convince Jack that he'll recover completely, and to do it I have to believe it will happen.'

'He's lucky to have you, Judy. If by some unkind twist of fate he doesn't regain the use of his legs, he's had the best education that we could afford to give him, and he'll be able to take over the business side of running the estate.'

'But he's such an active person. I don't know how he would cope with life as a cripple.'

'Jack has a much stronger character than his brother. Jay couldn't face responsibility of any kind.'

'But you loved him once,' Judy said shyly.

'Yes, I don't mind admitting it. I married him twice, didn't I?' Daisy laughed but there was no humour in the sound. 'You and Molly were my bridesmaids at our spring wedding.'

Judy smiled. 'I remember my dress and the little baskets filled with herbs and flower petals that Molly and I strewed in your path. It was a lovely day.' She eyed Daisy warily. 'I mean it seemed lovely to us, but that was before Jay disappeared.'

'That was a talent of his; that and marrying women bigamously.'

'I'm sorry. I didn't mean to remind you of unhappy times.'

'Don't apologise. I got over Jay a long time ago and I was lucky enough to meet Marius, who is the best of husbands and a wonderful father. I doubt if I would have been half as happy with Jay, who was selfish to the core. It was painful at the time, but I'm glad he left the country.'

'Jack isn't like his brother.'

'They're only half-brothers. You didn't meet the old squire, Jay's father, but he was a nasty character. He wanted me to marry him but I had the good sense to refuse his advances.'

'But he married Mary.'

'He did the right thing, but only because he knew

he was dying and he was afraid of going to hell. Anyway, he made Jay his heir. I suppose in the eyes of the law Jay still owns the manor house and the estate, but he won't come home to claim it back from his brother – not after all this time.'

'What makes you so sure?'

'I know Jay so well. He shies away from responsibility of any kind. I doubt if he'll ever return to Little Creek.'

Judy went back to Creek Manor with mixed feelings. Daisy had given her good advice, but she had put doubts in Judy's mind as to the eventual outcome of Jack's injuries. After all, Daisy had spent time as a probationer nurse at the London Hospital, and she had probably seen people with similar conditions, which made her an expert in Judy's eyes. She went straight to Jack's bedchamber without even stopping to remove her hat and gloves, and she found him wide awake, staring up at the ceiling. She could tell from his expression that he was in the grip of deep depression.

'Let me prop you up, Jack. You don't look comfortable.'

'You've been gone for hours,' he said peevishly. 'I've been here all alone, apart from Ma, who keeps trying to make conversation when I've nothing to say. What is there to speak about when I'm stuck here like this?'

Judy peeled off her riding gloves and plumped up

the pillows. She could not lift him and she did not try, but she dropped a kiss on his forehead.

'You can stop being grumpy, and I'll tell you what Daisy had to say.'

Jack turned his head away. 'Go on then.'

'Well, she said she was very sorry to hear about the accident, and she's going to ride over to see you.'

'I really don't feel like seeing anyone. It's bad enough having my sisters coming round every day.'

'You should be thankful that people care about you, Jack Fox. If you keep on like this I'll go away and leave you to sulk.'

He shot her a sideways glance. 'I'm not sulking.'

'Well, what do you call it then? I went to see Daisy to ask her advice, because someone has to take charge until you get better, and you will recover, Jack. I refuse to let you sink into a state of depression.'

'I might never walk again. What sort of man does that make me?'

'You are still the same Jack Fox that you were before the accident.'

'I'm as dependent as a baby. I can't do anything for myself.'

'That will change in time. Look at my mother: she's learned to live with her disability. You have every chance of a full recovery, so don't lie there feeling sorry for yourself. Dr Neville is coming tomorrow and maybe he'll let you sit up in a chair. If he does, then James could carry you downstairs.'

'Like a baby,' Jack said with a wry smile. 'I'm sorry, Judy. You've been working so hard to keep up my spirits. I will try to be a better patient.'

She leaned over to kiss him on the cheek. 'Just try to be positive, Jack. I'm doing my best.'

Having left him in a slightly better mood, Judy went to her room to change out of her riding habit. She put on a simple grey cotton gown with a starched white collar and cuffs, and brushed her fair hair into a chignon at the nape of her neck. Small tendrils curled around her forehead, as if rebelling against her attempts to tame her thick tresses, but she was not concerned about her appearance, she had work to do. She began with Cook, her old friend and mentor Nell Pearce, and they sat at the long kitchen table, drinking tea and discussing topics as diverse as laundering the kitchen maids' uniforms, stocking the larder and the cold room, as well as the menus for the coming weeks.

When Judy left the kitchen she went straight to the housekeeper's office and found Ida Ralston poring over an accounts book. Judy had grown up in awe of Mrs Ralston, but now they discussed the housekeeping duties like equals, although Judy was careful to defer to Ida's age and experience, and they parted on the best of terms. That left Molesworth, who was getting a bit rheumaticky, but was still eager to show off the contents of the cellar and explain his method of cataloguing the wines, spirits and barrels of ale. His one complaint was that the days of dinner parties and large-scale entertainments were over, and there was little call for his expertise. Judy sensed that he was worried about his future at the manor house and she did her best to assure him that he would not be replaced by a younger man, and that he was virtually indispensable.

She was exhausted when she made her way to the drawing room to tell Mary about her visit to Colneyhurst, and she was surprised to find her mother seated on the sofa in deep conversation with Mary. They both looked up with a start when she walked into the room, putting Judy in mind of two children caught doing something naughty.

'Is there something I should know?' Judy looked from one to the other.

'Wilfred has asked me to marry him,' Hilda said, blushing rosily. 'I know it's quite sudden, although we've known each other for ten years, and quite ridiculous for a woman my age, but . . .'

'But nothing, Ma.' Judy rushed over to give her mother a hug. 'Don't be silly. If you love each other, of course you must marry him.'

'That's what I said.' Mary smiled smugly. 'Faulkner is a good man and he's been here for as long as I can remember. I don't see what's stopping you, Hilda.'

'My leg,' Hilda said in little more than a whisper. 'He hasn't seen me undressed, and I'm afraid he might find me repulsive.'

'Of course he won't.' Judy squeezed in between them on the sofa and put her arm around her mother's shoulders. 'He must know about your injury. You've never kept it a secret.'

'I know, dear, but it's different when you're married.' Hilda glanced anxiously at Mary. 'It's one thing having a kiss and a cuddle, but when you're married you share a bed . . . well, Mary knows what I mean.'

'I'm not a child, Ma.' Judy released her mother with one last hug. 'If it worries you so much just show him.'

'What?' Hilda cried. 'Lift my skirt in front of a man? I'd die from mortification.'

'Ma, you want to marry him, don't you?'

'I'm considering his offer.' Hilda pursed her lips primly.

Judy looked from one to the other, shaking her head. 'I don't see how you can get round it in any other way. Although, I suppose if you were to sit behind a screen, and I lifted your skirt for you, we could show Wilfred without causing either of you any embarrassment.'

Mary covered her mouth with her hand, barely disguising a chuckle. 'That sounds sensible, Hilda.'

'I don't know. I'd still find it awkward.'

'You won't see him,' Judy said firmly. 'You'll be hidden except for the bit of you that is causing the problem. If he finds it disturbing, I'll know by his expression.'

'It's the most practical solution, Hilda.' Mary rose from the sofa. 'I think I need a glass of sherry wine. You must both join me. I never drink alone.'

She moved swiftly to the bell pull and tugged it so hard that Judy was afraid she might pull it down.

Judy turned back to her mother. 'Well, what do you think?'

'I don't know, dear. It all sounds a bit theatrical, not to say embarrassing. There's no getting round the fact that I look like something from a freak show.'

Judy leaped to her feet. 'Nonsense. I won't have you say things like that about yourself. You're the bravest, kindest woman I've ever met and you deserve to be happy.'

Mary nodded emphatically. 'I agree with Judy. It sounds a bit extreme, Hilda, but if you can't bear to reveal your poor damaged limb in any other way, I don't see the harm in it.'

'I wonder what Grace Peabody would say if she knew,' Hilda said with a wry smile.

'Heaven forbid!' Mary sank down on a chair by the fireplace. 'Where is that girl? I really could do with a glass of sherry.'

'I'll fetch the decanter and glasses from the dining room,' Judy said hastily. 'Just in case words gets out that the mistress of Creek Manor has taken to drinking in the afternoon. That really would scandalise the vicar's wife.' She left the room, almost bumping into the parlour maid. 'It's all right, Lizzie. The mistress has changed her mind.'

'Yes, miss.' Lizzie turned on her heel and hurried back in the direction of the servants' quarters, leaving Judy free to fetch the decanter.

After two glasses of sherry, drunk in quick succession, Hilda finally plucked up the courage to agree, and they decided to put Judy's stratagem into action the following afternoon.

Later, when Judy had taken Jack's supper to his room, she told him what they were planning and had the satisfaction of hearing him chuckle.

'You're a witch, Judy Begg,' he said, grinning. 'Who else would think of something like that?'

'It's common sense,' she countered. 'Ma is afraid that Wilfred will be horrified when he sees her poor injured leg, and both Mary and I said that if he really loves her he will take it all in his stride.'

'Unlike poor Hilda,' Jack said, laughing.

Judy smiled. She knew that Jack was not being callous, it was merely his wry sense of humour struggling to get through the haze of misery that had held him in its thrall since the accident. He had always been able to see the funny side of a situation, and this was just the start of his recovery, or so she hoped. She waited until he had finished his meal, then she picked up the tray.

'Lizzie should be doing that,' Jack said sharply. 'And you should be seated at table in the dining room with my mother. Why are you still here with me?'

'I'm here because this is where I want to be, and I eat in the servants' hall, as always.'

'But that's ridiculous, Judy. You aren't a servant, and you should be treated as a member of the family.'

'You're wrong, Jack. I am still a servant, even if my position has changed slightly.'

'I won't have that. You're my . . .' He met her gaze with a puzzled frown. 'I mean, we've been together for so long that you're part of me.'

'Not in the eyes of the family, or anyone else, if it comes to that. We're not engaged or even thinking about it.'

'Of course not. I'm a cripple and likely to remain so. I can't marry you, or anyone while I'm in this state.'

She could see that he was getting agitated and she headed for the doorway. 'Don't worry about it, Jack. It will all work out in time.'

'That's what people say when they don't know what's going to happen,' he said bitterly. 'Look at me, Judy. I'm supposed to be lord of the manor in Jay's absence, but everyone knows that I'm not up to it. I wasn't before the accident and now I'm completely useless. I can't even elevate you from the servants' quarters to the family table.'

'I won't listen to this.' Judy balanced the tray on her knee while she opened the door. 'I'll come back after I've had my supper.'

'Don't bother. I'll probably be asleep.'

'All right, if that's the way you want it, I'll say good night.' She left the room, knowing that she would return later and he would be pleased to see her, even if he pretended otherwise. She loved him dearly, but he was behaving like a fractious child.

She took the tray to the kitchen where she found her mother in conversation with Cook and Ida Ralston, but Judy was quick to note the worried look on her mother's face.

'What's the matter, Ma?'

'Oh, Judy! I really can't make up my mind. I don't know what to do.'

'What do you mean?' Judy asked wearily. 'Is this about your feelings for Mr Faulkner or embarrassment because of your amputation?'

'Yes, my dear,' Cook said with a sympathetic smile. 'If you have any doubts about marrying the fellow, I'd say think again.'

'Yes, indeed.' Ida Ralston nodded in agreement. 'What exactly is worrying you, Hilda?'

The sound of booted feet on the flagstone floor made them all turn with a start and Judy was surprised to see Wilfred Faulkner standing in the doorway, the smell of the stables hanging over him in a cloud.

'Well, this is charming,' he said, grinning. 'Are you spreading the good news, Hilda, my dear? We're to be married, ladies. My Hilda has yet to name the day, but it can't be soon enough for me.'

Nell nudged Hilda in the ribs. 'Go on, then. Tell him what you want him to do.'

Chapter Six

It was all set up. The following afternoon, in the seldom-used Blue Parlour, Hilda sat in a chair behind a tapestry screen. Her damaged limb rested on a stool, and the wooden leg lay on the floor beside her. She had been ready to give up, but a glass of sherry had steadied her nerves, and Wilfred had been sent for, although he had not been told the reason for their meeting. Judy stationed herself on the other side of the screen, ready to pull it back just far enough to reveal the stump. It had seemed like a brilliant idea when first mooted, but now she was beginning to think it was a bit too theatrical, and might have the opposite effect to that planned. Everything now depended upon Wilfred and his reaction; she would know immediately if the sight of Hilda's injury made him recoil in horror.

The sound of footsteps in the corridor made Judy

panic for a moment, but she took a deep breath, forcing herself to sound calm.

'He's here, Ma. Just sit tight and leave the rest to me.'

'I could do with another tot of sherry wine, Judy.'

'Nonsense. Do you want him to think that you are a toper? Sit quietly and let me do the talking.' Judy waited for the rap on the door, then moved swiftly to open it. 'Come in, Mr Faulkner. I expect you're wondering why I asked you to come here today.'

Wilfred Faulkner was a big man, used to working in the stables and apparently more comfortable when he was with horses than he was at this moment. He stepped into the room, clutching his cap in his hands. 'I was a bit curious, miss.'

Judy opened her mouth to explain, but Hilda cut her short.

'Wilfred, it's me, Hilda. I'm here behind the screen.'

His mouth dropped open and he cleared his throat noisily. 'What are you doing hiding behind that thing, Hilda?'

'There's something I want you to see before I give you my answer to the question you asked yesterday.'

'I'm hoping that you will accept my offer, Hilda. I haven't got much, but what I do have will be yours if you'll agree to marry me.'

'That's just the point,' Hilda said softly. 'You know about my injury, but you haven't seen it. I want you to take a good look, and if you can't abide the sight of my stump, then we'll say no more about it. I don't want us to marry and then you have the shock of your life.'

'Hilda, me dear, I can't believe you would think that of me. Wasn't I a boy soldier sent out to fight in the Crimean Peninsula in '53? I saw many things what a boy of fourteen should not see, so you mustn't worry about your poor leg.'

'But I do, Wilfred. I want you to take a good look before you commit yourself to marriage.'

'My dear, I've loved you from afar for the last ten years, only I thought I wasn't good enough to propose to a lady like you. I would count myself the luckiest and happiest man in the world if you would marry me.'

Judy wiped a tear from her eyes, wishing she had had the forethought to put a hanky in her pocket. 'Shall I pull back the screen, Ma?'

'Yes, but only to show the worst of it.'

Judy folded back part of the screen to reveal the pitiful stump just below her mother's knee. She studied Wilfred's face and saw that he, too, was crying. Tears trickled down his weather-beaten cheeks, disappearing into the soft fluff of his neatly trimmed beard and moustache. He said nothing as he moved the screen aside and he went down on one knee.

'Hilda Begg, I loves you, girl. I wants you to be me wife more than anything in the whole wide world, and to me you're the most beautiful woman I've ever seen. Will you do me the honour of being my wife?'

Hilda threw her arms around his neck and burst into tears. 'Oh, Wilfred, yes I will, with all my heart.'

Judy mopped her eyes on her apron as she hurried from the room, giving the lovers the privacy they deserved. She found Mary loitering in the corridor.

'Well? What happened, Judy? Why are you crying? Didn't it work out?'

'Oh, yes, it did. It was quite beautiful and I think they'll be very happy together.'

'I'm glad.' Mary hesitated, frowning.

'What's the matter?' Judy asked anxiously.

'Nothing really, it's just hearsay, but I believe Faulkner can be a bit hot-tempered at times.'

'But he seems so gentle with Ma. Perhaps he's different with men.'

'Yes, I'm sure you're right, and he has a lot of responsibility looking after the horses and training the young boys. I'm sure they can be a handful, and I've no complaints about his work.'

'I've never heard my brothers complain about him, but perhaps I ought to warn Ma.'

'No, don't do that, Judy. Your mother deserves a good life with a loving husband, and they will have the cottage.' Mary gave Judy a calculating look. 'You'll stay here, of course.'

'I hadn't thought that far ahead, but thank you. I'd better start organising the wedding. I don't suppose Ma is in a state to make the necessary arrangements.'

'We'll do this properly,' Mary said firmly. 'It will

be a summer wedding, not on a grand scale like Daisy's, but your mother will have the best we can give her. She will be a June bride, and there's much to do before then.'

The forthcoming wedding had the household in the grip of a race against time. Mary decided to pay for everything, given that Hilda had earned very little during her time at Creek Manor and Faulkner's wages as head groom would not cover the bare essentials. Hilda had wanted a quiet wedding, but Mary was eager to show off her home and her position as the squire's widow, although she passed most of her responsibilities on to Judy, including the organisation of the wedding.

Judy's first task was to help Hilda select the material for her wedding gown. Hilda insisted that it must be a sensible style that could be worn as her Sunday best. Miss Creedy, the village dressmaker, was given the task of making it, together with dresses for Judy and Molly, who were to be maids of honour. It also fell to Judy to organise the wedding breakfast on a very limited budget, although Mary refused to acknowledge the fact that funds were low. Judy, Cook and Mrs Ralston put their heads together, and with Molesworth's help they chose food and wine that would suit all the guests.

Both Faulkner and Hilda were well known in the village, and Little Creek was such a tight-knit community that it would have been easier to invite everyone, but Judy had to be practical. With a limited budget she had to be ruthless when Hilda presented her with a long list, and they sat down together and managed to cut it down to a reasonable size. Judy spent several afternoons laboriously writing out the invitations, which were then delivered by Nate and Pip. Both boys said they were pleased to welcome Wilfred into the family, although Judy thought she detected unspoken criticisms of their mother's choice behind their warm words. However, it was obvious that Hilda was radiant, and Judy would not have said anything to mar her mother's happiness, so she kept the niggling concern to herself.

The only person who was not excited about the coming nuptials was Jack, who was able to sit up in bed, but had not regained any feeling in his legs. Dr Neville gave him exercises to perform in an attempt to strengthen his muscles, but Jack was not a good patient, and he expected miracles. Judy suggested that he might feel more cheerful if James or one of the grooms were to carry him downstairs to the drawing room, but Jack refused on the grounds that it would be humiliating. Judy had done her utmost to humour him, but even she was beginning to lose patience. In the end she turned to Nick Neville after one of his regular visits to see Jack.

'I've been thinking,' she said cautiously. 'I saw people being pushed along in chairs with wheels. They weren't the old-fashioned Bath chair, but something much more practical.'

'I know what you mean, Judy. They're quite a modern invention, and probably expensive, but maybe we could get a second-hand one. I'll contact Dr Marshall and see if he can help.'

'Oh, would you? I'd be so grateful. Jack is trying everyone's patience, and I'm at my wits' end to know what else to do for him.'

Dr Neville patted her on the shoulder. 'I understand. Leave it to me.'

Three weeks later the wheelchair arrived in the back of Farmer Johnson's cart. When unloaded and brought into the great hall it looked a bit dilapidated and dusty, which was explained by the fact that it had been left in an outbuilding after the previous owner had passed away. Judy decided that there was nothing that a lot of beeswax polish and elbow grease could not solve, and she set about cleaning it up, working all afternoon on the chair until it gleamed like new.

Daisy had called in to see Jack, bringing her youngest son with her as Timmy was not yet old enough to join his older brothers in the schoolroom, but his eyes lit up when he spotted the wheelchair, and he demanded a ride. Judy pushed him round the great hall while his mother went upstairs to see Jack, and Timmy had to be physically prised from the chair when his mother came downstairs to take him home.

'At least I know it works,' Judy said, smiling. 'I

just hope Jack approves of it as much as young Timmy.'

'No, Timmy. You can't ride home in the wheelchair.' Daisy restrained her young son by seizing him round the waist and lifting him off his feet. 'If you misbehave I won't bring you here again, and I most certainly won't ask Nate to take you for a pony ride.'

Timmy subsided at once, and was set free. 'I'm sorry, Mama.'

'What a good boy.' Judy ruffled his curly hair. 'Next time your mama brings you here, I'll make sure that one of my brothers is free to take you for a ride.'

Timmy's face lit up with a huge grin and he gave Judy a hug.

'I've been thinking,' Daisy said slowly. 'Both your brothers work in the stables, don't they?'

Judy nodded. 'They do.'

'And Nate is particularly good with Timmy. I was wondering if he'd be interested in working for us at Colneyhurst. I imagine he would stand more chance of promotion, when he's older, of course. He's still very young, isn't he?'

'He's thirteen, but he'll be fourteen soon. I can't speak for Nate, but he might be interested.'

'I'll have a word with Marius, and our head groom, but I'd like all my boys to be good riders, and Nate seems to have more patience with young children than most boys his age.'

'Would you like me to find out if he'd consider

a move? He's very close to Pip and he might not want to be parted from his brother.'

'Yes, Judy. Find out how he feels, because I wouldn't want him to be unhappy or homesick. They're both good boys. I'd take the pair of them if it were possible.' Daisy took Timmy by the hand. 'We must go now, but I hope the wheelchair works for Jack. He's very depressed, poor fellow.'

'It's all I can think of at the moment.'

'His accident is one reason why I want my boys to learn to ride while they're young, and to be taught by someone who's learned the right way to do things. Anyway, I mustn't stand chatting. Goodbye, Judy. You're doing a wonderful thing for Jack. I hope he realises how lucky he is to have you.'

Judy waved goodbye to Daisy as she left the house, holding her youngest son by the hand. Even though she had been a child at the time of Daisy's disastrous marriage to Jay Tattersall, Judy had great respect for the way Daisy had dealt with the heartbreak and humiliation. She had come through the bad times, and if Jack could follow her example he might recover at least some of his old spirit, instead of giving up on life, as he seemed to be doing now. Judy sighed and pushed the wheelchair into a corner out of the way. It was too late in the day to ask Jack to try it out, but tomorrow she would broach the subject. The wedding was in two weeks' time and it would be wonderful if Jack could be present.

*　　*　　*

Next day, after a great deal of persuasion, Jack allowed James to carry him downstairs and Judy had the wheelchair waiting for him. James lowered him gently onto the seat and then backed away.

'Well?' Judy could hardly contain her excitement. 'Is it comfortable? Would you like to go outside and get some fresh air? It's a lovely day.'

Jack said nothing for a long moment and Judy was afraid he was going to refuse, but then he nodded. 'I suppose so. Are you going to push this contraption?'

'Yes, although I'll need James to help me get it down the steps. From then onwards it's easy.' Judy beckoned to James, who stepped forward, and together they managed to get the chair down the front steps and onto the gravelled drive. 'Thank you, James.' Judy began to push the chair towards the parterre garden, but Jack raised his hand.

'Not there. I'd like to go to the stables to see Conqueror.'

Judy hesitated, trying in vain to think of a plausible excuse. She was worried that seeing his horse again might rekindle memories of the accident, but Jack was adamant, and against her better judgement she agreed. Even so, it was good to see the fresh breeze whipping some colour back into his pale cheeks, and the pleasure he exhibited on seeing his horse again was heart-warming. Conqueror rubbed his head against Jack's shoulder, whinnying softly.

'He's missed you, Jack,' Pip said, grinning. 'He's trying to say he's sorry you got hurt.'

'It wasn't his fault.' Jack raised his hand to stroke Conqueror's soft muzzle. 'I misjudged the jump. It was lucky he didn't break a leg.'

'Don't think about it,' Judy said hastily. 'He's obviously pleased to see you.'

'Horses don't bear grudges, not like people.' Jack's smile faded. 'If he had broken a leg he'd have been shot. It's a pity they couldn't do that for me.'

'Jack!' Judy gasped. 'Don't say things like that.' She glanced at her brother and saw that he too was upset. 'Jack doesn't mean it, Pip. He was joking.'

Pip nodded, but he did not look convinced. 'Shall I take Conqueror back to his stall?'

Jack shrugged and turned away. 'You might as well. I'll never ride again. Take me back to the house, Judy. I'm tired.'

'Is it my fault?' Pip whispered.

Judy shook her head. 'No, of course not. Maybe we'll come again tomorrow.'

'Get me out of here, please, Judy.' Jack's voice broke on a suppressed sob and she pushed the wheelchair out of the stable. They emerged into bright sunshine and she did not stop until they were clear of the stable yard.

'Do you really want to go back to the house? Would you like to see the lake?'

'I want to go back to my room.'

'Of course, but wouldn't you like to have tea in the drawing room first? Your mother would love that.'

'I can't think of anything worse. I don't want

107

people fussing over me, Judy. Just do as I say, take me back to the house and James can carry me upstairs like the cripple I am.'

Judy sighed, but she knew Jack well enough to realise that arguing was futile. They returned to the house in silence, and when Jack had been taken to his room Judy stowed the wheelchair out of sight. It seemed now that her initial reservation about visiting the stables had been well judged. The memory of the accident had stirred up all the anger and emotion that Jack had been feeling, and had made matters worse. She stood stiffly, staring out of one of the tall windows with unseeing eyes. The glory of the early summer's day and the beauty of the grounds did not register in her mind. All she could think of was Jack, immured, it seemed for ever, in his room upstairs.

The sound of a horse's hoofs and the clatter of wheels brought her abruptly back to the present and she saw Dr Neville's chaise approaching the carriage sweep. It was with a huge feeling of relief that she ran to the door and wrenched it open. Dr Neville was the only person with whom she could speak openly about Jack's problems. Mary became distressed if she suspected that Jack was not making progress and Hilda was too involved in her wedding plans to offer any words of encouragement. Judy stood on the top step and waited while Dr Neville climbed down from the vehicle, and to her delight he was followed by Dr Godfrey.

Maybe Dr God could live up to his name and offer a treatment for Jack that would give him hope of recovery.

'It's good to see you again, Judy,' Dr Godfrey said, smiling.

'And you, Doctor. I'm so glad you've come. Jack is very downhearted at the moment.'

Dr Neville nodded. 'It's only to be expected. I remember Jack when he was a boy and he was always up to something. I treated him when he fell from a tree and broke his arm.'

'Is it convenient for me to see him now?' Dr Godfrey asked politely. 'I take a particular interest in his injury, although I can't promise a cure.'

'If you could just give him some hope,' Judy said quickly. 'He thinks he'll be like this for the rest of his life. He won't, will he?'

'I don't know.' Dr Godfrey shook his head. 'I wish I could give you some hope, but I've done some research and it might be something the doctors are calling spinal shock. If that's so, then he will recover, although it's impossible to say how long it might take.'

'And if not?'

'Then he might spend the rest of his life as a cripple.'

'Come along, Ben,' Dr Neville said impatiently. 'We won't know if there's been any improvement until we've seen the patient.'

'Of course.' Dr Godfrey gave Judy a rueful smile.

'We'll do everything we can for Jack.' He followed his colleague up the grand staircase, leaving Judy staring after them. She wanted so much to believe that Jack would recover the use of his limbs, but she knew that she must prepare herself for the worst. No matter what the outcome she would always stand by Jack and support him in every way possible. She hurried to the drawing room to tell Mary that the doctors has arrived.

Mary had wanted to go upstairs to be with her son, but Judy had managed to dissuade her, and they settled down to wait. After half an hour Mary was becoming restive and she jumped to her feet. 'I think I'd better go and see what's keeping them.'

'Jack won't thank you for barging in, Mrs Tattersall. I'm sorry to be so blunt, but you know what he's like.'

Mary subsided back onto her seat. 'I suppose so. But he's still my boy, no matter how old he is.'

'I can hear someone coming.' Judy turned her head at the sound of the door opening and Dr Neville entered first, followed by Dr Godfrey. Judy glanced from one to the other, but their expressions were carefully controlled and gave nothing away. 'How is he, Doctor?'

'Is there any improvement?' Mary added anxiously. 'Ring the bell for Lizzie, please, Judy. I'm sure the doctors would like some refreshment.'

'A cup of tea would be most welcome,' Dr Neville said, smiling.

Judy stood up and reached for the bell pull. 'Is it good news, Dr Godfrey?'

'There's little change from when I last examined the patient,' Dr Godfrey said carefully. 'But there is no deterioration in Jack's condition, so I remain hopeful.'

Mary's hands flew to cover her flushed cheeks and she uttered a cry of relief. 'I'm so glad. But where are my manners? Please sit down, gentlemen.' She waited until they were settled. 'So what exactly are you saying, Dr Godfrey? Will my son recover fully, or not?'

'I would love to be able to give you a definite answer, Mrs Tattersall, but I'm afraid I cannot. All I can say for sure is that Jack is young and strong, and it is just a matter of time, although you can help him by keeping up his spirits.' Dr Godfrey turned to Judy. 'I gather you took him out in the wheelchair this afternoon. That is just the sort of thing he needs.'

Judy shook her head. 'I thought so, but now I'm not so sure. Jack insisted on going to the stables to see his horse, and he was very upset. I think he's afraid that he'll never ride again.'

'Oh, Judy, that was a silly thing to do,' Mary said crossly. 'You ought to have known better.'

'I didn't set out to take him there, Mrs Tattersall. It was Jack's idea.'

'And we all know that Jack can be very determined when he sets his mind on something,' Dr Neville said, chuckling. 'I wouldn't let that put you off, Judy. Maybe in a day or two you might suggest another outing, and this time take him in the opposite direction.'

'I could take him out in my carriage,' Mary suggested eagerly.

'Perhaps at a later date, ma'am.' Dr Godfrey exchanged meaningful looks with his colleague. 'I mean, of course it would do him good to get out and about, but the jarring on his spine simply getting in and out of a carriage is not advisable at this stage.'

Judy could see that Mary was affronted by Dr Godfrey's dismissal of her project, but the arrival of Lizzie created a diversion.

'You rang, ma'am?'

'Yes, Lizzie. We would like tea and cake. Judy will give you a hand.' Mary nodded to Judy, adding in a low voice. 'Go and help the girl. You know she gets things wrong, and I expect Jack would like some refreshment after undergoing the examination. As the doctor said, we must keep up his spirits.'

Judy had little choice other than to rise from her chair and follow Lizzie from the room. She avoided looking at Dr Godfrey, although what he must think of her was anyone's guess. Mary had not done it deliberately, Judy knew that, but she had been put firmly in her place. Judy Begg was nothing more than a servant, and as such she was expected to wait on Mary and her visitors.

'I ain't stupid,' Lizzie said over her shoulder as

she hurried towards the servants' quarters. 'I can put up a tea tray and cut some slices from a cake.'

'Of course you can, but I expect Mrs Tattersall wants to talk to the doctors in private.'

Lizzie cast her a pitying glance. 'You're stuck then, aren't you? I mean you're not one of them, nor really one of us neither. It's a shame because I like you, Judy.'

'And I like you, Lizzie,' Judy said, forcing a smile. 'If you'll see to the tray for the drawing room, I'll take some tea and cake up to the master.'

Lizzie pulled a face. 'He ain't much of a master now, though. He's a poor cripple what can't leave his bedchamber, never mind anything else. We're all very sorry for him, and you too. Cook says—'

'Never mind that now,' Judy said hastily. 'Let's get on with this, shall we?' She hurried towards the kitchen with Lizzie clomping along behind her. Judy came to a halt and spun round. 'What have you got on your feet?'

Lizzie giggled and raised her skirt a couple of inches, revealing a pair of men's boots, caked in mud. 'Sorry, miss. My shoes are at the cobbler's being mended. These belong to me elder brother.'

'Are they all you could find this morning?'

'I didn't think anyone would notice under me frock.'

'No wonder you fall over your own feet. When you've taken the tea to the drawing room I want you to go and find Mrs Ralston. Perhaps she can help.' Judy could see the slow working of Lizzie's mind as she tried to think of two things at the same time. 'Never mind,' Judy added hastily. 'I'll see if I can find you a pair of decent shoes. Just do what Mrs Tattersall asked.'

Grinning with relief, Lizzie clattered on ahead, tripping over a raised flagstone and only narrowly saving herself from falling as she clutched the kitchen doorpost.

'You'll break your neck one day, you silly girl,' Cook said crossly. 'What did Madam want?'

Lizzie stuck her thumb in her mouth, glancing anxiously at Judy.

'Mrs Tattersall wants tea for three in the drawing room.' Judy could see that Lizzie had forgotten her instructions and she set about laying a tray with crockery. 'Make two pots of tea, please, Lizzie. On second thoughts, I'll make the tea in case you scald yourself. You can fetch the cake from the larder.'

Lizzie shambled off, repeating Judy's words over and over as she went.

'I don't know why we keep her on,' Cook said, shaking her head. 'I'd sack her today if it was up to me.'

'She's one of seven children and their father worked on the railway.'

Cook's hand flew to her mouth. 'Of course, I remember now. Wasn't he killed in an accident on the track?'

'That's right. The family are struggling and her mother takes in washing. The children who are old enough do anything they can to earn a penny or two. The small amount that Lizzie takes home, together with her brother's wages from the Johnsons' farm, just about keeps them all from the workhouse.'

Cook lowered her voice to a whisper as Lizzie lumbered out of the pantry carrying a plate of cakes. 'I'll make more of an effort, Judy, I really will, but she's enough to try the patience of a saint.'

Judy made the tea, laid the tray and cut the cake into dainty slices. 'There you are, Lizzie. Take this to the drawing room.' She gazed down at the toecaps of Lizzie's brother's boots peeping out from beneath the grey cotton dress, and she changed her mind. 'I'll carry it as far as the drawing room and you can take over from there. Follow me.'

'Yes, miss.' Lizzie licked a crumb of cake from the corner of her mouth and chuckled. 'That's good, but I only took a little pinch, Cook. I never stuck me finger in it.'

Cook rolled her eyes and turned away to stir a pan on the range. Judy picked up the tray and headed for the drawing room. 'Don't trip over anything,' she said in a low voice when they reached the door. 'Put the tray on the tea table beside the sofa and leave Madam to pour. Have you got that, Lizzie?'

'Of course I have. Do you think I'm stupid, or something?'

Judy ignored this and knocked and waited for an answer. 'Just try not to spill anything.' Judy opened the door and stood aside. She crossed her fingers as she walked away. If there was a god of clumsy girls, Lizzie needed his help now.

Judy related this episode to Jack a little later when she took him tea and cake. He listened quietly to her description of Lizzie's antics and then he laughed. She could have hugged him with delight, but she resisted the temptation. This was a normal conversation after the fiasco of the outing in the wheelchair, and she felt a little more hopeful. She was tempted to ask him what the doctors had said, but thought it best to leave him to tell her in his own good time. She waited until he had drunk his tea and eaten a slice of cake, hoping to resume the conversation, but he lapsed into silence and turned his head away to stare out of the window. The brief interlude had cheered her temporarily, but now Jack seemed to be slipping back into the dark world of depression. There was little she could do other than to make him as comfortable as possible, and leave him to rest.

Downstairs, she was on her way to the drawing room to see if Mary wanted anything when she met Dr Godfrey in the hallway.

'I was looking for you, Judy. You left us rather abruptly.'

'It's difficult, sir.' Judy dropped her gaze. His

charming smile invited confidences, but she was wary of saying too much.

'I can see that,' he said gently. 'I know a little of your history, and Nick explained how Mrs Tattersall came to be mistress of Creek Manor. It's an incredible tale, worthy of gothic novel.'

Judy looked up and met his humorous gaze with a giggle. 'I don't think Mrs Tattersall would appreciate that, Doctor.'

'Are you coming, Ben?' Dr Neville strolled up to them. 'I have a couple of calls to make on my way home. I'd value your opinion.'

'Yes, of course.' Dr Godfrey turned back to Judy with a smile. 'There's very little I can do for Jack. I'm afraid it's a matter of time and, of course, the good care he's receiving, but if you need someone to talk to, or if I can be of help in any way, you can reach me at the hospital.'

'Goodbye, Judy,' Dr Neville said affably. 'You know you can send for me at any time. If I don't see you before, I'll see you at your mother's wedding. It's the talk of the village.'

'Really?' Judy stared at him nonplussed. 'I don't see why.'

Dr Neville looked away. 'Don't take any notice of the gossips, Judy.'

'What are they saying? I want to know.'

He shot her a sideways glance. 'Oh, you know the type of thing. They talk about the curse of Creek Manor, no doubt referring to the days when the old squire was here and the goings-on then, and the fact that Jay abandoned Daisy on their wedding day. You know the rest. It's all nonsense, of course. I'm sure that your mother's wedding will go off smoothly.'

Chapter Seven

Judy took the small posy of rosebuds and forget-me-nots from her mother and went to sit beside Molly in the front pew. They exchanged watery smiles as the Reverend John Peabody intoned the words of the marriage service, and Judy took her handkerchief from the pocket of her new gown, fashioned by Miss Creedy's clever hands. She wiped her eyes and at an insistent tug at her sleeve from Molly, she passed her the hanky. Molly might be bright and beautiful, but to Judy's knowledge her sister had never in her whole life had a hanky when she needed one. She glanced at Pip and Nate, who were looking uncomfortable in their Sunday best, and Nate kept running his finger around the inside of his starched white collar, his ruddy cheeks turning scarlet from the heat.

Judy could see that both her brothers were hot and uncomfortable and eager for the wedding ceremony to be over so that they could get on with the party. She smiled to herself and felt better. Things would soon get back to normal, although quite how she would get on with her new stepfather was an unknown. She liked Wilfred Faulkner well enough, but she had seen slight changes in his demeanour over the past few weeks. He had always been pleasant enough, but recently she had seen another side to his character. Wilfred did not like to be crossed, and he had shown signs of being possessive towards Hilda that Judy did not appreciate. He had sworn that he would not come between a mother and her children, but Judy was not so sure. Wilfred had already made it clear that Nate and Pip would be expected to remain in their quarters above the tack room. He had stated in no uncertain terms that he expected Hilda to spend more time at home after they were married, although he had not forbidden her to work for Mary. However, Judy had the uncomfortable feeling that this would happen sooner or later. Even so, one look at her mother's happy face as Wilfred slipped the ring on her finger was enough to convince Judy that her worries were groundless. The main thing was for Ma to have a good life with the man she loved, and Wilfred had promised to love and honour her, so all Judy could hope for was that he was a man of his word.

At last they were husband and wife and the congregation rose to their feet as the happy couple made their way to the vestry to sign the register.

When they processed down the aisle Judy was aware of smiling faces on all sides. It seemed as though the whole village had turned out to celebrate the nuptials of Hilda and Wilfred, with one major exception – Jack had refused to leave his room. He had stubbornly turned his face to the wall and nothing anyone said made any difference. In the end Judy had given up, as had his mother, and he had been left in the house with only Molesworth to tend to his needs.

A cheer went up as the happy couple stepped outside into the blazing heat of a June day. Rice and rose petals were strewn across their path as they made their way to the flower-decorated landau, loaned by Mary for the occasion. She had also allowed Judy to organise the wedding breakfast in the great hall at the manor house, although it would not be such a lavish affair as the one ten years ago given in honour of Daisy and Marius. Daisy herself had been a great help when it came to organising the food and drinks, and the kitchen staff had been busy for days previously.

'Crikey, I'm glad that's over,' Pip said, wiping his brow on his sleeve. 'I'm sweating like a pig.'

'Maybe,' Judy said, chuckling. 'But don't let Ma hear you talking like that.'

'You always were mouthy, Pip,' Molly added crossly. 'I think you've got worse since you started living over the stables.'

'Well, you're stuck-up now that you're living at

Colneyhurst.' Pip stuck his tongue out at his sister and Molly cuffed him none too gently round the head.

'That's enough of that, both of you,' Judy said sternly. 'Remember whose day this is and behave yourselves.' Judy turned to Nate, who was giggling. 'And that applies to you, too. Come on, let's go and get the ferry. If we wait for everyone else to go first there won't be any food left for—' She broke off as the boys raced off in the direction of the chain-pulled ferry.

'Typical,' Molly said scornfully. 'Mention food and they're off like a shot.' She linked arms with Judy. 'Let's go. I'm starving. I hope Cook has done us proud.'

'Of course she has.' Judy set off at a slow pace, but the rest of the congregation were already marching towards the crossing.

Molly quickened from a walk to a near run, dragging Judy along despite her protests, and when they reached the ferry Molly elbowed her way to the front.

'Move aside, if you please, for the maids of honour.' With a triumphant laugh she boarded the ferry, followed by Judy, who smiled apologetically at Linnet and Elliot.

'I'm sorry, Mr and Mrs Massey,' Judy said hastily. 'But we have to be there waiting for the bride and groom when they arrive.'

Elliot's reply was lost as the boatman began to wind the crank and the boat jerked into motion.

'I'm sorry, Mrs Marshall,' Judy said as she

stumbled against Daisy's aunt, who was clutching her husband's arm as if terrified that the small craft would sink.

'That's all right, dear. But please don't rock the boat or we'll go overboard and drown.'

'Don't be silly, Eleanora.' Sidney Marshall patted his wife on the arm. 'The creek isn't deep enough here to drown you.'

She tossed her head. 'Well, it would ruin my new gown and my best shoes, Sidney. You might like spending your life up to your knees in cold water, but it's my worst nightmare.'

Molly giggled and Judy nudged her in the ribs, giving her a warning look. 'We need to get to the house before the happy couple,' Judy said earnestly. 'Fuller should have sent the dog cart for us, but the rest of the party will have to walk up the hill to the house.'

After a relatively quick crossing Judy was relieved to find one of the under grooms waiting with the dog cart, onto which she and Molly climbed and hung on precariously while the vehicle jolted up the hill to the house. Barely waiting for it to come to a halt, Judy climbed down and hurried up the steps to find Molesworth waiting for her. He gripped her arm, which in itself was unusual as he rarely made any physical contact with the servants.

'We've got a problem, Judy,' he hissed close to her ear. 'A very big problem, I'd say.'

She gazed at him in astonishment, never having seen him display any emotion whatsoever. 'What's wrong, Molesworth?'

'Nothing is wrong, my dear.' The voice was familiar and yet she could not put a name to the person until she turned her head to look at him.

'Mr Tattersall?' she murmured nervously. 'Is it really you?'

'I think Squire Tattersall is the correct form of address.' The tall, sun-bronzed man descended the last few steps on the grand staircase and strolled towards them, eyeing Judy curiously. 'Is it? No, surely you can't be skinny little Judy with the snub nose and freckles?'

'Yes, sir. I'm Judy Begg.' She exchanged anxious glances with Molesworth. 'But I thought you were in Australia. I mean, that's what everyone said.'

'I was,' he said agreeably, 'and now I've come home to claim my inheritance, and it seems that I arrived at an opportune moment.' He glanced over his shoulder at the tables groaning beneath the weight of the food that Cook and her underlings had prepared. 'Well, now everyone can celebrate the return of the squire.'

Molly rushed into the house, followed more slowly by Eleanora and Sidney.

'Who is he?' Molly demanded, staring at the intruder, wide-eyed. 'He looks a bit familiar.'

'I have the advantage,' Jay Tattersall said, grinning. 'I remember you, young Molly. Although you were quite small when I left for the Antipodes. You've grown into your looks, I must say. You're quite a little peach.'

'I think I'm going to faint,' Eleanora leaned against her husband, covering her eyes with one hand. 'I don't know how you've got the nerve to turn up like this, Jay Tattersall.'

'Eleanora, my dear aunt-in-bigamy, and Sidney, too. This is an unexpected pleasure.'

Sidney grasped Molly by the hand. 'Run and warn my niece, will you, please?'

Molly shook her head. 'It's too late, sir. Look behind you.'

'Jay!' Daisy Walters stood in the doorway, staring at him in a mixture of horror and amazement.

'You've got a nerve, sir.' Marius Walters placed a protective arm around his wife's shoulders. 'I'm astounded that you dared show your face here.'

Jay shrugged and smiled. 'I am the legal lord of the manor, Walters. Do I take it that you've made an honest woman of my erstwhile wife?'

Marius leaped forward, but was restrained by Nick Neville, who had followed them into the house.

'Don't waste your energy on him, Marius,' Nick said angrily. 'Jay loves to create a stir, no matter who gets hurt in the meantime.'

'I say, Nick, that's not true. I'm a most reasonable chap, and I would have expected a warmer welcome home after all these years. Anyway, what's going on? You're all dressed up so it looks like a wedding.'

Jay glanced round at his stunned audience as the rest of the party began to arrive. 'Don't tell me that Ma has tied the knot with some other old codger who's likely to pop off and leave her a fortune.'

Daisy wriggled free from her husband's grasp and stepped forward, her eyes blazing. 'How dare you speak of your mother in those terms? You should be ashamed of yourself.'

Before he could answer, his sister Dove pushed past Nick. 'Jay Fox, you are a disgrace. I can't believe you said that. How dare you come back to Little Creek and start causing trouble?'

'You can go away again as far as I'm concerned.' Linnet moved swiftly to her sister's side. 'We don't want you here after what you did to Daisy. This is Hilda's day, so mind your own business and keep quiet. We'll sort you out later.'

'Really?' Jay threw his head back and laughed. 'I think I have the upper hand, little sister. I have come back to take up my position as lord of the manor.'

'You wretch!' Daisy moved too quickly for anyone to restrain her. She rushed at Jay arm raised, and before he had a chance to dodge the blow she slapped his face. The sound echoed off the high ceiling, and there was a sudden hush as everyone stared at them, open-mouthed.

Jay nursed his red cheek, and then he laughed. 'You wouldn't have done that ten years ago, Daisy, my love.'

'Maybe not,' she said icily. 'But it's time someone

took you to task. Jack has received a good education, and, due to your continued absence, he's the lord of the manor now. You can't take that away from him.'

'What I do no longer concerns you, Daisy Marshall. You are nothing to me.'

'I'm Mrs Marius Walters and have been for the last ten years, but I'm very fond of Jack and Mary, and I don't want to see them hurt.'

'The lady in question has just walked into the house,' Jay said casually. 'Mother, it's me. I've come home.'

The guests who had crowded into the great hall moved aside, and Mary walked slowly towards her son, her face ashen and her lips moving soundlessly.

Dove rushed forward but Mary shook off her daughter's restraining hand. 'So you've turned up again, like the bad penny you are, Jay Fox.'

'Oh, Ma, don't play games with me. You of all people know who fathered me – I'm Jay Tattersall, and I am the master here now. I've spoken to Jack, and at least he is overjoyed to see me, which is more than I can say for the lot of you.'

A ripple of disapproval ran through the onlookers, but it seemed that no one had the courage to speak out. Judy stood frozen to the spot. She felt as though she was watching a drama on the stage, and as a member of the audience there was nothing she could contribute to the scene. But there would be no applause at the end of this performance.

'How could you do this to us, Jay?' Mary said sadly. 'Why did you come back after all these years? Aren't you ashamed of the trouble you've caused?'

'All right, since you've pressed the point, Ma, I'll tell you all the truth. I have come back to claim my inheritance, and I intend to sell the estate, lock, stock and barrel. Then I'll return to Australia, where I have done rather well. I invested money in a gold mine, but I need more capital. As soon as I've got the means I'll be returning to New South Wales. You can come too, Ma, but only if you behave yourself and promise not to nag me.'

'How can you treat your mother like this?' Daisy turned away and went to stand beside her husband. He placed his arm around her waist and held her close. Jay's sisters clung to each other, and Dove was in tears, although Linnet scowled angrily at her brother. Judy was waiting for someone to speak up when the sound of the landau arriving outside made heads turn. It seemed to Judy that everyone were holding their breath as they waited for the bride and groom to enter. She had the eerie feeling that even the old house was waiting to see what happened next.

Arm in arm Hilda and Wilfred walked into the great hall, but they were greeted by silence. Hilda came to a halt, gazing round wide-eyed until she spotted Jay, and then she dropped her posy and her hand flew to cover her mouth. She broke away from her husband and hurried to Mary's side.

'What's going on? Why is he here?'

Mary shook her head. 'Jay has come to put us all out onto the street. He's so like his father that it's unbelievable.'

'I'd ask you all to leave my house,' Jay said casually, 'but it seems a shame to waste good food. Eat and drink and celebrate the return of the master. Oh, and by the way, congratulations, Faulkner, you've made a wise choice. Hilda is all right. In fact I'd say she's too good for the likes of you, but there's no accounting for taste.' He paused, gazing round at the stunned faces of the guests. 'Come on then. Start celebrating or I'm afraid I'll have to throw you all out.'

'You're a bastard, Jay,' Nick said in a low voice. 'In every sense of the word you are rotten to the core.'

Jay shrugged and turned away. His gaze fell on Judy and he beckoned to her. She hesitated, looking round in the hope that someone else would step forward. However, most of the guests seemed to have taken Jay at his word, and had hurried off to help themselves to the food and drink. Daisy and her husband had remained, but Jay's sisters had walked away, leaving their mother to deal with her errant son.

'Leave Judy out of this, Jay,' Mary said nervously. 'She's served me well since she was a child.'

'Maybe she'd like to accompany us to Australia.' Jay leaned towards Judy, fixing her with a hard stare.

'You're fond of my brother, so he tells me, and he needs someone to take care of him during the voyage.'

'You haven't changed,' Daisy said bitterly. 'You're still playing games with people's lives, and it's cruel, Jay.'

He ignored her, focusing his full attention on Judy. 'You can speak for yourself, I'm certain. What do you say?'

'I want to see Jack.'

Jay stood aside. 'Of course you do. Up you go, young lady. Mop his brow and whisper sweet nothings in his ear, while I enjoy some of that excellent-looking food, and a glass or two of wine. Come along, Daisy. Let's be friends again – you too, Walters. No hard feelings.' Jay extended his hand to Marius.

'I can never forgive you for the way you treated Daisy,' Marius said stiffly. 'If I had my way I'd horsewhip you, but we're civilised people, and that's not acceptable. Just don't expect me to befriend you, Tattersall.'

'That goes for me, too.' Daisy slipped her hand through the crook of her husband's arm, and they walked away.

Mary was the only person left, apart from Judy, who remained at her side.

'Well, Ma?' Jay faced her with a supercilious smile. 'Are you going to tell me off, or threaten me with some dire punishment?'

'Why are you doing this?' Mary asked in a voice that shook with emotion. 'Why do you always have to spoil everything that's good?'

Jay looped his arm around his mother's thin shoulders. 'Come on, Ma. Let's eat and drink – it's a wedding party, after all. We'll talk about the details later.' He glanced over his shoulder. 'Go upstairs and talk it over with Jack, there's a good girl, or I might withdraw my offer, and then you'll be out of work, like the rest of the servants.'

Judy drew herself up to her full height. 'You are a very bad man, Mr Tattersall. I wouldn't cross the creek for someone like you, and if I can persuade Jack to remain here, then so be it.' She turned on her heel and walked slowly and deliberately upstairs, holding her head high. She had learned to deal with bullies at an early age, and she decided that Jay Tattersall was the worst of his kind. She did not look back, and when she was certain that he could not see her, she broke into a run. She arrived in Jack's room breathless, and with her flower-trimmed hat tilted at a dangerous angle.

'You've seen my brother?' Jack's faced glowed pink with excitement and there was a hint of the old sparkle in his eyes. 'Did he tell you that he's going to take us to New South Wales where he has shares in a gold mine, and he's building a hotel? We'll be rich as Croesus.'

'You don't know that, Jack. From what I've heard of your half-brother, he's more likely to lose money than to make his fortune. Why do you think he wants to sell Creek Manor if he's doing so well?'

'All businesses go through bad times; Jay told me so and I believe him. Anyway, I'm sure the sea voyage will set me back on my feet.'

Judy went to kneel beside the chair where Jack spent many hours each day. It was placed close to the window so that he could look out and enjoy the view over the park.

'Is that what you really want?' she said gently. 'I mean, do you really want to give up the manor house and all your friends here in Little Creek? You might hate Australia.'

He gave her a steady look. 'Why are you saying these things? I'm not a child, Judy. I know what I want, and it isn't being stuck here day in and day out like the cripple I am. Jay wants to sell up here so that he can double his investments and make even more money.'

'That's all very well for your brother, but are you sure it's best for you, Jack? Would you get the medical treatment you need?'

Jack curled his lip. 'You mean like the amazing cures that your Dr God has offered me? All he and Nick can say is that in time I might be able to walk again, but they can't promise anything. In reality what they're trying to tell me is that they don't know how to treat me, and they don't really think I'll ever walk again. I broke my back – and that's the end of it. Jack Fox, crippled for life.'

'You mustn't think like that. You know that the doctors said it might be the condition they call spinal shock, and one day you might simply get up and walk.'

'I don't want to talk about it now, but I want you to come with me.' Jack reached out to clutch her hand. 'Say you will, Judy. I need you.'

She withdrew her hand gently. 'I don't know about that. I'll have to think about it.'

'What is there to think about? You say you love me, so you must want to be with me.' His arched eyebrows drew together in a frown. 'Or do you love Creek Manor more? Is that why you've been so attentive? Did you want to marry the squire?'

Judy leaped to her feet. 'That's so unfair and it's not true. I can't believe you said that, Jack. You're the one who should give the matter more thought.'

'What are you saying?'

'Your half-brother isn't to be trusted. Look what he did to Daisy and the other women in his life.'

'His private life has nothing to do with it.' Jack turned his head away. 'But I'm not going to argue with you. Anything is better than being cooped up here in my room. I might as well be dead.'

'You could have broken your neck,' Judy said angrily. 'Then you would have died. You're alive and you have a loving family and friends to look after you. If you go with Jay you're risking everything.' She hurried from the room. There was no reasoning with Jack when he was in this mood. If she stayed any longer the argument would go round in circles, getting nowhere. She decided to join the party. After all, it was Hilda's day, and Jay must not be allowed to ruin it for the newlyweds.

Despite the initial upset everyone seemed to be enjoying themselves. Molesworth had made certain that there was enough wine, cider and ale to keep the party going, and Cook had excelled herself when it came to the wedding breakfast. Molly was the first person Judy saw and she met her enquiring look with a shrug.

'Jack wants me to go to Australia with him and Jay,' Judy said bluntly.

'What did you say to that?'

'I said no. I don't trust Jay, and I think Jack would be making a terrible mistake. It might be different if he could walk, but in his present state I don't think it's a good idea.'

'Did you tell him so?'

'Of course I did, but you know Jack: he's stubborn.'

'And so are you,' Molly said with a wry smile. 'Surely you won't let him go all that way without putting up a fight.'

'You know Jack as well as I do. If he's made up his mind, nothing and no one will stop him doing exactly as he wants.' Judy shook her head. 'I really don't know what to do.'

'I'd go with him, if it were me,' Molly said stoutly.

'It would be so exciting. Far better than being stuck in a nursery with naughty babies and their mischievous brothers.'

'I thought you were happy at Colneyhurst Hall.'

Molly tossed her head. 'I am, I suppose. It's just that sometimes I long to do something different. I want to have some excitement in my life, Judy. Can't you understand that?'

'I suppose so. You and I are so different, Molly. I often wish I could be more like you.'

'Don't! You're all right as you are, Judy Begg. We all love you, so don't change.' Molly gave her a quick hug. 'Leave Jack to think about what he's about to do. Maybe he'll change his mind. It's yourself you ought to worry about.'

'Me? What do you mean?'

'If Jay is determined to sell the property you'll lose your job here, as will everyone else, including Ma and Wilfred.'

'Yes, of course. I'm so busy worrying about Jack that I forgot everyone else.'

'He should be the least of your concerns, if you ask me. Think of yourself for once, Judy. You've only been away from Creek Manor once since we moved here, and that didn't last long. It was Jack's accident that cut short your time in London, but you mustn't allow him to rule your life. Let him go to Australia with Jay, and see how he likes it, but you don't have to go with him. Why don't you go back to London and take up your job in the hospital?

Maybe you could do what Daisy did and become a probationer nurse.'

Judy was about to answer when she spotted Wilfred heading their way. She greeted him with a smile. 'It was a lovely wedding ceremony.'

'Thank heaven it was Constable Fowler playing the organ and not Miss Creedy. She might be a good dressmaker, but she had no musical talent whatsoever. Anyway, what are you two girls doing lurking here? Come and join the party. That's an order from your new father.' Wilfred was smiling, but Judy could see that he was serious, and she felt Molly stiffen. Judy recognised the stubborn look on her sister's face. Although Molly had only been six years old when their father was killed in the same accident that crippled their mother, Judy knew that her sister had loved Pa, as she had. Despite his many failings, his passing had left a huge gap in their lives, and Wilfred Faulkner could not simply step into their father's shoes.

'You might be our stepfather,' Molly said curtly, 'but we don't need you to tell us what to do.'

Judy stepped in between them. 'Aren't you a bit concerned about what Mr Tattersall just said? If he sells the manor house and the estate we'll lose our jobs.'

Wilfred's smile faded into a frown. 'I don't think he was serious. I've known Jay since he was a boy. He wouldn't do a thing like that. It's all talk, so stop worrying and join the party or people will think you don't approve of me marrying your ma.'

'Heaven forbid,' Molly said sharply. 'We can't have that.' She shot a meaningful look at her sister. 'Let's eat before those greedy pigs scoff the lot.'

Despite the tempting dishes laid out on pristine white tablecloths, Judy found that her appetite had deserted her. She managed to greet her mother with a hug and a kiss on the cheek, and she was pleased to see her looking blissfully happy, but there was a nagging doubt at the back of Judy's mind. She could not agree with her stepfather when it came to Jay's sudden announcement: he had not been making a wild claim. Jay had been deadly serious and the outlook for everyone at Creek Manor was bleak. When Dr Neville approached her later, she could tell from his expression that he agreed with her.

'What will you do, Judy?' he asked in a low voice. 'Jay is quite capable of going through with his plan to sell the place.'

'Jack wants me to accompany them to Australia.'

'It could be a good opportunity for you, I suppose,' Nick said doubtfully. 'But Jay is a wild card. You never know what he'll do next. You and Jack could find yourselves in a worse situation than if you remained here.'

'That's what I'm afraid of, and it's the other side of the world. We might end up penniless and friendless.'

'It's your decision, but I could always find work for you at Creek Hall. I couldn't pay you very much, but you could live in, and I know that Mrs Bee would feed you like a turkey cock.'

'But I'm not a nurse.'

'It would be more like the work you were asked to do at the London Hospital. Even though you had such a brief time on the ward, Dr Godfrey was very impressed with the way you set about the most menial task without a word of complaint. What do you say, Judy?'

'Would you mind if I didn't give you an answer right now?' Judy eyed him warily. She did not want to turn down the offer outright, but her whole world had just turned upside down and she was not in a position to make such a decision.

Nick smiled and nodded. 'Of course. Perhaps we'd all better wait and see. As I said, Jay is unpredictable. He might be saying things simply to create a stir.' He glanced over Judy's shoulder. 'My wife is beckoning to me. I'd better go and see what she wants.' He strolled off to join Dove, who was standing in a small group with Sidney and Eleanora Marshall, Daisy and Marius.

Judy turned her head to see Jay walking purposefully to the middle of the great hall. He clapped his hands and called for silence.

'Ladies and gentlemen, I want you to enjoy yourselves because this is the last time you will get anything from Creek Manor. The truth is that I'm selling the estate, and your employment here is terminated. I'll give you a month in which to find alternative accommodation.'

There was a stunned silence, and then everyone began to talk at once. Judy found her mother and Wilfred standing at the table where the wedding cake was waiting to be cut. Hilda was deathly pale and bright spots of colour were raised on Wilfred's weathered cheeks.

'How can Jay do this to us?' Hilda said in a low voice. 'We'll lose our home. Oh, Judy! What will we do?'

Chapter Eight

No one knew how the fire started. Just days after the manor house was sold and the last person left, the house was razed to the ground, and everything in it was consumed by the flames. It was rumoured in the village that one of the dispossessed servants had set it ablaze out of sheer malice, but this was simply hearsay. However, fingers were pointed at several people who had the most to lose, and one of them was Wilfred Faulkner. It was well known in the village that he had a long-standing grudge against Jay, considering him an upstart and an unworthy heir to the estate. Faulkner had been with Squire Tattersall since he was a boy, and had been devoted to him. But all these whisperings were largely ignored, and some blamed the curse of Creek Manor, saying it had finally done its worst.

As far as the family were concerned, Jay had left

for Australia before the conflagration, taking his mother and Jack with him, and it was the new owner who was the loser. No one knew his identity, nor had they seen his mysterious person, and it now seemed unlikely that they ever would. The only buildings left standing were the stable block and coach house, but the horses had been sold off and the only occupants were rats, mice and bats. Pip and Nate had lost their jobs and their home above the tack room, and it was Marius Walters who came to their aid by offering them work in the stables at Colneyhurst Hall. Daisy had taken pity on young Lizzie and had employed her as a tweeny, although Judy suspected that Daisy might regret her generosity when she discovered Lizzie's innate clumsiness.

Everything had happened so quickly, and there had been so much to do after Jay's shock announcement that the manor house was for sale, that Judy had only a short time in which to brood over Jack's decision to leave the country. He had tried to persuade her to go with him, but as far as she could make out he seemed to have fallen out of love with her and was now totally obsessed with the idea of gold mines and the large hotel that Jay was having built. Jack was convinced that a long sea voyage would effect a cure, but it seemed to Judy that he wanted her more as a nurse or unpaid servant than the woman he had once professed to love. She had spent many sleepless nights trying to come to a decision, and it hurt her more than she could have imagined when she had to tell Jack that she would not go with him. He had been angry at first, and then he had pleaded with her, but she was convinced that he was making a terrible mistake. She neither liked nor trusted Jay, and with good reason. He had turned his back on the people who had worked at Creek Manor for most of their lives, and some of the older members of the household were facing a poverty-stricken future.

Amongst those worst hit was Clem Guppy, who had been cast aside despite the fact that he had a large family to support. Another land agent had been employed by the new owner, although it was clear from the start that this was not going to be a happy relationship. Judy knew all the tenant farmers and they were all up in arms due to the fact that their rents had been doubled and Cosgrove, the agent, was not a patient man. If they failed to pay the full amount each quarter they stood in danger of being evicted, which had already happened to some of the smallholders.

Hilda and Wilfred had been forced to vacate their home and they were now renting the cottage where Jay and his siblings had been born and raised. With no alternative, Judy had to sleep on a truckle bed in the one room downstairs, which served as kitchen and parlour, while her mother and stepfather slept in the bedroom on the first floor. It was not a comfortable arrangement and Wilfred seemed to be in a permanent bad mood. Hilda tried to excuse his outbursts of temper, putting them down to the fact that he was unemployed and they were living on the pittance she and Judy earned at Creek Hall. Judy, however, was unimpressed. After a week of living under the same roof she knew that she disliked Wilfred Faulkner and that the feeling seemed to be mutual. He made it obvious that he resented her close relationship with her mother, and although he never put his feelings into words, he managed to make it clear that Judy was an unwanted lodger in the marital home.

Both Judy and her mother had been taken on as domestics at Creek Hall, but Judy had missed the opportunity to live in, due to the fact that several of the servants from the manor house had already applied for positions at the small hospital. Judy tried to make light of it when Nick apologised, and he promised that if anyone left she was more than welcome to take their place. Mrs Bee and Dove were sympathetic, but Judy assured them that all was well at home, and she was careful not to criticise her stepfather. She had lived in Little Creek long enough to know that titbits of gossip like that would fly round the village in no time, and if they reached Wilfred's ears he would take pleasure in throwing her out of the house.

The situation came to a head one evening in late September when Judy arrived home before her mother. Hilda had stayed on at the hospital to have a cup of tea and a chat with Mrs Bee, and Judy had enjoyed a solitary walk. It was a golden evening and the leaves were turning from green to russet, tipped with scarlet, and the air was fresh and clean. It had been a good day at work, with many of the patients showing signs of improvement, which was always satisfying. However, it had been a long and hectic day and Judy was tired. She filled a bucket with water from the village pump and, having got the fire going, she put the kettle on the trivet to make a pot of tea. She was wondering what they would have for supper when Wilfred's large frame momentarily blocked the last of the daylight as he stood in the doorway. Judy glanced over her shoulder, saying nothing. She always waited to find out what sort of mood he was in before she started a conversation. She went to the cupboard and was wondering what to do with the meagre contents when she realised that he was standing close behind her. She waited for a few seconds, thinking he was simply trying to get past, but then she felt his arms around her waist and his breath was hot on her neck as he cupped her breasts in his hands. She froze, hardly able to believe that this was the man who had married her mother.

'You're beautiful,' Wilfred whispered close to her ear. 'I could make your life so much better, if you would be nice to me.'

That was enough to galvanise Judy into action and she spun round, giving him a mighty shove that caught him off balance and sent him sprawling onto the flagstone floor.

'Get off me,' she cried angrily. 'Do that again and I'll tell Ma and the whole village what sort of man you are.'

He scrambled to his feet. 'It was your fault, you little slut. You tempted me.'

'I did no such thing. You disgust me.'

With a savage swipe of his hand he caught her round the side of her head, knocking her against the cupboard door, and she fell to the ground, jarring every bone in her body.

'Breathe a word to your ma and I swear I'll kill you.'

'You wouldn't dare.' Judy scrambled to her feet. 'If you harm me you'll go to prison.'

'Get out.' He grabbed her by the arm and dragged her to the doorway. 'I'll never get any peace with you in the house, always giving me sly looks and driving me mad.'

She clung to the doorpost. 'Let go of me. You can't do this. Ma won't allow it.'

'You'll go far away from here, or I'll tell your mother that you tried to lure me into your bed like the harlot you are. Come here again and I swear I'll strangle you.'

Judy backed away from him. 'You haven't heard the last of this. My mother will find out what you've done and you'll be the one to leave the village.'

Wilfred picked up a bundle of clothes that lay on Judy's bed for want of anywhere else to put them, and he tossed it after her. 'Good riddance.'

Bruised, shocked and dazed by the suddenness of the attack, Judy picked up her belongings and limped away, not knowing what to do or where she would go. Her first thought was to run to Creek Hall, but then she would have to tell her mother that the man she married was a monster, and very soon the whole village would know. It was tempting, but Judy needed time to think. One thing was as clear as the babbling waters of the creek: she could not stay here a minute longer. The blow on the head and the fall had left her dazed and feeling sick, but it was getting dark and she needed to find somewhere to spend the night. There was only one place where she could go, and that was Colneyhurst. Daisy would take her in, but then Judy would have to tell her brothers and Molly what had happened, and she would have to explain why she had left home so suddenly. Her head was throbbing and by morning she would have a bruised cheek and maybe a black eye, making it impossible to hide the injuries caused by Wilfred's savage blow.

Without having a plan in mind, Judy started walking. There were plenty of friends in the village who would give her shelter for the night, but that would mean explanations and she would be forced to reveal the part that her stepfather had played in her sudden flight. Her only thought at this moment was to protect her mother, who had been through enough hard times and heartache. Wilfred was a brute, but her mother seemed happy with him.

There was no accounting for what a woman in love would put up with, and Judy was certain that Ma must be head over heels in love with the man she had married. Judy trudged along the road that led out of the village. Perhaps she would find a barn where she could shelter until morning. It had started to rain and she needed to find somewhere quickly.

She was about half a mile out of Little Creek when she heard the sound of horses' hoofs and the rumble of wheels. There was nowhere to hide and with tall hedgerows on either side of the road there was no escape. She flattened herself against the prickly hawthorn, hoping that the driver would go past, but the passenger was peering out of the window and he thumped on the roof, shouting to the coachman to come to a halt. The door opened and Dr Godfrey leaped out.

In the light of the coach lamp there was no hiding place and Judy met his shocked gaze with a steady look. 'I walked into a doorpost,' she said gruffly.

'The hell you did.' Ben Godfrey lifted her chin with the tip of his gloved finger. 'I've seen that sort of injury all too often. Who did this to you?'

'I'm all right,' Judy said stubbornly. 'I mustn't detain you, Doctor.' She started to walk away, but he caught her by the wrist.

'Where are you going? It's dark and wet and you're soaked to the skin.'

Her head ached and each step caused her more and more pain. She was wet, cold and hungry, and she felt her resolve weakening. 'I'm going to visit a friend.' It was a poor lie and she could see that he remained unconvinced.

'Then I'll take you there. Please get in the carriage.'

There seemed to be little alternative and Judy allowed him to help her into the vehicle. He waited until she was settled before climbing in to sit opposite her. 'Where were you headed, Judy? I'll tell the coachman to drive you to the door.'

'I don't know,' she said wearily. 'Just as far away from Little Creek as possible.'

Dr Godfrey tapped on the roof with his cane. 'Drive on.'

'We're heading back to Little Creek,' Judy said in a sudden panic. 'Tell the coachman to stop. I can't go home.'

'I'm taking you to Creek Hall. I was on my way there anyway. You need those cuts and bruises attended to.'

'You don't understand,' Judy said in desperation. 'I can't allow anyone to see me in this state. If it gets back to Ma—' She broke off, covering her mouth with her hand. She had said too much, and even in the dim light she could see from his expression that Dr Godfrey understood.

'I've met your stepfather on a couple of occasions,' he said calmly. 'I didn't take to the fellow. Is he the reason you were running away?'

'I don't want to talk about it, but please, Dr Godfrey, I can't go to Creek Hall.'

'Don't worry, I'll make sure that no one knows apart from Nick and his wife.'

'You won't keep anything from Mrs Bee, and some of the servants from Creek Manor now work at the hospital.'

'Mrs Bee is the soul of discretion, I'm sure. You'll have to trust me, but I can't allow you to wander the country lanes alone and at night.' He took off his overcoat and laid it over her. 'When we get there just sit tight and wait for me to come out and get you. That way we'll make sure no one sees you.'

'My mother and I have been working there,' Judy said through chattering teeth. 'She mustn't find out.'

'I understand your concern, but I don't agree with you.' He held up his hand. 'But I promise to do as you wish. I know that Nick and Dove will want to help you, as I do.'

Judy huddled beneath his coat and the warmth began to seep back into her tired bones. Despite her pain and distress she found herself drifting off to sleep, comforted by the scent of maleness, bay rum and a mere hint of carbolic, no doubt from the hospital.

'Judy, wake up.'

She opened her eyes and found the interior of the carriage suffused with light from a lantern held by Dr Godfrey. 'Where are we?'

'We're at Creek Hall. There's no one about to see you.' He held out his hand and Judy allowed him

149

to help her down from the carriage. 'I won't be needing you again tonight, Carter. Dr Neville's man will see that you're fed and find you a bed for the night.'

'Yes, Doctor.' Carter drove off in the direction of the stables, leaving Judy to follow Dr Godfrey into the house.

Nick and Dove were waiting for them in the entrance hall, and Dove rushed forward to fling her arms around Judy. 'Don't worry. No one will know you're here. Come with me and I'll find you some dry clothes.'

Judy was too exhausted to argue and allowed Dove to lead her upstairs. In the sanctity of Dove's bedroom she made Judy sit down while she went through the garments in a clothes press. 'I was shocked when Ben told us that you'd been assaulted, but you can trust us to be discreet. However,' she added, taking a soft woollen wrap from the press and a fine lawn nightgown, 'he mustn't be allowed to get away with such behaviour.'

'No, you don't understand. He'll deny it and he'll say I encouraged him. I don't care for myself but I won't have my mother upset.'

'My dear, it will be even worse if she finds out the hard way. How would you feel if Faulkner turned on your mother?'

'He won't, or at least, I don't think he would hurt her. He's just a disgusting man. I'd rather not talk about it.'

'I understand. Let's get you out of those wet clothes, and into something warm and dry. Nick will take a look at your injuries and then Mrs Bee will make up something tasty for you to eat.'

'She might tell Ma what he did to me.'

'You can trust her implicitly. Mrs Bee is a good sort and she won't say a word, if that's what you want.'

'Yes, it is, and tomorrow I need to get away from Little Creek. I can't live in the same village as that brute.'

'No, of course not, but we'll talk about it again when you're feeling better. I'm sorry, Judy, I know you've had a bad time since Jack left for the other side of the world. I wish he'd stayed, but there's no gainsaying Jay when he sets his mind on something.'

Judy was too tired to argue and she undressed as obediently as a small child. Dove uttered a gasp of disgust. 'Just look at those bruises on your side and back. That man should be in prison for what he's done to you.'

'We all thought he was a decent enough fellow, although I had heard rumours about his quick temper. Nate and Pip spoke highly of him in the beginning, but maybe he's different when he's working with men. Ma loves him, and that's enough for me. I don't want to break her heart.'

Dove pursed her lips as she slipped the clean nightgown over Judy's head, and helped her into the warm woollen wrap. 'I'd break something over his head if I had my way.' She opened a cupboard door and took out a pair of slippers. 'Put these on and then I'll get Nick to look you over, although I don't think you've broken any bones, and the cuts on your face are nasty, but they don't look deep enough to need stitching.'

Judy smiled and winced at the pain from her cut lip. 'That's one mercy, I suppose.'

'At least you haven't lost your sense of humour,' Dove said with a smile. 'I've made up a bed for you in the next room. The servants don't come to this wing of the house every day, so no one will bother you. I'll bring you some supper.'

A hot meal and a dose of laudanum, prescribed by Nick, had a soporific effect, and Judy slept well that night. She awakened early and for a moment she could not think why she was in a room at Creek Hall, but as she tried to sit up the pain from her bruises was a sharp reminder. Nick and Dove had both tried to persuade her to stay and shame Wilfred Faulkner, but Judy had made up her mind to leave before anyone saw her. She had a little money saved from her earnings, which she reckoned was just enough to get her to London, where she was sure that Mrs Marshall would once again help her to find work. It would be a new beginning far away from Little Creek and the unhappy memories that had almost ruined her life. She dressed in the garments that were more or less dry and she opened the door carefully. There was no one about, although she could hear sounds coming from the wing where the patients had their rooms, but that was on the far side of the building. If she left now she would be in time to catch the first train to London. With her bundle tucked under her arm she crept downstairs and was about to cross the hall to let herself out of the front door when she saw a familiar figure coming towards her.

'Ma! What are you doing here so early in the morning?'

'I came to take you home, love.'

'No. That's not a good idea, Ma.'

'Don't worry about him. He's gone. I threw him out with the aid of me walking stick.'

'But how did you know?'

'Nancy Noon heard the goings-on, and she popped out of next door like a Jack-in-a-box to warn me. I found Wilf in such a state as I'd never seen before, and when I saw the broken stool and a smear of blood on the cupboard door, I knew that Nancy was telling the truth. He tried to give me some cock-and-bull story about you trying to make up to him, but I knew he was lying.'

'I'm not trying to excuse him, Ma, but he's your husband. You had that beautiful summer wedding before the old manor house burned to the ground. It was a lovely day.'

'No one hurts one of my kids,' Hilda said defiantly.

'He's gone and he ain't never going to set foot in our house again. It's you and me from now on.'

Judy eyed her mother curiously. 'It's really early, Ma. How did you know I was here?'

Hilda's lips curved in a wry smile. 'She told me not to tell you, but Dove sent a note with Billy, the head groom. She said that Dr Godfrey had found you on the road to Maldon and brought you here.'

Judy acknowledged this piece of information with a nod. She had asked Dove not to tell anyone of her whereabouts, but she could hardly blame her for breaking that trust. Perhaps running away was not the solution. She gave her mother a hug. 'I'm glad she did, Ma. And I'm sorry you found out about Wilfred like this.'

Hilda sniffed and turned her head away. 'I'd seen things in him that I didn't see before we were married, but he was good at hiding his nasty side. Our marriage would have come to grief sooner or later, Judy. I'm just sorry you had to suffer. Anyway, let's go and put the kettle on. We'll have a quiet cup of tea before the others come down to start work.'

It was obvious when the rest of the staff arrived that news of Wilfred Faulkner's appalling behaviour had spread throughout the village, but everyone maintained a tactful silence, and work went on as usual. Judy opted to remain at the Hall, and she carried on as well she could, although she was limited by the pain from her bruised ribs. She was very conscious of the bruises on her cheek, her swollen lip and the cut on her forehead, but she was lucky to have escaped a black eye, and she was grateful to her friends for their tactful silence. The events of last evening were something she would rather forget, and her mother was there at her side, like a protective guard dog.

Judy was polishing the floor in the Nevilles' private parlour when Dr Godfrey walked into the room. She scrambled to her feet.

'I'll come back later, Doctor.'

He held up his hand. 'No, please don't go on my behalf. I came to see how you are.' He gave her a critical look. 'You should be at home, resting.'

'No, really, I'm better off here. It takes my mind off my aches and pains,' Judy said with an attempt at a smile.

'I heard that your mother had sent the brute packing. I admire her spirit, and yours, too.'

'Thank you, Doctor.'

'What will you do now, Judy? Will you stay on here?'

'For the time being, I suppose. Although, even with both of us working, we can barely make ends meet. I'm grateful to Dr Neville for keeping me on, but I need to find something that will pay better.'

'Will you sit down for a moment? I have something to say that might interest you.'

Judy eyed him warily, but she could see that he was serious and she perched on the edge of an upright chair. 'I'm listening.'

Dr Godfrey sat down in an armchair, facing her. 'Nick and I have been talking things over. It was his suggestion in the first place, but I can see the benefits to both of us and the community.'

Judy stared at him nonplussed. 'I'm sorry, I don't understand.'

'I'm putting this badly, but it concerns Creek Manor.'

'Which is just a pile of ashes now.'

'Precisely, and the person who bought the manor and the title is no longer interested in it. The whole estate is up for sale again, and Nick and I are trying to find investors so that we can buy the land and rebuild the property.'

'You want to be lord of the manor?'

'No, not at all. We want to build a proper hospital, one that is modern and large enough to serve the whole area, not just the village. I want to specialise in orthopaedics, and in particular the rehabilitation of people crippled by spinal injury.'

'Like Jack.'

He nodded. 'Yes, like him and many other unfortunates who are destined to spend their lives dependent on others, or begging on the streets. Once we have the money we will put in an offer for the estate and build a splendid hospital. I think that you would make a very good nurse, Judy. You could train and specialise in orthopaedics. I would be more than happy to have you on my team.'

He smiled and Judy was struck once again by the warm golden lights in his brown eyes. She could imagine how he must soothe his nervous patients, but she was in no mood to be charmed, and she shook her head. 'Thank you, Doctor, I think a new hospital is a wonderful idea, but I don't think I'm cut out to be a nurse.'

'That's a pity, but I'm sure we could find work for you, and your mother, too.'

It was Judy's turn to smile. 'I think we'd better wait until the hospital is built before we come to a decision.'

'You're right, of course, and if you don't mind me saying so, it's good to see you haven't lost your fighting spirit, Judy.'

'I was born and raised in Green Dragon Yard, and you have to be tough to survive in that place.'

'All the more reason to admire your courage.' Dr Godfrey went to open the door, but he hesitated, looking back over his shoulder. 'I want you to think of me as a friend, Judy. Perhaps we could start by you calling me Ben.'

'They call you Dr God at the hospital.'

'I answer to anything but that,' he said, laughing. 'But I hope you'll come to me if you have any more problems. I'm returning to London tomorrow, where I hope to raise the money to buy the land when it comes up for sale, but I'll be back in Little Creek quite often.'

'But what will happen to Dr Neville's hospital if you build a larger one on the other side of the creek?'

'We've talked about that, and we will work together to make sure that Creek Hall Hospital remain the centre of excellence for the village, but it's too small for our purposes. The new venture will be more specialised.'

'It sounds very exciting,' Judy said earnestly.

'It is. I can hardly wait to begin.' He hesitated in the doorway. 'Don't work too hard. You need to look after yourself, Judy.'

Judy acknowledged this statement with a brief nod, but she did not respond to his engaging smile, and as he left the room she went down on her knee to resume her work. She admired Dr Godfrey tremendously, but it would take her a long time to recover from Jack's sudden departure, and she might never cease to wonder if she had made the right decision. As things were, she had no interest in exploring a new relationship.

'Judy! Haven't you finished in here yet?' Hilda stood in the doorway, arms akimbo. 'You should have gone home and rested, as I said.'

'I'm all right, Ma.' Judy stood up with difficulty. She did not want to admit it, but her mother was right, and now every bone in her body ached. 'I'm coming now.'

'I should think so. Anyway, Dr Neville has given

me a bottle of arnica to put on your bruises, and I want you to have a lie-down when we get home.'

'Yes, Ma.' Judy had no wish to return to the tiny cottage overlooking the creek, but she had no choice.

Nancy Noon was leaning against her doorpost when Hilda and Judy arrived. 'I thought he was going to kill you, duck.' Nancy took the clay pipe from her lips and puffed smoke into the air. 'I thought about coming round to help you, but I know what men are like when they get like that. I need to take care of meself so that I can look after my aged ma.'

'Yes, Nancy. Thank you.' Hilda unlocked the door and hurried into the gloomy living room.

'Are you all right?' Nancy asked, peering at Judy. 'He didn't – you know what, did he?'

Judy shook her head. 'I've got a few cuts and bruises, but otherwise I'm fine. Thank you for asking.' Judy hurried after her mother and closed the door before Nancy could hop over the low fence and follow her inside. Nancy was the village busy-body. She knew everyone's business, and it was best to avoid her if possible.

Judy looked round the grim interior and shuddered at the memory of her stepfather's sudden and unexpected assault. 'We can't stay here, Ma. This is a horrible place.'

Hilda was already on her hands and knees trying to coax the fire to light. 'We haven't any choice in the matter, love. Where would we go?'

'I've heard that Lemuel Fox was a violent man, and he beat Jay when he was a boy, which is why he ran away to sea. Perhaps it's this cottage that makes men violent.'

'Well, if it is, we don't have to worry because Wilfred will be far away from here by now.'

The words had barely left her lips when the door opened and Wilfred burst into the room. 'I heard what you said, and you're wrong. This is my home and you are my wife.'

Judy threw herself between them. 'Leave my mother alone.'

'She's my property, just as this cottage is rented in my name. You can get out, you harlot, but Hilda stays with me.'

Judy picked up her mother's walking stick and brandished it like a sword. 'Touch me or Ma and I'll beat you senseless.'

Hilda cupped her hands round her mouth. 'Nancy Noon – fetch Constable Fowler.'

Chapter Nine

'Have you gone mad, wife?' Wilfred demanded furiously.

Hilda shook her head. 'Nancy will have her ear to the wall. You'd better be ready to explain yourself to Constable Fowler.'

'You're my wife,' Wilfred said through clenched teeth. 'And she's nothing but trouble.' He advanced on Judy, his hands clenched into fists. 'You can get out of my house or I'll fetch you one.'

'I'm not afraid of you.' Judy spoke boldly and she stood her ground, but inwardly she was quaking. She was still sore and aching from her last confrontation with her stepfather.

Hilda rushed to Judy's side. 'Go to Colneyhurst, Judy. You'll be safe there. Daisy will take care of you.'

'I'm not leaving you here with him, Ma.'

'Please go. He won't hurt me.' Hilda cast a wary glance in her husband's direction. 'Tell her, Wilfred.'

'I'm no wife beater,' Wilfred said sulkily. 'But you tempted me, girl. You're a brazen hussy.'

Hilda opened the door and a gust of cool air filled the stuffy room. 'Go, Judy. I'll be all right.'

Judy hesitated in the doorway, but Nancy Noon appeared suddenly and peered over her shoulder. 'What's going on? Shall I run and fetch Constable Fowler?'

'No, it's all right, ta, Nancy,' Hilda said hastily. 'Wilfred was larking around and he scared us, but we're fine now.'

Nancy looked from one to the other. 'He looks a bit cross. Are you sure he won't beat you up the minute I turn me back?'

Wilfred uttered a growl and took a step towards Nancy, who hid behind Judy. 'Get out,' he bellowed, 'and take that harpy with you.'

'Go, please,' Hilda pleaded. 'I'll be fine.'

'I should do as she says,' Nancy whispered in Judy's ear. 'I'll keep an eye on things, or perhaps I should say I'll listen, and the first sign of trouble I'll be off down the lane to fetch the constable.'

Hilda nodded and Judy was left with no choice other than to do what her mother wanted, even though it felt completely wrong. She turned to Nancy, grasping her by the hand.

'Promise me that you'll watch out for my mother.'

Nancy's small eyes glittered with excitement. 'I

most certainly will. You can't trust men. I'm glad I never tied meself to one, although I had offers. I was pretty once.'

'I'm sure you were,' Judy said vaguely. 'I'm sorry, Nancy, but I have to start walking. It's three miles to Colneyhurst and it'll be dark by the time I get there.'

'Good luck, love,' Nancy said gloomily as she climbed over the low wall and disappeared into her cottage, slamming the door behind her.

Faced with a long walk in the gathering gloom, Judy set off, heading towards Colneyhurst. The road took her along the margin of the saltings and as it grew darker she could see the tiny darting lights of the will-o'-the-wisp that had lured many a traveller to wander into the marshes. It was not until she reached the headland that the moon came out from beneath a thick blanket of clouds and the calm waters were bathed in a silver light. It was then that she spotted the almost forgotten and long-deserted smugglers' inn. The landlord of this infamous hostelry, a relation of the notorious Dorning brothers, had been arrested and jailed along with his accomplices, and the pub had been empty for as long as Judy could remember. She could only imagine what it must have been like when the gangs were in operation, and the surrounding villages had been complicit in helping them to evade the revenue men.

Her feet were sore and she was exhausted, but she walked on despite the pain from her injuries. The road was deserted and she saw no one until she had almost

163

reached Colneyhurst, but by this time it was pitch-dark and growing colder by the minute. Her thin cotton gown was no protection and she sighed with relief when she saw the lights of the Georgian mansion glimmering like tiny diamonds amongst the surrounding trees. An old man tipped his cap as he walked past her, and she acknowledged him with a nod.

'If you're planning on visiting the Hall, you'll not find the master and mistress at home,' he said gloomily. 'Gone to London, they have.'

'Thank you,' Judy murmured as she hurried past him. She had been banking on finding Daisy at home, but perhaps Molly was there and she could share her room or, failing that, there were Pip and Nate. She headed for the servants' entrance at the rear of the building and was met by a startled scullery maid. When Judy explained that she had come to visit her sister, the girl looked even more worried.

'Molly's gone to London town, miss. She's looking after the little 'un, although Master Henry and Master Edward don't need no nursemaid. They're big boys now.'

'Yes, thank you.' Judy turned to go but the girl caught her by the hand.

'It's getting late. I expect Cook would give you a cup of tea or something.'

'Thank you, that's kind, but I'm going to the stable block to find my brothers.' Judy walked off before the curious girl had a chance to ask any more questions. She picked her way across the cobbled yard to the stable block, and a dim light over the tack room indicated the presence of the stable lads. None of the doors was locked and Judy made her way in the darkness to the ladder leading up to the place where the boys slept. The smell of unwashed adolescent bodies hit her forcibly as she reached the loft, which was dimly lit by a couple of oil lamps. Pip, Nate and two other boys were sprawled on their beds, and the eldest boy was smoking a clay pipe. He jumped to his feet when he saw Judy and hid the pipe behind his back.

'There you are, Davey. I told you you'd get caught smoking that filthy tobacco,' Pip said gleefully. 'Lucky for you it's only my sister.'

Judy looked round at the chaotic jumble of clothes, boots, empty beer bottles and racing papers. 'What a mess. Aren't you ashamed of yourselves, living like pigs?'

Nate scrambled to his feet and gave her a hug. 'Don't scold us, Judy. I'm pleased to see you. How's Ma getting on?'

'We haven't seen her for weeks,' Nate added angrily. 'Pip and me walked all the way to Little Creek on our one day off in a month, only to be turned away by Faulkner. He said she was too busy to see us.'

The boy called Davey swaggered nonchalantly towards Judy with the pipe clenched between his teeth, although the rising spiral of smoke made his eyes water. 'Won't you introduce us, Pip, old chap?'

'It's nice to meet you, Davey,' Judy said, trying

not to laugh at the boy, who could not have been much older than twelve-year-old Pip. 'The same goes for you, too,' she added, smiling at the lad who was sitting cross-legged on the floor.

He jumped to his feet and bowed, causing the other boys to roar with laughter.

'Pleased to meet you, miss.'

Judy shook his hand solemnly. 'What's your name?'

'That's Eric,' Nate said importantly.

'Why are you here, Judy?' Pip gave her a searching look. 'What happened to your face?'

Judy hesitated. She did not want to tell her brothers the whole story, especially with Davey and Eric listening intently. 'Just a bit of an argument at home. Nothing to worry about.'

'It must be something bad to bring you here at this time of the evening,' Pip insisted. 'Did he do that to you, Judy? If he did I'll fetch him one. I ain't afraid of Faulkner.'

'He did, but I don't want either of you to get involved.'

Pip glowered at his curious friends. 'Can you give us a bit of private time, lads? I want to talk to my sister.'

The two older boys shuffled off to the far end of the large loft, taking one of the lanterns with them.

'Sit down, Judy,' Pip said, taking the lead. 'Tell us what happened?'

She sat on the floor next to Nate and told them

what had occurred between herself and their step-father, without giving too many details, although both the boys were plainly shocked and upset. Nate jumped to his feet and fisted his hands.

'I'll give him what for.'

Pip tugged at his brother's shirt-tails. 'Sit down, you looney. We can't do anything without making things worse for Ma. What we have to do is get her away from that brute.'

'Yes,' Judy said, nodding. 'That's right, Pip. I think I have an idea, but I'm not saying anything yet.'

Nate grabbed her hand. 'Will it include us? I like it here, but I miss Creek Manor. Mrs Marshall is very kind, but it's not the same.'

'If my plan works things might fall into place. I can't say any more than that.' Judy glanced into the shadows beneath the sloping roof. 'Is there room for me to sleep here tonight? I haven't anywhere else to go.'

Pip pointed to his palliasse. 'You can have my bed, Judy. I'll double up with Nate, even if he does talk in his sleep. But you'll have to leave very early in the morning, because Old Puckett, the head groom, wouldn't approve of a girl sleeping up here, even if you are our sister.'

'She can share my bed any time,' Davey called out from the far end of the loft and was immediately leaped upon by Eric, who pinned him to the floor.

'That was rude. Say sorry to her.'

Davey threw his smaller friend off with the ease of a dog shaking off a flea. 'Pick on someone your own size, you little tiddler.'

At this insult, Eric threw himself once again at Davey and they rolled around on the dusty floor like a couple of playful puppies.

Judy smiled at their antics. It was good to be with her brothers again, and if her plan worked out maybe she could reunite her family and they could all live together.

'I'm worn out,' she said, yawning. 'Would you mind if I turn in now, Pip? I'm sorry to take your bed, but as you say, I'll leave at crack of dawn.'

It was not the best night's sleep that Judy had ever had. The palliasse was well used and she could feel the floorboards through the crushed straw. Davey snored loudly, while Eric talked in his sleep. She was awakened time and again by the sound of Eric calling for his mother, and the boy's obvious homesickness wrung her heart. She wondered if that was how Nate was feeling, although he would be too proud to admit such a weakness.

She was still awake when the first light of dawn filtered through the gaps in the roof where tiles had blown off in the gales last winter. The boys were sleeping soundly and she had not the heart to wake her brothers. She had slept fully clothed, removing only her boots, and she picked them up and tiptoed across the creaky floorboards to the ladder, which led down to the tack room, but as luck would have it she found she was not alone.

A middle-aged man was bending over the fireplace, poking at the embers and swearing volubly. He turned with a start and glared at Judy.

'Who the hell are you? Women ain't allowed in here.'

Judy drew herself up to her full height, hoping he had not noticed that she was in her stockinged feet. She hid her boots behind her back. 'Are you Mr Puckett?'

'What if I am? What's it got to do with you? Who are you, anyway?'

'I'm Pip and Nate's sister. I came here to see Mrs Walters, but I'm told she's gone to London.'

'That's right.' He looked her up and down. 'You look a mess. What's a young lady like yourself doing sleeping in the stables?'

'It's a long story and I won't bore you with it, Mr Puckett. I'm on my way now, so you can forget I was here.'

He straightened up, pushing his cap to the back of his head. 'Are you any good at lighting fires, Miss Begg? I don't seem to be having much luck.'

Judy hesitated. 'I really should be on my way.'

A wry grin creased his leathery face into a maze of tiny wrinkles. 'You won't get far without shoes on your feet. If you get the fire going I'll make a brew and you can have a cup of tea before you go.'

Judy smiled. Perhaps Old Puckett was not as bad

as the boys thought. 'All right. That's a fair swap.' She placed her boots on the floor and set about lighting the stubborn fire. With luck on her side she got it going quite quickly and Puckett placed the smoke-blackened kettle on a trivet in front of the flames. He took a chipped Brown Betty teapot from the shelf and placed it on the table in the middle of the tack room, together with a poke of tea leaves and another filled with coarsely grated sugar.

Judy sat down and put her boots on while they waited for the kettle to boil. 'I really should go before my brothers wake up,' she said warily.

'You're going back to Little Creek? That where you come from, ain't it?'

'It is, but I wasn't planning to return so soon.'

'It ain't none of my business, but you seem to be in a bit of bother.'

'You might say that. I had a difference of opinion with my stepfather.'

Puckett gave her a straight look. 'He done that to you, I suppose.'

Judy's hand flew to the cut on her forehead and she nodded wordlessly.

'Some men can't keep their fists to themselves,' Puckett said drily. 'So you got nowhere to go?'

'I was hoping that Mrs Walters could help.'

'Well, she ain't here, so what now?'

It was a good question and one for which Judy had no answer. 'What do you know about the old smugglers' inn on the headland?' she asked cautiously.

'What's that got to do with you? That place has been empty for at least ten years to my knowledge.'

'Do you know who owns it?'

Puckett shook his head. 'Don't think anyone does right now. Certainly no one has taken it over since old Abel Parrish got hisself transported to Australia. Why do you ask?'

'I need somewhere to live and I need to keep myself and my mother, if I can get her away from the brute she married. We haven't had a decent home since Creek Manor was sold, and now it's no more.'

Puckett stood up and reached for the kettle. 'I heard that some toff from London bought the place before someone put a torch to it. Maybe he's going to build hisself a mansion to rival the old house.'

'I wouldn't know,' Judy said carefully. 'But I want to be independent. I don't want to rely on any man.'

Puckett made the tea and replaced the kettle on the trivet. 'Well, good luck to you, that's all I can say. I tell you one thing, though. If you try to reopen the Crooked Billet, you'll get a rough crowd of customers. It's always been the sort of place that attracts wrong 'uns.' He filled a cup with tea and handed it to Judy.

'I'm not planning to encourage a smuggling ring. I don't think they do that sort of thing these days.'

'You'd be surprised.' Puckett raised his cup in a toast. 'Good luck to you, anyway, Miss Begg. You've got spirit, I'll say that for you.'

* * *

Half an hour later Judy was back on the road, only this time she was retracing her steps and walking in the direction of the abandoned pub on the headland. It was still very early but the sun had risen and it was already warm, with the promise of a fine autumn day ahead. As she drew nearer to the building she could hear the creaking of the inn sign as it dangled from one rusty hook. The sound of the waves lapping on the foreshore mingled with the mournful cry of the seagulls as they soared overhead, adding to the desolate atmosphere of the deserted inn.

Judy was apprehensive, but determined. She approached the building nervously and she was tempted to retreat, but the thought of another night sleeping on the floor in the loft over the tack room was enough to make her continue her investigation. She tried the front door but, as she had suspected, it was locked, and she made her way round to the back of the building.

There was a stable and a store of some sort, plus a couple of sheds that might have had many uses. A pump sat rusting away in the middle of a yard where grass and moss had almost obscured the cobblestones. A little further away was a privy, which she examined briefly and then closed the door. It might not have been used for many years, but the smell lingered, and it was obvious that the last land-lord had not been too particular when it came to cleanliness. She crossed the yard and tried the back door, but that, too, was locked, and most of the windows were closed, even though some of the panes had been broken.

She was wondering who had the keys when she spotted a small window that was partly open. If she stood on one of the empty kegs she might be able to climb into the building. It was a risky thing to do, but she was driven by necessity. Her feelings of apprehension were replaced by the desire to investigate further, even though she remembered the ghostly tales about the old inn that had circulated in the village. However, it was broad daylight and she doubted if any of the ghouls or ghosts would bother her today. She hitched up her skirts and raised herself up on a keg, balancing with difficulty as she opened the window wide enough for her to climb through.

It was dark inside the building and she dropped onto the floor in what appeared to be a small storeroom. Cobwebs brushed her face and a huge spider landed on her arm. She shook it off, stifling a cry of alarm, and let herself out into a narrow passageway where she came to a halt. She stood very still, hardly daring to breathe as she listened for any sound that might indicate another presence.

'Is anyone there?' she asked anxiously, but the only answer was an echo of her own voice.

Emboldened, she began to explore the ground floor. The main taproom was still furnished with tables and chairs, and a multitude of spiders, cockroaches and probably a few rats, although the rodent population kept well out of sight. Cautiously, she opened the shutters and allowed the sunlight to filter through the salt-encrusted windowpanes. She had expected complete devastation, but oddly enough the taproom and its furniture seemed intact, although filthy, and the hearth by the inglenook was covered in cinders and ash. The shelves behind the bar were empty and if any bottles or glasses had been left behind, these must have been looted years ago. The same was true in the snug bar and in the kitchen. All the cupboards were empty and although she did not venture down to the cellar, she was quite certain that there would be nothing of value down there.

A private parlour at the rear of the pub had been stripped of its furniture, and there were oblong patches on the walls where pictures must have once adorned the room. The flagstone floor was muddied and bare of rugs, and the whole ground floor smelled of damp, must and the stench of cockroaches and rat droppings. She needed to take a look at the upstairs room, but her nerve began to fail her now that she was in the sombre shell of the building. She plucked up the courage to make her way to the first floor, and her heart was pounding when she reached the top of the stairs. She took a deep breath: she had come this far and she was determined to see the investigation through.

There were six bedrooms, all empty except for iron bedsteads minus their mattresses. A narrow flight of stairs led to three small attic rooms, which were filled with the rubbish that the last tenant had left behind, and that had been unwanted by looters. Judy closed the door on the higgledy-piggledy mess, but by the time she reached the ground floor she had made up her mind as to what her next move would be. She secured the window in the storeroom and a search of the drawers in the kitchen produced a bunch of rusty keys, one of which opened the back door. To her delight another key unlocked the front door. It was obvious that the persons who broke into the building were not domesticated, or they would have thought to search more thoroughly for the keys that would give them freedom to return as often as they pleased.

With the set of keys in her pocket she left the inn and set off at a brisk pace for Little Creek. It was midday by the time she reached Creek Hall and she found her mother in the kitchen with Mrs Bee. They both welcomed her as if she had been gone for a year, and Mrs Bee made her sit down at the large pine table while she ladled mutton stew into a bowl. Judy was made to eat before she was allowed to tell them where she had been all night. She ate ravenously, mopping up the last of the soup with freshly baked bread, still warm from the oven.

Hilda sat back in her chair, eyeing her expectantly. 'Now then, love. Tell me everything. I've been out of my mind with worry. I didn't know where you had gone. Not that it was your fault – you didn't have much choice.'

'Where is he now?' Judy asked anxiously. 'Is he still around?'

Hilda and Mrs Bee exchanged meaningful glances. 'Well,' Hilda said slowly, 'I dare say he's still there, although I don't know what he'll do when the rent collector turns up. I've been paying the rent ever since we moved in, and I doubt if Wilfred has any money on him.'

Mrs Bee had been sitting quietly on the opposite side of the table, but she nodded vigorously. 'He's been living off you, Hilda. What sort of man does that?'

'You're not to go back there, Ma,' Judy said firmly. 'You deserve better.'

'I'm his wife, as he keeps pointing out. I don't have much choice, dear.'

'Yes, you do,' Judy cried passionately. 'I think I've found the ideal place for us. Well, perhaps it's not ideal, and it needs a bit of work, but nothing we can't do and it would put a roof over our heads.'

'You know you can stay here, Hilda,' Mrs Bee said hastily. 'I'm sure that Dove would be happy to have you here, and the doctor is too busy to notice. Besides which, you're a good worker and they wouldn't want to lose you. That goes for you, too, Judy.'

'And I'm very grateful to both of them, Mrs Bee.' Hilda reached across the table to pat Mrs Bee's hand. She turned back to her daughter. 'But what's your idea, love?'

Judy glanced warily at Mrs Bee. 'Promise you won't tell anyone.'

'You can trust me, my dear. I could set the stones alight if I was to tell all the secrets I've been privy to over the years.'

'Go on, Judy,' Hilda urged. 'Please tell me. I'd give a lot to turn the clock back to when I was a simple widow, but if you can think of a way to get me free from Wilfred I'll do almost anything.'

'How do you fancy being a pub landlady, Ma?' Judy said, smiling.

Hilda gasped and stared at her wide-eyed. 'You're joking, aren't you?'

'No, Ma. I'm deadly serious, but it's not going to be easy and we'll have to find the money somewhere to stock the bar and to pay for essentials.'

Mrs Bee was suddenly alert. 'Where is this public house?'

'It's an inn. The Crooked Billet on the headland.'

'No!' Mrs Bee clapped her hands to her mouth. 'That place has been empty for more than ten years. It has a terrible reputation, Judy. You wouldn't be able to make a living there.'

'It closed soon after we came here,' Hilda said slowly. 'I seem to remember there was a lot of talk about it being used for smuggling, but then so was Creek Manor when the old squire was alive.'

'I'm not suggesting that we encourage free-trading,' Judy said, laughing. 'I think we could run an inn together, and the boys could manage the stables and help in the bar. We would have a home again, Ma, and it would be ours.'

'There's just one problem.' Mrs Bee looked from one to the other. 'The building might be empty but it belongs to someone. Have you thought of that, Judy?'

Chapter Ten

No matter what anyone said, Judy was not going to be put off, and she had a surprising ally in Dove, who took her side when Nick was adamant that taking over the Crooked Billet was a terrible mistake. It was Dove who insisted that they take Hilda to view the premises later that afternoon.

'After all,' she said, fixing her husband with a steely look, 'it was my brother who let Judy down. They were all but engaged before Jack took off for Australia with Jay and our mother. My brothers have a lot to answer for, especially Jay.'

Nick shook his head. 'You can't hold yourself responsible for the sins of your brothers, my love. But the Crooked Billet has a terrible reputation, and even if we could find out who owns the land on which it's built, I doubt if anyone could make an honest living out there.'

'I think you're wrong,' Judy said firmly. 'All we want is a home and enough money to live on. I don't expect to make a fortune, but we would run an honest business.'

'Of course you would.' Dove slipped her arm around Judy's shoulders. 'They deserve a chance, Nick.'

'I can't stop you.' He sat down at his desk and opened a ledger. 'Take the carriage and Billy will drive you out there, but make sure you get home before dark.'

Dove smiled and blew him a kiss. 'Thank you, Nick. I promise to give them the best advice I can. If I think it's impossible, I'll say so.'

'Shall we go now?' Judy said anxiously. 'We don't want to be there after dark, unless you have a lantern or two we could take.'

'We'll leave as soon as Billy brings the carriage round.' Dove opened the door, turning to her husband with a gentle smile. 'We'll be back in time for supper, darling.'

Judy was anxious as Billy drew the carriage to a halt outside the Crooked Billet. A cold east wind set the inn sign swinging wildly on its one remaining hook. Dark clouds obscured the horizon and Judy felt the first drops of rain as she unlocked the front door. She held it open for her mother and Dove to enter the building, leaving Billy to see to the horses.

Hilda and Dove exchanged horrified glances as they looked round the desolate taproom.

'Just imagine that the place is clean and smells fragrant, and there's a fire burning in the ingle-nook,' Judy said eagerly. She lit the lantern that they had brought with them, and held it above her head, throwing a beam of light on the bare shelves behind the bar. A rat chose that particular moment to race from one end of the counter to the other.

'You'll need the services of the rat catcher before you do anything else,' Dove said, shuddering.

'Or else get a couple of big tomcats to do the job for nothing,' Hilda suggested, wrinkling her nose. 'It stinks in here, Judy.'

'There's a small snug bar and a private parlour behind that,' Judy said in desperation. 'And a nice large kitchen with a big range.'

'I can imagine the state that must be in if this part of the pub is anything to go by.' Hilda braced her shoulders. 'Bring the lantern, Judy. Let's see the worst that the Crooked Billet has to offer.'

They explored the building, treading carefully to avoid the carapaces of dead cockroaches. Hilda was impressed with the size of the kitchen, but she shook her head when she examined the long-neglected range. Dove thought the parlour at the rear of the building could be made comfortable with suitable furniture and some carpet, and, to Judy's surprise, it was Dove who was the most enthusiastic about reopening the inn to the public. They discussed the possibilities on their way home, but Hilda was reluctant to take a risk in a pub with such a dreadful reputation.

It was not easy, but eventually, after a lot of persuasion, Judy succeeded in winning her mother over. They spent the next two days armed with mops, brooms and scrubbing brushes, and the first thing Judy did was to clean the kitchen range. It took the best part of a morning to clear the ashes and attack the grease and rust, and when she had stripped it down to the cast iron, she applied a generous coating of black lead.

Nick's gift to start them off in their new home was a supply of fuel delivered by the coalman, who was upset when he discovered that there was no beer to make up for the distance from the coal yard at the station to the pub on the headland. Judy promised him that when he delivered their next supply he would have a pint of their best ale, but he muttered something about there not being a next time and stamped out of the taproom, slamming the door behind him.

However, once the fire was going in the range and a kettle singing on the hob, the kitchen became a much friendlier place. Hilda had swept the dust, dirt and dead leaves from the taproom, and after a cup of strong tea, sweetened with a lump of sugar, she set about mopping the floor with the luxury of hot water and lye soap. Dove had also come to help and she had brought Linnet with her. They rolled up their sleeves and set to work, swapping jokes about the 'old days' when they were poor and lived in the cottage that Hilda had just vacated. There was another surprise when Daisy drove up in the chaise accompanied by Pip and Molly although Nate could not be spared by Mr Puckett, and soon they were all occupied with one task or another. Windows were cleaned, bedrooms were swept, scrubbed and the windows thrown open as soon as the rain-bearing clouds passed over. Daisy set to with a will, but Molly's contribution was to flit from room to room, wielding a feather duster.

Daisy had had the forethought to bring a hamper filled with food, and at midday they gathered round the huge kitchen table to enjoy a feast of mutton pies, cold chicken, cakes, fruit and copious amounts of tea.

'This reminds me of old times at Creek Manor,' Daisy said, smiling. 'We only need Mrs Ralston and Cook to complete the set.'

'Don't forget Molesworth and James,' Judy added. 'It's such a shame that the old house burned to the ground.'

'Well, there's some good news,' Dove said importantly. 'Our dear friend, fondly known as Dr God, had proved his omnipotence by securing part of the finance necessary to buy the land and rebuild Creek Manor, but this time it will be a hospital big enough to serve the whole county.'

Pip looked up from the slice of fruit cake he was about to devour. 'Will there be a chance of employment for local people, Mrs Neville?'

'Are you thinking of leaving our employ, Pip?' Daisy asked anxiously. 'I thought you were happy with us.'

'I am, Mrs Walters. But I don't want to be a stable boy all my life. I would like to help people with injuries like Ma. We all saw how she suffered and still suffers.'

'Just think of all those handsome young doctors,' Molly said, smiling dreamily. 'I might end up like you, Mrs Neville.'

'Trust you to think of yourself.' Pip glowered at his sister.

'Do you want to spend your days making wooden legs, Pip?' Molly stifled a giggle.

Hilda frowned at them and shook her head. 'Don't laugh at him, Molly. I think it's a very good thing to do. I know how grateful I was to the kind fellow who made my first wooden leg. I would be a cripple in a wheelchair if he hadn't set out to help me.'

Judy laid her hand on Hilda's shoulder. 'Of course, you're right. I'm sure Molly didn't mean to make fun of you, Pip. I think wanting to help others is a very laudable ambition.'

Molly tossed her head. 'Everyone is so serious these days. Perhaps things will become livelier when you open for business. I think I quite fancy working behind the bar.'

'It's not the place for a young lady,' Hilda said firmly. 'You're better off where you are.'

'More cake, anyone?' Judy handed the plate round, and there was a brief silence while everyone finished their food.

When the last morsel had been eaten, Judy rose to her feet. 'I want to thank you all for your hard work. All we need now are some mattresses and bedding, and of course some beer and spirits to stock the bar. At this rate we could open for business in a few days.'

'You'll need some form of transport,' Daisy said thoughtfully. 'There's the old farm cart in the coach house, and Major is almost ready to put out to grass, but he's got a few more miles in him. He's a good steady horse and you're welcome to have him, if that would help.'

'It would indeed.' Judy gave her a grateful smile.

Daisy rose to her feet. 'I think this is a very exciting venture, Judy. I hope it will prove to be a great success.'

The inn sign was cleaned and oiled, and Pip fixed it securely so that it swung gently and silently in the breeze. Daisy had supplied several old mattresses, taken from the storeroom, and some bedding that was considered too old for use at Colneyhurst, even for the servants' quarters. Hilda set to and neatly darned the blankets, all of which were washed and hung out to dry in the fresh air. The most worn of all were consigned to the family rooms, which left the largest bedchamber for any traveller who might want a bed for the night. Similarly, the only refreshment they could offer, apart from tea and coffee, was a barrel of beer that Pip and Nate had manhandled onto a trestle behind the bar, before they returned to their duties at Colneyhurst. The menu was equally limited and unless their future customers wanted anything other than rabbit stew and freshly baked bread, they would have to go elsewhere, but as the only other hostelry was the one in the village, more than two miles away, Judy was hopeful that they might attract passing trade.

On the first day they opened for business there was a steady flow of customers, especially in the evening, but Judy was quick to realise that it was curiosity that had brought the fishermen and farm workers to the door of the Crooked Billet. No one wanted the rabbit stew, one burly workman saying that he could get better at home for next to nothing. Judy dropped the price that evening until they were almost giving the food away, but it was cash in hand, and the money they took on the cask of ale would just about cover the cost of buying a replacement next day. When the ale ran out there was a grumbling exodus of dissatisfied customers, leaving Judy and Hilda to collapse on the settle by the fire with what was left of the stew for their own supper.

'Have we made a terrible mistake, as Nick said?'

Hilda paused with her spoon halfway to her mouth. 'I doubt if we've made any profit today.'

Judy broke off a piece of bread and dipped it in her bowl. 'It's only the first day. We have to build up a reputation, and we need to get more stock.'

'What with?' Hilda demanded crossly. 'I haven't got another penny. What about you?'

'No, but there's the cash we've taken. That will buy a keg of ale, and at least we have somewhere to sleep, and food to eat.'

Hilda did not look impressed and they finished their meal in silence. Outside the wind had got up and it was howling mercilessly around the building, like souls in torment.

'You go to bed, Ma,' Judy said as she piled the plates on a tray. 'I'll lock up.'

'I'd feel safer if the boys would move in with us, although I don't suppose they will.' Hilda rose slowly to her feet. 'But I think I could sleep on a washing line tonight – I'm so tired.'

Judy kissed her on the cheek. 'We'll do better tomorrow. I'm sure of it.'

Hilda limped off in the direction of the staircase and Judy went to lock and bolt the front door. If any weary traveller wanted a bed for the night they would have to go somewhere else. She was too exhausted to care one way or the other.

Next morning, after a surprisingly good night's sleep, considering the storm that raged around the headland and the strange creaking sounds from the contracting timbers of the old building, Judy rose from her bed refreshed and ready for whatever the day might bring. Failure, as far as she was concerned, was not an option. She was going to succeed in bringing the inn back to life, there was no question about it, although when she sat down at the breakfast table and counted out yesterday's takings it was not very encouraging. There was enough for another keg of ale and a few supplies, but no profit from their hard work. She nibbled a stale roll and washed it down with tea, although there was no milk. It was warm in the kitchen and the milk that was left in the jug had soured overnight. She was about to throw it down the stone sink when Hilda entered the kitchen.

'What are you doing, Judy?'

'The milk has gone off. I'm throwing it away.'

'Don't do that.' Hilda crossed the floor with surprising speed. 'It will make cream cheese. All you have to do is to mix it with some salt and place it in a piece of butter muslin, hang it over a bowl for the whey to drip out and tomorrow or the next day it will be delicious. We can't afford to waste a thing.'

Judy stared at her in amazement. 'I suppose I was used to working in the kitchens at Creek Manor where food was plentiful. I don't remember doing this to sour milk.'

'Well then, this is the start of being very careful with what we have. I was used to doing so when we lived in Green Dragon Yard, and even in the cottage on the estate I had to watch the pennies.'

'Yes, of course you did, Ma.' Judy eyed her mother thoughtfully. 'I wonder if you'd like to take the cart to Maldon. It would be a day out for you, and you'd probably get far more for the little money we have than I would.'

Hilda's eyes lit up with a delighted smile. 'I'm not sure I could handle the reins for that long, but I could call at Colneyhurst and maybe Nate or Pip would drive me. It would be a trip out for both of us.'

It took both Judy and her mother to harness Major and get him between the shafts, but somehow they managed it and the old horse munched stoically on his nosebag, rolling his soft brown eyes occasionally when either of them made a mistake.

Judy watched her mother drive off, hoping that Major knew more about pulling a cart than Hilda did about driving one, but they seemed to be getting on reasonably well and they only had to get as far as Colneyhurst Hall. Judy hoped that either Pip or Nate would be allowed to drive the cart to Maldon. Old Puckett was not such a mean old man as the boys had made out.

Judy set about cleaning the taproom ready for business that day, and having swept and dusted, she opened the front door and shook out the duster. It was a fine October morning and the sun was shining from an azure sky. The water trapped by the marsh grasses at low tide sparkled in the bright light, and the sea beyond the headland was a deep ultramarine, dotted with the tan-coloured sails of the working barges. It was a picture of peace and calm, and Judy felt almost ridiculously optimistic. They might not have made a profit on their first day of trading, but they had not made a loss. She was about to go back indoors when she heard the sound of a horse's hoofs and she waited, hoping that it might be passing trade. Perhaps word had got round that they were open for business. She shielded her eyes against the bright light and to her surprise she saw Dr Godfrey himself holding the reins. He drew the horse to a halt and dismounted.

'Good morning, Doctor,' Judy said, smiling.

'Good morning, Judy.' Ben Godfrey looped the reins over the horse's head and tied them to the inn sign. 'I don't suppose you have a stable boy yet.'

'No, but I think Ma is trying to persuade my brothers to come here and help. Won't you come inside, Doctor?'

He followed her into the taproom. 'I thought we had decided that you would call me Ben?'

She turned to give him an enquiring look. 'If you're a customer I don't think it would be right for me to call you by your Christian name.'

'What if I'm a privileged customer?' he asked, laughing. 'Besides which, I don't see anyone here to complain that we're breaking the rules.'

'Well, Ben, I'm afraid you're out of luck if it's a drink you want. I'm waiting for Ma to return with a fresh keg of ale, so I can only offer you tea or coffee.'

'Coffee would be most welcome.' He walked round to the bar and studied the empty shelves. 'How do you propose to make a living without any stock?'

'We'll manage,' Judy said stiffly. 'Please take a seat and I'll fetch your coffee. I've only just lit the fire, but it won't take long for the kettle to boil.'

'I didn't mean to offend you.' Instead of taking a seat as she had asked, Ben followed her to the kitchen. 'You don't mind if I look round, do you? It's an interesting old building.'

She shook her head. 'No, but there's not much to see. We're starting from scratch.'

'Yes, that's what Nick told me.' He pulled up a chair and sat down at the table. 'I'll come straight to the point, Judy. I plan to come down to Little Creek much more often. We have backers for the project to buy Creek Manor. I want to supervise every detail of the design and building, so it would be very useful if I could book a room here on a permanent basis.'

'But you always stay with Dove and Nick.'

'And they've been most hospitable, but I prefer to be more independent. They have their own lives with their family, and if I were to reside here I'd be that much nearer to Creek Manor.'

Judy eyed him doubtfully. 'It's not luxurious accommodation. We have a guest room, but it's quite basic.'

'All I need is a comfortable bed and a good night's sleep with a decent breakfast in the morning, and some supper when I return in the evening. I know that you're a good cook because Mrs Bee told me you'd been trained in the kitchen at Creek Manor.'

'I can show you the room, and you can decide then,' Judy said warily. She finished grinding the coffee beans and tipped a measure into a jug, filling it with boiling water from the kettle. She allowed it to stand before pouring the dark liquid into a cup. 'I'm afraid we haven't any milk or cream,' she said apologetically, 'but there is some sugar.'

'It's perfectly all right like this,' he said, chuckling. 'Stop worrying, Judy. I'm not here to criticise, in fact the very opposite. I admire your spirit and I'm here to help.'

She sat down opposite him. 'In what way?'

'This inn would get a lot of trade when the building work starts on the new hospital. You might find yourself almost too busy, but you will need to stock the bar and cellar, and the larder, too.' He held up his hand as she opened her mouth to argue. 'I know what you're going to say, but I can help by reserving your best room for my personal use when I'm in the vicinity. I can pay in advance.'

'Why would you do that?'

'Because the pub in the village wouldn't be able

to cope with the sort of influx of workers, surveyors and architects that will come to Little Creek. Besides which, there is a landing stage and a slipway, which means that barges carrying the materials for building the hospital could unload here and be transported to Creek Manor by road. It's in the interests of the new hospital to keep the Crooked Billet in business.'

Judy was not convinced. 'But the docking facilities haven't been used for as long as I've been living in Little Creek.'

'That's not a problem. They could be rebuilt if necessary and I've already received part of the funds necessary. I'm putting up some of my money and the investors will be contributing the rest. What do you say, Judy? Will you allow me to help you?'

Judy glanced at the bare shelves in the larder and she knew that this was an offer she could not refuse. She nodded. 'Thank you. It would certainly keep us in business.'

Ben raised his cup to her in a toast. 'Here's to the future, Judy.'

'Perhaps you'd better see your room before you make a final decision, Doctor.'

Judy's efforts at creating a comfortable guest bedroom were rewarded by Ben's enthusiastic comments, and he booked the room there and then.

'It's a priceless view,' he said earnestly. 'I've grown used to looking out at the backs of terraced houses in London, with stray cats howling all night and feral dogs barking. Even in a respectable square the privies still smell appalling, but here I can breathe easily and enjoy the scent of the countryside and the view of the sea in its ever-changing moods.'

Judy stared at him in surprise. 'My goodness, I didn't realise you were so poetic. I know you're a good doctor and I'm beginning to suspect that you're an excellent businessman. You are full of surprises.'

He turned to her with a rueful smile. 'I must seem like a very dull chap to someone like you.'

'I never thought of you in that way,' Judy said hastily. 'I was told that they worship you at the London Hospital.'

He laughed. 'All because of the silly pun on my name. It doesn't mean anything.'

'That's as may be, but you are highly thought of. I can tell you that from first-hand experience.'

He gave her a searching look. 'Do you share their opinion?'

His comical expression made Judy laugh and she shook her head. 'Now you're fishing for compliments. Are you saying yes to the room? If so I'll try and find some more rugs to make it more homely, and maybe I can find a better mattress for you.'

'Stop worrying. Of course I'll take the room. Don't even think of allowing anyone else to book that one. I can return to London safe in the knowledge that I have a place to lay my head even if I arrive late in the evening.'

Judy held out her hand. 'I agree to that.'

'We'll be a partnership of sorts, Judy.' He held her hand rather longer than was necessary to seal a bargain. 'Now there's just the question of money. I suggest we go downstairs and discuss the price.'

Judy had good news for her mother when she returned from Maldon late that afternoon. They unloaded the meagre amount of supplies that Hilda had brought back with her, leaving the keg for Nate to bring into the taproom when he had finished unharnessing Major. Judy was bubbling with excitement, and she could not wait to show her mother the princely sum that Ben had left to secure the reservation of the best room. She hurried her into the parlour where she had stowed the leather pouch behind a cushion on one of the chairs.

'I've never had so much money,' Hilda whispered, glancing over her shoulder as if she were expecting someone to be spying on them.

'I know,' Judy said, smiling. 'This solves all our problems for now at least, but if Ben is right and work starts very soon, we should get really busy.'

'Nate said he would like to live here, but of course I'd have to speak to Daisy first. It's only polite, considering she's been so good to the boys.' Hilda fingered the coins as if touching precious metal. 'We need somewhere to keep this safe. I suspect some of the customers we had last evening would rob their grandmothers if they could get away with it.'

'I've thought of that.' Judy led the way to their

private parlour and she kneeled down to prise up a loose floorboard. 'We'll keep out what we need and put the rest down here. With a rug over the top no one would think of looking there.'

'I certainly hope not.' Hilda watched while Judy stowed the leather pouch in its hiding place. 'I'm starving,' she said faintly. 'I haven't eaten since that slice of stale bread for breakfast.'

'Neither have I,' Judy admitted reluctantly. 'I was working so hard getting the place ready to open that I forgot about food.'

'There are two meat pies in the basket,' Hilda said eagerly. 'Let's eat.'

But a noise coming from the taproom and a male voice shouting Hilda's name made them both freeze.

'It's him,' Hilda said faintly. 'He's come to get me.'

Chapter Eleven

Judy grabbed Hilda's walking stick. 'Stay here.' She ran from the parlour and made her way to the taproom where Wilfred was pacing the floor.

He came to a halt. 'Where is she?'

'My mother doesn't want to see you.' Judy faced him bravely, although inwardly she was quaking.

Wilfred was a big man, and he was obviously furious. His hands shook and his eyes were bloodshot, veins stood out in his neck and his chest rose and fell as if he had been running and was short of breath.

'She's my wife and she's going to come home with me.'

Judy could see that he was beyond reason and she raised the stick, pointing it at him. She was afraid, but she was not going to let him see that she was trembling. 'No, she isn't. Ma wants to stay here, and that's good enough for me.'

Wilfred uttered a bark of laughter, but there was no humour in the sound. 'Who's going to stop me? A slip of a girl with a stick? Get out of my way.' He advanced on her, fists clenched, but at that moment the pub door flew open and Nate rushed into the taproom brandishing a shotgun.

'Get away from her,' he cried, his voice breaking, but there was a steely look in his eyes and a determined set to his jaw. It was as if overnight the youth had become a man. 'I know you've come to get Ma, and I ain't going to let you near her.'

Wilfred spun round, but he backed away when he saw the gun. 'Where did you get that? You don't know how to handle a firearm.'

Judy could see that Nate was nervous but his gaze was fierce and resolute.

'Yes, I do,' Nate said angrily. 'The gamekeeper at Colneyhurst taught me how to shoot so that I could kill rats in the barn, and I ain't afraid to use it.'

Wilfred took a step towards him. 'You haven't got the nerve to pull the trigger, son.'

'Don't call me "son". You ain't my pa, and you ain't good enough for Ma. I heard how you've been treating her.'

'Put the gun down.' Wilfred advanced purposefully.

'Stop this at once.' Judy flung herself between them. 'You're not welcome here, Wilfred Faulkner. I'm telling you to go.'

'And so am I.' Hilda marched into the taproom,

head held high. 'I'm not coming back to you, not ever. You pretended to be a good, kind man, when all the time you're just a bully, and I'm not going to put up with it. Now do as Judy says and get out.'

Nate cocked the gun and pointed it at his stepfather, and this seemed to have the desired effect. Wilfred backed towards the doorway. 'All right. I'm going, but this isn't the last you'll hear from me, Hilda. You'll come running back to me when this place closes, and I'll make sure that it does.' He opened the door and stormed out of the taproom.

Judy sank down on a wooden settle by the inglenook. 'Put the gun down, Nate. Where did you get such a dangerous weapon?'

'Like I said, the gamekeeper loaned it to me so that I could keep the rats down. I reckon that Faulkner is a big rat.' Nate made the gun safe and laid it on the nearest table. The colour left his cheeks and he collapsed onto a chair. 'I really would have shot him, Ma. If he'd tried to hurt you I'd have pulled the trigger.'

Hilda hurried to his side and gave him a hug. 'You shouldn't have taken the shotgun, Nate. Don't ever do something like that again.'

'But I saved you, Ma.'

She hugged him again. 'Yes, you did, and I'm proud of you, but please keep away from Wilfred. He's a mean man when he's crossed.'

Nate pulled a face. 'I know that well enough. I

had many a beating from him when I was at Creek Manor.'

'You never said.' Hilda stared at him in horror. 'Why didn't you tell me?'

'We all got beaten by him or one of the other grooms. It's part of the job, I suppose.'

'Well, it shouldn't be,' Judy said angrily. 'I think that's awful, and if you'd told Mrs Tattersall she would have sorted those bullies out. She wouldn't have stood by and seen you ill-treated.'

'I don't know about that,' Nate said wearily. 'Is there anything to eat? I'm blooming starving.'

'Of course, there is, love.' Hilda ruffled his curly hair. 'I bought meat pies and there's bread and cheese. Come through to the kitchen and I'll put the kettle on.' She glanced over her shoulder. 'Are you coming, Judy?'

'Yes, in a minute.' Judy stood up and threw a log onto the fire, watching the flames lick round the bark, sending sparks flying up the chimney. She believed Wilfred when he said that this was not the end of his attempts to force Hilda back to the marital home, and she did not doubt that he was capable of violence in order to get his own way. She could hear Hilda calling to her and she was about to follow her mother and Nate to the kitchen when the pub door opened. A tall, broad-shouldered man entered carrying the cask of ale on his shoulder.

He dumped it down on a table. 'I think this is yours, miss. You don't want to leave such as this lying around or someone not as honest as Rob Dorning might come along and help themselves.'

Wilfred Faulkner's sudden arrival had put all thoughts of unloading the cart out of Judy's head. 'Thank you. I'm afraid it's a bit heavy for me and Hilda to lift on our own.'

'It's no light weight, that's for sure. Where do you want it?'

'On the trestle behind the bar, if you please.' Judy watched in awe as the man hefted the cask in his arms and placed it as she had directed.

'Maybe I should try a glass or two, miss. Just to make sure that the brew is all right.'

His grin was infectious and Judy found herself warming to him even though he was a complete stranger. She struggled to place the name. It sounded vaguely familiar, but she could not think where she had heard it before.

'All right,' she said slowly. 'You have to tap the barrel first.'

'Aye, I reckon I've done that a few times.' He set about the task so efficiently that Judy did not doubt him. He filled a tankard with ale. 'Of course it should be left to settle for a while to clear the sediment, but I don't mind a cloudy pint.' He raised the pewter mug to his lips and drank thirstily.

'Do you live round here?' Judy tried to sound casual, but she was curious. 'I mean, I haven't seen you before.'

He drained the last of the ale and went to stand

with his back to the fire. 'It's getting chilly these evenings.'

'Then you aren't from these parts?'

'I didn't say that. My family are well known along the coast.'

'I'm sure I've heard the name Dorning mentioned, but I can't place it.'

'I'm surprised to find someone like you working in a place like this. It's always had a bad reputation.'

'I'm running it with my mother,' Judy said firmly. 'I believe this pub went through a difficult time, but it's going to be different now.'

His blue eyes lit with amusement and he pushed his cap to the back of his head, revealing a mop of fair hair, streaked almost white by the sun. 'Well, I wish you luck with that. What do they call you?'

'Miss Begg,' Judy said primly. 'Judith Begg.'

'Judy. I like that name.' He moved to the settle and sat down, sprawling his long legs in front of him. 'I could do with some supper, Judy. What have you got to offer a hungry man?'

She laughed. 'Are you speaking as a paying customer, or do you expect to be fed for nothing because you did me a favour?'

'Either would be good. I have money if you want to charge a fellow who saved your ale from being stolen. You don't leave things unattended round here, Judy. This is a rough area.'

'I spent the first ten years of my life living in Whitechapel. You probably don't know London very well, but this place has nothing on Green Dragon Yard.'

'So how did you come to live in Little Creek?'

'It's a long story, but we used to live in Creek Manor. Ma worked for Mrs Tattersall.' Judy eyed him warily. 'Anyway, I don't suppose that's of any interest to you.'

'I wouldn't say that, but I am very hungry and I can pay for my supper.' He took a handful of coins from his pocket and laid them on the table.

Judy smiled. 'Well then, I'll see what we have to offer, Mr Dorning.'

'It's Rob.'

Judy acknowledged this with a nod, but she was still wary. Despite his friendly demeanour, good looks and candid smile, she was uneasy, and she hurried to the kitchen to see what supplies her mother had brought back from Maldon.

Nate was seated at the table munching away on a meat pie. A dribble of gravy ran down his chin and his mother tossed a cloth at him.

'You're not a baby, Nate. Don't gobble.'

'Sorry, Ma, but it tastes so good. We don't get grub like this in the stables. Mostly it's some kind of stew or potatoes cooked in the fire and a bit of cheese.'

'I knew they weren't looking after you boys properly,' Hilda said, sniffing. 'I want you to stay here, Nate. I know this isn't like Creek Manor, but Judy and I can find work for both you and Pip, if he wants to come here.'

Judy nodded. 'That's true. Of course we couldn't pay you much to begin with, but things will improve.' She turned to her mother. 'I have a paying customer who wants something to eat. What can we offer him?'

'There's your meat pie. I gave mine to Nate, otherwise it'll be bread and cheese. I would have brought some bacon but I didn't have enough money.'

'I'm sure Mr Dorning would rather have the pie.'

Hilda dropped the plate she had been about to wash and it fell to the floor, smashing into shards on the flagstones. 'Dorning?'

'That's right. His name is Rob Dorning.'

'We don't want his sort round here,' Hilda said urgently. 'The Dorning family are notorious. You were too young to know what was going on, but they caused no end of trouble for Jay before he went off to Australia.'

'It was a long time ago.' Judy unwrapped the pie and placed it on a plate together with a thick slice of bread and butter and a chunk of cheese. 'This will have to suffice. Anyway, he might never come here again, so I'm not going to worry.'

'The Dornings are bad news,' Hilda said darkly. 'You ask Daisy. She'll tell you all about them.'

Judy shrugged. 'He seems harmless enough. Maybe things have changed after all these years. Anyway, he is probably just passing through.'

She took the plate through to the taproom. 'I'm afraid this is all I can offer you at the moment,' she said apologetically. 'We've only just taken over the inn, so we aren't quite up to scratch as far as serving food is concerned.'

He took the plate from her with a smile that would have melted the hardest heart. 'I understand, and this looks excellent.' He picked up the pie and took a large bite, eating with obvious enjoyment.

'I suppose you are just passing.' Judy scooped a shovelful of coal from the scuttle and threw it onto the fire, adding a log for good measure.

Rob put his head on one side, grinning. 'Someone has been telling you stories about my family's exploits.'

Judy felt the blood rush to her cheeks and she turned away, wiping her hands on her apron. 'People gossip.'

'I feel I should put your mind at ease. That particular branch of the family paid the price for their crimes, although in those days most people who lived along the coast were involved in free trading in one way or the other.'

'I remember the secret passage that led from Creek Manor to the cove,' Judy said, frowning. 'The old squire was involved in free trading, as you call it.'

'It doesn't pay well enough now.' Rob finished the pie. 'That was good, but I'm sure you could make better pastry.'

Judy stared at him in surprise. 'What makes you say that?'

'You were at Creek Manor as a child. It follows

that they put you to work very young, and I suspect you might have been sent to the kitchen.'

'How did you know?'

He chuckled and reached out to take her hand. 'Your hands are too smooth and soft to be those of a skivvy or a laundry maid.' He stroked her fingers gently. 'And your hands are cold, just right for making pastry, I'd say.'

She drew away, startled by the accuracy of his comments. 'I did work in the kitchen, although it was because I wanted to learn how to cook and Mrs Pearce was kind to me.'

'Then I can't wait to sample your efforts.' Rob rose to his feet. 'I have to go now, but I'll be back sometime soon. Then I hope to enjoy a meal cooked by you, Judy Begg.' He took his cap from the settle where he had left it and sauntered out into the darkness, closing the door behind him.

Judy stared after him. He had worked out her past with surprising accuracy and yet he had not given away anything about himself. She picked up the plate and saw the bread and cheese had been left untouched even though he had paid handsomely for the meal.

Nate chose that moment to rush into the taproom. 'I have to go now or I'll be in trouble at the stables.' He eyed the bread and cheese. 'Is that going to waste?'

Judy smiled and handed the plate to him. 'Take it to eat on the way, but do be careful. You've made an enemy of Faulkner – I refuse to call him our stepfather – and who knows what he might do next?'

Nate wrapped the slice of bread around the cheese and stuffed it in his pocket. 'I've eaten, but I'll take this for Pip. He's always hungry, and I'd better return the gun, or I'll be in trouble.'

'You will think about what Ma said, won't you, Nate?' Judy asked anxiously. 'I mean you and Pip are more than welcome to live here. We've plenty of room and, to be honest, we could do with the help. It would be wonderful to have the family together again. Maybe Molly might come and live here one day, too.'

Nate nodded eagerly. 'I'll see what Pip says, but I'll definitely be back.'

'Without the gun next time,' Judy said firmly.

He laughed. 'You don't have to worry. I've already promised Ma.'

Next day Judy set out for Colneyhurst to discuss the release of the boys from their apprenticeship at the stables, but that was not the only thing she wanted to ask Daisy. As luck would have it, Daisy was at home and Judy was shown into the drawing room.

'This is a lovely surprise, Judy.' Daisy motioned her to sit down. 'We'll have a tray of coffee and cake, please, Lizzie.'

'Yes'm.' Lizzie grinned at Judy as she left the room. 'I can see that you have something exciting to tell me,' Daisy said, smiling. 'You never were good at keeping your feelings secret.'

'It's nothing really. I came to ask you if Nate would be allowed to leave your employ and come to work with us at the Crooked Billet.'

'Yes, of course. It was only meant to be a temporary arrangement anyway. I took the boys on to make sure they had somewhere to live, but I can see that you might need at least one of them.' Daisy sat back in her chair, eyeing Judy curiously. 'You don't want to rob me of Molly, too?'

'I didn't come with that in mind,' Judy said tactfully. 'Molly always does as she pleases.'

'There'll be another baby in the nursery next spring.' Daisy patted her belly. 'I didn't mention it before because it's early days, but now I'm certain.'

'That's wonderful. Do you mind if I pass the good news on to Hilda?'

'No, of course not. I really thought that after my last difficult birth that I wouldn't be able to have any more children, but it seems I was wrong. Marius always wanted a large family, so now we're well on the way.' Daisy smiled and relaxed against the silk cushions. 'But here am I going on about our good news, and there's something else on your mind, Judy. I can always tell.'

'I wanted to ask you about the Dorning family,' Judy said slowly. 'Hilda said you knew all about them.'

Daisy's happy smile faded. 'They're a bad lot, all

of them. You don't want to get mixed up with them in any way.'

'What did they do to turn you against them? Who are they? Hilda won't tell me much.'

'They ran a smuggling gang in the Burnham area for many years, and most of them went to prison, or were transported to the penal colony in Australia. Unfortunately, Jay got himself mixed up with them, and it caused no end of problems. I hope they haven't come back to cause more trouble.'

'A man walked into the pub yesterday and he said his name was Rob Dorning. He had a drink and something to eat and he was very pleasant, but he wouldn't talk about himself. I was just curious.'

'And I suppose he was quite good-looking,' Daisy said, smiling. 'I'm just teasing you, Judy. I don't know him personally, but he could be related to the Dornings. Although it doesn't mean that he's a criminal like the others.'

'Ma was very suspicious.'

'The family have a dreadful reputation, but he might be a perfectly decent fellow. I'd just say be careful.'

'Why is that? Please tell me anything you know.'

'It was a long time ago, Judy. You would have been too young to take much notice of what went on around you, but Jay had somehow become involved with the Dorning brothers. Anyway, I was desperate for information and I went looking for them.'

'Did you find them?'

Daisy shook her head. 'No. I was told they

frequented a disused chapel on the edge of the marsh, some three miles south of Little Creek. Perhaps it was fortunate for me, but they weren't there and I had to return home, having achieved nothing.'

'I do remember the servants talking about Jay, but I didn't pay much attention to what they were saying.'

'Jay was bold and charming, and I was quite smitten with him at first,' Daisy said with a rueful smile. 'Just be careful, Judy.'

'I can understand why you were attracted to Jay, as I was to Jack. But that's all over now.'

They were interrupted by the arrival of Lizzie with a tray. She placed it on the table without mishap. Judy was suitably impressed and she smiled at Lizzie as she made her way to the door.

Daisy filled a coffee cup and handed it to Judy. 'Do I detect a hint of regret?'

'I don't know what you mean.'

'It's not long ago you were devastated because Jack went off to Australia, and to my knowledge you haven't shown interest in anyone else, unless you count the handsome Dr God. Although to my mind he's too good to be true.'

'Really?' Judy stared at her in surprise. 'Why do you say that?'

'I'm probably being very unfair to the poor chap, but somehow he's too charming and I wonder if it's quite genuine.'

'What would he gain from pretending to be something he isn't?'

'Trust, I think is the right word. He's talking investors into putting hundreds of pounds, maybe thousands, into building the hospital for which they might not get any return on their investments. I just thank heaven that my brother isn't wealthy enough to risk his money in such a way.'

'Do you think it will be a failure?'

Daisy shook her head. 'I don't know what to think, but Marius is very dubious and he's a very good businessman. Ben Godfrey approached him at the start but Marius wouldn't have anything to do with the scheme.'

'It seems such a worthy cause,' Judy said slowly. 'I believe Dr Godfrey is a good man.'

'Maybe he is, but that doesn't make him a good businessman.' Daisy picked up the plate of dainty cakes and offered it to Judy.

'I suppose not.' Judy selected a cake. 'This looks delicious, thank you.'

'Changing the subject, and I don't want to offend you, Judy, but are you all right for money?' Daisy asked anxiously. 'I mean it can't be easy setting up in business on a shoestring.'

'Dr Godfrey has paid in advance for his room, and that's helped us enormously. He says he's going to stay very often when the building work commences, and he was talking about renovating the old slipway so that materials could be shipped to Little Creek.'

Daisy frowned. 'It all sounds very ambitious and extremely costly. I do hope he's gone into it properly, because so many local people have contributed to the scheme.'

'Why don't you like him?' Judy eyed her curiously. 'Has he upset you?'

'No, not at all. In fact he's always been charm itself when I've met him, but I can't help being a little suspicious.'

Judy shook her head. 'I think you're wrong. At least I hope you are, because we're depending on the money he advanced to keep us going.'

'Maybe I'm being overcautious,' Daisy said hastily. 'I hope so for your sake.'

'So do I, but it would be wonderful to see something good rising from the ashes of Creek Manor. It almost seems that there really was a curse on the old house.'

'Not that I believe in that superstitious nonsense, but it doesn't seem as though the house was ever a happy one. Maybe you're right and whatever is built there now will have a brighter future.'

Judy ate the cake with relish. 'I could almost imagine that Mrs Pearce had made this delicious fancy.'

'You're right, she did. My cook left suddenly to look after an ageing parent and I went to find Nell. I'm afraid Jay treated the servants very badly, but at least I've been able to help out a little.'

'I'm so glad. Mrs Pearce was like a second mother

to me while I was growing up.' Judy rose to her feet. 'Anyway, thank you for the tea and cake, and the good advice. Don't worry about me, Daisy. I'll mind what you said about Dr Godfrey, although I think you're wrong.'

'I hope so, too. But time will tell.'

'Is it all right if I go to the stables now and take Nate home with me? We really need him.'

'Of course it is. I'll make sure that he gets any wages owing to him. Goodbye, dear, and please remember what I said about the Dornings.'

Several weeks went by without any further visits from Wilfred. Slowly the customers began to trickle into the pub, but these were mainly farm workers on their way home from toiling in the fields, and a few fishermen. They drank a pint or two of cider or ale and then they went on their way. There had been no carriage trade, and there had been no sign of Dr Godfrey or the rush of business that he had predicted. Winter was almost upon them, and the proposed building of a new hospital seemed as far away as ever. Judy was beginning to wonder if Daisy had been right about Dr Godfrey. He might be well-meaning dreamer, or worse, a man who was prepared to take money from others with no intention of fulfilling his promises. Judy did not want to think ill of him, and his room was kept ready for him.

There had been no sign of Rob Dorning after his

initial visit and it seemed to Judy that she had been correct in thinking that he had been passing through. She had put him out of her mind when, one frosty morning at the end of November, he strolled into the pub as if he had never been away.

Judy happened to be on her own in the taproom. She was polishing the oddments of old horse brasses that she had found in the stable, and had pinned to the beams that surrounded the bar. She was enveloped in a large apron with a scarf tied around her head, and she had not expected to see much trade until later in the day.

'Good morning, Judy,' Rob said cheerfully. 'I can see that you're busy.'

She wiped her hands on her apron. 'I'm never too busy to serve a thirsty customer.'

'Then I'll have a pint of ale and something to eat, if you have your kitchen organised by now.'

Stung by his casual remark, she took off her soiled apron and laid it on the bar counter. 'Of course we have. There's a very good stew or . . .' She racked her brains to think of something she could conjure up from bread and a heel of cheese, and then she remembered the apple pie that Hilda had made for their supper the previous evening. 'There's apple pie, too.' She crossed her fingers behind her back, praying silently that Nate had not eaten the last slice.

'A bowl of stew will be fine,' Rob said easily. He went to sit in the inglenook while Judy pulled a pint of ale. She placed it on the table in front of him.

'Have you got business in this part of the world, Mr Dorning?'

'Rob,' he said, reaching for the tankard. 'Please call me Rob. As to business, you might say that, yes.'

She could not let it rest. Daisy's words had been bothering her ever since their last conversation. 'Might I ask what it is that brings you to Little Creek?'

He opened his mouth to reply, but at that moment the door burst open and Wilfred Faulkner erupted into the taproom. 'Where is she? Heaven knows I'm a patient man, but I won't wait another day for the trollop to return home.'

Judy took a step towards him. 'You had her answer weeks ago, Mr Faulkner. I'm asking you politely to leave.'

'I ain't going nowhere without Hilda.'

Rob had been sitting in the inglenook, unseen by Wilfred, but now he rose swiftly to his feet. 'You heard what Miss Begg said.'

'Abel Dorning. By God! He's dead and gone and you ain't no ghost. You're the spitting image of him.' Wilfred's jaw dropped and his eyes bulged. 'Keep away from me, Dorning. I don't want no trouble.' He wrenched the door open and fled.

Chapter Twelve

Judy turned to Rob, staring at him in amazement. 'Do you know that man?'

He shrugged. 'I've never seen him before.'

'But he seems to know you,' Judy said warily. 'And he was terrified.'

'I must remind him of my late uncle. Who is Hilda?'

'She's his wife, but she left him because of the way he treated her.'

'I can't say I blame her if that's an example of the way he behaves.' Rob sank down on the settle. 'Anyway, thanks to Uncle Abel, he seems to have fled. So what about that stew?'

'I'll go and fetch it for you.' Judy hurried to the kitchen where she found Hilda leaning against the pine table, her face pale and drawn.

'I heard him. Where is he now?'

'He's gone. He took one look at Rob Dorning and left in a great hurry.'

'That's really odd. I never saw Wilfred scared of anyone.'

'It seems your Wilfred knew Abel Dorning. When Wilfred saw Rob he was terrified, and the family likeness was enough to send him packing. Anyway, more to the point, Mr Dorning wants a bowl of stew.'

'There's no meat in it,' Hilda said ruefully. 'It's just vegetables. If we could afford to buy better ingredients we might attract more customers.'

Judy set about cutting slices from a freshly baked loaf of bread. 'We can't afford meat unless Dr Godfrey sends some trade our way, but I must admit I'm getting worried, Ma. Daisy said he might have taken on more than he can handle, and she wasn't very impressed with his plans to build the new hospital. I don't know what to think.'

'Handsome is as handsome does,' Hilda said darkly as she ladled the savoury-smelling stew into a bowl. 'Tell Mr Dorning there's apple pie if he's still hungry after he's eaten this.'

Judy spread butter more lavishly on the slices of bread than was strictly necessary. 'I already have. But I must say he's a mystery. I wish I knew more about him.'

'I have a feeling you're not going to let it go at that,' Hilda said, chuckling. 'Take that awful scarf off and take the food to him. I'm sure you can turn the conversation your way, if you really want to.'

Judy placed the plates on a tray, together with a spoon and fork. 'I'll treat him like any other customer, Ma. Heaven knows, we've few enough, so I don't want to lose a single one.'

Rob was warming himself by the fire and he looked up, smiling as she placed the tray on the table in front of him. 'Thank you.'

Judy hesitated. She was eager to talk to him, but she could not remain without a valid excuse. Seeming to guess her thoughts, he paused with the spoon halfway to his lips.

'You haven't any other customers. Why don't you take a seat and keep me company? I hate eating alone.'

Judy pulled up a chair. 'I can spare a few minutes, I suppose. We will be busy later. It's always quiet at this time of day.'

He tasted the food and nodded appreciatively. 'This is as good as I hoped. I'll eat and you can tell me how you came to be running a smugglers' haunt.'

The twinkle in his blue eyes was irresistible and Judy laughed. 'It might have been so at one time but I promise you we're totally respectable now. I don't know what else I can tell you.'

He nodded. 'Start at Green Dragon Yard – that was where you were born, wasn't it?'

Despite her reservations Judy found herself telling him the story of her life so far. She tried to sound casual when she mentioned Jack, but she could see by the alert expression on Rob's face that he suspected there was more than she was admitting.

However, he refrained from asking questions and ate slowly, savouring every mouthful until the bowl was empty. He leaned back in his seat, eyeing her thoughtfully.

'So where is this benefactor of yours now? The saintly doctor, I mean.'

'I don't know,' Judy said softly. 'We keep his room ready for him, but it's been a few weeks since he was last here.'

'And Mrs Walters suspects that he is taking money under false pretences.'

'She didn't say that exactly, but she thinks there is something not quite right.'

'And you say you keep a room ready for him to occupy at a minute's notice?'

'Yes, we do.'

'I have business in this area and it would suit my purpose if I stayed here tonight. I take it you aren't expecting the doctor to arrive?'

'No, but he asked me to keep the room just for him.'

'But he hasn't turned up.'

'Not yet.'

'Then the room is free and I'm a paying customer. I'd like the room for tonight and maybe tomorrow, and a meal this evening. Can you do that?'

Judy thought quickly. The deposit that Dr Godfrey had left to secure the room had run out, and this was a chance to earn money. She nodded. 'Yes, of course. I'll show you to your room when you're ready, but I'll go and light a fire to take the chill off before you go upstairs.'

'Haven't you got a servant to do that?'

Judy laughed and shook her head. 'There's just Ma and me, and my brother Nate manages the stables and acts as a potman in the evening. We manage very well.'

'But your doctor friend told you that the building of the hospital would bring more trade. How would you manage then?'

'We'll meet that eventuality when it happens.' Judy rose to her feet. 'You've finished. Would you like some apple pie?'

'No, thank you. That was excellent, but I've eaten my fill, and now I must go, but I'll be back this evening.'

'Don't you want to see your room first?'

He smiled. 'I'm sure it will be perfect. Thank Hilda for her efforts in the kitchen. Tell her I look forward to supper.' He picked up his cap, gloves and riding crop and left the taproom with a cheery wave.

Judy took the tray back to the kitchen.

'Well?' Hilda said eagerly. 'Did he enjoy his meal?'

'Yes, he did, and he's coming back this evening for dinner, and he wants the room we've kept for the doctor.'

Hilda stood arms akimbo. 'Well, since that gent hasn't turned up, I see no reason why we can't let it to a paying customer. I reckon the advance Dr Godfrey gave you has run out by now.'

'You're right,' Judy said, placing the tray on the table. 'But I'd love to know what business Rob Dorning has round here. Maybe I can find out when he returns this evening.'

'I'm sure there must be a good reason.' Hilda picked up the coal scuttle and handed it to Judy. 'Be a dear and fill this for me.'

'That reminds me,' Judy said, frowning. 'I'd better light a fire in his room. Heaven knows when Dr Godfrey will put in an appearance.'

The taproom was quiet as usual in the early evening with only a few customers. Eli, the old man who looked after Colonel Catchpole's pigs, and smelled worse than all the animals in his care, was a regular. He always sat in the corner of the bar, nursing a pint of mild beer, which would last him the whole evening, unless someone bought him a drink. Seated near the fire was the gamekeeper from Colneyhurst Hall, and his son, Davey, whom Judy recognised as one of the stable lads who worked with her brothers. He kept eyeing Judy and grinning at her, but she chose to ignore him. She was not in the mood for banter with a cheeky fourteen-year-old. Nate was in the kitchen eating his supper, but he would be in the bar later, collecting empty tankards and serving when required.

She had just thrown another log on the fire when the door opened and Dr Godfrey walked into the taproom, bringing with him a gust of ice-cold air and a dusting of dead leaves. Judy's heart sank, but she managed a welcoming smile. 'Good evening, Doctor.'

He took a seat as far away from the other customers as was possible. 'Brandy, please, Judy. Bring me the bottle.'

She did as he asked and placed a glass and the brandy bottle on the table in front of him. 'Are you all right?'

A wry smile curved his lips. 'It's usually me asking that question of a patient, but since you seem to sense my mood, I'll have to say no.' He uncorked the bottle and poured himself a generous tot, which he downed in one and refilled the glass. 'I've had the devil of a day, and now I'm ready for a decent meal and a comfortable bed.'

A meal she could provide, although pie was the only item on the menu. Nate had snared a rabbit and Hilda had done what was necessary to make a tasty meal, but that was the least of Judy's worries. Then, to her dismay, the door opened again and this time it was Rob himself who strolled into the taproom. He was carrying a saddlebag, which he placed on a stool at the bar counter. He shot a curious glance at Ben and nodded.

'Good evening.'

Ben acknowledged him with a curt nod. 'Who is that?' he asked in a low voice.

'He's a customer,' Judy said softly. 'Would you like to eat now, Doctor?'

'Not yet. I'll tell you when I'm hungry. I hope my room is ready.'

Judy shot a wary glance at Rob, who was watching them with mild interest. 'I'm afraid not, but I can offer you alternative accommodation.'

'What?' Ben leaped to his feet. 'I've had the most dreadful day, and now you tell me that my room is being used by someone else.' He turned to glare at Rob. 'I suppose this is your doing, sir. I don't know you, but you appear to be the only person in the bar who could afford a bed for the night.'

Judy clutched his arm. 'Please lower your voice, Doctor. These people are my bread and butter. I don't want them offended.'

Ben shook off her restraining hand and marched over to Rob. 'You look like a gentleman, so I'm assuming that you will understand when I tell you that the room you were to have is no longer available. I have a long-standing agreement with Miss Begg that the bedchamber in question is mine when I need it, and tonight is that night.'

'I'm afraid you're out of luck, sir. I booked the room at midday, therefore I believe I have prior claim. Unless you've given Miss Begg due notice I don't see how you can expect to simply walk in here and make such unreasonable demands.'

'I'm not in the mood to be crossed by a complete stranger. I've had a very trying and unprofitable day.'

'I suppose you're referring to the purchase of the Creek Manor estate,' Rob said casually.

'What is it to you?' Dr Godfrey eyed him warily.

'Your offer was turned down.' Rob turned to Judy. 'Perhaps the doctor would like another glass of brandy.'

'I'll order my own drinks,' Ben snapped. 'What do you know about the sale?'

'I was there, although I kept in the background. You were so wrapped up in your own self-importance that you didn't see me.'

'What business is it of yours, anyway?' Dr Godfrey thumped his hand down on the counter. 'Who are you?'

'The name is Dorning, Robert Winters Dorning to be exact, and I am the new owner of the Creek Manor estate.'

There was a sudden silence in the taproom. The only sounds were the gentle ticking of the grandfather clock and the snap and crackle of the log as the sap leaked out into the flames. Judy gazed at Rob in disbelief.

'You bought the Creek Manor estate?'

He laughed. 'There's no law against it, is there?'

Judy looked from one to the other. 'But Dr Godfrey was going to build a new hospital.'

'I can speak for myself, Judy,' he said crossly. 'This is an outrage, sir. That land is perfect for what we wanted.'

'You had your chance, although I doubt if you could raise the sort of money you would need for such an ambitious project.' Rob picked up his saddlebag. 'I'm going to my room, Judy. I'll have supper later, if that's all right with you.'

'Yes, of course.' Judy stepped in front of Dr Godfrey, blocking his way. 'Please don't make trouble. I know you're disappointed, but you must have known that there would be other bidders.'

He sank down on a chair by the bar, holding his head in his hands. 'I'm ruined.'

'No, surely not,' she said anxiously.

'You don't understand.'

'I might, if you told me what's wrong.'

He shook his head. 'I persuaded people to invest in the project.'

'But you can give them back their money.'

'That's the problem.' He turned his head away. 'I don't know why I'm telling you this.'

'Sometimes it helps to talk to someone about your problems.'

He uttered a mirthless bark of laughter. 'I can't repay all the money. There were expenses.'

'But surely the investors will understand that.'

'I was so certain that I could get the land at a good price. I gave up my position at the London Hospital and I travelled all over the country, visiting other medical institutions to see how they were run. The fact is that I spent more than half the money I took from the investors, and I have no hope of repaying them. I'm ruined.'

Judy was at a loss for words. She raised her hand to give him a comforting pat on the shoulder, but dropped it to her side. After all, he had used other people's money to follow his dream, and his gamble had failed. There was nothing she could say that would either help or comfort him. She refilled his glass from the brandy bottle.

He accepted it with a nod and tossed the drink back in one swallow. He rose unsteadily to his feet. 'I'd better go.'

'It's getting late,' Judy said reasonably. 'Where will you go at this time of night?'

'I don't know. Anywhere but here.'

'There is another room you can have. It's smaller, but it has a view of the estuary, and I'm sure you'll find it very comfortable. I'll light the fire while you're eating your supper.' She pressed him back onto the chair. 'I'll bring you some pie. A good night's sleep is what you need, and you'll be able to think more clearly in the morning.'

His eyes were bloodshot as he met her anxious gaze. 'Why are you doing this for me?'

'Because everyone at the hospital said that you are a good doctor. You might have been unlucky in business, but I'm sure you can come to some arrangement with the people to whom you owe money. Perhaps Dr Neville could help you to find another position.'

He poured himself another glass. 'Who will trust me now?'

Judy shook her head. 'I can't answer that, but feeling sorry for yourself won't help. Stay there and

I'll bring you some food, and then I'll prepare you a room.'

'I don't deserve your kindness.'

'Now you're being maudlin. That's what Jack would say, although I had to look the word up in his dictionary. Anyway, think of it as repayment. You helped us over a difficult time when we first moved into the Crooked Billet, and now I can return the favour.' She left him to finish his drink while she went to the kitchen.

Having served him a plate of pie and mashed potato, she went upstairs to make a room ready. Dr Godfrey's confession was shocking, but it paled into insignificance compared to Rob Dorning's announcement that he was now the owner of the Creek Manor estate.

Judy's mind buzzed with questions as she lit the fire. Who was Rob Dorning? And how could he afford to purchase a country house and an estate? All these thoughts went through her head as she made up the bed with fresh sheets and added a couple more blankets. She smoothed the coverlet and then crossed the floor to draw the curtains on the wild night outside. Through the rain-spattered windowpanes she could just make out the white crested waves as they pounded the foreshore, whipped up by the wind as it howled around the building, rattling windows and sending the inn sign swinging to and fro so that it looked as if it might take off and fly away. She pulled the thin material together and moved the oil lamp to a safer place. The room looked inviting enough, although she doubted if the doctor would notice much when he eventually staggered up the stairs to bed. She had been startled by the sudden change in his demeanour. The Dr God she had first met in the hospital seemed to be a very different person from the broken man who slumped against the bar, feeling sorry for himself. She left the room and went downstairs to help Hilda.

Nate met her at the foot of the stairs. 'Can you do something with the doctor, Judy? He's squiffy but he wants another bottle of brandy. What shall I do?'

'Don't worry. I'll sort him out.' Judy hoped she sounded more confident than she was feeling as she walked over to where Dr Godfrey was slumped over the table. 'Come on, Doctor. I'll show you to your room.'

'I want another drink.'

'I'll bring some to you later.' Judy beckoned to her brother and together they managed to get Dr Godfrey to his feet. It took both of them to get him upstairs to his room, where he collapsed onto the bed and closed his eyes.

'Are you going to leave him like that?' Nate asked warily.

'I'm not going to undress him and put him to bed, if that's what you mean. He'll have to sleep it off.' Judy ushered her brother from the room and closed the door. Nate hurried downstairs and she followed more slowly. It was sad to see a man like Dr Godfrey, who was so respected in his chosen profession, reduced to drinking himself into oblivion. Dr God was paying for his mistakes, and she was sorry for him. She walked into the taproom and was met by Rob.

'I'm starving,' he said, smiling. 'I think I smell rabbit pie.'

'I'm afraid that's all we have on the menu.'

'That's fine by me. I love pie.'

'It's quiet in the bar,' Judy said cautiously. 'Would you like to eat with us in our private parlour? Or if you prefer to eat alone . . .'

'No. I hate eating on my own. I would like that very much.'

'Nate has already eaten and he'll keep an eye on the bar, although I doubt if we'll get many customers in this evening. People tend to stay at home when the weather is bad.'

She led the way to the parlour and laid the table while Rob made himself comfortable by the fire.

'It won't be long,' she said, smiling.

'Where is the doctor? Do we have to share a table with him, too?'

'He's in his room. He's a bit tipsy, but I hope he'll sleep it off. The new hospital was his dream – he just couldn't make it happen.'

'That's just it, Judy. It was an impossible dream. I gather he was representing a group of investors, but he was out of his depth in the business world.

He should stick to what he knows and concentrate on healing the sick.'

'You are a very cynical man, Rob Dorning.'

He chuckled. 'Thank you, Judy. I'll take that as a compliment. Now where's that pie? I'm really looking forward to my meal.'

Judy bit back a sharp retort as she left the room. She knew in her heart that what Rob said was true, and Ben Godfrey was at fault, but she resented the criticism of someone who had wanted to do something good for his fellow men.

She marched into the kitchen. 'Mr Dorning is hungry,' she said, taking plates from the dresser and slapping them down on the table.

Hilda looked up from the sink where she had been straining cabbage. 'I thought you liked him. What's he said to upset you?'

'He was being very judgemental about Dr Godfrey.'

'What has the doctor done?'

'I'll tell you later. I made the mistake of inviting Rob to eat with us in the parlour. Let's get supper over and then we can relax.'

Hilda sliced the pie and put a large piece on a plate together with a generous helping of cabbage and a couple of boiled potatoes. She handed the plate to Judy. 'Give him that to be going on with, and don't forget the jug of gravy. In my experience all men love a good gravy.'

This made Judy laugh. 'And most women, too, I

suspect. You always put things in perspective, Ma. What would I do without you?'

'You'll have to one day, dear. When you get married you won't need me.'

'That won't happen, Ma. You and I have been through so much together. Whoever marries me, if anyone ever does, he will have to take you on as well. I wouldn't marry a man who didn't get on with my mother.'

Hilda threw a drying cloth at her. 'Take the food in while it's hot.'

Judy knew better than to argue and she served the food, taking care to put the gravy within Rob's reach. He was helping himself to a generous amount when Hilda entered the room, bringing two plates of food. She smiled and nodded approvingly and she set one in front of her daughter.

'I said you'd appreciate a good gravy, Mr Dorning.'

He looked up and smiled. 'Thank you, Mrs Begg. This looks and smells wonderful.'

'Eat up, then.' Hilda sat down and picked up her cutlery. 'There's more outside, sir. If you want it, that is.'

He swallowed a mouthful of food. 'This rabbit pie is really delicious. When I rebuild Creek Manor I'll need a good cook.'

Judy dropped her fork with a clatter. 'You are going to rebuild the manor house?'

'Of course. Why else would I buy the land?'

She shook her head. 'I don't know. Will it be like the old house?'

'Not exactly. I fancy something in a more modern style. Perhaps in the Italianate design, but it will be about the same size.'

'And you plan to live there?'

'Maybe. I haven't decided yet. My business takes me away for much of the time.'

'You'll need a small army of workmen to construct the building,' Judy said thoughtfully.

He smiled. 'You're thinking about trade.'

'Yes, it's very important to us. If we don't start making money we'll have to leave here.'

'That would be a shame,' he said agreeably. 'But you could find work elsewhere.'

'I suppose you'll be on the lookout for kitchen maids.' Judy spoke more sharply than she had intended and she dropped her gaze.

'I will, of course, but I wouldn't insult a business-woman like yourself by offering you such a menial position.'

'Now you're laughing at me.'

'No, indeed I'm not.'

Hilda sent her daughter a warning glance. 'Changing the subject, sir, you must have a fortune to spend so liberally.'

'You're wondering how someone as young as I could afford such a project. Am I right?'

It was Hilda's turn to blush and look away.

'You must be a very astute businessman, Mr

Dorning.' Judy modified her tone. 'I'd really like to know how to make a lot of money.'

'You'd like to know, would you?' Rob regarded her with a wry smile. 'I have to admit I did nothing to earn the fortune I inherited, but my father and grandfather paid the price for their misdeeds. They were transported to the penal colony in Australia, but the authorities didn't manage to get their hands on the money they'd made. Free trade is what brought me Creek Manor. Ironic, isn't it? I believe the old squire was one of the ringleaders of their gang, but he died before it could be proven.'

'Well, I never did!' Hilda stared at him in amazement. 'The sly old fox. We always knew he was up to no good, but he was obviously better at being a crook than we thought.'

'That's just about it.' Rob turned to Judy with a questioning look. 'I suppose you'd like me to leave now. A respectable woman like you wouldn't want anything to do with a man whose family were notorious smugglers.'

'You're determined to put me in the wrong,' Judy said, laughing. 'We look forward to your invaluable custom, Mr Dorning.'

'Now you're laughing at me,' Rob said equably. '*Touché.*'

Before Judy had a chance to respond in kind, the parlour door flew open and Nate rushed into the room. 'Judy, come quickly. I think the doctor's going to kill himself.'

Chapter Thirteen

Judy leaped to her feet, as did Rob, and they hurried after Nate, with Hilda following more slowly. The pub door was swinging violently in a gale-force wind, and rain lashed down in torrents. Judy ran outside and a flash of lightning revealed Ben Godfrey teetering on the edge of the cliff.

'He's going to jump,' she cried, turning to Rob, but he was already on his way and he threw himself at Dr Godfrey, bringing him down just as he was about to plunge into the churning waves below.

Nate rushed to his aid and together they raised him to his feet and half-dragged, half-carried him back to the safety of the taproom. Judy raced upstairs to fetch a blanket and some towels. When she returned she found Dr Godfrey seated by the fire, clutching a glass of brandy. She wrapped the blanket around his shoulders.

'You stupid man,' she said angrily. 'You would have died if it hadn't been for Rob.'

He bowed his head. 'You should have let me end it all. I'm finished.'

Rob pushed his wet hair back from his forehead. 'If that's all the thanks we get for saving your life, then go ahead and throw yourself off the cliff.'

'What would you do if you were me?' Ben Godfrey said wearily. 'You'd feel exactly the same. I owe good people a lot of money that I can't repay.'

'You should have thought about that before you encouraged them to invest.' Rob shrugged off his wet jacket and hung it over a chair by the fire. 'You're no businessman, Doctor. You should stick to what you do best.'

'I don't think this is helping,' Judy protested, handing Ben a towel. 'What you need is a good night's sleep.'

Hilda had been hovering in the background, but she nodded in approval. 'I'll make him some cocoa. That will help.' She turned to Nate, who was standing by the fire with steam billowing off his wet clothes. 'And you can go upstairs and change out of those wet things, or you'll be down with a fever and no good to man or beast.' She bustled off in the direction of the kitchen and Nate headed for the stairs.

'I'll mind the bar,' Judy said hastily, 'although it's unlikely that we'll get any more customers this evening.'

'You need to get dry, too,' Rob said firmly. 'I'll stay down here and make sure this idiot doesn't do anything stupid, and if anyone comes in I can serve a pint of ale as well as the next man.'

'I'll go to my room,' Dr Godfrey said tiredly. 'Don't worry, I won't try that again – the moment has passed. I'll have to face up to what I've done.'

Judy took the glass from his hand and placed it on the table. She helped him to his feet. 'I'm going upstairs, you can lean on me.'

He smiled ruefully. 'It's a case of "physician, heal thyself". But I don't think I'm clever enough to do that.'

'Everything will look better in the morning,' Judy said gently. 'Come on, Doctor.'

'I think after this you really ought to call me Ben.'

She smiled. 'All right, if it makes you happy. Come on, Ben.'

Judy slept little that night. She had pinned all her hopes on the fact that Ben had promised to send trade their way, and he was not the only one who was suffering from his ill-judged actions. She was left wondering how they would survive the rigours of winter out here on the headland. It was not surprising that past landlords had encouraged the smugglers to use the premises, but those days were long past. There must be another way, but a solution to their problems escaped her. Rob might intend to rebuild Creek Manor, but he had given no assurances, and perhaps she had been naïve in assuming that goods and workers would arrive by sea and bring much-needed custom to the Crooked Billet.

After sleeping fitfully Judy awoke next morning having come to a decision. She got up, washed, dressed and put her hair in a neat chignon before going downstairs to the kitchen, where to her surprise she found Ben seated at the table, drinking coffee.

He looked up and smiled sheepishly. 'I'm so sorry for the way I behaved last evening.'

'You gave us all a terrible fright. But no harm came to you, that's the main thing.'

'You're right, Judy. It's time to put it all in the past, Ben.' Hilda placed a plate of bacon and eggs in front of him. 'Eat that. You need all your strength to set matters straight. Those creditors aren't going to be very happy when you tell them what you've done.'

'That's not helping, Ma.' Judy stifled a chuckle. How typical of her mother to put things so bluntly. She was right, of course, but that did not make it any easier for Ben, who was obviously bitterly ashamed of his actions.

'I don't know what to do,' he said, draining the last of the coffee from his cup. 'I gave up my position at the London Hospital because I thought I was going to organise everything for the new hospital. It didn't occur to me that it might not go through.'

'Forget that for a moment.' Judy pulled up a chair

and sat down opposite him. 'You will have to tell your creditors, of course, but you need to find another job or you won't be able to pay your rent.'

He shook his head. 'I doubt if I can afford it anyway. I'll have to find somewhere a lot cheaper, and then when I start earning again I can begin to repay the rest of the money.'

'I know who might be able to help you,' Judy said thoughtfully. 'Dr Marshall is your friend, isn't he? His wife was very kind to me when I went up to London, looking for work.'

Ben frowned. 'I don't like to impose on Toby. I got myself into this mess, and it's up to me to find a way out.'

'There's no shame in asking for assistance when you need it,' Judy said firmly. 'I'll come to London with you, if that would make things easier. There's little enough for me to do here, and you did help us out at the beginning. Call it the return of a favour, if you like.'

He buried his head in his hands. 'If I have to depend upon a woman for courage, what sort of fellow does that make me?'

Hilda refilled his coffee cup. 'Never mind your pride, Ben. Let Judy do what she suggests. She's very determined when she makes up her mind to do something. Nate and I can manage here for a few days.'

'What do you say?' Judy asked eagerly. 'Let me do this for you, Ben. You're too good a doctor to mope around because you failed when it came to such a big undertaking. You weren't to know that Rob Dorning would appear as if from nowhere and outbid you.'

Ben nodded tiredly. 'You're right, of course, and I must return to London. I can do nothing more here.'

'Has anyone seen Rob this morning?' Judy looked to her mother for an answer and Hilda nodded.

'Yes, he left earlier. He didn't say where he was going, but he paid handsomely for the room. We could do with more guests like him.'

Ben Godfrey's lodging house in Raven Row came as something of a shock to Judy. It was a narrow street close to the London Hospital, which was probably why so many of the staff chose to lodge there. It was a rundown building and Ben's room was sparsely furnished with scant attention to comfort. A trivet in front of the small fireplace was the only means of heating a kettle, and would do little to warm the draughty room. The bare floorboards were splintered and worn and the two rag rugs looked as though they could do with a good wash. The narrow iron bedstead might have come from the servants' quarters in a larger house, and it looked as though it had been discarded as being unsuitable even for the youngest, newest member of staff.

'Why do you live here?' Judy demanded crossly. 'Surely as a doctor you could afford better?'

He shrugged and dropped his battered leather valise onto the bed. 'It's cheap and it's handy for the hospital.' He shot her a sideways glance. 'I've been saving my money so that I could invest in a project such as the hospital in Little Creek. It's a lifelong ambition of mine to provide medical care for the poor and needy. I've seen such terrible things in this part of London, and I've visited homes that were overcrowded hovels. I've seen families of seven or eight living in damp cellars together with complete strangers, but even they are better off than the people with nowhere to go. If you walked the city streets at night you would see terrible sights – people living in doorways, and all too often dying there.'

'And you put all the money into your scheme?'

'Every penny, and now I'm broke. At least I was able to settle my bill at your pub, but the railway fare back to London used up the last of my money.'

'I'm so sorry, Ben.' She glanced round the depressing room and sighed. 'I wish I could help, but I've nothing to give you.'

He smiled. 'I wouldn't take it from you anyway. But don't worry about me. We'll walk to the Marshalls' house, as planned, and then I'll see you safely on the train back to Little Creek.'

'I thought they were moving to a larger establishment.'

'There was some delay, but that's all to the good. It's not very far to Sidney Square.'

'Let's go then,' Judy said eagerly. 'I'm sorry, Ben,

but this room is so dreary it makes me want to cry. I don't know how you've stood it for so long.'

He held the door open. 'I only sleep here. It's not so bad.'

'Well, I think you could do better. Let's see what Dr Marshall says.'

Minnie was delighted to see them and she welcomed Judy with a hug and a kiss on the cheek. She smiled and extended her hand to Ben. 'We were so worried about you. Why did you leave without telling us?'

He raised her hand to his lips. 'I'm sorry, Minnie. I suppose I got carried away with my new venture. I thought it would work out wonderfully, but it hasn't.'

Minnie looked from one to the other. 'Sit down, both of you. I'll ring for some refreshments. You look exhausted.'

Judy sank down on the sofa. 'We left Little Creek first thing this morning, and we've just walked from Raven Row.'

'I've always said you ought to move somewhere better, Ben.' Minnie tugged at the bell pull. 'I think a glass of sherry might be what's needed, and you must stay for luncheon. Toby will be back soon and you can tell him everything, Ben. But I really want to hear Judy's news, if you don't mind.'

'Not at all. My tale of woe can wait. It's not something I care to repeat over and over again.'

Minnie shot him a sympathetic look as she took a seat beside Judy. 'Well, then. Tell me all the news from Little Creek. It's so long since we were last there. How are Daisy and the children? Do you see them often?' She looked up as the door opened and Sukey sidled into the parlour.

'You rang, ma'am.'

'Yes, Sukey. Please fetch the sherry decanter and four glasses, and tell Cook there will be two extra for luncheon.'

Sukey bobbed a curtsey and backed out of the room, closing the door carefully behind her.

'Your protégée has improved,' Judy said, chuckling. 'I seem to remember she was all feet and elbows when I was here last. She could hardly move without falling over or dropping something.'

Minnie pulled a face. 'Don't speak too soon. She has learned a lot but sometimes she gets excited and forgets what she is supposed to be doing. However, I'm fond of the child and I have hopes for her. She'll be coming with us when we move to Harley Street in a week's time. You're lucky to have caught us at home. Now tell me everything, Judy.'

Judy had just finished regaling Minnie with tales from Little Creek, although she was careful not to mention the reason for Ben's sudden return to London, when Toby Marshall breezed into the room, smiling cheerfully.

'Ben, old chap. Sukey told me that we had visitors.'

He slapped his friend on the back as Ben rose to greet him. 'And Judy, too. This is an unexpected pleasure. How are you and your family?'

'They're all well, thank you,' Judy said, smiling. 'I've just been passing on all the gossip from home.'

Toby reached for the sherry decanter and poured himself a drink. 'There's always plenty going on in a small village. But what brings you back to London, Ben?'

'I was outbid at the sale.' Ben sank back onto his chair, shaking his head. 'I've let everyone down, myself included.'

'I'm sorry to hear that, but there'll be other plots of land, surely?' Toby sipped his drink and sat down in a chair next to his friend. 'It's not the end of the world.'

'I was so convinced that the land would go for a song. I used a lot of the investors' money in order to further my plans,' Ben said gloomily. 'I can't repay them and I'll be bankrupted when this gets out.'

'I'm so sorry.' Toby frowned thoughtfully. 'But surely if you explained to them and promised to repay the money, they'll be willing to wait. I mean, investing in any project is a risky business. They must have considered that.'

'Maybe, but I haven't got a job and I can't even afford to pay next month's rent. I've been a complete fool, Toby. I don't know where to turn next.'

'You're a good doctor and a good man,' Toby

said firmly. 'You aren't cut out for a business career, and that's a fact, but there must be a way round this. I suggest we have our meal and talk about it later. You will stay here tonight, of course.'

'Thank you, but I still have my room in Raven Row, and Judy needs to get home to Little Creek.'

'I can get the next train,' Judy said stoutly. 'Don't worry about me.'

'You'll do no such thing. You must both stay here for tonight at least and perhaps we can help you to sort out your problem, Ben.' Minnie stood up, brushing the creases out of her silk morning gown. 'We have room for you, and it will be delightful to talk about something other than the move to Harley Street. I hope you don't mind the fact that there are packing cases everywhere, but we'll make you as comfortable as possible. Do say yes, Judy.'

The thought of travelling home late in the afternoon had little appeal. She had warned her mother that she might stay in London overnight, and it was good to be away from the worries and pressures of running the inn. She realised that Minnie was waiting for her response. 'Yes, of course. I'll go home tomorrow, I'm sure they can manage without me for another day.'

After luncheon Toby had to return to the hospital, leaving Minnie, Judy and Ben to finish their coffee in the parlour. Toby had been unable to offer any encouragement when it came to finding Ben a new position. The doctor who had been taken on at short notice to fill the gap left by Ben's sudden departure had proved to be very good at his job, and everyone was satisfied with his work. Toby knew of no other vacancies in the hospital, but he promised to ask his colleagues if they had heard of any positions waiting to be filled in other institutions.

'It serves me right.' Ben toyed with his coffee cup. 'I should have thought it through instead of acting on impulse, but I was so certain I could succeed.'

Minnie gazed at him with a thoughtful frown. 'But if you'd spent so much of the investors' money, how did you think you would have enough to buy the land?'

'That's a question I keep asking myself. I thought I could go back to them, and providing I bought the land cheaply, they would stump up the rest of the money. I suppose I was naïve, if not downright foolish.'

'You're being too hard on yourself,' Judy said hastily. 'In any event, the people who loaned the money must have expected you to have expenses. They might be much more reasonable than you think. After all, they must be very wealthy to have considered such an investment in the first place.'

'I'll visit them all in person and explain. It's the least I can do, but first I must find somewhere else to live, and I think I know someone who might help me.' He put his cup back on its saucer. 'Would you mind if I go out now, Minnie? I don't want to abuse your hospitality, but I need to see this person urgently.'

'Of course,' Minnie said hastily. 'Treat our home as if it were yours, Ben.'

He turned to Judy with an eager smile. 'Would you like to come with me? You'll be interested in the work Sarah does in such a poor parish.'

'I think I know who you mean.' Minnie leaned forward, her eyes alight with interest. 'Is it Sarah Holden, the woman who runs the soup kitchen and shelter in Limehouse? I've heard she does amazing work with the poor and destitute.'

Ben nodded. 'Yes, she was a nurse at the orthopaedic hospital where I qualified. She would have made a fine doctor had it been easier for a woman to enter the profession, but she hasn't let it stop her from doing a tremendous amount of good. She might know of cheap rooms that I can rent.'

'I'd like to meet her,' Judy said eagerly. 'Where does she live?'

'She took over a near derelict warehouse in Juniper Row some years ago, and she has a room there, but the rest of the building she's turned into a refuge for the most needy.'

'And this place is in Limehouse? I don't know the area.'

'You don't want to either,' Minnie said firmly. 'It's a rough place, Judy. I'm not sure you ought to go with Ben.'

Judy tossed her head. 'If Sarah Holden is brave

enough to live there, I'm sure I can face a visit this afternoon.'

As Ben had intimated, the old warehouse had seen more prosperous days. The narrow street was lined with similar buildings, although most of them were in a better state of repair, and many of them were connected by covered walkways high above the street. Ben rapped on the door, which looked as though someone had attempted to break it down at some point, and it had been repaired with more enthusiasm than skill. They waited, shivering as a cold wind hurled itself at them from the direction of the river, bringing with it the stench of sewage, silt and the smell of hot engine oil. Judy waited impatiently for someone to let them in, and after a couple of minutes the door opened just a crack.

'Who's there?'

'Is that you, Sarah? It's me, Ben Godfrey.'

The door opened wide and a tall, well-built woman flung her arms around Ben. She gave him a hug that almost swept him off his feet.

'Where have you been all these months, you devil?' Sarah's voice was deep and gravelly, but her smile was genuine. She released Ben to give Judy a curious glance. 'Who have you brought to see us in Juniper Row?'

'This is Judy Begg, a good friend of mine. May we come in, Sarah? It's a bit chilly out here.'

Sarah backed into the gloomy interior. 'Of course.

Where are my manners? But we seldom get visitors, other than those who are desperate for help. Come in, please.'

The inside of the old warehouse was only slightly less welcoming than the exterior. Judy found herself in a small, dark lobby, which led into a narrow corridor that ended in a barn-like room filled with a collection of beds and straw-filled palliasses laid end to end on the brick floor. She recognised the smell of carbolic, mingling with the odour of sickness and chamber pots filled to overflowing. A young boy was seemingly delegated to emptying these, but he moved so slowly, taking one at a time to a communal privy somewhere outside. Judy could see that it was a losing battle, and she tried not to wrinkle her nose at the stench.

It was cold and the wind whistled through gaps in the brickwork above their heads. Shapeless mounds lying on the beds huddled beneath coarse woollen blankets. The only sign that these shapes were human was the occasional grunt, snort or moan.

'You get used to it,' Sarah said as if she could read Judy's thoughts. 'These people can't afford to pay a doctor, and it's doubtful whether the charity hospitals would take most of them in. This is the best they can expect.'

'You're doing a splendid job,' Ben said earnestly.

'I wish I could help more people.' Sarah's grey eyes darkened and her generous lips pulled down at the corners. 'There is so much suffering out there. I can only help a few.'

'Would you like me to look at any of your patients?' Ben asked tentatively. 'Free of charge, of course.'

'You know the answer to that.' A chuckle escaped Sarah's lips and she slapped Ben on the back. 'Thank you, Doctor. But first, tell me what prompted this visit? You haven't come to this part of Limehouse for the good of your health.'

'Ah, there you have me. I've made a mess of things, Sarah. I thought I was cleverer than I am, and I've landed myself in financial difficulties. I gave up my position at the London so that I could organise the building of a new hospital on the Essex coast, but I was outbid for the land, and now I can't repay the investors the full amount. I need somewhere cheap to live while I try to sort myself out.'

Sarah eyed him thoughtfully. 'That's a shame, Ben. You're a very good doctor and I'd be more than happy to have you here to help me, but I couldn't pay you anything. We depend upon charity and there are many other worthy causes vying for funds. Having said that, there's plenty of room here, and you're more than welcome to stay; that is if you don't expect any sort of luxury.'

'That would be wonderful.' He grasped her hand and held it to his heart. 'It might be just what I need. At the moment I feel as if I've let everyone down, including myself. Perhaps a little real hardship will make me feel that I'm paying for my misdeeds.'

'I think that's a bit strong,' Judy protested. 'You made a mistake; you didn't set out to swindle the investors. There's a difference, Ben.'

'Yes, there is.' Sarah withdrew her hand gently. 'Stop feeling sorry for yourself and do something useful, and you can start right away.' She pointed to a bed at the far end of the room. 'I think that old fellow is slipping away. Perhaps you'd take a look at him and see if there's anything more we can do for him.'

Ben nodded and shrugged off his greatcoat, handing it to Judy. 'Yes, of course. Can you lend me a stethoscope? I left my medical bag at the Marshalls' house.'

'Yes, of course.' Sarah produced a stethoscope from the pocket of her voluminous apron. 'His name is Bert Huggins, and he worked on the docks for most of his life.'

Ben nodded and hurried off, picking his way through the beds and bodies lying on the floor until he reached the old man's bedside.

'I do my best,' Sarah said sadly. 'But there's very little I can do to alleviate the problems these people have, and poverty is the main cause.'

As her eyes grew accustomed to the dim light, Judy could see a small family huddled around a gaunt-faced woman, who had a baby at her breast, but the infant was clearly unsatisfied and mewling like a kitten. The other children were stick thin, dirty and hollow-eyed. Their very stillness was unnerving, especially when Judy compared them to the youngsters in Little Creek – dirty they might be, but they were bright-eyed and energetic, and none of them went hungry.

'How do you manage without funds?' Judy asked anxiously. 'How do you feed all these people?'

'We rely on charity, as I said. Maybe Ben could use his talents to help our cause. These are forgotten people and no one cares whether they live or die. I do what I can, but it's never enough.'

'What happened to that family?' Judy asked in a whisper. 'Why can't she stop her baby from crying?'

'I found them crouched under a railway arch early this morning. The poor woman hasn't got enough milk to feed the infant. I've given them some gruel, but they're so close to starvation that they can only take a little at a time.'

'Will they be all right? Will the baby die?'

'I can't answer that one, Judy. I'll do what I can, but it might be too late for the youngest child. Very few children survive up to the age of five in this area. They either die of malnutrition or one of the many childhood diseases.'

'Where is the woman's husband?'

'As far as I can gather he was killed in an accident on the docks. It happens all too often.' Sarah peered into Judy's face. 'Are you all right? You're very pale.'

'My father died in a street accident in Whitechapel when I was a child. This brings it all back to me.'

'I'd offer you a cup of tea, but I gave the last of the milk to the little ones.'

'No, thank you,' Judy said hastily. 'Perhaps I can do something useful while Ben is treating the sick? I can see that you're very busy.'

'There are chamber pots to empty in the privy at the end of the back alley. Or are you too much of a lady to do such work?'

'I worked briefly as a ward maid at the London Hospital, which is how I met Ben. I'm more than happy to help.'

It was dark by the time they reached Sidney Square and the street lights cast a warm glow on the pavements. Men dressed in the formal attire of city clerks were arriving home in time for dinner, and scenes of well-ordered domesticity were clearly visible through windows where the housemaids had not yet drawn the curtains. It was not a particularly rich area but the contrast between this place and the poorest parts of Limehouse was quite shocking.

Minnie was in the parlour saying good night to her twin girls, who were in their spotlessly clean nightgowns, their faces pink and healthy and their eyes bright with mischief as they pleaded to be allowed to stay up for a while longer. The scene, lit by warm mellow gaslight and a roaring fire, brought tears to Judy's eyes. This was how life should be for all children, but she could not forget the vision of the poverty-stricken family she had seen in Limehouse. She blinked and forced a smile.

'Good night, girls. Sleep tight.'

'And don't let the bed bugs bite.' Lottie, the boldest of the twins, gave Judy a cheeky grin.

'Where did you learn that vulgar saying?' Minnie demanded.

'Sukey says worse than that, Mama.' Evie eyed her sister warily. 'Well, she does.'

'Don't start arguing now it's bedtime. I'll come upstairs and tuck you in soon,' Minnie said, giving them each a loving hug and a kiss. 'Papa will come up too when he gets home.' She waited until the door closed after them before turning to Ben. 'Well, how did it go in Limehouse? Did Sarah have any suggestions for you?'

'I'm going to stay there for a while,' Ben said slowly. 'Sarah's desperate for help.'

'But surely she can't afford to pay you?' Minnie gave him a searching look. 'How will you survive without an income, Ben?'

Judy cleared her throat in order to gain their attention. 'I think I have an idea.'

Chapter Fourteen

At that moment the door opened and Toby strolled into the parlour. Minnie leaped to her feet to embrace her husband.

'You're home early, darling. The girls have only just gone to bed if you want to go upstairs and give them a good night kiss.'

Toby smiled and gave her a gentle hug. 'Yes, I will, in a minute, but it looks as though I've interrupted something. What's going on?'

'Ben and Judy have been to Sarah Holden's establishment in Limehouse. Ben says he's going to work there for nothing. What do you think of that?' Minnie resumed her seat, gazing up at her husband as she waited for his response.

'I think it's a splendid idea, although it's not going to solve your money problems, Ben.' Toby walked to the side table where a decanter and glasses were laid out in readiness. He filled four glasses and handed them round before taking a seat. 'It's been a long day.' He sipped his drink, eyeing Judy curiously. 'I believe you were about to say something when I walked in and interrupted you.'

'I was shocked when I saw the state of the people in Sarah's care, and I think Ben is a hero if he's willing to give his time to help them.'

'But even a hero has to eat, and there will be creditors wanting their money back,' Minnie said softly. 'You said you had an idea.'

'Ben is obviously very good at persuading people to invest their money, so why not continue with the quest to create a new hospital?' Judy looked at each of them, gauging their reaction. 'It seems to me that a charitable institution in the poorest part of London would be far more appropriate. I think Ben could use his persuasive powers to convince his investors that this is a far better plan, and that their money will be put to good use.'

Ben frowned. 'But I couldn't promise any profit on the scheme, excellent though it may be.'

'They're all wealthy people, aren't they? They would benefit from knowing that they were doing something good for those who were less fortunate. I would gladly give up my time to work with Sarah had I not responsibilities at home.'

'I'm flattered that you think so highly of my persuasive powers, Judy,' Ben said seriously, 'but I can't share your optimism. I think the investors who believed in me will turn away, especially when I can't repay them.'

'I think you're wrong. If you put it to them that you will give your time for nothing in order to help the poor and desperate, how could they argue with that?'

'Judy has a point,' Minnie said thoughtfully. 'What do you think, Toby?'

'It's certainly worth a try, considering the mess that Ben has got himself into. Sorry, old chap, I don't mean to sound harsh, but you must expect some people to be cynical.'

'I do,' Ben said earnestly. 'I mean I'd be prepared for that sort of reaction. If I could turn this situation round and something good came out of it, I would be more than happy.'

'I know that when Daisy was in financial difficulties and she had to let Creek Manor out to Mrs Harker, it ended up with that lady raising funds to support Dr Neville's hospital in Little Creek. I'm sure it could be done here.' Judy turned to Minnie with a persuasive smile. 'What do you say? Would your well-off friends want to help?'

'I'll certainly do what I can,' Minnie said enthusiastically.

'I'll put a good word in with the powers that be,' Toby added. 'When we move into the house in Harley Street I'll be in a better position to spread the word. Maybe turning the business proposition into a charity is the answer. Good luck to you, Ben.'

*   *   *

Judy had intended to return home the following day, but she was so touched by the scenes she had witnessed that she decided to stay on for a few more days. There was little she could do other than to give Ben moral support when he went to visit the investors who had put money into the Creek Manor scheme, and she spent most of her time in Limehouse, helping Sarah to the best of her ability.

At night, when she retired to bed exhausted but found sleep evaded her, she recalled happier days. She had tried to forget Jack, but he was rarely from her thoughts. If something amused her, she imagined him laughing with her. She could not blame him for deserting her. She knew that in his crippled state he considered himself only half a man, and although that was untrue, she realised that it was not good enough for Jack – he was a perfectionist. The only cure for heartache was hard work, and a worthwhile project to occupy her mind.

On the fourth day after their arrival in London, Ben returned home with good news. One of his largest investors had been persuaded to back the new charity hospital in Limehouse, and at least two others were considering his proposition. Judy was relieved and delighted. It was a thoroughly worthy cause, even though it meant that Little Creek would lose its new hospital. Minnie invited her to stay on, insisting that she would be an invaluable help when they moved house. Judy was tempted to accept, but anything could have happened at home, and it was there that she was needed most. In the end there was no choice: she missed her family and Little Creek was her home.

Judy had not expected to be met when the train chugged into Little Creek Station, but to her surprise she saw Rob Dorning standing on the platform. At first she thought that he must be waiting to board the train, but he held out his hand to take her valise.

She hesitated. 'Did you come to meet me? Or is this just a coincidence?'

'Dr Godfrey sent a telegram to the inn. I've been staying there while you were away. It's very convenient for my purposes, and I think your mother was relieved to have someone there in case Faulkner turned up again.'

'He hasn't, has he?' Judy handed her ticket to the collector as they walked through the barrier.

'No. He hasn't shown his face, but I have people keeping an eye on him.'

'You employ spies?'

'I have a lot of people working for me, and Faulkner is so well known in the area that it's not difficult to keep tracks on him.' Rob handed her into the chaise and took the reins from a small boy, tossing him a coin as he climbed onto the driver's seat. 'Walk on.'

Judy shot a wary glance at him as he handled the horse with considerable expertise. It was obviously a thoroughbred amongst carriage horses, and the chaise itself was brand spanking new. She knew very little about Rob's past, but she sensed that he was a very private person and she did not like to pry.

It was a crisp winter's day and a pale buttercup-yellow sun shone on the frosty hedgerows and sparkled on the grassy banks. The creek bubbled merrily over the shallows and slinked silkily where it was deepest and greenest in the shade of the trees on the water's edge. Bright red berries glowed amongst the dark green spiky leaves of holly, and the clock in the church tower struck one, its sonorous sound echoing off the surrounding cottages and the village pub. Judy smiled to herself; it was good to be home. She had not realised how much she loved this part of the world until she went away. She could not help wondering if Jack felt similar pangs of homesickness, or perhaps he had forgotten his old life and was getting on well in the Antipodes. She could only hope that he was happy, and that, by now, he could walk again.

'You look sad.'

Rob's comment jerked her out of her reverie. 'I was just thinking how things have changed,' she said, forcing a smile. 'Not so very long ago we were like one big family at Creek Manor, but that is all gone now.'

'Creek Manor will rise again, like the phoenix from the ashes.'

'Is that what you intend? You want to rebuild the old house and call it Creek Manor?'

'It's still the same plot of land, and I imagine the manorial rights still hold. I am now the lord of the manor, although the title means nothing to me.'

'Why did you buy the estate? Do you intend to live there, or will you sell it to someone else for a huge profit?'

He took his eyes off the road ahead and turned his head to give her an amused look. 'You have a very poor opinion of me, don't you?'

'I am struggling to form an opinion, if you must know. I can't make you out, Rob Dorning. Why would a young man like you want to saddle yourself with running an estate like Creek Manor?'

'I'll have an estate manager. In fact I'll employ Clem Guppy, who I believe filled the position very efficiently before he was ousted. I'll let the tenant farmers do all the physical labour, and I'm quite capable of organising myself and the household, but more importantly, I want a permanent home. My father was jailed when I was a child, along with my uncles, and my mother died penniless. I was brought up by my Aunt Adeline, who's a wonderful woman, but times were hard. Now I'm in a position to improve her lot as well as mine.'

'But why did you pick Creek Manor? If you're wealthy you could have bought a grand mansion that was ready to move into.'

'That wouldn't do for me. The coast and the salt marshes are my part of the country, and I want to build something that fits in with the landscape but is very modern inside. I want to install indoor plumbing and bathrooms where you can turn on a tap and have unlimited hot water.'

It was Judy's turn to laugh. 'I've never heard of anything so odd. It would be wonderful, but surely it's just a dream.'

'It's possible, and I intend to make it a fact. Maybe we'll be the first people in Essex to have such a thing.'

'You're married?'

'I didn't say that.'

Judy felt herself blushing and she turned her head away. 'You said "we" – I just assumed . . .'

'No, I'm not married and I have no plans to alter my bachelor state, at the moment.'

'Not that it's any of my business,' she said hastily.

He laughed and flicked the reins to encourage the horse to quicken its pace. Judy's attention was caught by a group of women, huddled together with their shawls wrapped around them in an attempt to keep warm. They looked up at the sound of the approaching vehicle and Judy recognised Miss Creedy, Annie Maggs and Nancy Noon. Judy smiled and waved and they acknowledged her, but she could tell by the way they turned their backs and put their heads together that she and Rob Dorning were now the subject of speculation. She shot him a sideway glance and he turned to her with a smile.

'They'll have us engaged before the day is out.

I was born and raised in a village near Burnham-on-Crouch. I know exactly what the gossips are like.'

Judy relaxed against the squabs. 'I can't quite make you out, Rob Dorning. You are a mystery to me.' She groaned. 'Oh dear, and there's Mrs Peabody, the vicar's wife, talking to Daisy's aunt, Mrs Marshall, and they've seen us.'

'Don't worry, Judy. Let them talk.'

'It's all right for you, Rob. You don't live in Little Creek.'

'Not yet, although I've spent the last few days at the Crooked Billet while I sort out the details of the new house, and I expect to be here much more often while the building is taking place.'

She fixed him with a hard stare. 'Don't you have work to do? I mean, are you really a gentleman of leisure?'

'I wouldn't claim to be a gentleman, but I can afford to spend my time as I wish, thanks to the money left to me by one of my relatives who was transported to the penal colony in New South Wales. He made a fortune in the goldfields but he died childless.'

'I thought your family were smugglers.'

He chuckled. 'Yes, among other things. I want to make the name of Dorning respected, if that doesn't sound too pretentious.'

'No, I don't think it does in the slightest.' Judy turned her head away, staring at the creek as it splashed over rocks and fallen tree branches. Soon she would be home.

The pale sun shimmered on the silky waters of the estuary and the Crooked Billet seemed to slumber in the hazy light. Smoke curled up from the chimneys and as Rob drew the chaise to a halt outside the front door Judy could see her mother peering out of the window. Within seconds the door opened and Hilda limped out to throw her arms around Judy, hardly giving her time to alight from the carriage.

'I've missed you, darling girl. Have you have a good time in London? What happened to Dr Godfrey? Did he sort out his money problems?'

Judy returned the hug, chuckling. 'Give me a moment, Ma. I can't answer all your questions at once.'

'Of course not. You must be famished after that journey from London. I've made a cheese and potato pie especially for you.' Hilda turned to Nate, who had come running from the direction of the stables. 'Come and get your dinner when you've done what you have to. We'll have a family meal together for once.' She hustled Judy into the taproom where Eli, the pig man, was supping ale by the fire. Judy could smell him from where she stood. She smiled and acknowledged him, and a group of fishermen, who frequented the pub after a good catch. The tang of the sea and the aroma of fish hung in the air, battling with the farmyard odour of pigs.

Judy followed her mother to the kitchen where the table was laid with four place settings. 'There are only three of us.'

'It's Rob. He's taken to having his meals in the kitchen. He says it's nicer than dining on his own.' Hilda opened the oven door and took out a large pie with a glistening golden crust, placing it on the table. 'Now tell me everything before the others join us. What happened to the doctor?'

Judy had a sudden vision of Ben on the night when he attempted to fling himself off the cliff, and she brushed it aside, remembering instead the calm, capable man who treated the destitute patients in Limehouse. She sat down at the table, resting her arms on the scrubbed pine surface as she related the events in London. She came to a halt as Nate burst into the kitchen, bringing with him a gust of cold air, and he threw himself down at the table.

'That pie looks good and I'm starving. Wait until I tell Pip what we had for dinner today. I'm going to the Hall to see him tomorrow.'

'Then you may take a slice of pie,' Hilda said, smiling. 'That is if there's any left. Judy looks hungry and Rob has a good appetite.'

'You must cut a piece for him now.' Judy held out her plate. 'He can have half of mine if everyone else is being greedy.' She winked at her brother and Nate grinned back. 'And don't forget Molly. She might be living well at Colneyhurst, but she loves Ma's pies.'

'Heavens above.' Hilda threw up her hands. 'I'd have made two pies if I'd known you were going to fight over them.'

Judy looked from one to the other. It was good to be home with the people she loved most in the world. If Pip and Molly were here it would be perfect. She looked up as Rob strolled into the kitchen, pulled up a chair and sat down as if he too were part of the family.

'That smells wonderful, Hilda. You are a superb cook. I hope you'll be generous enough to share your recipes with my cook, whoever she might be, when I move into my new home.'

Judy was amused to see her mother blush as she cut him a large slice of pie.

'You're a flatterer, Rob Dorning,' Hilda said with mock severity. 'But I'll gladly do as you ask, and if you've got any sense you'll employ all the servants that used to work at the manor house. You'll not get any better.'

'That sounds like good advice,' he said, nodding. 'I'll bear it in mind.'

Judy eyed him sceptically. She suspected that Rob Dorning would do what he wanted no matter how much good advice he received. She tasted the pie and smiled. 'This is one of your best, Ma. I think we should have this on the menu every day.'

'My pies do seem very popular,' Hilda said thoughtfully. 'I might see if George Keyes wants some for his shop. It would be a way of making a little extra money as we're not taking much in the bar. The bad reputation this pub had in the past won't easily be forgotten in these parts, and we have the worst part of the winter to come.'

Rob put his knife and fork down. 'You can count on me. I'll be staying here until I can move into Creek Manor, and the architect I've employed will probably want a room for a while, at least.'

'So you're definitely going ahead with the rebuilding of the old manor house?' Hilda sat down opposite him and helped herself to a small portion of pie. 'It's not going to fall through like it did for the doctor?'

'No. I've had the preliminary plans and I'm off to Chelmsford today to confirm the details with a builder I've hired. The foundations of the old house are already there and the site is being cleared as we speak. In fact it's almost ready for work to begin.'

Judy eyed him curiously. 'How long will it take before you can move in?'

'The main body of the house should be habitable within a year, maybe sooner. I've told the builder to hire as many men as it takes to get the job finished as quickly as possible.'

'That will bring employment to the village,' Hilda said with a nod of approval. 'But it will cost a lot of money.'

'It will be worth it.' Rob held out his plate. 'Another slice of pie would be very acceptable, Hilda, my dear.'

She laughed, shaking her head. 'You know how to get your own way, Rob.'

'Yes,' he said, turning to Judy with a wry smile. 'I do.'

Nate jumped to his feet. 'I'd better fetch more coal before the fires go out, but I'll take that last slice of pie with me. I won't mention it to the others when I see them.' He rushed from the room before his mother had a chance to stop him.

'That boy will be the death of me,' Hilda said faintly. 'Whatever happened to manners?'

'He's all right, Ma.' Judy stifled a giggle. 'I have missed you all. It's good to be home.'

Hilda sighed and shook her head. 'Let's hope business picks up soon, or it might not be home for much longer.'

'Don't worry, Hilda.' Rob reached across the table to pat her hand. 'I'll bring in as much trade as I can. I wouldn't want to see this old place closed or, worse still, going back to the bad old days.'

'You're a good man, Rob.' Hilda squeezed his fingers.

Judy was suddenly apprehensive. Rob Dorning seemed to have charmed Ma and had moved in on a more or less permanent basis. She could not help being suspicious of his motives, but she did not want to upset her mother by challenging him. Men had a way of turning the tables: Faulkner had been charm itself until he achieved his ends; Jack had professed to love her, and then deserted her. As for

Dr Godfrey, he had let everyone down, including himself, and was now desperately trying to make amends. What possible reason could Rob Dorning have for working so hard to ingratiate himself with her family?

Judy rose to her feet. 'I'd better check the bar or Eli will be helping himself to a free drink.' She left the kitchen without waiting for a response and made her way to the taproom.

'Yes, Eli?' She held out her hand to take the empty pewter tankard. 'Another pint?'

'No, ta. Got to get back to me pigs or the colonel will dock me wages and the missis will throw a fit.' He tipped his greasy cap and hurried out of the pub, leaving a waft of the piggery in his wake. Judy picked up a nosegay of dried lavender and held it under her nose, inhaling the delicate scent. She washed the tankard in a bowl of water beneath the counter and was drying it with a clean cloth when Rob joined her.

'You don't believe me, do you, Judy?'

The question took her by surprise. 'What do you mean?'

'I could see by the look on your face that you thought I was simply bragging.'

She turned away to replace the tankard on the shelf. 'I never said anything of the sort.'

'You didn't have to.' He reached across the counter and caught her by the hand. 'Look at me. I'm not exaggerating and I'm not lying. I have the means and I have the determination to see this through. When the manor house is rebuilt it will give employment to all your friends who now face difficulties, and in the meantime it will bring business to you and to the village as a whole.'

She snatched her hand free. 'But why would you act like a great benefactor? You don't owe the people of Little Creek anything, and there's no reason for you to bother about us. We've faced worse than this, and we'll survive.'

'I don't doubt it,' he said easily. 'But you're wrong about me. I'm not doing this for glory.'

'Then why? I could understand why Ben wanted to do something good – he's a dedicated doctor – but you are the son of a convicted criminal, and you've also profited from the money your predecessors made in a penal colony. Why would you wish to spend it all in Little Creek?'

'I have my reasons, as I told you.'

'I think there's something more.'

Judy would have questioned him further, but the pub door opened and Constable Fowler strode into the taproom. She could tell by his expression that this was not a social visit. Mick Fowler was a popular member of the community and Judy had known him since she was a child. 'Is there anything wrong, Constable?'

He took off his helmet and tucked it under his arm. 'Is Mrs Faulkner at home, Judy?'

'Yes, she's in the kitchen. Shall I fetch her?'

Constable Fowler glanced at the group of fish-ermen who were taking a sudden interest in what was going on around them, whereas previously they had been laughing and joking amongst themselves.

'It might be best if I spoke to her in private, Judy. You should be there, too.'

'I'll mind the bar,' Rob said calmly.

'No, Mr Dorning. You'd better come too. This concerns you as well. I'll wait in the parlour if you'll fetch your ma, Judy.' He held up his hand. 'Don't worry, I know where it is. This isn't the first time I've been here on police business. I'm afraid it's not good news.'

Chapter Fifteen

Hilda sank down on the nearest chair, her hand clasped to her mouth. 'No. He wouldn't do such a thing.'

'I'm sorry, Hilda,' Constable Fowler allowed himself to bend a little. 'Wilfred was caught in the act of setting fire to your old cottage on the Creek Manor estate, which I believe now belongs to you, Mr Dorning.'

'The devil he did!' Rob said, frowning. 'You're right, Constable. I am the landowner.'

'But why would he do such a thing?' Judy slipped her arm around her mother's shoulders. 'There's nothing of ours left there.'

'Only memories,' Hilda said, sighing. 'We were happy there, you and I, Judy.'

'Maybe that was his reason for burning the place to the ground,' Constable Fowler said grimly.

'He seems proud of what he's done and he claims that it was he who started the blaze at the manor house.'

Hilda fanned herself with her hand. 'Wilfred had worked there since he was a boy. I can't think what would make him behave in this way.'

'Who's to say what goes on in a man's head? He was caught red-handed by Farmer Johnson and Will. They said that Faulkner was laughing like a maniac. I'm sorry to be the bearer of such bad news, Hilda.'

'He's a violent man,' Judy said quickly. 'He threatened Ma, and he attacked me and then he threw me out of the house because I wouldn't let him have his way with me. I hope the judge gives him the longest sentence possible. He deserves it.'

'He seemed so nice and kind at the start.' Hilda mopped her streaming eyes on her apron. She stood up, somewhat unsteadily. 'But it's over now and I've got work to do. Is that all, Constable?'

'Why don't you sit down a little longer, Ma?' Judy reached out to steady her mother, but Hilda brushed her hand away.

'I'm all right, ta. It was a bit of a shock, but I'm not really surprised. He couldn't get what he wanted so he destroyed the one place where we were happy, and he knew I loved that little cottage.'

'But it doesn't explain why he wanted to burn the manor house to the ground,' Rob said slowly. 'It doesn't make sense, Constable.'

'He admitted it, but he wouldn't say anything

further.' Constable Fowler backed towards the doorway. 'I don't need you to do anything, Hilda. I just wanted to tell you before it became public knowledge.'

'Will I have to give evidence at his trial?' Hilda asked nervously.

'I doubt it. He'll be brought up before the magistrate tomorrow and then it's my guess he'll be sent to the assizes in Chelmsford. I doubt if you'll be seeing him again for a very long time. I'll say good day to you all.' He left the room, ramming his helmet on his head as he went. His footsteps echoed on the bare boards, leaving the air trembling with silence.

Judy was the first to speak and her voice shook with emotion. 'Oh, Ma, I'm so sorry.'

'It's all right, dear. I knew something bad was going to happen. I'm just glad he took it out on the building and not on any of us. I'm just sorry that I brought that man into our family.'

'No, you mustn't think like that.' Judy cast a desperate look in Rob's direction and he nodded.

'Judy's right, Hilda,' he said earnestly. 'I didn't know Faulkner personally, but I know his type. They can be very skilled at presenting a different face to the world. You weren't to know.'

Judy eyed him curiously. 'But Faulkner was scared of you, Rob. Can you explain that?'

He shook his head. 'Maybe it was the name Dorning that frightened him, or maybe a fleeting family likeness. Perhaps he had fallen foul of one of my uncles before they were caught and sent to prison? Who knows what went on in the man's head?' Rob turned back to Hilda with a sympathetic smile. 'Try to forget him. As the constable said, you won't be seeing Faulkner again for a very long time.'

'Yes, I know you're both right. I'll try to put it out of my mind, but I can't help feeling a bit responsible for all our friends losing their livelihoods and their homes. I brought my children here but we've always been regarded as newcomers in Little Creek, and now we've brought shame and hardship to the village.'

'That's not true, Ma,' Judy said in desperation. 'No one will blame you for what Wilfred's done. You'll see.'

'I don't think I can show my face in the village again,' Hilda said, sighing. She held up her hands as Judy went to give her a comforting hug. 'I'm all right, dear. What I need is to keep myself occupied. Why don't you go back to the bar with Rob, and I'll clear up the kitchen? Anyway, I need to make more pies for the evening's trade. That's if anyone ever comes here again.' She hurried from the room, leaving Judy staring after her in dismay. She had never seen Ma brought so low, not even after the accident that left her permanently maimed.

Rob laid his hand on her shoulder. 'Your mother's right. Come into the taproom and I'll show you the plan for the new building. The sooner work starts on it the better.'

She nodded wordlessly and walked slowly to the taproom.

The fishermen had left and Nate was stoking the fire. He straightened up and turned to give them a curious stare. 'What's going on? I saw the copper leaving. What did he want?'

'Don't let Ma hear you calling Constable Fowler "a copper",' Judy said with a reluctant smile. 'You know she's brought us up to respect the law.'

Nate shrugged and wiped his grubby hands on his trousers. 'You're as bad as she is sometimes, Judy. Anyway, you haven't answered my question.'

Rob hesitated at the foot of the stairs. 'I'll go and get the plans while you tell your brother what's happened. It's my guess that it will be all round the village by now.'

'Sit down, Nate,' Judy said wearily. 'It's not good news, I'm afraid.'

'The old devil,' he said when she had finished speaking. 'I never liked the fellow, especially when he beat me for nothing, but I never said anything because I thought he was good to Ma. I wish I'd known what he was up to. I'd have knocked some sense into him.'

Her brother's pugnacious stance both touched and amused Judy, but she managed to keep a straight face. 'Then it's as well you didn't know. He's a strong brute, as I discovered to my cost. Anyway, I'm glad he's out of the way now, and I hope I never see him again.'

'I've finished here unless we get any passing carriage trade, which I doubt.' Nate shrugged on the jacket he had discarded. 'I'm going to saddle up Major and ride over to Colneyhurst to tell Molly and Pip. They need to know.'

'Yes, of course. You're so grown-up now, Nate. I'm proud of you. But,' Judy added hastily, 'be careful what you say to Ma. She's pretending to be strong, but I could see how upset she is. She thinks the whole village will be against us.'

Nate pulled a face. 'Why would they think it was our fault?'

'Because we only came here a relatively short time ago. Most of them have been born and bred in the village, as have their parents and grandparents. We're newcomers and we've brought trouble and disgrace to Little Creek. That's how Ma sees it.'

'That's stupid. They'd better not say anything in my hearing.' He fisted his hands. 'I won't have anyone spreading untruths about my family.' He stamped out of the taproom, slamming the door behind him.

'He took that well, then?' Rob came towards her, clutching the architect's drawings. 'Only to be expected from a lad of his age, I suppose.'

'Nate won't allow anyone to criticise Ma,' Judy said defensively. 'Neither will I.'

Rob unfolded the large document and laid it on one of the tables. 'I don't think you're giving the people of Little Creek credit for common sense. I'd be very surprised if there was any resentment against your family. Anyway, forget all that for a moment. Come and look at the plans for the new manor house. You knew the old one so well, and you might have some useful ideas. I need a woman's point of view.'

Somewhat reluctantly, Judy moved to his side and studied the expertly drawn outlines of what would soon be built on the site of the old manor house. To her surprise the layout was very similar, although greatly simplified and not as rambling. The original sixteenth-century building had been added to greatly over the years, but somehow the heart and soul of the dwelling had been captured and put down on paper.

'What do you think, Judy?'

She looked up, meeting his serious gaze with a feeling of surprise, and she realised that he was genuinely interested in her opinion. She studied the plans carefully, pointing out anything that would not work well when it came to running the house, especially from the servants' point of view.

'For one thing,' she said seriously. 'It makes sense to have the dining room a bit closer to the kitchens. If you'd ever tried to get hot food to the table when you had to negotiate draughty corridors and flights of steps, you might understand better.'

He smiled. 'It's not something I'd considered, but I can see the sense in what you're saying.'

'And these rooms set aside for washing and

bathing,' Judy said, shaking her head. 'It would be better if they were closer to the main bedchambers.'

'That's easily done. I'll pass your advice on to the architect.'

She eyed him warily. 'Are you making fun of me, Rob Dorning?'

'No, certainly not. I want this house to be a comfortable home for both the master and the servants.'

'Then you could put proper washing facilities on the top floor where the servants sleep,' Judy said firmly. 'If you'd had to carry ewers filled with hot water up several flights of stairs—' she broke off as he started to laugh.

'I know, Judy. You don't have to spell it out for me, and you're quite right. I should consider those who work for me as well as my own comfort and that of my guests and family.'

'You said you haven't any family, apart from your aunt Adeline. Will she live with you?'

'I'm going to do my best to persuade her to move in with me, but Aunt Adeline is a very independent woman and extremely stubborn. One day I hope I might find a woman who will put up with me.'

'With all your money I don't think that will be difficult. I'm sure the young ladies in the county will be falling over themselves in an attempt to gain your good opinion when you move into Creek Manor.'

'You're forgetting my background. My fortune

was made through ill-gotten gains. Who would want to be associated with such a man?'

'Who indeed?' Judy eyed him warily. The teasing light in his eyes was disconcerting, and she had a feeling that involving her in the design of his new home was merely a way of taking her mind off the problems that beset her. She glanced over her shoulder as the door opened and, to her surprise, it was Colonel Catchpole who strode into the taproom, closely followed by two yellow Labradors and a small terrier.

'Sit!' The colonel's strident tone made the dogs skid to a halt and sit down, tongues hanging out as they gazed up at their master.

'Good afternoon, Colonel.' Judy went behind the bar. 'What can I get you, sir?'

'I'll have a tot of rum to ward off the cold. It looks like snow to me.'

She poured him a measure of the spirit and he knocked it back in one mouthful. 'Could your mother use a side of bacon, Miss Begg? Got a surplus, so to speak, so she'd be doing me a favour in taking it off my hands.'

'I'm sure she could, Colonel. If you're sure you can spare it. How much do we owe you?'

He shook his head. 'Another tot of rum will settle the bill, my dear. We all do our bit for each other in Little Creek.' He downed the drink in one and turned to leave. 'I'll have it sent round in the morning. Come, boys.'

The dogs leaped to attention and followed him out of the building, tails wagging.

'What did I tell you?' Rob said, grinning.

'He can't know what my stepfather did already.'

'Eli must have told someone and it came to Constable Fowler's attention. As I said before, Judy. Word flies round faster you can blink in Little Creek. The colonel obviously doesn't blame your family for what Faulkner's done, so why should anyone else?'

Starting later that afternoon they received a constant trickle of visitors, led by Grace Peabody and Eleanora Marshall, who arrived at the Crooked Billet to lend their support to Hilda and her family. Women who would never normally put a foot over the threshold came with small gifts: a couple of fresh eggs, a few onions or anything they could spare. Judy knew it was their way of showing sympathy for Hilda, quite contrary to her expectations of being branded a pariah. It seemed that far from being considered outsiders, Little Creek had taken the Begg family to its heart and their struggles had not gone unnoticed. Their prospects looked even brighter when Rob's architect booked a room for an indefinite period. The building of the new manor house was about to begin, despite the sudden change in the weather. Christmas was almost upon them and the cold snap gave way to rain and howling gales.

At Rob's suggestion Nate took the cart to the grounds of Creek Manor and he arrived back at the Crooked Billet with a huge load of berried holly, and a large bunch of mistletoe. He helped Judy to decorate the taproom and their private parlour, and Rob provided a Christmas tree.

'It's lovely,' Judy said wistfully, 'but all the decorations were lost in the fire at the manor house.'

'I've thought of that. Get your cape and bonnet, we're going to Maldon.'

She hesitated. 'I don't know about that. I can't leave Ma to do all the work.'

'Nonsense. I've asked Hilda and she says you've earned a day off, besides which she needs some things and she's writing a list as we speak.'

Judy glanced out of the window at the dreary overcast weather, and she smiled. 'Well, it would be nice to go to town. I haven't been anywhere since I returned from London.'

'That's settled then. I could do with some time away from the site of the old house, and I'll enjoy a day out with you, Judy. Fetch your things and we'll be off.'

The drive to Maldon was uneventful and the rain held off, although a cold east wind made Judy huddle beneath the rug that Rob had placed over her knees. He, however, seemed oblivious to the cold and the sharp slaps of the wind as it reddened his cheeks and threatened several times to snatch his hat from his head. He merely laughed and held it on with one hand while holding the reins in the other.

Nothing seemed to bother him and he was in a good humour, keeping Judy amused with tales of his misspent youth that made her chuckle, and the time passed so quickly that she was surprised when they reached the outskirts of the town.

They strolled arm in arm around the market and Judy purchased the items on her mother's list, while Rob bought up every strand of tinsel and glass bauble that he could find. Judy had a little money of her own and she bought a pair of warm mittens as a Christmas present for her mother and a silk scarf for Molly. She decided on socks for her brothers, which would be sensible, and to make their gifts more festive she added slabs of toffee and Fry's Chocolate Cream bars, a rare treat. Rob was more of a problem. He was a friend, but he was also a patron of the inn and as such needed to be treated with a degree of reserve. She waited until he was absorbed in bargaining for a box of glass decorations, and she purchased a leather-bound notebook and a pencil. It was the only thing she could think of that was relatively cheap and useful – he could make notes on the building progress and costs, or whatever came into his mind. She tucked the little present into her basket beneath the socks.

'There,' Rob said, turning to her with a beaming smile. 'We'll have the best decorated Christmas tree in Little Creek, and when I move into the manor house I intend to have an enormous tree every year.' His smile faded. 'You look chilled to the bone. We'll get something to eat before we set off for home.'

She managed to stretch her cold lips into a smile. 'Yes, that would be good. I'm starving.'

He tucked her hand in the crook of his arm. 'We'll drive down to the quay. I know the landlord at the inn there and his wife is an excellent cook.'

Judy fell into step beside him. 'I really hope so.' She glanced up at the sky, which had darkened significantly since they arrived and the stallholders had lit the naphtha flares that were normally only used at dusk. 'I think we're in for a storm.'

'No matter. We have to eat, and my horse needs sustenance, too, and a rest in the stables. Don't worry, Judy. I'll get you home safe and sound.'

It had started out such a pleasant day, even if it was cold. The sun had shone and Judy had enjoyed every minute of their shopping expedition. It was good to get away from the confines of the inn and the day-to-day chores that seemed never-ending, but with the fickleness of the weather, particularly at this time of year, the rain started in earnest just as they reached the inn on the quay. The taproom was crowded with fishermen, seafarers and dock workers, and the landlord led them to a private parlour where a fire burned brightly in the grate, and boughs of holly decorated the mantelshelf. Polished brass andirons vied for attention and admiration with a gleaming copper coal scuttle, and two long tables were laid with cheerful gingham cloths. The room was lit by oil lamps, the atmosphere was both cosy and welcoming, but outside the sky was darkening and the storm seemed to be gathering strength. Rain turned into hailstones that battered the windowpanes and bounced off the cobblestones in the yard, scattering like a broken string of pearls.

'It's not going to be a pleasant drive home,' Judy said anxiously.

'We can't leave while it's like this.' Rob took his watch from his waistcoat pocket and frowned. 'It will be dark soon and I wouldn't want to risk the roads in this storm. We might have to put up here for the night if the weather doesn't improve.' He looked up as the landlord entered the room, bringing with him the aroma of roasting meat, wood smoke and a hint of hops.

'Might I recommend the roast venison, sir? It's a particularly fine joint, if I say so myself, and my good wife is an excellent cook.'

'So I've heard,' Rob said pleasantly. 'I'm happy with that. What about you, Judy?'

'Yes, indeed. I'm starving.'

The landlord's flushed cheeks wobbled into a grin. 'Then I suggest you start with the soup, miss. It's chicken broth with barley. Very good.'

'Yes, thank you,' Judy said, smiling. 'That sounds delicious.'

'I'll have the broth also, and I'll have a pint of your best ale. What would you like to drink, Judy?'

'I'd love some lemonade.'

'Very well, miss.'

Judy waited until the landlord had left the parlour before turning to Rob. She leaned across the table, fixing him with a hard stare. 'We can't stay here tonight. Ma will be frantic with worry if I don't get home.'

'I think she'll realise that we've been held up by the storm.'

Judy frowned. 'But it won't look good. I don't normally care what people say, but even friends might jump to the wrong conclusion.'

'I promise you that my intentions are honourable,' Rob said, chuckling. 'Don't look so worried. No one will know apart from your mother and Nate, and I'm sure they would believe us.'

'Perhaps it will clear,' Judy said hopefully as she gazed out of the window.

Rob turned to look round as the landlord entered, bringing their drinks and two bowls of soup.

'What do the locals say about this storm, Landlord? Do they think it will blow over soon?'

The landlord wiped his hands on a beer-stained apron. 'No, sir. I'd say it's going to get worse. The fishermen didn't go out today and all the barges are alongside, although there's one ship that's just anchored and they're having a struggle to row ashore in the jolly boat. I'd have stayed put if it were me.'

'Even if the hail turns back to rain the roads are going to be treacherous, especially in the dark,' Rob said thoughtfully. 'Have you a couple of rooms vacant, Landlord?'

'No, sir. There's but one, and it's not the best room. That was booked just now by the ship's agent. I'm afraid it will be the same all over town.'

'Then we'll take the one room.'

'Very good, sir.' The landlord flicked a quick look at Judy and his lips twisted in a wry smile. 'One room it is.'

Judy waited until he left the parlour. 'We can't stay here. We must try to get home.'

'You can have the room, Judy. I'll get the landlord to provide some cushions and a blanket and I'll sleep in here.'

'I don't know. It doesn't seem fair.'

He shrugged. 'It doesn't look as though there's much choice. I can bear it, if you can.'

They finished their meal not exactly in silence, but the pleasure had gone from the outing for Judy. She knew that Ma would be worried sick, and there was no way of contacting her to allay her fears. The sound of raucous laughter and loud voices filtered through from the taproom, and she found herself wishing that the Crooked Billet had as many customers, but the thought of spending the night in such a rowdy place was even less appealing. It was late afternoon and it was already dark outside. They had just finished their coffee when the landlord sidled into the parlour.

'I have two gentlemen who would like to dine in private, so perhaps you would like to see your room, miss. I'm sure you wouldn't mind retiring to the snug, sir? It's very congenial.'

Judy shot a wary glance in Rob's direction, hoping that he would refuse to budge, but he merely smiled and nodded.

'Excellent idea,' Rob said a little too heartily. 'I'm sure you'd like to see where you'll spend the night, Judy.'

Left with no alternative other than a point-blank refusal, Judy followed the landlord into the taproom, but she came to a sudden halt, staring at two men who were propping up the bar. She backed into the parlour and slammed the door.

'What's the matter?' Rob rose to his feet. 'You look as if you've seen a ghost.'

She attempted to speak but she seemed to have lost her voice and she was finding it hard to breathe. The landlord stood in the doorway, looking red in the face and flustered.

'The young lady just bolted, sir. It wasn't anything that I said or did.'

Rob guided Judy back to the settle and pressed her gently onto the seat. 'I think the lady is unwell. A glass of brandy, if you please.'

The landlord disappeared again, closing the door quietly behind him.

'What did you see that upset you?' Rob demanded anxiously. 'For heaven's sake, speak to me, Judy.'

'I saw a ghost from the past, or at least I think I did. I have to leave now. I won't stay here another minute.' She jumped up and made a grab for her cape and bonnet. 'I'm going home even if I have to walk all the way.' She opened the door almost bumping into the landlord, who was holding a glass of brandy in his hand. 'Is there a way to the stables without going through the taproom? I'm leaving this instant.'

'Turn right and straight ahead . . .'

Despite protests from both Rob and the landlord, Judy left the parlour and ran.

Chapter Sixteen

Judy had barely reached the back door when Rob caught up with her.

'Where do you think you're going?'

She wrapped her cape around her shoulders and pulled up the hood. 'I'm going home. I can't stay here. Don't try to make me.'

'But it's madness to make the journey in this weather, and it's pitch-dark. The roads will be treacherous.'

'I don't care,' she cried passionately. 'I'm not going back in there. You don't understand.' She wrenched the door open and ran out into the raging storm. Rob caught her up as she barged into the stable.

'Will you tell me why you are in such a panic? Why won't you stay here?'

She rounded on him furiously. 'Did you go into the taproom? Did you see who was standing at the bar?'

'No. The landlord was as surprised as I am by your reaction. I threw some money at him and chased after you. For God's sake, tell me what's wrong.'

Judy beckoned to the stable boy. 'We're leaving. Harness the horse to the chaise, please, and do it quickly.' She glanced over her shoulder. 'They might have seen me.'

Rob took her by the shoulders, holding her firmly so that she could not escape his iron grasp. 'Who are they? I won't ask again. If you don't tell me I'm going to carry you back to the inn and set you down in the taproom. Then you can point out these monsters.'

'You wouldn't dare.'

'Try me.'

Judy took a deep breath. 'It was Jay and I couldn't see his face but I'd swear that Jack was there also.'

'You mean the Fox brothers? Or Tattersall, whatever Jay calls himself these days.'

'Yes, it was definitely Jay and if it was Jack, he was cured. He was standing unaided and he must have walked into the bar.'

'There's nothing to be afraid of,' Rob said gently. 'I'm with you, and surely they were your friends.'

'Once upon a time, yes. But I haven't heard from Jack since they left for Australia. He obviously doesn't want to know me, and I hadn't the slightest notion that he was cured. I don't want to meet him like this. Please, Rob, take me home or I'll drive the chaise myself.'

He nodded to the boy, who was hovering a little way from them, gazing uncertainly as if waiting for his confirmation. 'All right. Do what the lady says.' He tossed a coin and the boy caught it with a grin and set about putting the harness on the horse.

'Thank you,' Judy said, sighing.

Rob went to help the stable boy and within minutes they were climbing into the chaise and setting off into the storm. Despite the fact that the hood was pulled up it gave very little protection from the rain and sleet. The horse plodded against the wind and even though Rob had wrapped the travel rug around her, Judy was cold and wet before they had gone even half a mile.

'Just remember,' he said through clenched teeth, 'this was your idea, not mine.'

'You wanted to stay for the night,' Judy countered angrily. 'We could have left hours ago and be home by now.'

His reply was lost in the pounding of the horse's hoofs, the sound of the rain lashing on the leather hood and the wind howling around them like spirits in agony. Rob had to concentrate on the road ahead, attempting to guide the horse away from the deepest of the ruts and huge puddles. Judy clung on for dear life as the chaise swayed dangerously from side to side. It was a light vehicle and much better suited to travelling in more clement weather. She was beginning to regret her impulsive decision to run away. Maybe it would have been better to brave a night at the inn and a possible embarrassing reunion with Jack. She huddled beneath the blanket, although it was impossible to keep warm and she leaned against Rob's tense body as he struggled to control the frightened animal. Now they were faced with winding lanes and the wind whipped the over-hanging branches into a frenzy, lashing the hood as if intent of causing damage. It was impossible to sleep, but Judy kept slipping into a state somewhere between waking and dreaming. At one moment she imagined she was curled up by a roaring fire, and then cold reality brought her back to the present with a start. She was sliding into another more pleasant place when suddenly there was an almighty crack. The horse uttered a horrific sound so like a human scream that Judy covered her ears with her hands. Seconds later the chaise tilted to one side and the horse reared up in the shafts as the vehicle toppled over. Rob was thrown to the ground but somehow Judy managed to hang on, although one leg was trapped in the buckled woodwork, and a tear-inducing pain in her ankle made her cry out.

'Rob.' She called his name again and again but there was no reply. One carriage light had been smashed, but in the dim glow of the other one she could just make out one broken shaft. As if by a miracle, the horse remained upright, although trapped and obviously terrified. Of Rob there was no sign. That side of the wrecked carriage was in complete darkness and his silence was even more frightening. Very carefully she pulled herself to a sitting position and slowly, and with great difficulty, she managed to free her ankle from the splintered footwell. She sat upright, not daring to move for a few agonising moments, and then she leaned over to massage the injured ankle. Her boots had saved her from a more serious injury and she could wriggle her toes, even though it was painful. She could only hope that it was a bad sprain and nothing worse. But her main concern was for Rob and she edged herself over the wreckage, calling his name, but still there was no answer.

She slid down into the tangle of metalwork and splintered wood, and felt about in the darkness as best as she was able. She was limping badly and the wind had tugged off her bonnet and dragged her hair from its confining snood. Rain-soaked and blinded by the water dripping into her eyes, she almost fell on top of Rob's inert body. She went down on her knees regardless of the deep puddle of muddy water, and as she ran her hands over his body she realised that he was trapped by a branch of the fallen tree that had caused their accident.

For a terrible moment she thought he was dead and her breath hitched in her throat, but as she struggled to free him she heard a faint moan, and she used all her strength to drag the thick branch away.

'Rob.' She bent over him, putting her lips close to his ear. 'Can you hear me?'

Another faint groan made her heart beat even

faster as she attempted to lift him from the muddy bank, but he was too heavy and reluctantly she abandoned her effort. There was another and more urgent call on her energies and that was the terrified horse. He was thrashing about as he tried to free himself from the remaining shaft, and Judy raised herself to her feet. She made her way with difficulty over the debris, and despite the pain in her ankle she managed at last to calm the frightened animal. It took a while to free him from the tangled harness, but eventually her numbed fingers managed to undo the straps that held the traces in place and the horse bolted into the darkness, leaving her alone with an injured man.

She threw back her head and screamed with frustration. If she had managed better she might have ridden off to find help, but now they were marooned in a remote country lane, surrounded on all sides by darkness. She limped back to where Rob lay and she dragged the rug from the chaise. Even though it was sodden it made a pillow for his head, and she huddled beside him, attempting to use the warmth from her own chilled body to protect him from the bitter cold. A further examination in the flickering light of the carriage lamp did not reveal any obvious injuries and the only blood she could see was on a gash on his forehead.

'It's all my fault, Rob,' she whispered, chafing his cold hands. 'If I hadn't panicked and made you drive out into the storm this wouldn't have happened.'

He groaned again and this time his eyelids flickered and opened. She touched his cheek gently. 'Rob, speak to me.'

He muttered something unintelligible and closed his eyes again. Judy gave him a shake.

'Don't do this. You can't go to sleep here. You'll die of cold.' She was suddenly desperate. It was happening all over again – he would be crippled for life, as it had seemed to be with Jack – and it was all her fault. She shook him harder this time. 'Open your eyes, Rob. Talk to me, please.'

'Stop nagging me.'

The words were faint but clear, and tears of sheer relief rolled down Judy's cheeks.

'You'll be all right. Can you move at all?'

He opened his eyes, frowning up at her. 'What happened?'

'I don't know exactly, it was all so sudden. I think the fallen tree must have crashed onto your side of the chaise and toppled it over. You ended up on the ground, and I freed the horse but the wretched animal bolted. I'm afraid we're stuck here until a passer-by finds us.'

Rob raised himself with difficulty. 'My head hurts, but I don't think I've broken any bones, although I'm sore all over.'

'Can you stand up?' Judy scrambled to her feet. 'We might be able to find somewhere to shelter, if you could walk, that is.'

'I'll try. Give me your hand.'

Slowly, with Judy's help, he managed to raise himself to a standing position.

'That's good,' Judy said carefully. 'Can you take a step or two?'

He raised his hand to his forehead, grimacing as his fingers found the bloody gash. 'I feel as if I've got a hundred imps with pickaxes hammering at my skull, but there's no use remaining here. There's unlikely to be any traffic until morning.'

'Then we have to make a move.' Judy winced as she put weight on her damaged ankle. 'I'm game, if you are.'

'You're hurt.'

'Just my ankle. I can walk, if you can.'

'Maybe we'll find that blasted animal grazing somewhere along the way. At least one of us can ride.'

'That's right. We'll take it in turns.' Judy proffered her arm. 'I'll lean on you and you can lean on me. We can do this, Rob.'

'Most of the women I know would be having hysterics right now.'

'Not this woman,' Judy said, laughing. 'I'm made of sterner stuff, and it was my fault in the first place. I'm sorry I made you leave the comfort of the inn for this, Rob.'

He tucked her hand in the crook of his arm. 'Never mind that now. Let's get moving before we both succumb to lung fever or worse.'

'You could have been more gracious about it,'

Judy grumbled as pain shot upwards from her injured ankle. 'I rarely admit I'm wrong.'

He laughed. 'Why doesn't that surprise me?' He looked up into the lowering clouds. 'It's stopped raining but it's started to snow. We'd better walk faster.'

They tramped along the muddy lane with Judy limping painfully and Rob having to stop every few minutes to catch his breath. The rain had turned to sleet and then to snow and the world around them was rapidly turning from darkness to shining silvery white as the hedgerows and fields took on a mantle of snow. It felt a little warmer and the wind had ceased, but Judy was uncomfortably aware of her wet garments and when she glanced up at Rob she could see that he, too, was in pain. She did not voice her fears, but she suspected he might have broken a few ribs when he was thrown from the chaise, and the fallen branch had caught him across the chest, adding to her worries.

They trudged on until suddenly Judy spotted the swinging lights of carriage lamps not too far ahead. 'Look, Rob. Someone's coming.'

As it drew nearer she realised that it was a farm cart, driven by a man who was well-muffled against the cold. He drew the vehicle to a halt.

'I knew it,' he said triumphantly. 'Didn't I tell my pa that there was an accident somewhere on the way? I've come to help you.' He leaped to the ground and swung Judy up on the driver's seat without giving her a chance to protest. 'Can you climb onto the cart, mate?' he asked, peering closely at Rob. 'That be a nasty gash you got on your forehead. I bet that stings.'

'Yes, I can manage, thanks.'

'I'm Seth Trundle. I knew there was trouble when the horse trotted into our yard half an hour ago. I says to my pa, that's no old nag, Father. I bet there's trouble up yonder. I'd best go and see who needs help.' He climbed up to sit beside Judy. 'We'll be home in no time at all. I told Ma to put the kettle on the hob because some poor soul must be suffering in the cold. Nasty weather, and likely to continue for some days.' Seth flicked the reins. 'Walk on Skipper.'

Judy's teeth were chattering too much to allow her to speak, and Seth did not seem to need answers to the questions he fired at them, barely stopping for breath. Rob was silent as he was bounced around on a bed of straw in the back of the cart, and Judy sighed with relief when she saw the lights of the Trundles' farm getting closer. Seth actually stopped talking for a while as he helped her to alight and then turned his attention to Rob. Two sheepdogs raced up to them, but subsided instantly at a word from Seth.

'Come this way, if you please,' he said politely. 'Ma will look after you, lady. And Pa will tend to you, mate. He's used to patching me up when I've had a fight. I got a fierce temper when roused, but you don't need to worry about me. I'm as docile as a lamb with people what I like, and I consider that I likes the pair of you.'

Judy exchanged amused glances with Rob as they followed Seth into the farmhouse.

'Ma, I found 'em. I reckon as how they'll be ready for a cup of tea, and the lady has hurt her ankle. I could hardly hear myself talk for the sound of her teeth chattering together.'

Mrs Trundle rushed forward. 'Pull up a chair for the young lady, Seth.' She guided Judy towards the table. 'Sit down, my dear. I'll give you a nice hot cup of tea and then we'll see to your injury.'

Farmer Trundle rose from his seat by the range. 'So what were you doing driving out on a night like this, I might ask, sir? Is it an elopement? If it be then I cannot condone such behaviour, being a God-fearing man.'

'No, indeed, sir,' Rob said firmly. 'Miss Begg and I are just friends. Our journey was ill-judged, I admit, but it's easy to be wise in hindsight.'

Judy picked up the cup and sipped the hot, sweet tea that Mrs Trundle had placed on the table in front of her. 'It was my fault, Mr Trundle. I insisted on getting home to Little Creek tonight. I knew that my mother would be worried sick if we didn't arrive.'

'Well, miss, you might have perished out there in the bitter cold if my boy had not had the forethought to go looking for you.'

Seth took off his cap and tossed it across the kitchen so that it hung on a wall peg. 'You can thank your horse, mate. A fine animal, if ever I seen one, but you was lucky he come here and didn't make his way back to his own stable.'

'Never mind all that.' Mrs Trundle handed a steaming mug of tea to Rob. 'You'd best sit down, too, mister. That gash on your brow needs attention.' She turned to her husband. 'You'd best see to him, Joe. I'll go upstairs and make up two beds.'

Judy cast an anxious look in Rob's direction. 'No, really, we can't put you to so much trouble, ma'am.'

'It's no bother, I can assure you, miss. You can't go anywhere if your vehicle is damaged, and it's no good trying to sort it out until morning.'

'We're very grateful, Mrs Trundle,' Rob said hastily. 'And we can pay for the night's board.'

Mrs Trundle smiled and shook her head. 'No call for that, sir. We'd do the same for any travellers in distress.' She hurried from the kitchen.

Farmer Trundle knocked the dottle from his pipe into the fire. 'Let me see that cut, son. It looks quite deep. It might need a stitch or two.'

'It'll be fine, sir,' Rob said hastily. 'No need to worry.'

'Scared of the needle, are you, son? It's better than having a scar or the wound turning nasty. Sit tight and Seth will fetch Mother's sewing box. We'll have you sorted in minutes.'

'I told you that Pa would know what to do,' Seth said triumphantly.

'Stop talking, son, and fetch the sewing box, and

some hot water from the kettle. I'll have to wash the blood off first.' Farmer Trundle turned to give Judy an appraising look. 'If you're squeamish best look away, miss. I'll get to you and take a look at your ankle when I'm done here.'

'You seem to know a lot about medical matters, Mr Trundle,' Judy said nervously.

'I tend my animals, miss. There ain't much difference when it comes to fixing up injuries of any kind, although horses and cattle can't talk.'

'And they can't complain either.' Mrs Trundle bustled into the kitchen armed with a copper warming pan. 'This belonged to my parents, but it still does the job.' She scooped a few glowing coals from the fire and placed them in the pan. 'This will make your bed nice and cosy, miss. If you'd follow me I'll find some dry clothes for you and then you must join us for supper.'

Farmer Trundle selected a large needle and a spool of thread from the sewing box. 'Best leave her here, Mother. I need to look at her injuries.'

'I can tend a sprained ankle well enough, Joe. There's no need to make a song and dance about it. Come with me, miss.'

Judy cast an anxious glance in Rob's direction. He looked pale and the cut was still bleeding, although not as much as before. 'Will you be all right, Rob?'

He curved his lips in a wry smile. 'I'll try to be brave.'

Judy followed Mrs Trundle to the bedroom upstairs where a fire had been lit in the grate.

'This is the only spare room we have, my dear,' Mrs Trundle said apologetically. 'But don't worry, your young man will have to double up with Seth, although I'm afraid my boy snores.'

'My mother will be worried,' Judy said, sighing. 'This is all so unfortunate, but of course we're very grateful to you for taking us in.'

Mrs Trundle ran the warming pan over the sheets. 'I'll do that again before you turn in, dear. The damp gets everywhere at this time of the year.' She tipped the coals into the fire and a warming blaze roared up the chimney, sending a shower of soot onto the hearth. She laughed and wiped a smut off the tip of her nose. 'Oh, Lord! I forgot that the chimney hasn't been swept for a while. Anyway, let's get you out of those wet things.' She opened an oak chest and took out a plain woollen gown that was at least two sizes too large for Judy's small frame. 'This will have to do until your clothes are dry. Now let's get that boot off so that I can take a look at that ankle.'

'Thank you, Mrs Trundle. You've been so kind.'

'It's Prudence, dear. No need to be formal.' She helped Judy to take off the boot and examined her ankle. 'It is just a sprain. You'll need to rest as much as possible, but it will soon get better. Now let's see to those wet garments.'

Half an hour later, wearing Mrs Trundle's old grey dress and with her hair hanging loose around her shoulders, Judy went downstairs to join the others. She was pleased to see that Rob's wound had been neatly stitched and was no longer bleeding. He had swapped his wet clothes for an old pair of trousers and a shirt that probably belonged to Seth, and the colour had returned to his previously ashen cheeks.

'You should wear your hair like that more often,' Rob said, smiling.

'You're a very pretty lady,' Seth added.

'Mind your manners, son,' his father said, frowning. 'We don't make personal remarks, do we?'

'Leave the boy alone, Joe.' Mrs Trundle proceeded to arrange their damp garments on a clothes horse in front of the range. 'Set the table, please, Seth. I'll serve supper as soon as I've done this.'

'Is there anything I can do to help?' Judy asked anxiously.

'No, miss. You're a guest in our humble home and we don't allow guests to lift a finger. Seth, do you hear me? Lay the table.'

Joe Trundle pulled up a chair and sat down at the head of the table. 'We'll go out first thing in the morning to see what damage is done to your carriage, Rob. There's nothing we can do until then.'

'Has it stopped snowing?' Judy took her seat beside Rob. 'How will we get home to Little Creek?'

'You can ride, Judy. I'll remain here to help move the wreckage or at least to see if it can be salvaged. Is there a smithy near here, Joe?'

Judy smiled to herself at the familiarity that had

sprung up between the two very different men. Joe Trundle was old enough to be Rob's father, and Rob was a wealthy landowner, but that did not seem to bother either of them. She glanced at Seth, who was scowling like a spoilt child and it was obvious that he resented the fact that his father seemed to have taken a liking to the stranger in their midst.

'I can take you home on the cart, miss,' he said sulkily. 'It ain't a smart vehicle like your chaise, but it'll get you to where you want to go.'

'That's very kind of you, Seth.' Judy flashed him a sympathetic smile. 'We might still be suffering had you not decided to come out and look for us. We're very grateful to you, aren't we, Rob?'

'Yes, indeed. You showed great presence of mind, Seth. Thank you.'

Mrs Trundle placed a heavy iron pan on the table and when she lifted the lid a delicious aroma filled the kitchen. 'Hand the plates round, Seth. There's a good boy. I'll take the bread from the oven and then we'll eat.'

'We'll say grace first,' Joe said, glaring at each of them in turn as if he expected someone to object. 'And when we've eaten it's bed for all of us. We're early risers here,' he added, fixing Judy with a hard stare. 'Five o'clock and we're up and about. There's milking to be done and animals to feed.'

Prudence pulled out a chair and sat down. 'Don't take any heed of my husband, Judy. You get up when it suits you. No one expects you to earn your board. Do they, Father?' She gave her husband a stern look.

He folded his hands and closed his eyes. 'For what we are about to receive, may the Lord make us truly thankful. Amen.'

Next morning Judy was awakened by the sound of activity. Doors banged, heavy footsteps trod the stairs and she could hear cows lowing as they waited to be milked. She rose from the bed and shivered as her feet touched the bare boards. The water in the ewer on the washstand had frozen and the fire had died to nothing but ashes. She drew back the curtain and even though it was still dark the snow gleamed white and sparkling in the moonlight. She wrapped the coverlet around herself and went downstairs to the warmth of the kitchen. As she had hoped, the men had gone about their work, leaving Mrs Trundle to her household duties.

'Good morning, Mrs Trundle.'

'It's Prudence, dear. As I told you last evening. Did you sleep well?'

'I did, thank you. Is Rob still asleep?'

'No, my dear. Not much chance of that when he was sharing with Seth. They went out together to see what can be done with your vehicle, if anything.'

'I left my Christmas presents in the chaise,' Judy said, sighing. 'I don't know if they'll have survived the accident, but I'd really like to go and see.'

Prudence filled a cup with tea and handed it to

her. 'Not before breakfast, dear. I make it a rule that everyone has to have something in their belly before they go out, especially in this dreadful weather.' She ladled porridge into a bowl and slapped it on the table. 'There you are, Judy. I don't want any arguments.'

Smiling, Judy sat down. 'You sound like my mother. She'll be out of her mind with worry.'

'Of course she will, and so would I in the circumstances. Anyway, you heard my Seth last evening. He said he would drive you home in the farm cart, that's if you don't mind travelling in such a way.'

'No, of course I don't. I'd be most grateful.' Judy drank her tea and then started on the porridge, which was very good. She finished it with a sigh of satisfaction. 'Thank you, that was really lovely.'

'Your clothes are dry, so I suggest you take them upstairs and put them on, and then you can borrow my woollen cloak. It's old-fashioned but it's warm, and from what Seth told me it's about a mile along the road to Maldon that you'll find your vehicle.'

'Thank you. I will go because I spent my last penny on the gifts and my family will be very disappointed if I go home with nothing.'

'My dear, I think they will just be pleased that you came home in one piece. Now go and get dressed, and for heaven's sake wrap up warm.'

As Prudence had predicted, it was bitterly cold out of doors. An east wind bullied the powdery snow into fantastical shapes, and it slapped at Judy's cheeks as she walked, head bent and her feet sinking up to her ankles in the snow. Each breath felt like icicles stabbing her lungs, but she was determined to rescue anything she could from the wreckage. It seemed like much further than a mile, but eventually she spotted what remained of Rob's chaise and she quickened her pace. Rob and Seth were attempting to move the damaged vehicle to the side of the road, but it was an almost impossible task.

'It's no use,' Seth said, straightening up. 'I'll have to get Pa and a couple of the heavy horses to move this, but I don't fancy your chances of getting it fixed, at least not in a hurry.'

Rob kicked the broken shaft out of the way. 'You're right. Who would imagine that a falling tree could cause so much damage?' He looked round. 'What are you doing here, Judy?'

'I came to retrieve the presents I bought yesterday. Unless someone has taken them.'

Seth chuckled. 'Look at the road, miss. Not a sign of cart tracks or footprints. It would have to be a big bird that flew in to pinch your things.'

Judy said nothing as she climbed over splintered wood and the spokes of a shattered wheel, but there, beneath the driver's seat, she spotted the basket containing her purchases and she reached in to retrieve it. 'There it is.' She opened the frozen paper with trembling fingers and sighed with relief. 'All here and, as far as I can see, undamaged.'

Rob turned to Seth. 'Is there anywhere we could hire any kind of vehicle that would get us home?'

'No, mate. I said I'd take you back to Little Creek, but you'll have to wait until I've finished my chores around the farm. Pa is very particular about that.'

Judy was about to walk back to the farm when the sound of muffled hoofs and the rumble of wheels made her hesitate. 'Maybe we could beg a lift, Rob?' She shielded her eyes against the white glare of the snow, but when she recognised the man driving the barouche, she knew that there was nowhere to hide. The pain and humiliation she thought she had conquered now came flooding back, but she braced herself for the inevitable encounter with the past.

Chapter Seventeen

'Judy! Good God, so it was you I saw at the inn.' Jack leaped down from the driver's seat, leaving Jay holding the reins. He came towards her, smiling delightedly.

Judy struggled to maintain a calm exterior. 'You can walk again, Jack.'

'It was as your Dr God said. After a while I found I could stand, and then slowly I regained full movement, as you can see.' He eyed her warily. 'Aren't you pleased to see me?'

'You left without a word,' Judy said in a low voice. 'You didn't tell me that you were going away with your brother. I had to hear it from someone else.'

'I was a sick man, Judy. Surely you can understand that?'

'Might I suggest we continue this touching reunion

at a more appropriate time?' Jay climbed down from the carriage. 'Looks like you had a serious mishap,' he said, turning to Rob.

'Seems so, but we'll manage.' Rob met Jay's amused glance with a straight look. 'You don't remember me?'

It was a statement as much as a question and for a moment Jay looked at a loss, but he recovered quickly. 'No, you have the advantage.'

'It will come back to you, I expect.'

'Is this some sort of riddle?' Jay demanded irritably. 'You have a strange way with words.'

Judy shivered. 'This is ridiculous. We don't need your help, Jay. Why don't you go on your way and leave us in peace?'

'Now that's not very nice, Judy,' Jack said, chuckling. 'I expected a warmer welcome from my girl.'

Judy was about to protest, but Rob placed a protective arm around her shoulders. 'It's too cold to stand about gossiping. There's room enough for you to get past, if you're careful.'

Jay nodded. 'Yes, easily. I stopped in case you needed help, but clearly you prefer to suffer.' He turned to Judy. 'We could take you back to Little Creek. Are you still living in the cottage on the estate?'

'Why are you here, Jay?' Judy eyed him curiously.

Jay puffed out his chest. 'I'm a very wealthy man now. I've decided to buy back my family home.'

Judy exchanged meaningful glances with Rob. 'You don't know then?' she said slowly.

'Know what? What's going on?' Jay leaned against the wheel of the barouche.

'You tell them, Judy,' Rob said casually. 'I need to talk to Seth about getting the chaise moved.' He beckoned to Seth, who had been listening to the conversation open-mouthed, and they moved a little further down the lane.

Judy looked from one to the other. 'Creek Manor burned to the ground. It's no longer there, and the original purchaser sold the entire estate. You are behind the times, Jay.' She had the satisfaction of seeing both the Fox brothers taken by surprise, and their shocked expressions might have been funny in any other circumstances.

'The old house needed to be razed to the ground. It was draughty and would have fallen down in time. However, I've made a fortune in Australia, and I want my son to inherit the estate and the title.'

'Creek Manor has a new owner who might not wish to sell.' Judy glanced at Rob, but he was deep in conversation with Seth. She was tempted to tell Jay that Rob was the new owner, but that could wait. She was so cold that she was losing the feeling in her feet and fingertips.

'Everyone has a price,' Jay said sulkily. 'I'll pay whatever is necessary.'

Judy shivered convulsively. 'I'm cold so you'll excuse me if I don't wait around.' She set off in the direction of the farm, but Jack caught her up before she had gone more than a few yards.

'We'll take you home in the barouche, Judy. There's no need for you to wait here unnecessarily.'

'Thank you, Jack, but I'm fussy about the company I keep.' Judy was about to walk on, but he caught her by the wrist.

'Judy, please. I came back to fetch you. I sent you letters.'

She turned to give him a searching look. 'I never received anything from you.'

'On my honour, I wrote once a month – well, maybe not that often, but I did send you a letter telling you that I had recovered. Let us take you home, please.'

'I don't know. I can't leave Rob here.'

'What is this fellow to you? Do I have competition?'

'Jack, I'm shivering and my boots are leaking. I refuse to have this conversation. Let me go.'

'Then I'll call on you at the cottage.'

'The estate was sold, Jack. We were evicted from the cottage months ago, and now that too is razed to the ground.'

'I don't understand.'

'Go and see your sisters. They'll tell you everything – just leave me alone.' Judy limped off in the direction of the farm. She was still getting over the shock of seeing Jack so unexpectedly, and even more confused by his attitude towards her. It was as if he had just returned from a term at university, and he expected everything to carry on as normal; but for her nothing would ever be the same. The closeness they had once shared was gone, as was the trust. She walked on, slipping and sliding on the icy surface of the snow, but determined to remain independent.

Prudence greeted her with a smile that faded into a worried frown. 'Are you all right, dear? You look peaky.'

'I'm cold and my feet are wet, Mrs Trundle. Might I sit by the fire for a while?'

'Of course, you may. I'll make you a nice hot cup of cocoa. That always works when my Seth is feeling low.'

Judy took off the cloak and hung it back on its peg before going over to warm herself by the fire. Prudence made two cups of cocoa and the delicious aroma of hot chocolate filled the kitchen. Judy sat down to enjoy it, resting her feet on the brass rail of the range.

'Thank you, Mrs Trundle. You've been so good to us. I wish there was something I could do to repay you.'

Prudence sipped her drink. 'Having female company is reward enough, dear. I love my menfolk, but sometimes I wish I had a daughter to talk to. There are things that husbands and sons just don't understand.'

Judy nodded. 'Sometimes I think we speak a different language than they do.'

'Yes, indeed. Have a rock cake, dear. They're still

313

warm from the oven.' Prudence took a cake from the cooling rack, placed it on a plate and handed it to Judy. 'These will be gone in a flash when Joe and Seth come home, so eat up while you have a chance.' She pulled up a chair and sat down. 'Perhaps you feel like telling me what's upset you since you left the house this morning. You were bright as a button first thing, but when you came in that door I thought, my goodness, something or someone has upset the poor girl.'

'It's a long story,' Judy said apologetically.

'That don't matter, dear. I've got all morning. It'll take the men that long to shift the wrecked vehicle.' Prudence sat back, sipping her cocoa and listening in silence while Judy talked.

'Well, dear, that's some story indeed,' Prudence said when Judy had finished speaking.

'I don't know what to do, Mrs Trundle. I think I still love Jack, but I didn't believe him when he said he had written to me. Jack was always very bad at letter writing. The truth is that he left me without a word, and I don't feel I can ever trust him again.'

'It seems to run in the family, from what you just told me. I mean his brother didn't treat his women well, although I think you said that they're only half-brothers.'

'That's right. Jay's father was the late squire, and not a nice character at all. Jack's father was a good man at heart, I suppose, but he was also a bully.'

'And how do you feel about Rob?'

Judy almost dropped her plate. Prudence's question had taken her by surprise. 'Rob is a guest at the inn. There's nothing between us.'

'Are you sure about that, dear? He seems quite taken with you.'

'No, you're wrong. We're just friends.'

'In that case perhaps you do still love Jack. The only way you'll find out is to talk to him.'

Judy was about to answer when the sound of men's voices and loud footsteps announced the return of Rob and Seth. The door opened and a blast of cold air rushed round the warm kitchen, sending a gust of steam into the icy world outside.

'Seth has agreed to take us back to Little Creek, Judy. Can you be ready in five minutes?'

It was Christmas Eve and Judy had seen nothing of Jack or Jay since their meeting in the country lane. Nate had come home armed with the latest gossip after a brief visit to see Pip at Colneyhurst. It turned out that Jack was staying with Nick and Dove at Creek Hall, while Jay had imposed on his sister Linnet and her husband. Jay was apparently making extensive enquiries as to the identity of the new owner of the Creek Manor estate, and it was only a matter of time before he discovered the truth. Although it was inevitable that his enquiries would lead him to the Crooked Billet, Judy was caught by surprise when he walked into the taproom at midday. She was about to serve Eli with a pint of ale.

Jay strode up to the bar, giving Eli a withering glance. 'You smell a bit ripe, mate. I suggest you take your drink and move downwind of me.'

Eli shot him a baleful glance and shambled off to his usual seat in the corner.

'That was mean, Jay,' Judy said crossly. 'He looks after Colonel Catchpole's pigs. Eli can't help it if the odour of the piggery clings to him.'

'That's his problem – I don't want it thrust on me. Any chance of a hot rum punch? It's freezing outside.'

Judy sighed. 'Yes, of course, if that's what you want.' She lifted the hatch in the counter and went to the fireplace where she placed the poker amongst the red-hot coals. 'It'll take a few minutes to heat up.' She returned to the bar, took a tankard from the shelf and began mixing rum with dark sugar and spices. 'How long do you intend to stay in Little Creek?'

'That's a leading question, sweetheart. But as it's you, I'll admit that I plan to remain here until I have the deeds of the Creek Manor estate. I've been told that your friend Rob might have the answer to my problem. Is he here?'

'He had business in London,' Judy said carefully. 'I don't know when he'll return. He comes and goes as he sees fit.'

'What about the other chap? The architect who's supposed to be designing the new house.'

'He returned to London yesterday. What's this all

about? What do you hope to gain by staying in Little Creek when you know that the property belongs to someone else?'

'I want my inheritance back. All right, I know I sold the estate in the first place, but now I have the money to buy it back and I have a newborn son who will inherit everything when I die. The name of Tattersall will go on.'

Having added water to the mixture, Judy retrieved the poker from the fire and shook off the ash. She immersed the red-hot tip in the tankard and waited while it hissed and bubbled. She walked slowly back to where Jay was standing.

'I wish you luck with that, but if you want my honest opinion I think you said goodbye to your inheritance when you sold the estate.'

He took the tankard from her and drank thirstily, despite the fact that the brew was still steaming. 'That was good. You make a decent barmaid, Judy. It's a pity you can't stay on here when I take over.'

She stared at him in astonishment. 'What did you say?'

'You should have tried harder to find the true owner of the Crooked Billet, my love.'

'What do you mean? I did make enquiries but no one knew who it was.'

'This pub was not part of the Creek Manor estate. It was a separate parcel of land that my late father owned, and it came in very handy I've no doubt.'

'Everyone knows that he was involved in

smuggling, but I never heard it said that he owned this place.'

'Well, it is so, and when I sold the estate the inn was not included. I needed somewhere to come home to, and now I am here. So I want you and your family gone. Is that clear enough?'

'I need proof of ownership,' Judy said faintly. 'You can't just toss us out on the street.'

A grim smile curved his lips. 'Oh, but I can.' He put his hand inside his jacket and pulled out a folded sheet of parchment. 'These are the deeds of the Crooked Billet. Look at them closely, Judy.' He spread the document out on the bar counter.

It took only a few seconds for Judy to scrutinise the elegant copperplate writing. The deeds confirmed what Jay had claimed, and she could see that he was in no mood to be generous.

'At least give us time to find alternative accommodation.'

'I'm a reasonable man. You have until six o'clock this afternoon, and then I'm taking over. You will have all your belongings removed by that time or they will be forfeit. Do you understand?'

She nodded mutely, too shocked to put up an argument, besides which, he seemed to have the law on his side. It was her fault, she thought miserably as she watched him finish his drink with obvious relish. She should have gone into the matter more thoroughly, but they had been desperate, and now matters were even worse. It was the depths of winter, it was Christmas Eve, and by late afternoon they would again be homeless. She shot him a wary glance – Jay was enjoying her discomfort. He could have told them this when he first arrived in Little Creek, but he had obviously chosen today because it suited him to be melodramatic.

'What have we ever done to you?' she demanded angrily. 'Why are you treating us this way?'

'I had to get the deeds from my solicitor in Chelmsford, or I would have claimed my birthright sooner.' Jay's urbane smile faded. 'I'm serious, Judy. I want you all out of here by six o'clock and no excuses. That goes for your gentleman friend also. I'm the legal owner of this establishment and you and your family are squatters.' He strode towards the door, pausing by Eli. 'And you are barred from this pub as of this evening. Show your dirty face here again and I'll take great pleasure in throwing you out.' He left the building, slamming the door behind him.

Eli looked up, scowling. 'That 'un will come to no good, miss. I'll tell you that for nothing.'

'Maybe, but for now he has the upper hand. I need to speak to Ma urgently. Call me if anyone comes in, please, Eli.' Judy left the bar and hurried to the kitchen where she found her mother and Nate enjoying a cup of tea and a chat. 'Ma, you'd better pack your things. You, too, Nate.'

Hilda looked up, frowning. 'Why? What's the matter, Judy? You're white as a sheet.'

'Jay Tattersall has just shown me the deeds of the Crooked Billet. He owns it, Ma. It belonged to the old squire and it wasn't included in the sale. Jay has given us until six o'clock this afternoon to get out.'

'But it's Christmas Eve,' Nate protested. 'He can't do that.'

'I'm afraid he can,' Judy said miserably. 'We are here illegally. I should have gone into it properly, but I was so glad to have somewhere for us to live that I let things slide.'

'It's not your fault, dear.' Hilda pushed her cup and saucer away and rose to her feet. 'Where is he now? Maybe I could persuade him to give us a few days' grace. We won't find anywhere on Christmas Eve.'

'He walked out, and anyway, he wasn't prepared to listen. We'll have to leave, although I don't know where we'll go or who could take us in at such short notice.'

'This wouldn't have happened if Mary was still here. She'd have a fit if she knew what her son was doing to us.'

'Then there's Rob,' Judy said miserably. 'He doesn't know yet. He'll have to find somewhere to go, too.'

'He's got money, my love. He can afford to stay at a hotel or another wayside inn. We haven't enough to last us more than a night or two at the most. We are in trouble, Judy. Big trouble.'

'We must be practical,' Judy said urgently. 'I intend

to clear the shelves in the bar. We've paid for all that drink and we're not leaving anything for Jay. If he wants to run a pub he can buy in his own stock. We'll take the keg of ale, too.'

'What can I do?' Nate jumped to his feet. 'I'll stand up to Jay Tattersall. I ain't afraid of him.'

Judy smiled despite the turmoil inside her brain. 'That won't be necessary. Ma and I will pack all our belongings, including the bedding and anything we can fit into the cart. Then I want you to drive to Colneyhurst. I know Marius won't mind if we store our things in one of the empty stables, and you can stay with Pip until we find somewhere more permanent.'

'It breaks my heart to leave here when we've put so much effort into making a go of the place,' Hilda said bitterly. 'It's almost worse than when Wilfred turned on me, although that was bad enough.'

'He'll pay for what he did, Ma,' Judy said softly. 'Let's not think about anything for now other than collecting what is rightfully ours.'

Nate rose from the table. 'All right, I'll do as you say, but I don't like it. I'd rather fight him than let him do this to my family.'

'He won't profit from it, love.' Hilda began opening cupboards and taking out the oddments of china they had managed to collect. 'In my experience bad people get their comeuppance sooner or later.'

Nate muttered something beneath his breath and stormed out of the kitchen.

'Don't worry about him, Ma,' Judy said hastily. 'He's young and he'll get over it. Maybe this will be all to the good. We have to face the fact that the reputation of the Crooked Billet has been against us all the way, and we've made almost nothing, even after all the hard work.'

Hilda piled plates on the table, followed by bowls, cups and saucers. 'But we've had a home, Judy. We've had food and warmth, and we might have done really well when Rob started building his new house.'

'Even that looks doubtful now.' Judy lifted the old saucepans from the shelf above the range. 'Jay is clever and I don't think he'd do all this unless he was quite sure he could get the estate back.'

'And where is Jack in all this?' Hilda tipped the contents of the cutlery drawer onto the table. 'Why didn't he stand up for us?'

'I don't know, Ma.' Judy placed the last pan on the table. 'I'll go and start in the bedrooms. We'll have to leave the pieces of furniture we've acquired, but I'll strip the beds. I still can't believe that Jay would do this to us on Christmas Eve, of all days.' She left her mother to pack up the kitchen and she made her way upstairs to the chilly bedrooms.

In her own room she walked slowly to the window and gazed out at the turbulent grey waters of the estuary. The sound of the waves crashing on the rocks, and the rattle of the shingle on the shore was comfortingly familiar. It had lulled her to sleep every night for the past few months, and the creaking old inn had become their home and their haven. Her hands gripped the windowsill, and her knuckles whitened as she clenched her fists as anger raged in her breast. Jay was not going to do this to them. He might have a document with his name on it, but that did not give him the authority to throw them out on the street. The winter afternoon would be closing in soon and then it would be dark. This was not how she had envisaged spending Christmas. Judy hurried from her room and raced downstairs.

Having locked the front door and made sure that all the windows were securely fastened, she went to the kitchen.

'Ma, you can put everything back in the cupboard. We're not leaving – at least not yet.'

Hilda gazed at her with a puzzled frown. 'What do you mean? I thought you said that he wanted us out of here by six o'clock.'

'That's what he said, but we're not going. If he wants to get us out he can get a court order and that won't happen until after Christmas. It gives us a few days to think about what we're going to do and where we might go.'

'But he could fetch the police.'

'Do you seriously think that Constable Fowler will oblige him on Christmas Eve?'

'But Jay is the old squire's legal heir.'

'I know, he showed me the deeds. Let him go to court and prove he owns this place, which would take time. That gives us breathing space, Ma. Put the kettle on and make us a nice hot cup of tea. I'm going to the stable to catch Nate before he leaves for Colneyhurst.'

Judy snatched her shawl from its peg and wrapped it around her head and shoulders as she braved the bitter cold. The stable was only a few yards from the back door and walking on the packed snow made the going difficult, but she reached it without mishap and went inside.

'We're not leaving,' she said breathlessly. 'At least not yet. I'm not going to allow Jay Tattersall to throw us out today.'

Nate leaped down from the cart. 'I'm with you, Judy. I wasn't looking forward to taking poor old Major on the icy roads, to tell the truth.'

'Which makes it even more unlikely that Jay can actually do anything to get us out. He's very unpopular in the village, so I don't imagine he'll get any help there. I'm calling his bluff.'

'Just tell me what to do.'

'Bring anything you value into the house. Leave the horse with plenty of food and water in case we can't get out for a day or two.' Judy did not wait for a response. She had hoped that Nate would enter into the spirit of the thing, and would enjoy the drama of the situation, but this was no game. She knew enough about Jay Tattersall to realise that he meant what he said. He was intent on getting back what he considered to be rightfully his, and there would be no stopping him.

Braving the icy winds again, she left the stable and returned to the warmth of the kitchen where her mother had just put the last saucepan back on the shelf.

'What will we do about our customers?' Hilda asked wearily. 'Heaven knows, we don't get too many, but do we simply keep the doors locked?'

'We'll have to, at least for the time being. I'll put a sign up in the window saying we're closed for business. I just hope that Rob doesn't return tonight.'

'Did he tell you when to expect him?'

Judy shook her head. 'It's none of my business, Ma. We're just here to provide a service and he's paid for his room, so he can come and go as he pleases.'

Hilda sniffed. 'I thought there was more in it than that, at least on his side.'

'I don't know about that,' Judy said hastily. 'I can't think about anything at the moment other than the task in hand. I'm going to bring as many logs in as I can, and I'll get Nate to fetch coal and water. We're getting ready for a siege.'

Hilda put her head on one side. 'Someone's hammering on the front door, Judy. I think it's started.'

Chapter Eighteen

Judy stormed through the pub ready to take Jay on single-handed, but to her surprise it was Jack who stood outside, stamping the snow off his boots.

'Let me in, Judy.'

She hesitated. 'No. I can't. We're not leaving here, Jack. I don't care what you say.'

'I want to talk and I'll freeze to death if I have to stand here much longer.'

'Is this a trick?'

'No, on my honour it is not. Jay told me what he'd done and I don't agree with him. Let me in, please.'

She drew back the bolts and unlocked the door, opening it just far enough to look out and make sure that Jay was not loitering outside. 'Come in.'

He pushed past her and went straight to the fireplace where he stood, warming his hands.

Judy locked and bolted the door. 'Why did you come here, Jack? What do you want?'

'A tot of brandy might help to warm me up. I've grown used to a much balmier climate in Australia. You'd love it there, Judy.'

'You didn't brave the snow just to tell me that, did you?'

'It wasn't my main reason for coming. I do care about you, Judy, despite what you think of me. Jay told me what he'd done and I tried to persuade him to give you more time, but once he's made up his mind to something that's the end of it.'

'We're not leaving because we haven't anywhere to go. We're staying put at least for the time being and you can go back and tell Jay so.'

He straightened up, giving her a searching look. 'What happened to you, Judy? You used to be so biddable and nice.'

'I've learned to stand up for myself and my family. Jay might own this place, but he can't just throw us out on a whim. If he wants us to leave he'll have to prove ownership, and also give us time to find somewhere else to live.'

'Yes, I see that. But it's not my fault, Judy. I can't control my brother.'

'And yet you went with him to the other side of the world. You left without a word to me.'

'I asked you to go with me.'

'It was more of an order than a request. You expected me to leave my family and travel across the world. I might have ended my days as an unpaid servant.'

'I'd have married you eventually, Judy.'

She looked him in the eye. 'Would you really? Is that why you're here now? Are you asking me to marry you?'

'What am I supposed to say to that? I want you to come to Australia with me and build a new life.'

'I think you've answered my question. You're a spoilt child who refuses to grow up.' Judy went to the bar and poured a measure of brandy. She handed him the glass. 'Drink up and go back to Jay. You can tell him that I'm not easily bought by vague offers of a better life. For all I know, you might be like your brother and have a wife in Australia.'

He downed the spirit in one gulp. 'I'm hurt. You know me better than that.'

'Do I? Maybe at one time I did, but not now. I don't understand why your brother is so keen to get his hands on Creek Manor, but that's his business. All I'm concerned about is providing for my family and keeping a roof over our heads.'

'Is that your last word?'

'It most certainly is. Now go, please.'

'I don't want to leave you like this. You're placing me in a difficult situation, Judy.'

'What do you mean by that?' Instantly alert, she faced him angrily. 'Jay did send you to persuade me to leave here, didn't he?'

'Not exactly, but you know it would be better

all round. Honestly, Judy, where will you go? How will you live? Be reasonable and agree to leave of your own volition. Maybe Jay would allow you another day, if you promised me you would move out after Christmas.'

She eyed him curiously. 'Why does Jay want the Crooked Billet?'

'It belongs to him, Judy. It's the only part of the estate that he didn't sell, and we need somewhere to stay while we're here. He's set on getting Creek Manor estate back, and nothing is going to change his mind.'

'But you and he plan to return to New South Wales?'

'Yes, I made no secret of it. I'm being totally honest with you, and I truly want to atone for the way I treated you. I'll marry you, if that's what it takes.'

'It's too late for that. Nothing is as it used to be. Go away, please.'

'All right, I'll do as you say, but you belong with me, Judy. You'll see sense eventually.' Jack walked to the door where he hesitated, turning to give her a pitying look. 'You don't have to go through this. It's Christmas and all you have to do is agree to Jay's terms and we could all be together, as we were in the old days. Dove said she would love you to come to Creek Hall for Christmas dinner. We'll all be there.'

Judy crossed the floor in angry strides. 'Get out and let me lock up. Tell Jay that we're staying put.

329

Merry Christmas, Jack.' She slammed the door after him, locked and bolted it with such force that the timbers shook. The taproom echoed with silence and the Christmas tree in the corner suddenly looked tawdry and out of place. She had been looking forward to the festivities, but now her hopes for the New Year were dashed. How they were going to survive if they were forced to leave was the burning question, although the most pressing problem was how they were going to hold out if Jay came mob-handed. Judy could not imagine there would be many local men who would band together under his lead, but time alone would tell.

It was pitch-dark outside when Jay arrived promptly at six o'clock. She could not tell if he was alone or whether he had brought a small army of men to intimidate her family further, but she refused to answer his urgent demands to open the door. The kitchen door was barricaded and they had closed the wooden shutters on the downstairs windows, but Jay continued to hammer on the door and shout all manner of threats, which Judy chose to ignore.

After half an hour of constant harassment, Jay acknowledged temporary defeat.

'You win for now, Judy Begg. But we'll be back tomorrow. Enjoy your last night on my premises, because tomorrow you'll be thrown out.'

Judy leaned against the door, waiting for another round of abuse, but there was none.

'Has he really gone?' Hilda asked faintly. 'I thought he might break the door down.'

'He stopped at that, thank goodness.' Judy sank down on the settle by the door, her knees having turned to jelly. 'He'll be back, that's for certain.'

'Maybe we should have done what he said.' Hilda went to sit by the fire, wrapping her arms around her body. 'I'm sure Daisy would have taken us in, even if we had to sleep in the stables.'

Judy managed to rise to her feet and she made her way to the bar. Jack had been the last person to drink brandy, but now she poured measures for herself and her mother. Nate was nowhere to be seen. She took a glass to her mother and pressed it into her hand.

'Sip this, Ma. If you'd like Nate to take you to Colneyhurst Hall you have only to say so. I don't think Jay will bother us again tonight, but I'm sure he'll be back tomorrow.'

Hilda clutched the glass in her hand. 'I'll only go if you'll come, too. Don't be stubborn, Judy. You know he'll get his way in the end.'

'I don't know that at all, Ma. I refuse to be driven out of my home by someone who is wealthy enough to have property anywhere he chooses. Jay is doing this out of spite, for what reason I don't know.'

'Jack wants you to go with him.'

'You were listening?'

'It was impossible not to hear what was going on. You two were shouting at each other for ages.

331

You were always together when you were younger. I really thought you would make a match of it.'

Judy took a mouthful of brandy and swallowed it. She closed her eyes as the spirit hit her empty stomach like a cannonball. 'I don't know how I feel now, but I don't trust him. That's the worst of it, Ma. He can't just turn up and expect things to be as they were in the past. He's fallen under Jay's influence, and we all know how Jay treats the people who love him. He married two women without bothering to divorce his first wife, and that sums him up nicely. He takes what he wants, no matter what it does to others.'

'But Jack isn't like him, and they are only half-brothers.'

'I don't care, Ma. I need time to think, and this business with Jay has only made matters worse.' She turned her head at the sound of footsteps and Nate strolled into the taproom.

'What's for supper, Ma? I'm starving.'

Judy stifled a giggle. 'Of course you are, Nate. So am I, if it comes to that. You sit there and rest, Ma. Nate and I will see to supper. It might be the last meal we have in the Crooked Billet so let's enjoy it.'

Judy had half expected Jay to turn up again in the early hours, but, perhaps because of the bitter cold and the lying snow, they had an undisturbed night. Christmas morning dawned bright and clear with the pale sun sparkling on the calm waters of the estuary, and the wildlife in the saltings going about their daily business as usual. Judy quite envied them their settled routine and seemingly endless supply of food. The larder was not quite bare, in fact they had supplies to last for a few days, but there had been no time to bake mince pies or to go to market to buy a fowl for their Christmas dinner. That and the threat of eviction was bound to overshadow what should have been a festive occasion.

She rose from her bed, washed and dressed, and set about the routine chores of lighting fires and making breakfast. She decided to give Hilda a treat and take her porridge and coffee upstairs so that she could enjoy it in the privacy of her room. Hilda was sleepily grateful, but clearly upset because she had no present to give Judy, especially when she opened the wrapping paper on her gift.

'What beautiful mittens. They're just what I've always wanted, dear girl. How thoughtful of you, but I have nothing to give you in return. I haven't had time to go shopping.'

'I had time to purchase a few things in Maldon, and you don't need to give me anything, Ma. I can't help feeling a bit guilty for the trouble we're in.'

Hilda picked up her spoon. 'Why would you feel guilty, Judy?'

'If I'd given Jack some encouragement, or given in to Jay's demands, we might have been sharing Christmas dinner with Dove and Nick and the rest of Jack's family. Goodness knows what will happen later today.'

'We owe the Tattersalls nothing. Remember that.' Hilda swallowed a mouthful of porridge. 'This is delicious. I hope you've had yours. As to the rest, we'll deal with whatever comes.'

Judy smiled and nodded but she was close to tears as she left the room and descended the stairs. She had just reached the bottom when she heard someone tapping on the front door. For a moment she froze, but then she realised that it could not be Jay – he would be hammering on the door and shouting. She went through the motions of unlocking and unbolting the door and to her surprise she found Wilby, Colonel Catchpole's gardener, standing outside holding an item wrapped in brown paper.

'Merry Christmas, Miss Begg,' Wilby said, grinning. 'The colonel's compliments of the season and he says there was one too many birds made ready for the table, so perhaps you might have a use for this.' He unwrapped the brown paper, exposing a fine goose already prepared for the oven.

Judy accepted it with a delighted smile. 'This is so generous and quite unexpected. Please thank the colonel.'

Wilby tipped his cap. 'And the colonel says if you need any assistance he is ready to send troops.'

'That's most kind, and greatly appreciated.' Judy stood in the doorway watching as he walked off towards the waiting dog cart and clambered onto the driver's seat. 'Merry Christmas, Mr Wilby.' She closed the door and carried the offering to the kitchen where she laid it on the table.

Nate looked up from his empty bowl and licked the spoon. 'Where did that come from?'

'Colonel Catchpole's gardener just delivered it. I think Eli must have spread the word that Jay was causing trouble.'

'Who cares?' Nate said gleefully. 'We'll have a splendid Christmas dinner after all. We just need someone to send a plum pudding and some mince pies and we'll have everything we need.'

As the morning progressed there were more visitors, despite the freezing temperatures. Hepzibah Egerton's sister, Hannah, arrived at the back door with a Christmas pudding, again claiming that it was surplus to their needs. Half an hour later George Keyes, the village shopkeeper, knocked on the door and presented Judy with a basket containing a dozen mince pies, and close behind him came Clem Guppy, bringing a rush basket filled with eggs.

'We heard about your problems, Judy,' he said grimly. 'If you need me you know where I live. I don't hold with bullying women, nor do I think it right to turn people out of their homes, especially on Christmas Day.'

Judy managed a smile although the kindness of the villagers brought tears to her eyes. 'Thank you,

Clem. I really appreciate that, and the eggs are most welcome.'

He tipped his cap. 'Better get back to the family, but don't be afraid to ask for help if you need it.' He backed away and Judy closed the door quickly, just in case Jay happened to be hiding round the corner. She took the basket to the kitchen where her mother was about to place the goose in the oven.

Flushed and smiling, Hilda closed the heavy iron door. 'We'll have the best Christmas dinner ever. What have you got there, Judy?'

'Eggs from Clem Guppy. I can't believe how generous people have been.'

'It just shows that we are part of the village. I can't quite believe that they see us as anything other than newcomers, but it does seem as though they care about us.' Hilda's smile faded. 'What will we do if Jay returns? He might break the door down.'

'Let's try and forget Jay for now. Maybe his family will dissuade him from doing anything today, but I think we'll have to face the fact that he does own the property, and we will have to find somewhere else to live quite quickly.'

'I thought you said we would stay here,' Nate said, scowling. 'What changed your mind?'

'I said we'd stay here for Christmas, but we can't barricade ourselves in for long. This is an inn and it was our livelihood. I don't know what we'll do next, but let's not think about that now. I'm looking forward to a splendid dinner, thanks to our kind friends.'

'You'd better enjoy it,' Hilda said gloomily. 'It might be the last decent meal we ever have.'

They did justice to the goose and demolished the Christmas pudding. Nate even managed to eat three mince pies before finally admitting defeat. It was mid-afternoon and there had been no sign of Jay or his men. Judy was beginning to hope that Jack might have persuaded his brother to change his mind, but within the hour there was a loud thudding on the pub door. Judy raised herself from her chair in the parlour and went to stand by the door.

'Go away.'

'You leave me no choice other than to break the door down,' Jay shouted angrily. 'Don't make this any harder than it need be.'

'We will leave here, but only when we've found somewhere else to live.'

'That's not good enough. This place belongs to me and you are squatters. The law is on my side.'

'Then get the law to throw us out. I don't think you'll find any constable willing to come out here on Christmas Day. Go back to your family, Jay, and leave us alone.'

'You've been warned. Break the door down, men.'

His words were followed by a sickening thud on the door and the sound of splintering wood, but somehow the timbers remained intact. The first blow was followed by another and another, and then the final strike caused the wooden panels to splinter and collapse. Judy backed away with Hilda clutching her hand. Nate strode forward but was knocked to the ground by a burly man who barged in first, followed by Jay.

'Steady, Gittins,' Jay said sternly. 'There's no need for violence, providing the people here are willing to be reasonable.'

Hilda went down on her knees beside her prostrate son. Nate opened his eyes and attempted to sit up, but was obviously dazed by the sudden fall.

'You brute,' Hilda cried passionately. 'He's just a boy.'

'He got in the way.' Gittins glanced at Jay, who acknowledged his unspoken question with a nod. 'That's what happens to folk who take on the boss.'

'Someone is talking sense at last.' Jay slapped Gittins on the back. 'Wait outside. I don't think they'll give me any more trouble.'

Gittins ambled towards the door, but was shoved aside by Rob, who entered, bringing with him a flurry of snow.

'They might not give you trouble, Tattersall, but I will.' Rob faced up to Jay. 'Call your man off.'

Gittins grunted and made a move towards Rob, but Jay held up his hand.

'It's all right, Gittins. I can handle this fellow.' Jay waited until his man was out of earshot. 'What the hell d'you think you're doing, Dorning? You aren't welcome here.'

'Is that so?' Rob walked past him and helped Nate to his feet. 'Are you all right?'

'He caught me unawares.' Nate dusted himself down, glaring at Gittins.

'Just what I'd expect.' Rob turned to Jay with a scornful curl of his lip. 'Making war on defenceless women and boys is about your mark.'

Nate fisted his hands, glaring at Jay. 'Leave my family alone.'

'We're safe now, Nate,' Hilda said urgently. 'Go to the stables and make sure that the horse is all right.'

Nate looked as though he was about to argue, but Judy gave him a gentle shove in the direction of the kitchen. 'Do as Ma says. We'll be fine.'

'Your sister is right, old chap,' Rob said easily. 'I'll make sure your mother and sister are safe.'

'Get out of here, Dorning.' Jay squared up to Rob. 'I own this premises and I'm telling you to leave.'

'Please do as he says, Rob,' Judy said anxiously. 'This isn't your battle, it's mine.'

'You're wrong there, Judy. And it's Tattersall who is the trespasser. I own the Crooked Billet and the land around it.'

'You're lying,' Jay snapped. 'I have the deeds.'

'A forgery, I'm afraid. You see I have the original document. That's why I went to London a few days ago. Until now I've kept my identity to myself, but now I think it's time to put matters straight. I am the true heir to the Creek Manor estate and I can prove it.'

The colour drained from Jay's face and he turned on Gittins, who was hovering by the door listening to every word. 'Get out and wait until I call you.'

Gittins obeyed reluctantly, leaving the two men facing each other like gladiators ready for mortal combat.

'You're lying,' Jay said through clenched teeth.

'You are the bastard son of Esmond Tattersall and a young servant girl whom he seduced.'

'He repented and married my mother on his deathbed. He left the estate to me.'

Rob shook his head. 'My mother was Miriam Dorning, a member of the family who ran the preventive men ragged for nearly a century. Despite their own shortcomings, her family forbade her to have anything to do with Esmond Tattersall, but the couple eloped and I was born less than a year later. I am the legal heir to my late father's estate and I can prove it. I have all the documents here.'

'But he left everything to me,' Jay said dazedly.

'The will is not valid. It was written under duress and I have witnesses who will attest to that. Esmond Tattersall was a dying man, not in a fit state to know what he was doing, and anyway, you are illegitimate. You own nothing, my friend.'

Judy looked from one to the other. 'Heaven's above! That means you two are half-brothers.'

'I'll hire a good lawyer and I'll fight you through the courts, Dorning,' Jay said angrily. 'It was your rotten family who stole my ship and caused me no end of trouble. I never knew why the Dornings were so against me, until now.'

Rob shrugged. 'I can't be held responsible for that branch of the family. I inherited my fortune from a Dorning who was transported for life to Australia. It seems we are somewhat bound to that country, Tattersall. You've obviously done well enough for yourself out there, and you had the money from the sale of Creek Manor. I think you've come out of it very well.'

'You can't take my birthright away from me, Dorning. You'll hear from my solicitor. This is just the beginning.' Jay's dramatic departure turned to farce when his coat snagged on a nail as he stormed through the shattered door. He uttered an explosive stream of expletives as he stamped on the hard-packed snow outside. He slammed what remained of the door, sending a shower of splintered wood onto the floor.

Judy turned to Rob, staring at him as if seeing a stranger. 'I don't understand. Why do you call yourself Dorning? If it was such a love match, why didn't Squire Tattersall bring you up?'

'Tattersall abandoned my mother in favour of a wealthy heiress. He married her bigamously and it broke my mother's heart. She died when I was two, and, as I told you before, I was brought up by my aunt Adeline. She knew what Tattersall had done, and she impressed upon me that I was a Dorning. In fact I knew virtually nothing about my father until I was sixteen, when my aunt told me the whole story.'

Hilda sank down on the settle by the fire. 'Did you try to contact your father?'

'I did, just the once, and I was not impressed. I decided that I was a Dorning and not a Tattersall. I'm nothing like him and I certainly wouldn't behave as he did.'

'Then why do you want the estate?' Judy struggled to come to terms with what she had just heard. 'It doesn't make sense.'

'My father took what he wanted without a thought for anyone else. I don't want to end up like him, Judy. I didn't earn the fortune that was bestowed on me, but for my dead mother's sake I feel I need to make amends for what my father did. My mother was a good person and she didn't deserve to be cast aside because Tattersall had his sights set on marrying money, even if it was bigamously. It seems that Jay inherited that particular trait.'

'So you want to run the estate in a way she would have wanted,' Judy said slowly. 'Is that it?'

'I knew you'd understand. As far as I can see, Jay is just like our father. We might be half-brothers, but we couldn't be more different. If Jay owned Creek Manor he would be just like the old squire, and the so-called curse of Creek Manor would continue for ever.'

'Surely you don't believe in that story?' Judy studied his expression. 'Do you?'

'Not as such. I don't think the house was cursed. It was my father's lack of conscience that created such unhappiness. From what I've learned about Jay I can see the same thing happening again and again. If he has a heart he keeps it well hidden.'

'You're right,' Hilda said firmly. 'Judy was too young to realise just how much Jay hurt Daisy, and he cared nothing for the other young woman whom he also married bigamously, nor for the two children she bore him. He didn't appreciate Creek Manor, and he saw his tenants merely as a way to make money.'

'My family paid for their crimes, but I want to make the name Dorning stand for something other than greed and violence. I want my children to be proud of their father.'

'That's all very well,' Judy said, frowning. 'But what happens now? As Jay said, you'll have a legal battle on your hands, Rob. So where does that leave us?'

'I think the first thing to be done is to fix the front door, and then we can talk about what to do next.'

Hilda raised herself from the settle. 'You're right, Rob. It's freezing in here. Nate will help you. I'll ask him to find the tool box and some wood.' She hurried from the taproom.

'Ma is fine when she has something to do,' Judy said, smiling. 'That goes for me, too.'

'I'm sorry you had to go through all that. I was

going to tackle Jay in private, but he forced my hand.'

'I'm glad I know the truth. It makes life easier for me.'

'You don't have to remain here, Judy. I've given it a lot of thought and there's the gatekeeper's cottage on the estate. The old fellow apparently went to live with his sisters and so the cottage is vacant. You could all live there rent free for as long as you like.'

'We're not your responsibility, Rob. Besides which, we have to earn our living. I'm happy to stay here and run the inn. We're breaking even at the moment, and if trade improves then we'll make enough to pay rent, like real tenants.'

'You're a stubborn woman, Judy Begg.'

'Have you just realised that?' she said, laughing. 'Do you agree, and will you stay on as a paying guest? We can't make exceptions, I'm afraid.'

Chapter Nineteen

It was all over the village. Soon everyone knew what had occurred on Christmas Day at the Crooked Billet Inn. Judy could not go anywhere without someone stopping her to congratulate her and her mother for standing up to the bullying tactics of yet another Tattersall. Jay was, if possible, even more unpopular than his late father, but that did not seem to deter him and he continued to lodge with his sister and brother-in-law in the school house. Judy gauged local opinion when she went to the village shop where George Keyes was always happy to update her on the latest gossip, and if anything, trade at the Crooked Billet had improved. People seemed eager to show their support for Rob, despite his family's notoriety, although Judy suspected that most of the inhabitants of Little Creek had sympathy, and a certain nostalgia, for the old days when smuggling was rife. It was said that previous incumbents of the vicarage had condoned the trade, and that contraband had at one time been stored in the church crypt. Of course John Peabody denied this, as did his wife, but Judy suspected that there was an element of truth in the story, and the Dornings' reputation did nothing to prevent the farm workers and fishermen from patronising the inn.

Rob occupied his room each night, going off early every morning to Creek Manor where the erection of the new house had already begun. There did not seem to be anything that Jay could do, although Judy doubted if he would give up easily. Despite rumours, there had been no further mention of law suits, and Rob did not seem unduly concerned, but Jay's continued silence was a source of worry to Judy. She had had a long talk with Daisy, and had come away convinced that Jay was up to something that did not bode well for any of them.

The weeks went by and trade picked up considerably with the arrival of the itinerant workmen, most of whom lived in a camp set up in the grounds of Creek Manor. Far from home and working long hours, they came to the Crooked Billet for a brief respite, and in particular for bowls of Hilda's mutton stew followed by treacle pudding. Judy was kept busy from morning until late at night, working in the bar and helping her mother in the kitchen. Nate was both ostler and potman, and his cheeky good humour made him a favourite with all the customers.

It was a hard-working life and not what Judy had envisaged for herself and her family, but they were not in debt, and they had a roof over their heads and food in their bellies. They had won the respect of their friends and neighbours, and that was something neither Jay nor Wilfred had managed to take away from them.

On the odd occasion, when she had a few moments of quiet time, Judy found herself thinking about Jack. He had not contacted her again since their last meeting and that hurt. They might never be lovers, but there was no reason why they could not be friends, and knowing him as she did, she was amazed that he had given up so easily. It came as surprise when she heard that he was planning to return to Australia with Jay. Pip had passed on the news to Nate, having heard it from one of the Walters' kitchen maids, who was stepping out with Billy, the head groom at Creek Hall. It never ceased to astonish Judy how quickly gossip was passed from mouth to mouth in the village. However, the fact that Jack would leave the country for a second time without saying goodbye was both disappointing and hurtful. She would have liked to see him again before he left, even though it would serve no useful purpose. Their lives had taken different paths, and perhaps it was better that way.

It was early morning on a fine day. The snowy weather was just a chilly memory and there was a definite hint of spring in the air. Judy was in the back yard pegging the washing on the line when she heard the sound of a horse's hoofs in the lane behind the inn. She did not take too much notice. It was probably the postman or maybe an early customer and her mother would answer the door, but the horse came to a halt outside the stable. She was about to take the empty clothes basket into the kitchen when Rob strolled into the yard.

'Did you forget something?'

He shook his head. 'No. I've come to take you out. It's high time you had a day off.'

'I can't leave Ma to do all the work.'

'Yes, you can. I've arranged for an old friend of yours to come and help out.'

'You've done what?' Judy gave him a searching look. 'Is this some kind of a joke?'

'Not at all. Your mother and Nate both agree with me that you've been working too hard. Mrs Pearce is on her way here as we speak, and she's going to help in the kitchen. Pip is coming over from Colneyhurst to work in the stable, and Nate is going to man the bar with Molly's help.'

'My sister is coming here to work in the bar?' Judy stared at him in disbelief. 'Molly is too much of a lady to stoop to such a thing.'

'She overheard me talking to Pip and she offered to come and help. I think maybe she's tired of being with small children all the time.'

'You arranged all this?'

'With your mother's help. I didn't do it all on my own.'

'But where are we going? This is silly, Rob. You didn't need to go to all this trouble.'

'Don't argue. I'll give you fifteen minutes to get ready. Pip should be here with Mrs Pearce and your sister, and he'll drive us to the station.' He took the basket from her and shooed her into the kitchen where Hilda was preparing vegetables.

'Were you in on this, Ma?' Judy demanded.

'Yes, I was. Rob thought of it and he's right. You've been looking peaky for days, and you've been working from early morning until late at night. I know you've been poring over the accounts long after I go to bed, so it's time you had a break.' Hilda waved the paring knife at her daughter. 'Go upstairs and change into your Sunday best. I don't know what Rob has planned, but I'm sure it will be something entertaining.'

'Wear that bonnet with the blue ribbons that suits you so well,' Rob said, smiling.

'I can't,' Judy admitted reluctantly. 'It got ruined when I was caught out in the rain.'

'Then I'll buy you another one even better, but the same colour.' Rob threw back his head and laughed. 'Don't look at me like that, Judy Begg. This is my way of saying thank you for everything you've done for me.'

'Less of the chitchat,' Hilda said impatiently. 'You'll miss the train if you don't hurry.'

*   *   *

They travelled in the luxury of a first-class compartment, and when they alighted at Bishopsgate Station they took a hansom cab to Regent Street, where they lunched in style at the Café Royal. Rob entertained Judy with amusing anecdotes about his notorious family, and tales of the exploits that had landed them in so much trouble. The wrongdoers themselves had richly deserved the punishments they received, but Rob had a way of telling a story that made their nefarious activities sound hilarious. Judy laughed until the tears ran down her cheeks, and she patted them dry on a hanky that her mother had pressed on her before she left the inn.

'I don't know how you manage to make it all sound so funny,' she said breathlessly. 'Your family sound like monsters.'

'They were, and some of them are still creating havoc, wherever they happen to be. I'm the only sane one in the whole bunch, and that's why I'm so determined to make my life better than theirs. I plan to build a beautiful home on the Creek Manor estate, and I'll try to make up for my family's shortcomings by being a worthy lord of the manor. I've been footloose for so long, Judy. I need to make a success of this project.'

She met his intense gaze with a smile. 'I understand how you feel. I suppose my life has been similar, in that I've never had a real home, at least not one what belonged to me or my family. You can't imagine what Green Dragon Yard was like,

350

and it was Daisy who rescued us from that place after Pa died. I was in service from the age of ten, although they were all very kind to me, so I can't complain.'

'No,' he said seriously. 'You never do, and that's one of the things I admire about you. Jack Fox was a fool to let you go. He should have begged you to take him back.'

She recoiled with a start. 'How did you know about that?'

'It was quite obvious to someone who knows you well, and I think I do know you quite well by now.'

'He's returning to Australia with Jay. I haven't seen Jack since Christmas, and I doubt if we'll ever meet again.'

Rob toyed with the stem of his wineglass. 'How do you feel about that?'

'I realised that we were never meant to be together in the first place. It was a childish dream, and we were very young, but things are different when you grow up.' She managed a watery smile. 'Except that I don't think Jack has ever matured, not really. He's still a little boy who thinks he can have anything he wants, if he persists hard enough.'

'Perhaps you ought to see him before he goes away.'

'Why do you say that? What good would it do to open old wounds?'

'Maybe you need to be certain that they are healed.'

'Let's not talk about it any more, Rob. I was enjoying myself until you mentioned Jack.'

'I'm sorry. We'll forget about him for now.' Rob signalled to the waiter. 'I'll have the bill, please.' He turned back to Judy with a teasing smile. 'There are some really good shops near here. I haven't forgotten about the new bonnet. I'm afraid I don't like the one you're wearing.'

Judy chuckled in spite of her raw emotions. 'As a matter of fact I hate it, too. But Ma insists that it's suitable for a girl of my age.'

'You're a beautiful woman, Judy. You should wear only the best. Allow me to indulge myself.'

'Maybe I will. Just this once, of course, only don't tell Ma.'

Arm in arm they left the elegant restaurant and made their way up Regent Street, stopping to look in shop windows. The well-dressed men and women they saw made Judy very conscious of her old-fashioned clothes, and she did not argue when Rob insisted that she must try on a number of bonnets, ending with a pretty little confection of net, feathers and silk flowers. The hat she had fallen in love with was the height of fashion in London, but she could not imagine wearing it in Little Creek. Rob, however, saw no such problem and he insisted on buying it for her.

She hesitated, gazing at her reflection in the shop mirror. 'I can't accept it, Rob. Look at me. I look like a servant who's parading around in her mistress's bonnet.'

'It's not you, Judy, it's those drab garments you're wearing.' Rob glanced at the prim sales assistant. 'Perhaps you have a more fashionable mantle that might suit the young lady?'

'I'll fetch my colleague, sir.' The woman marched off to where a group of shop girls were waiting for prospective customers. She returned minutes later with another, much younger woman.

'I think I have exactly the right thing for you, miss. Will you come with me, please?'

'Go on, Judy. I'll wait here, but I want to see you in it before you commit yourself.' Rob settled back on a spindly gilt chair, leaving Judy little option but to follow the eager saleswoman.

'I believe you're enjoying this,' Judy said over her shoulder.

He smiled and tapped the side of his nose. 'I'd be lying if I denied it. Go on, choose something you really like.'

'I'm not letting him spend a fortune on me,' Judy said in a low voice as she followed the assistant into the next department.

'I wish I had a gentleman friend who was generous and good-looking.' The young woman winked saucily, and then her smile faded. 'Pretend you didn't hear that, miss. I'll lose my position here if Miss Banks finds out I've been familiar with a customer.'

Judy followed her gaze and saw the prim woman, who was standing with her hands clasped tightly in front of her, and a sour expression on her face. 'I won't say a word. Let me try on something and then we'll go on our way.'

Judy waited while the girl went through a rack of elegant outer garments and her breath caught with a gasp of admiration when she was shown a velvet mantle in a glorious shade of deep blue. 'It's like the midnight sky,' Judy breathed. 'And the silver buttons look like stars, but it must be every expensive.'

'It's the latest Paris fashion, miss.' The girl shot a wary glance at her superior. 'I haven't sold anything today and I'll lose my job if you walk away empty-handed.'

Judy fingered the material and sighed. 'It's far too good for me. I would love to have it, but I don't know when I would have occasion to wear such a fine garment.'

'I can't afford to be out of work. Miss Banks has it in for me because I get on well with the customers, but I try to be more like her.'

Judy met the girl's anxious gaze with a smile. 'Of course I'll try it on, and if it looks well on me I'll buy it myself even if I have to pay Rob back at a shilling a week for the rest of my life.' She allowed the assistant to help her off with her serviceable merino jacket, which was at least five years old, and she shivered with pleasure at the feel of the velvet as it caressed her body through the thin cotton of her blouse.

The expression on Rob's face when she walked towards him was enough to convince her that the mantle was worth every penny of the price, which she considered exorbitant.

'That looks wonderful on you, Judy. You look like a queen.'

'It's very expensive,' she said in a low voice. 'But I'll pay you back a little every week.'

He stood up, his smile fading into a frown. 'No such thing. I won't hear of it. This will be a thank-you present. You've done more for me than you can ever know.' He turned to Miss Banks, who was standing beside the anxious shop assistant. 'We'll take the hat and the mantle. Miss Begg will wear both, so perhaps you'd wrap her things and send them to the address I'll give you.' He flashed a disarming smile at Miss Banks. 'You run a very efficient department, madam. I'll be delighted to commend you to your employer.'

Wearing the expensive mantle and gloriously extravagant hat, Judy felt like the most elegant woman in London as they strolled towards Oxford Circus. 'Do you really know the owner of the shop, Rob?'

'Of course not, but to be fair to the staff I will write a commendation, especially of the younger woman who found this lovely mantle for you. Now she has good taste and she'll go far if the redoubtable Miss Banks will let her.'

'Why do you care about someone you may never meet again?'

'I felt sorry for her. I know what it's like to be poor. I haven't always had money, and I haven't forgotten what it is to struggle to make a living. But let's put all that aside. We're here to have a good time. Where would you like to go next?'

'I've never been to the zoo, but I've heard that there are lions and tigers and all manner of exotic animals to be seen.'

Rob raised his hand to hail a passing hansom cab. 'The zoo, please, Cabby.' He helped Judy to climb into the vehicle. 'We'll spend as much time there as you like,' he said as he sat down beside her. 'But I suggest tea at Gunter's before we head back to the station. What do you say to that?'

She leaned against him and sighed happily. 'It sounds too good to be true. I've really enjoyed today, Rob.'

'It's not over yet,' he said cheerfully.

Judy was entranced by everything she saw at the Zoological Gardens, although she did feel sad for the loss of freedom that the large animals must surely suffer, even though they were obviously well fed and cared for by their keepers. She and Rob strolled around taking in the sights for over an hour, but the sky began to darken and there was a hint of sulphur in the air, and a yellow tinge to the fog that had begun to creep up on them.

Judy had experienced this only too often as a child. 'It's the beginning of a peasouper,' she said urgently. 'I think we'd better leave, Rob. When it gets dark you won't be able to see your hand in front of your face, quite literally.'

'Yes, I was afraid of that. We'd better cut our visit short or we might be stuck in London overnight.'

They left the gardens but it seemed that the whole of the West End had realised what was happening, and everyone was making for home or shelter of some kind. Cabs rushed past them, but all were booked, and the air grew steadily thicker as the fog swirled around them. Eventually Rob managed to flag down a hackney carriage, but the roads were so congested that they were travelling at a snail's pace. The gas lamps were being lit and darkness was falling. The heavy cloud cover had forced the smoke from both domestic chimneys and manufactories to mix with the fog and had formed a choking yellow London Particular. Eventually the cab came to a halt.

Rob opened the door and leaned out. 'Where are we, Cabby?'

'I'm sorry, mister. This is the best I can do for you. We're at Charing Cross Station and with luck I'll make it to the cabmen's shelter at St Clement Danes church.'

'Is there any chance you could get us as far as Bishopsgate Station? I'll pay double if you can.'

'I'd like to oblige, but we'd never make it. The best you can do is to put up here, at the Charing

Cross Hotel. You won't get no further, I promise you.'

Judy caught Rob by the sleeve. 'We could try to walk there.'

'It's too far. The cabby's right, Judy. The fog is getting thicker by the minute. We haven't got much choice.' Rob alighted from the cab, holding his hand out to Judy.

She could only just make out his silhouette as the thick, choking pea-green fog closed in on them, but his fingers closed around hers in a warm clasp and a moment later she was standing beside him on the cobblestones. He paid the cabby and the vehicle moved off slowly, edging its way along the Strand, and was lost within a few feet of them.

'We haven't any choice,' Rob said, linking her hand through the crook of his arm. 'We'll have to stay here tonight.'

Judy shivered. 'You're right. We'd never find our way in this, and it's a long way from here to Bishopsgate.'

The foyer was crowded with people clamouring for rooms, and the overworked concierge was clearly at the end of his tether. The hotel manager was attempting to keep the would-be guests calm while they allocated rooms to those who had been marooned by the peasouper. Judy glanced round at the pale faces of the men who vied for attention at the reception desk. They were mostly businessmen, judging by their city suits and top hats, but there were some ladies, probably the wives of the more prosperous gentleman. Judy amused herself by trying to pair them off with their irate husbands while she waited for Rob to return from the mêlée.

After a long wait he emerged from the crowd brandishing two keys. 'It was a battle,' he said, smiling broadly. 'I thought it was going to come to fisticuffs, but I have the last two rooms.'

Judy made a move to join him, but the young woman who had been seated not far from her suddenly rose to her feet, swaying dangerously. Rob was nearest and he caught her as she collapsed in a faint. The young man who was with her relieved Rob of his burden.

'Thank you, sir. I'm afraid I wasn't quick enough. My poor wife is exhausted and I've just had to tell her that the last room has been taken.' He set his semi-conscious wife back on the chair.

'Is she all right?' Judy asked anxiously. 'She looks so pale.'

'We're expecting our first child. We came up to town to celebrate, but I'm afraid all this has been too much for her.' The man leaned over his wife, fanning her with his hands.

Rob exchanged meaningful glances with Judy and she nodded.

'You must have my room, sir,' Rob said firmly. 'There's no question about it, and it's on the first floor, so you haven't far to go.'

'Are you sure, sir? It's very kind of you.'

'Your wife's need is greater than mine,' Rob said, smiling.

The young woman opened her eyes. 'What happened, Henry?'

'You fainted, Clara. But this kind gentleman has given us the key to his room. Can you stand, my dear?'

She held out her hand. 'Yes, I think so. It was silly of me to faint, but I suddenly felt very hot and dizzy.'

'You need to rest,' Judy said calmly. 'Is there anything I can do to help?'

'No, you're very kind.' Clara rose to her feet with her husband's assistance. 'It's the fault of this wretched fog. I'll be fine now.'

Henry grabbed Rob's hand and pumped his arm up and down enthusiastically. 'I should introduce myself, sir. I'm Henry Parsons. Thank you again.'

'Rob Dorning and this lady is Judy Begg.' Rob proffered his arm to Judy. 'Come, my dear. We'd better go to our room.'

Judy snatched the key from his hand and walked away. 'My room, I think, my dear.'

'You wouldn't force me to sit up all night in the bar, would you?' Rob's eyes twinkled despite his pained expression.

Judy tucked the key into her reticule. 'Wouldn't I? Anyway, I'm starving. Do you think we could get something to eat?'

He took her free hand and tucked it into the crook

of his arm. 'We'll go to the dining room before these people descend upon it like locusts. Then we'll talk about where I'm to rest my head tonight.' He led her through the crowd, heading for the elegant sweep of a staircase that led to the first-floor dining room, where by a stroke of luck they were shown to a recently vacated table. The flustered waiter apologised for the fact that the cloth had not been changed, but Rob assured him there was no need to worry and they understood the situation. The waiter, who was perspiring freely, hurried off to get the bottle of wine that Rob ordered and to bring them the menu.

Judy sat back in her chair. 'This is getting to be a habit, Rob Dorning.'

'I don't recall bringing you here before?'

She giggled in spite of her attempt to be serious. 'You might have brought another lady here, but not me. In Maldon we were caught out by snow, and now we're stuck here in London because of a peasouper fog.'

'It's quite delightful having your company for longer than intended, but I promise you I didn't order the bad weather on either occasion.'

She smiled. 'You do realise how this is going to look when we get home, don't you? We'll be the talk of the village, yet again.'

'Then you'll just have to marry me, won't you, Judy?'

She eyed him cautiously. 'You need to be careful,

Rob. A joke like that could backfire on you. I might accept.'

'Would that be so terrible?'

She was prevented from answering by the sudden appearance of the agitated waiter, who had brought the wine that Rob ordered, and the menus, which he dropped on the floor and had to scramble around under the table to pick up. Having given them one each, he opened the wine and spilled some of it as he poured a little for Rob to sample. His hands shook as he filled their glasses.

'I beg your pardon, sir. I'm so sorry, but it's chaos in the kitchen, and people are queuing to get into the dining room. I've never seen it so busy.'

'It's all right,' Rob said easily. 'Don't worry. We're not in a hurry. We're going nowhere until the fog clears.'

The waiter backed away and Rob handed Judy a menu. 'Heaven knows what he'll do with the food. I half expect it to be delivered straight to my lap.'

Judy was still chuckling when the waiter re-appeared, only this time he was not alone. 'Sir, I beg your pardon, but this gentleman says he knows you, and he insisted on speaking to you.'

Judy looked up and saw Henry Parsons hovering behind the waiter.

'I do hope you don't mind this imposition, but my wife is terribly hungry, and the queue is halfway down the staircase. I saw you through the glass door, and I just wonder if we might share your table?'

Judy met Rob's amused glance with a smile of resignation. 'Of course we don't mind. Do we, my dear?'

Henry's jaw dropped. 'Oh! Are you two celebrating as well? I'm sorry I didn't mean to interrupt.'

'No, it's quite all right,' Judy assured him. 'Rob just proposed to me. I haven't given him my answer yet, but don't worry, Henry, I'm still thinking about it. Please do fetch Clara. We can't allow a lady in a delicate condition to go hungry, can we, Rob?' She smiled angelically and turned her attention to the menu.

Two can play at that game, Rob Dorning. She shot him a sideways glance. *Now you don't know what I'm thinking.*

Chapter Twenty

Clara was apologetic and clearly uncomfortable during the meal even though Judy tried to reassure her that they were not imposing. However, Clara's appetite did not seem to be affected and she ate well, although she refused wine and opted for water instead. When she finished the last spoonful of dessert she replaced her spoon in the bowl.

'I've been thinking, Henry.'

'Yes, my dear. What about?'

Clara shot him a sideways glance beneath long, dark eyelashes. 'Well, we've taken poor Rob's room, and I think it very unfair that he has no bed for the night.'

'I assure you I can sleep anywhere,' Rob said hastily. 'Please don't worry on my account.'

'But I do feel concerned.' Clara's green eyes filled with tears. 'The hotel is so crowded there will hardly be a seat free, let alone anywhere to lie down.'

'Don't upset yourself, my love,' Henry said anxiously.

'I'm quite all right, but what I suggest is that Judy and I share a room, and you and Mr Dorning have the other.'

Judy could see the sense in this, and she, too, had been concerned for Rob. 'I agree. If Clara doesn't mind, then neither do I. It seems to be the most sensible arrangement.'

Rob looked as if he was about to refuse, but Henry insisted that his wife was right and that it was the only fair way to allocate the accommodation.

'That's settled then,' Clara said firmly. 'I'm very tired and I'd like to retire now, Henry.'

He rose to his feet. 'Of course, my love. Shall I take you to your room?'

'That won't be necessary.' Judy was already on her feet. 'I'm exhausted, too. I'll see you in the morning, Rob. It's been a lovely day, even allowing for the peasouper.'

Rob half rose from his seat. 'Good night, Judy. I'll see you at breakfast. Good night, Mrs Parsons.'

Clara answered with a weary smile and allowed Judy to lead her from the dining room. 'I hope you don't mind sharing with me, Judy. It seems a terrible imposition.'

'Not at all. In such circumstances it's the least we could do.'

They walked on in silence until they came to the room that Judy should have had to herself and Clara flopped down on the bed. 'Are you going to accept Rob's proposal?'

Judy went to the fireplace and added another shovelful of coal. 'That was a joke. We weren't serious.'

'Oh, no. You're wrong, Judy. It's quite obvious that Rob is in love with you.'

Judy turned to give her a searching look. 'What makes you say that?'

'I don't know. I suppose it was everything really – the way he looks at you and the change in tone of his voice when he's speaking to you. I hardly know either of you, but I'm certain I'm right.'

'I don't know about that,' Judy said evasively.

'Well, who am I to tell you anything?' Clara chuckled and rose to her feet. 'Would you be an angel and unlace me, Judy? I really need to lie down, and I'm so sorry if we spoiled your evening.'

'I was ready for bed, so please don't worry. I think I'll sleep without rocking, as my mum always says.' Judy helped Clara off with her outer garments before tackling the tightly laced corset.

Clara breathed a sigh of relief and, still wearing her chemise, she climbed into the bed. 'I hope I didn't speak out of turn, Judy. You and Rob have been so kind to us.'

'You've given me something to think about,' Judy said candidly. 'The trouble is, I never know when Rob is serious or when he's teasing me.'

'He's a good man.' Clara yawned and turned on her side. 'Good night, Judy.'

Judy sat by the fire for a while, thinking over what Clara had said. Of course she was mistaken: Rob was not romantically inclined, and even if he were, the old spectre of social divisions would once again raise its ugly head. When the mansion was rebuilt Rob Dorning, the legitimate son of the old squire, would become the lord of the manor, and she would still be Judy Begg from Green Dragon Yard.

Judy sighed and rose to her feet. She could tell by Clara's even breathing that she was already fast asleep. Judy unlaced her boots before shedding her outer garments and her stays. She crept under the covers, lying back to back with Clara, and drifted off to sleep.

Next morning, after a rushed breakfast in the over-crowded dining room, Judy and Rob said goodbye to Clara and Henry, promising to keep in touch, although Judy knew that their different lifestyles would make it unlikely that they would ever meet again. Nevertheless she was very touched when Clara promised to call their baby Judy, if it turned out to be a girl, and Robert if it were a boy. They parted on the best of terms and then Rob and Judy caught a hansom cab to Bishopsgate Station, although now they were on their own Judy found herself unusually tongue-tied and shy. Clara's insistence that Rob was interested in her romantically had made Judy examine her own heart, and Rob seemed preoccupied during the journey home. When he did talk it concerned his plans for the new Creek Manor, and Judy listened politely, making suitable comments when required, but they had lost the easy friendship they had enjoyed the previous day.

It was something of a relief to reach the normality of home, although there were explanations to be made as to why they found it necessary to stay away overnight. Hilda, being a Londoner born and bred, understood perfectly, but Nate had been too young to remember the peasouper fogs and he was openly hostile. Rob changed out of his city clothes into riding breeches and a tweed jacket and he set off for the building site, leaving Judy to go through every detail of their day out together in order to please her mother. Hilda drank several cups of tea while listening to Judy's account of her exciting trip to London, although she was clearly worried about what people would make of the smart new outfit that Rob had bought Judy.

'You know what people are like, dear,' Hilda said, shaking her head. 'The hat and the mantle are lovely, but I think they should be kept for special occasions only.'

Judy chuckled. 'You mean I should put them away in the clothes press and forget about them.'

'Not exactly, but let's face it, Judy. We couldn't afford to buy such things even if we saved up for a whole year. And then there's the fact that you spent the night in Rob's company – you know what people will say about that.'

'But they would be wrong, Ma. I shared a bed with Clara, and Rob had to sleep with Henry, who apparently snored all night. The people round here won't ever have experienced a London Particular, so they don't know what it's like.'

'Very true, and the least said the better.' Hilda finished her tea. 'There's something I must tell you before you hear it from anyone else.'

'Really, Ma? What is it?' Judy tried not to sound too relieved at the change of subject – the cross-examination about her time in London was getting a bit wearisome.

'I heard last evening that Jack has left for Southampton. He didn't call in or send a message, which I think was very wrong of him. You two were close at one time and he should have had the courtesy to come and say goodbye.'

'Perhaps it's for the best,' Judy said cautiously. 'Did Jay go with him?'

'I'm not sure, dear. It was quite strange because he came into the bar last evening. I thought for a moment he was going to cause trouble, but he chatted quite normally and then he left. He did ask after you, though. I thought that demonstrated a certain degree of feeling on his part.'

Judy rose from the table. 'I'll go and change into my work clothes, Ma. I'm sure there's a lot to do.'

'I had plenty of help. Molly seemed to enjoy

working here for a change, and it was lovely to have time to chat with Nell Pearce.' Hilda smiled and the lines of worry on her face relaxed.

Judy went to her room and changed out of her travelling costume. Her work clothes felt even shabbier now than they had before she went away, but she tied on a clean apron and went downstairs to attack her tasks with renewed vigour. She had enjoyed her time with Rob, but she must put all that behind her and get on with the life that fate had handed out to her.

She swept the bar and polished the tables ready for the usual influx of customers later in the day. The workmen at the building site usually came for a drink when they had finished their shifts, and the aroma of cheese and onion pies and rabbit stew wafted through the building. It was late afternoon and getting dark outside when she realised that the scuttle was empty, and Nate had gone to the village on an errand for their mother. Judy picked up the brass scuttle and went outside to fill it with coal. She was on her way back to the kitchen when she heard footsteps behind her and something was clamped over her nose and mouth. She struggled and lost consciousness.

Judy opened her eyes and licked her dry lips. Her head ached and her whole body was being rocked from side to side with the motion of the fast-moving carriage. She attempted to sit up but a sudden bout of dizziness made her subside onto the stale-smelling leather squabs. It was dark inside and out, and she could hear the thunder of the horses' hoofs as they pounded on the road surface. Although she called out, her dry throat turned her voice into little more than a croak and she realised that she could not make herself heard. Moreover, her wrists and ankles were bound and movement of any kind was restricted. She closed her eyes, saving her strength for what might come when the journey ended. Who had abducted her and the reason for such a crime was a mystery, but she was too angry to be scared. The journey seemed to last an eternity and she fell asleep only to awaken when the vehicle came to a halt. The door was wrenched open.

'I'm sorry about this, Judy, but there was no other way.'

'Jay? Is that you?'

A hand pulled her to a sitting position. 'I'll untie your ankles if you promise to do as I say. You can't run away because we're in the middle of nowhere and it's pitch-dark. Do as I tell you and all will be well.'

'I won't run, but I want an explanation.'

'All in good time.' Jay cut the rope binding her ankles and he lifted her to the ground. 'As I said before, don't even think about trying to get away.'

It was a moonless night and a bitter east wind whipped at Judy's hair, dragging it free from the pins that had kept it neatly in place. She was wearing a linsey-woolsey dress, but the chill cut into her bones like knives. Jay dragged her across rough ground and she stumbled over stones and ruts in the lane. She could hear the sound of waves crashing on the shore and she could smell the sea, but she had no idea where they were. Eventually she saw a pinprick of light, which grew nearer and nearer until she could just make out the shape of a house, standing on its own.

'Where are we?' Judy demanded angrily. 'Why have you brought me to this place?'

'Shut up,' Jay snapped. 'All in good time. I've gone to a lot of trouble to get you here.' He dragged her to the front entrance and kicked the door open.

Judy found herself in the dimly lit kitchen of what appeared to be an old farmhouse. A fire burned feebly in the ancient range, issuing gusts of soot-laden smoke at intervals, and not a lot in the way of warmth. Jay pushed her down onto a wooden chair at the table.

'Sit there and don't move.' He strode over to the range and riddled the coals, sending sparks flying in all directions. 'The bloody chimney needs sweeping. In fact the whole damn building needs razing to the ground. However, it'll serve its purpose.'

'What is this place?' Judy demanded. 'Where are we?'

'This, my dear, was bought by my late father many years ago. I believe he used to entertain certain ladies here where he could be sure of complete privacy.

Hardly anyone knew about it apart from the old woman who kept house for him, and she died some time ago.'

Judy twisted round in the chair, staring at him in disbelief. 'What's happened to you? I don't remember you being like this before you left for Australia.'

'You were a nipper then and a servant. You didn't know what was going on, any more than you realise what's at stake now.'

He was angry and Judy sensed danger. She decided to humour him. 'I might understand if you would only talk to me.'

Jay took off his greatcoat and tossed it over the back of a chair. 'Here's what you'll do, Judy Begg. You'll stop asking questions and keep your mouth shut.'

She met his irate gaze with a straight look. 'You could at least untie my hands. I can't go anywhere, as you said, and you're twice my size, so I'm hardly likely to overpower you.'

He opened a drawer and took out a knife, which he used to slice through the cords. 'There, now you can shut up. I'll speak to you when I'm good and ready.' He stood back, glaring at her for a moment. 'You can cook, can't you?'

'Yes, of course I can. You must know that I trained under Mrs Pearce.'

'I can't be expected to remember every servant we employed. Anyway, I'm damned hungry. There's food in the bag. See what you can make of it because we might be here for some time.'

Judy followed his gaze and in the dim light she saw a bag spilling its contents onto the deal table. She was hungry too, or she might have refused, although she knew from experience that a good meal had a soothing effect on a bad-tempered man. There were potatoes, onions and carrots together with a large chunk of bacon, a loaf of bread, and a wedge of cheese.

'I can make a meal of this,' she said carefully, 'but I'll need water. Is there a pump in the yard?'

He shrugged. 'I don't know.' He caught her by the sleeve as she was about to make for the back door. 'No, you don't. I'll go – you stay here.' He picked up a bucket and went outside.

Judy could hear him stamping around in the dark and cursing, but then there was the swooshing sound of water hitting the pail, and she sighed with relief. At the bottom of the bag was a poke of tea leaves and another of sugar. That might sweeten Jay's temper a little.

He stamped back into the kitchen and put the bucket down with a thud.

'There you are. Now get on with it.'

Judy filled the kettle and placed it on the hob. She began to prepare the meal by peeling the vegetables. 'There's no need to be so surly, Jay Tattersall. I'm not your slave and I've no idea why I'm here, or why you're behaving like this.'

Jay sat down and put his feet up on a second chair. 'You caused my young brother a lot of misery. All he wanted was for you to accompany him to Australia, but you decided to stay at home. Perhaps you had your eye set on the next master of Creek Manor.'

'You don't know what you're talking about. I was heartbroken the first time Jack went off without a word. You planned it that way, didn't you?'

'Watch your tongue, girl. You're nothing to me and I don't give a tinker's cuss for your good opinion. You're here because I've got a use for you. You'll find out in good time – now get on with the cooking.'

Judy did not like to push him too far. This was not the Jay she remembered from childhood days. When he had first married Daisy he had been kind and cheerful and generally well liked. Even when he had lost his memory after his return from a long period of absence, he had been a polite, if slightly distant master to the servants at Creek Manor, but this man was a relative stranger, and an unpleasant one at that.

Judy prepared the vegetables, adding them to the pot together with chunks of salty bacon and topping it up with water. She made the tea and handed Jay a steaming mug, sweetened with a little of the sugar. He drank it in silence, staring moodily into space, and Judy occupied herself by searching the drawers and cupboards for bowls and cutlery. The items she found were in need of a wash, and she was glad of having something to keep her busy. All the while she was plotting her escape, but she would have to wait until Jay was asleep. It was true that she had no idea where they were, but when she went to the back door and opened it just a crack she could hear the sea. A walk along the coast would almost certainly bring her to a village or habitation of some sort. It was a cold night, but dry, with very little wind. All she needed was a shawl or a blanket to wrap around her shoulders and she could walk for miles. While the soup was cooking she had a good look round the scullery and found a lantern beneath the stone sink. There were a few candles in Jay's bag, together with a box of matches. He seemed to have thought of everything.

Judy closed the cupboard door and went back to stir the soup.

The sweet tea had done much to restore Jay's good humour, and he demolished two bowls of soup and a large slice of bread covered in slivers of cheese. Judy had tried to be economical in case they needed to stretch the food out to last a couple of days, although she did not intend to wait idly to find out what Jay had in mind for her. She had to force herself to eat, and her throat seemed to close up when she attempted to swallow. At the back of her mind she knew that her sudden disappearance would make Ma and Nate frantic with worry. She wondered if Rob would come in search for her, but he would not know where to start.

She waited until Jay had finished his meal. 'Why are you keeping me prisoner?'

He sat back in his chair, eyebrows raised as if the question had taken him by surprise. 'You're not a prisoner, Judy. You're what I would call an insurance.'

'An insurance against what? What are you up to, and how do I fit in?'

'I want my birthright back,' Jay said slowly. 'I am the rightful lord of the manor, and that upstart has taken it away from me.'

'If you wanted to keep the manor house, why did you sell it in the first place?'

'I needed the money, you stupid girl. Why else would I put my ancestral home up for sale?'

'But you're doing so well in Australia. I don't see why Creek Manor is so important to you.'

'Robert Dorning is an imposter and his family are criminals. I'll pay him a fair price, but I want the Creek Manor estate for my son.'

Judy gave him a searching look. 'You're doing all this to hurt Rob?'

'I regretted my decision the moment the estate was sold. Had I known that one of the Dorning family had his eye on the estate I'd have returned sooner.'

Judy eyed him curiously. 'I think you know more about the fire than you're saying.'

'I was on the other side of the world. You told me about the fire when I returned to Little Creek.'

'You couldn't have started the fire yourself, but

you might have paid someone else to do it for you,' Judy said slowly. 'Did you plan it all, Jay? Did you hope to get the estate cheaper because the house was a ruin?'

'Why don't you mind your own business, girl?'

'You brought me here against my will. That makes it very much my business.'

'All right, since you won't shut up, I'll tell you. Yes, I arranged for someone to start the fire. I didn't want the old ruin of a house; I wanted the land and the title for my boy, and I would have got it cheaply if Dorning hadn't turned up.'

'Did you know that the squire had a son by his first marriage?'

Jay thumped his fist down on the table. 'No, I did not. Now stop asking bloody silly questions and clear this mess away. Then you can get to bed. I can't stand the sight of you any longer.'

Judy rose to her feet, leaning her hands on the table. 'If you feel like that why did you bring me here? What do you hope to gain by all this?'

'Dorning has received a ransom note. If he doesn't agree to let me buy back the land and the title at my price, he'll never see you again.'

Judy stared at him aghast. 'You plan to kill me for a stupid title?'

'Nothing so dramatic. If he agrees to my terms you'll go free, if not you'll be coming with Jack and me to Australia.'

'You can't do that. I won't go with you.'

'You won't have any choice. Jack isn't in Southampton, he's on board the *Lazy Jane*, just waiting for me to join him. He's not party to this, by the way. Now do as I said and tidy up, then you can go to bed. There are plenty of rooms upstairs – take your pick.'

'This is outrageous,' Judy said angrily. 'You can't do this.'

Jay narrowed his eyes. 'Dorning has taken a fancy to you, so I have a hold on him.'

'I refuse to be a pawn in your devious plans, Jay Tattersall. Rob and I are friends, that's all.'

'I don't believe you. Anyway, time will tell. If he doesn't turn up at the meeting place tomorrow I'll know you're telling the truth.'

'And you'll let me go?'

'Maybe. Or perhaps I'll let Jack decide. If he still wants you then he can have you.'

Judy held her tongue with difficulty. It was obvious that arguing with Jay was a waste of time and she was in no position to bargain. She cleared the table and placed the dirty crockery in the stone sink.

'You can leave that until morning.'

She spun round to find Jay standing behind her. Her heartbeat quickened and she was suddenly afraid, but she faced him with a defiant stare.

'I'd prefer to leave everything tidy.'

He grabbed her by the arm. 'And I'd prefer it if you were safely locked in your room. I'm not going to sit up all night keeping watch in case you try to make a run for it. Without you I haven't any bargaining power, so come quietly or I'll toss you over my shoulder and carry you.'

Judy shook free from his grasp. 'There's no need for that. I'll follow you.'

Jay shook his head. 'I'm not stupid, Judy Begg. You'll go upstairs first. Take any room you like. They're all much the same.' He lit a candle from the one burning in the centre of the table and thrust it into her hand. 'My patience is limited so don't try me too far.'

There seemed little choice other than to humour him, and Judy climbed the stairs. She hesitated on the landing. There was a distinct smell of damp and it was bitterly cold away from the kitchen range.

'In there.' Jay pushed past her and flung the nearest door open.

A gust of icy air almost took Judy's breath away as she entered the room. 'I'll need coal for the fire,' she said crossly. 'You can't expect me to sleep here.'

'You'll have to make do.' Jay backed out onto the landing. 'I'll let you have the candle, but I'm locking you in. I'll let you out at dawn.' He slammed the door and the key grated in the lock.

Judy held the candle high so that she could get a clearer picture of her prison, for that was what it felt like. Jay had her trapped in this isolated house, and there seemed to be little likelihood of escape. She spotted another candle on the mantelshelf, and she lit it from the one in her hand. The extra light was comforting, and she crossed the floor to check the window. It opened easily enough, but it was a dark night and she could not see the ground below. Shivering violently, she closed the window and drew the curtains, but the material was rotten and they fell to pieces in her hands.

The bed did not look inviting. The bare mattress was lumpy and felt damp, but by this time Judy was exhausted and she knew that there was nothing to be done until morning. A search of the cupboards revealed very little other than dead cockroaches and mouse droppings, but in an old sea chest she found a horse blanket, which was coarse and smelly, but infinitely better than nothing. Still fully dressed, she lay down on the bed and curled up beneath the rough woollen cloth. The old timbers of the house creaked and groaned, as if it too were settling down for a night's sleep. The wind whistled through the ill-fitting windows, thrashing the branches of the trees like an irate schoolmaster. Judy closed her eyes, shutting out the world in which she had found herself. She would find a way to escape from Jay but she would think about that in the morning.

Chapter Twenty-One

Judy was up and sitting on the edge of the bed when she heard the key turn in the lock. There was no telling what sort of mood Jay might be in, and she braced herself to face whatever might happen that day.

The door opened. 'You're awake. Good – I want my breakfast.' Jay stomped off and she could hear his booted feet clattering on the stairs.

Judy decided to play along with him, but at the same time she would look for a way of escape, and she followed him downstairs to the kitchen. He went to the range and began riddling the ashes, cursing loudly.

'Here, let me do that.' She edged him unceremoniously out of the way. 'Is there any coal outside, or some logs?'

'I'll go and look. You stay here and don't even

think of trying to get away. The front door is locked and I have the key.'

Judy set about clearing the ashes away from the embers and she used the bellows to coax them into flames, adding what was left of the coal. There was a decent blaze by the time Jay returned with a basket of logs and a bundle of dried furze. Minutes later the kettle was on the hob and bacon sizzled in the pan.

Jay took his place at the table. 'You'd be useful on board ship,' he said, grudgingly. 'Our cook should be tossed overboard for the rubbish he serves up.'

Judy turned the bacon and added a couple of slices of bread. 'I'm not volunteering for that job.'

'You might not have much choice if your friend doesn't turn up at the meeting place. If I can't get what I want we'll be setting sail sooner than planned.'

Judy served the food and slapped his plate down in front of him. 'So all this will have been a waste of time. Why don't you give up and be satisfied with what you have in Australia? It sounds like a good life over there.'

'If I don't get my way you'll find out for yourself.' Jay attacked his food with obvious enjoyment.

Judy took a seat opposite him. 'What do you think you'll gain by this? And what good will it do keeping me prisoner here?'

'If Dorning wants to see you again he'd better let me buy back the Creek Manor estate. I don't want something for nothing – I can pay whatever he asks.' Jay bolted his food and when he had finished his breakfast he rose to his feet. 'I'm leaving now and I'll be gone for a while. If Dorning agrees to my terms, he's welcome to you.'

Judy's taut nerves threatened to get the better of her and she had to curb the desire to fly at Jay and slap the smug smile from his face, but she managed to retain her self-control.

Jay reached for his greatcoat. 'Don't try to escape. You won't get very far on foot in this weather, and it's several miles to the nearest village.' He swaggered to the front door and let himself out.

Judy ran to the window. She watched him as he made his way to the stable, and minutes later he emerged, leading the horse all tacked up. With an agile leap he mounted and rode off, leaving her feeling alone and even more vulnerable. She returned to the table, but she had lost her appetite and she pushed her plate away. Jay was using her as a pawn in his twisted game, and she had no intention of making life easy for him. Her determination to escape grew by the second and she jumped to her feet. Outside the wind was battering the old building and rain lashed the windows. She had only the clothes that she stood up in, and if she was to brave the weather she would need to wear something warmer.

Upstairs, she rifled through the cupboards in every bedroom, and in the last room she found a moth-eaten woollen cloak. She put it on, wrinkling her nose at the smell of naphtha, which someone had used to keep moths at bay. It did not seem to have done its job very well but it was better than nothing, and she was desperate. She hurried downstairs, but the back door was locked. She searched frantically, pulling out drawers and scattering the contents on the floor, but she could not find the key. In the end she climbed onto a shelf in the larder and with a great deal of effort she managed to push out the screen window. She dropped to the ground and wrapped the cloak more firmly around her as the sleety rain poured down from a gunmetal sky.

She was free from the farmhouse, but she had no idea which way to go. In an effort to get her bearings, she followed the sound of waves crashing on the shore, but the bitter wind took her breath away and filled her lungs with icy shards. When she reached the clifftop she uttered a gasp of dismay. Anchored out to sea she saw a vessel that she recognised as the *Lazy Jane*. Jay had not lied, and she knew instinctively that he would carry out his threat to abduct her if Rob refused to co-operate. She did not stop to wonder if Jack was complicit with Jay's plans – she turned inland, and ran.

Buffeted by wind and blinded by the driving rain, Judy knew that she was heading south but there were no discernible landmarks to guide her. Eventually she was forced to stop in order to catch her breath, and she sank down in the lee of a stunted tree. She was shivering violently and the wet cloak gave her little protection from the elements. After a while the rain eased, but, as if to add to her problems, a sea fret rose up and swirled around her in a dense white cloud, blotting out the landscape and chilling her to the bone. She stood up, knowing that she must keep moving. Common sense told her that she must eventually come across some kind of dwelling, where she could ask for directions. Shrouded in mist, she walked slowly across a rutted field. If she kept on going she must surely come to a road or even a cart track.

She had lost all sense of time. She seemed to have been walking for hours when she stumbled over what appeared to be a gravestone. She fell heavily, landing with her right ankle twisted beneath her. A sharp pain caused her to cry out, and when she attempted to rise to her feet, she fell back gasping. It was the same ankle she had sprained when Rob's carriage overturned in the snow, and she closed her eyes, biting back tears of pain and frustration. She had come this far, and if there was a graveyard there must be habitation nearby. After a few minutes the agony lessened, providing she kept the injured limb absolutely still. She opened her eyes and found herself in an overgrown graveyard surrounding a small chapel. The mist had cleared and a wintry sun had pushed its way between the dark clouds.

Judy eased herself carefully to a sitting position and looked round, hoping to see a sign of life. The eerie silence was broken by the sound of someone whistling a cheerful tune.

'Ho, there,' she shouted. 'Help me, please.'

Moments later a youth appeared, seated on a donkey. He rode closer, eyeing her suspiciously.

'What's up with you?'

'I've hurt my ankle.'

The boy dismounted. 'Who are you?'

'I'm Judy Begg from Little Creek. Can you tell me where I am?'

'You're sitting on Abel Dorning's gravestone. That's where you are, miss. I'd move, if I were you, miss. He's likely to take exception.'

Judy gave the boy a searching look. She was not sure if he was trying to be funny, but he appeared to be serious. 'Dorning,' she repeated dazedly. 'Do you know the Dorning family?'

'I should say I do, miss. Almost everyone in the village is related to them in one way or another.'

Pain and fatigue were getting the better of Judy. 'What's your name, boy?'

'I'm Walter Dorning. What's it to you?'

'Would this be Crouch village?'

'Not exactly, miss. It's yonder.' He pointed vaguely in the direction of a stand of trees.

Judy struggled to remember the name of Rob's aunt. 'Do you know Miss Dorning? Miss Adeline Dorning?'

'I do. She's my aunt.'

Judy could hardly believe that her luck had changed so suddenly. 'Could you take me to her, Walter? I'd need you to help me because I don't think I can walk.'

He put his head on one side. 'I suppose I could let you ride.'

Judy attempted to rise, but fell back, stifling a sob. Walter grabbed her by the hand and looped her arm around his shoulders.

'I'm stronger than I look. Up you get.' He managed to heave her to a standing position, and they made their way slowly to where the donkey was munching grass. After pushing and heaving from Walter, and a determined effort by Judy, she was finally astride the animal, although completely exhausted. She clung to the donkey's mane as Walter led the animal to the village, which seemed to be a collection of half-timbered cottages surrounding a small pond. Sheep grazed contentedly on the green, and hens wandered at will, pecking at the ground.

'Here we are.' Walter came to a halt outside a pretty thatched cottage on the edge of the village. He led the donkey up the garden path and rapped on the door. 'Aunt Adeline, are you at home?'

The door opened and Judy knew instantly that this must be Rob's aunt. The genuine smile that lit Adeline's blue eyes, and the kindly expression on her weathered features were so reminiscent of Rob that Judy had to hold back tears of relief.

'Who have you brought to see me, Walter?'

'Her name is Judy – I can't remember the rest. I found her in the graveyard. I thought at first she was a ghost. She's hurt her ankle.'

'I really don't want to be any bother,' Judy said hastily.

'You're more than welcome, Judy. Let's get you

into the house, preferably without the donkey. You'll have to help me, Walter.'

Between them they managed to get Judy off the donkey and into the house. She cried out when she attempted to put her weight on the injured limb, but Adeline looped Judy's arm around her shoulders.

'It's all right, my dear. Lean on me.' She helped Judy into the parlour and set her down on a sofa upholstered in dark green velvet. 'Let's make you comfortable, and then I'll take a look at that ankle.'

'She's better than them medical men,' Walter said proudly. 'Everyone comes to Aunt Adeline when they're sick.'

'Get along with you, Walter.' Adeline took the sodden cloak and hung it over the back of a chair. 'I can look after Judy now, but if you go into the kitchen there are some cakes cooling on the table. You can have two, but I know exactly how many there are, so I'll know if you help yourself to more.'

Walter grinned and hurried off to claim his cakes. 'I might have to cut the laces on your boot,' Adeline said as she examined Judy's injured limb. 'The ankle is very swollen.'

'Do you think it's broken?' Judy asked anxiously.

'I'll know more when I get your boot off.' Adeline reached for a wooden sewing box and selected a pair of scissors, which she used to snip the laces. She eased the boot off and gently examined the ankle. 'I think it's just a bad sprain, but you must keep off it for a few days to give it a chance to heal.'

'My mother will be frantic with worry. I need to go home.'

'Where do you live, Judy?'

'Little Creek, Miss Dorning. I live in the Crooked Billet with Ma and my brother Nate.'

'I guessed who you were, my dear. Rob has told me so much about you that I recognised you from his description, and he wasn't exaggerating.'

Judy felt herself blushing. 'I could say the same of you, Miss Dorning. Rob speaks very fondly of you.'

'He's like a son to me.' Adeline eyed Judy curiously. 'But that doesn't explain why you arrived here in such a state.' She fingered the muddy hem on Judy's damp gown. 'I'll find you some dry clothes.'

'Thank you, but I really need to let my mother know that I'm safe and well.'

'You can't go anywhere with that ankle. I'll have a message sent to your family, and you're welcome to stay here until you're fit to travel.'

'But you don't understand. I have to go back to Little Creek. It concerns Rob and it's urgent.'

'You can tell me all about it later, my dear. I'll fetch you a cup of tea and maybe you could manage some porridge, or perhaps some bread and honey from my own beehive.'

Judy lay back, frustrated by the frailty of her own body, but hunger pangs reminded her that she needed food. 'Bread and honey sounds lovely. Thank you.'

'That's a good girl.' Adeline smiled benevolently. She left the room, returning moments later with a woollen robe, which she handed to Judy. 'Take off your wet things, and put this on.'

Left on her own, Judy changed out of her damp gown and wrapped the robe around her. It was soft and smelled of lavender, and she lay back against the cushions. She relaxed as the warmth seeped into her chilled body, and she tried to ignore the pain in her ankle by focusing her attention on her surroundings. The cosy room, with its comfortable, well-worn furniture, must have been Rob's childhood home. There was a window seat with a view over the small front garden and the village green beyond. Shelves on either side of the chimney breast were crammed with an assortment of books. In the place of honour, next to a brass clock on the mantelshelf, was a photograph of a young army officer, and he bore a striking resemblance to Rob. Judy rubbed her eyes and yawned. Maybe there was one respectable member of the notorious Dorning family. The scent from bowls filled with spring bulbs coming into flower wafted over Judy, and sunshine filtered through the small windowpanes. She fought against sleep – Rob must be warned that Jay was out to cause trouble.

She sat up as the door opened to admit Adeline.

'I have to get home urgently, Miss Dorning. Is there anyone who could take me back to Little Creek today?'

'I very much doubt it. The only people who have their own vehicles are those who live on outlying farms.' Adeline placed the tea tray on a stool beside the sofa. 'This is my very best china, Judy. I save it for special occasions.'

Judy sipped the tea. 'Thank you, Miss Dorning, but it is important that I let my family know where I am.'

'You're obviously in some kind of trouble, Judy. Have something to eat and then you can tell me all about it.'

Judy bit into the bread and honey and savoured the delicate sweetness. 'This is so delicious.'

'My bees feed on clover all summer. Honey has great healing properties, you know.'

'You don't understand, Miss Dorning. It's Rob who might be in trouble now. I must get word to him.'

'This must be something to do with that cursed place. I told Rob that no good would come from purchasing Creek Manor. That house was cursed from the moment it was built.'

'You do know that it was razed to the ground in a fire?'

'Rob told me last time he was here. He also told me that he was having trouble with his half-brother. I've never met the fellow, but if he's anything like the old squire, he's best avoided.'

'Jay Tattersall is the reason why I've ended up here, Miss Dorning. It's a long story.'

'My dear, I have all the time in the world to sit here and listen, but first perhaps you'd better write a note to your mother and I'll get Walter to take it to her, although it might cost me a few more cakes.'

Adeline took out a sheet of paper, pen and ink from a small writing desk in the corner of the room.

Later that evening, Judy and Adeline were seated by the fire in the parlour. Judy had regained her appetite, and enjoyed a supper of fish caught fresh that day by another member of the Dorning family, and potatoes that Adeline had grown and stored for use in the winter months. Walter had returned from Little Creek with a note from Hilda, saying that all was well now that they knew Judy was safe, and she was trying to arrange transport to bring her home. There was no mention of either Jay or Rob, which left Judy feeling even more anxious.

Adeline put her sewing down, giving Judy a sympathetic smile. 'Fretting won't make matters better. After everything that's happened to you in the last twenty-four hours, you need to rest and relax. There's nothing you can do tonight, so try not to worry.'

'I know you're right, but I believe Jay could be dangerous. He and Rob might be half-brothers, but they are totally different.'

'Rob is more like his mother,' Adeline said, sighing. 'Miriam was a sweet and beautiful girl, but she and I were Dornings. We were tarred with the same brush as the men in our family.'

'Why was that, Miss Dorning?'

'Adeline, please. Everyone in the county knew that our family had been involved in free trading for over a century, and the chances of Miriam or myself marrying out of our class were unlikely, to say the least. When the squire showed an interest in her the poor girl succumbed to his charm, even though we all warned her against the match.'

'But it didn't work out well.'

'No, it wasn't a happy union. Shortly after she conceived Rob, the squire was up to his old tricks. He couldn't stay faithful to one woman, or so it seemed. Then he met a wealthy heiress and married her, even though he was still legally wed to Miriam. I think the shock and the disgrace were largely to blame for my sister's early demise. She took sick and died, and I raised Rob like my own child.'

'You never married?'

'No, dear. Like I said, when you're a Dorning the family's reputation goes ahead of you.'

'I'm sorry.'

'Don't be. I like being on my own, but I worry about Rob. He's a good man, but he bears the tainted Dorning name, even though he's legally a Tattersall.'

'Perhaps the name Dorning is more acceptable to him than that of his father. The squire was hated locally, and Jay seems to have inherited his father's bad traits.'

'I kept Rob away from Creek Manor for as long as I could. I didn't want my boy corrupted by Esmond Tattersall. Heaven knows, Rob was disadvantaged enough by being born into the Dorning family, without adding his father's dreadful reputation to his name.'

'Do you see Rob often, Adeline?'

'He usually visits me regularly, but I haven't seen him for a week or two. He's very good to me,' Adeline said, smiling tenderly. 'He keeps me in comfort, and I don't have to worry about money.'

'But you live here all alone,' Judy said slowly. 'This is a tiny cottage.'

'It's my home, Judy. I don't wish to live in a grand house.'

Judy smiled. 'You might not have a choice. I have a feeling that Rob will insist that you move into his mansion when it's built.'

Adeline gave her a searching look. 'You don't seem very keen on Rob's plans for the new Creek Manor.'

'It's not that,' Judy said hastily. 'There was a plan to build a new hospital on the site, but it fell through when Rob outbid the would-be purchaser.'

'It sounds like a very ambitious plan, Judy.'

'It was. The doctor whose idea it was mismanaged the scheme, and he's landed himself in debt.'

'Have you talked this over with Rob?'

'Not really. He does know about Dr Godfrey, but it isn't his problem.'

'You might be surprised. He's very public-spirited, and I'm sure he would think a new hospital was an excellent idea. People in these parts rely on someone like me. I have a limited knowledge of traditional cures that I use to treat their ailments, but a modern hospital with fully trained medical staff would be wonderful.'

'I agree entirely,' Judy said earnestly. 'I spent only

one morning working as a ward maid at the London Hospital, but that was enough to make me wish that I could be a nurse, or even a doctor. Although I doubt if I'm clever enough for that.'

'Maybe you'll get your chance one day.' Adeline glanced at the clock on the mantelshelf. 'You look tired, Judy. Will you be all right sleeping on the sofa, or would you like to try to make it upstairs?'

Judy stifled a yawn. 'I'm quite comfortable here, thank you, Adeline.'

'I'll make you some cocoa, dear.' Adeline bustled into the kitchen.

Judy lay back against the cushions and closed her eyes, but she knew it would not be easy to forget the way Jay had behaved. He seemed to be obsessed with the inheritance that he had sold so carelessly when he needed the money. The desire to pass on the land and the title to his son had taken over his whole life, and it had become like a disease that was eating away his mind and body. Worse still, he had involved Rob, who was the innocent victim of his hatred.

Judy raised herself to a sitting position. She would go home tomorrow, even if she had to limp all the way to Little Creek. Rob needed to know that Jay was plotting against him.

'Here's your cocoa, Judy.' Adeline emerged from the kitchen. She placed the cup on the table she had moved close to the sofa. 'I hope you sleep well, dear. Things will look better in the morning. They always do.'

Chapter Twenty-Two

Despite her worries, Judy slept surprisingly well. She was awakened by the sound of someone rapping on the door and she raised herself on one elbow. She could hear voices, and she reached for the robe that Adeline had provided. She was about to rise from the couch when the door burst open and Molly rushed into the parlour.

'We've come to take you home, Judy.' Molly drew back the curtains. 'You look awful. Are you in a lot of pain? Miss Dorning told me briefly what happened to you, but I can't wait to hear the whole story.'

Judy sat up, the last strands of sleep clearing from her brain. As always her sister looked like a fashion plate, although Judy did not recognise the charming pale blue velvet outfit trimmed with fur or the matching hat, perched at an angle on Molly's golden curls.

'What are you doing here?' Judy demanded.

Molly pulled up the stool and sat down. 'Ma has been going mad with worry since you disappeared, and she insisted that we came to get you.'

'I thought you'd be back at Colneyhurst by now.'

'I had so much fun working at the Crooked Billet that I decided to stay on. I've had enough of caring for small children, and I enjoy meeting the customers at the inn.'

Judy pulled a face. 'You mean flirting with them, don't you?'

Molly fluttered her thick golden eyelashes. 'I realise now what I've been missing all these years. Maybe I wasn't cut out to be a nursemaid after all. I told Daisy yesterday afternoon, and she was very good about it. She even gave me this outfit because it doesn't fit her any more. Do you think it suits me?'

In spite of everything, Judy chuckled. Molly was irrepressible. She managed to turn every situation to suit herself, but she did it with such charm that her faults went unnoticed. 'You look lovely, as always.'

Molly's smile faded. 'Here am I, thinking of myself as usual, and all the time you were being held prisoner by Jay Tattersall. Why did he abduct you? Was it romantic? Does he want to marry you and make you his fourth wife, or would it be his fifth wife? I've lost count.'

'Certainly not! Jay is a dangerous man.'

'Surely not dangerous? Ma told me all about the

way he treated Daisy, but that doesn't make him a villain.'

'You don't understand. Jay intended to blackmail Rob into selling him the estate, using me as his hostage, but I ran away. I was lost and that's how I ended up here.' Judy brushed her tousled hair back from her forehead. 'I must speak to Rob as soon as possible.'

Molly frowned. 'Well, here's the thing. I talked it over with Jack, and—'

'You did what?' Judy stared at her in dismay. 'Are you mad? Of course he's on his brother's side. Anyway, I thought Jack was on board the *Lazy Jane* and about to set sail for Australia.'

'Don't shout at me, Judy.' Molly's baby-blue eyes filled with tears, and her lips pursed in a pout.

'Blame me, not Molly.' Jack strode into the room followed by Adeline.

'I tried to stop him,' Adeline said apologetically. 'He told me that he's Jay's brother, but I don't think he means you harm, Judy.'

'That's right.' Jack perched on the edge of Judy's bed. 'You know me well enough, Judy. I never meant to hurt you. The abduction was Jay's idea and I was totally against it, which is why I came ashore and went straight to the Crooked Billet. I had hoped to stop him before he did anything rash, but I arrived too late.'

'You didn't plan it with him?' Judy gave him a searching look. She knew Jack well enough to judge whether or not he was telling the truth.

He met her gaze with an apologetic smile. 'I should have warned you that Jay might do something stupid, but I had no idea that he would go so far. Believe me, Judy.'

'I do. But what happens now? Where is Jay?'

He shook his head. 'I don't know.'

'Didn't you put two and two together and come to the conclusion that his disappearance coincided with Judy's?' Adeline demanded crossly. 'What a silly pair you are, to be sure.'

'Of course I did, Miss Dorning.' Jack's smile would have melted ice and his tone was pure honey. Judy had seen it all before and she remained unimpressed. Jack was like a little boy who knew exactly how to handle an irate parent.

'I didn't.' Molly's eyes brimmed yet again. 'I couldn't imagine anyone doing such a wicked thing to my sister.'

Jack reached out to grasp Molly's hand, and the gesture was not lost on Judy. The expression on his face betrayed his feelings. Once upon a time he had looked at her in the same way and Judy experienced a brief pang of jealousy, but it went as quickly as it had come.

'Neither Molly nor your mother suspected anything,' Jack said firmly. 'But I know my brother, and I felt sure that he was the culprit, although I had no idea where he might have taken you.'

'Jay planned it all in an attempt to make Rob sell him the estate.' Judy managed a weak smile. 'He's obsessed with the idea of regaining the land and the title. He confessed that he'd paid someone to burn the old house down in order to buy the estate back cheaply.'

'The man must be deranged,' Adeline said, shaking her head. 'You'd best remain here, Judy. I'll look after you until your ankle is healed.'

'Begging your pardon, Miss Dorning,' Molly's voice shook with emotion, 'I think that's up to my sister. Daisy, I mean Mrs Walters, allowed us the use of her carriage, which is very comfortable, so that we could take Judy home.'

Adeline turned to Judy, eyebrows raised. 'Is that what you want?'

'I'm very grateful for your kindness, but I must go home.'

'Very well. I'll see if your clothes are dry. I hung them up in the kitchen overnight, so they should be aired by now.' Adeline retreated to the kitchen, closing the door behind her.

'I'm grateful to Daisy for allowing you to borrow her carriage,' Judy said with a wry smile. 'But is there anyone in Little Creek who doesn't know my whereabouts?'

'We did what we had to do, and Daisy won't breathe a word to anyone. She's been so kind to me.'

'What about Rob?' Judy asked anxiously. 'Has he even noticed that I'm not at home?'

'He was the first to realise that something was wrong,' Molly said hastily. 'He came into the taproom soon after I arrived, and he asked for you. I thought perhaps you were in your room, so I went upstairs to look. That's when we started searching outside, in case you'd fallen and hurt yourself. He discovered the upturned coal scuttle and there were signs that someone had been dragged across the muddy courtyard. He said he was going to look for you and he rode off. We haven't seen him since.'

'I really need to speak to him,' Judy said anxiously.

'Then I suggest we leave as soon as you're ready.' Jack made a move towards the door. 'Shall I tell the coachman we're leaving in ten minutes or so?'

'What do you say, Judy?' Molly asked urgently. 'Jack can carry you out to the carriage and we have a fur rug and a foot warmer, so you'll be quite comfortable. Mother will be so relieved to see you.'

'Of course I'll come with you. I doubt if Jay could do anything to harm Rob, but he really needs to be warned.'

Jack frowned. 'Don't underestimate my brother, Judy. I have a feeling that he's not beaten yet. I don't know what he's planning, but he won't give up easily.'

'Can't you persuade him to return to Australia without upsetting everyone even more than he has done?' Judy asked anxiously. 'Surely we don't need all this trouble? Jay shouldn't have sold the estate if he wanted to keep the title.'

'I think it goes deeper than just owning the estate,' Jack said slowly. 'Jay always knew he didn't fit in at home, and I don't think he could understand why

Pa was so harsh with him. According to Ma, the old squire was on his deathbed when he admitted that Jay was his son. The discovery that Rob Dorning is the true heir was the final insult.'

Judy shrugged. 'I'm afraid I have no pity for Jay. I think he suffers from a form of madness. You didn't see his face when he was threatening me. I was really scared.'

'And I can't forgive him for that,' Jack said earnestly. 'I was going to return to Australia with him, but only if you and I had come to an understanding, Judy. I've been worrying about you ever since I left without setting things straight.'

'I know, Jack. I think I've been doing exactly the same as you. We were childhood sweethearts but we've grown up, and now nothing is the same.'

'You understand. Thank God for that. I know I did wrong by you, but perhaps it was for the best that circumstances came between us.'

'Well, I don't understand.' Molly looked from one to the other. 'You two always did talk in riddles. You seemed to know what the other one was thinking.'

'That's no longer true,' Judy said with a wry smile. 'Jack will always be like a brother to me, but that's all.'

'It's hard to let go of a dream.' Jack turned to Molly, raising her hand to his lips. 'But that's all it was. I realise that now, and maybe I needed to go to the other side of the world to find out who I am, and what I want out of life.'

Judy could hear footsteps and she held up her hand. 'Adeline is coming. Please don't say anything about Rob that might upset her. She's been like a mother to him.'

Jack jumped to his feet and went to open the door for Adeline, who was carrying a heavy tray. She placed it on the table.

'You'll want something inside you before you leave for home.'

'Thank you, Miss Dorning.' Molly rose to her feet to hand round the cups of tea and slices of cake. 'You're very kind and I know Ma would want me to thank you for looking after Judy so well.'

'It was nothing. I'm sure your mother would have done the same for my Rob.' Adeline turned to Judy, raising an eyebrow. 'Do you think you're well enough to travel?'

'My ankle only hurts if I try to put weight on it.'

'Well, if you're sure, dear. Although I think you ought to stay here for another day or two in order to build up your strength.'

'We'll take care of her, Miss Dorning,' Molly said with a sweet smile. 'You've been so kind. I can't thank you enough.'

When Judy arrived home she was met by her mother, who was furious when she learned the full extent of Judy's suffering at Jay's hands.

'You might have died from lung fever or been set upon by gypsies,' she said angrily. 'You're lucky that all you suffered is a sprained ankle, but you should be resting it.' She poured tea into a cup and handed it to Judy. 'You are a stubborn girl.'

Judy smiled. 'I wonder where I get that from, Ma.'

'Don't be cheeky. Just because you've had a bad experience doesn't give you the right to talk back to your mother.' Hilda's words were stern, but her eyes were twinkling. 'It's good to have you home, dear, but if Jay Tattersall comes near this pub I won't be held responsible for my actions.'

'I don't think he will, Ma. Jack thinks now that Jay's gone to London to find a lawyer who will take his case. He intends to fight Rob through the courts for a share in the estate, although I doubt if he stands a chance of success. I certainly hope not.'

'If by some mischance he should succeed he won't find himself very popular in Little Creek. The people here have taken Rob to their hearts, but Jay is too much like his late father for anyone to trust him.'

'Jack isn't like him, thank goodness.' Judy sipped her tea, eyeing her mother over the rim of the cup. 'Molly seems to be very taken with him, and he with her.'

'I always thought that you and Jack would make a match of it.' Hilda punched the bread dough she was kneading. 'It seems a bit sudden to me, but then I suppose they've known each other for most of their lives.'

'Sometimes it happens like that, Ma.'

'Well, if you're not upset by his change of heart,

who am I to say anything? Molly will do as she pleases anyway.'

'She could do a lot worse than Jack. I'm still very fond of him, but we were never meant to be together. I realise that now.'

Molly chose that moment to waltz into the kitchen. She came to a halt, looking from one to the other. 'Have I missed something? Were you talking about me?'

'I was telling your sister that she should have gone to bed and rested that injured ankle,' Hilda said firmly. 'But then neither of you young ladies pays any attention to me now. I don't know why I waste my breath.'

Judy and Molly exchanged amused glances. 'Of course we pay heed to what you say, Ma.'

'Yes, we do,' Molly said, nodding. 'Anyway, I came to see if the soup is ready. Eli is hungry. He says his wife hasn't given him his midday meal because he stayed here late last evening and went home tipsy. He's in disgrace.'

Hilda wiped her hands on her apron. 'I don't blame her for being angry. Eli spends all his money on ale, when he should be taking it home for his family.' She bustled over to the range and ladled soup into a bowl. 'Here, Molly. Give him this, although he doesn't deserve it.'

Molly cut a slice of bread from a loaf just taken from the oven and buttered it lavishly.

'Poor old Eli, he's always in trouble with his wife.

I don't blame him for coming here and enjoying a pint or two.'

Hilda resumed her attack on the dough. 'You'd say differently if you were married to him.'

'Jack would never behave like that,' Molly said complacently.

'You've only just got to know him again, girl.' Hilda shook her head. 'He's a charmer like his brother. Don't let him gammon you.'

'Ma!' Molly said, rolling her eyes. 'I've had soft soap from the male servants at the Hall ever since I went there. I'm not likely to fall for anything like that from Jack.' She flounced off with the food on a tray.

'She would never be told.' Hilda shrugged. 'I just hope that Jack isn't simply amusing himself with her. Molly thinks she knows it all, but she's a child really.'

'Not any more,' Judy said, chuckling. 'I think my little sister knows exactly what she's doing, Ma. Molly is nobody's fool, and Jack is good at heart. I love him like a brother.'

The sound of footsteps made Judy turn her head and Nate rushed into the kitchen. He glanced at Judy and grinned. 'You gave us all a fright, Judy. I'm glad you're back.'

'Did you want something, dear?' Hilda slapped the bread dough into a baking tin.

Nate snatched a hot roll from the cooling rack. 'I'll be back for my soup when I've seen to Rob's horse. He's just arrived.' With a cheery wave he left the kitchen, slamming the back door behind him.

'Rob was out all night looking for you, Judy. We were all frantic with worry.' Hilda wiped her hands on her apron. 'You'll want to speak to him in private. Why don't you go into the parlour and sit by the fire? I'll send Rob in to see you. If that's what you want, of course.'

'Yes, Ma. I really do need to talk to him.' Judy raised herself slowly from the chair and made her way to the parlour, each step an effort. She had just settled herself in a chair when Rob rushed into the room.

'Judy, how are you?' He shed his hat and riding cape as he crossed the room to kneel beside her. 'You look pale. Are you feeling all right?'

She smiled. 'I'm better for seeing you.'

'I'm so sorry you were involved in this, Judy. If Jay's hurt you he'll answer to me.'

'He tried to scare me, but I was more frightened than hurt.'

'He'll answer for that, Judy, I promise.'

She shook her head. 'Don't have anything to do with him. Let him go back to Australia where he belongs.'

'I wish I was so forgiving, but I'm not.' Rob rose to his feet. 'I could kill him at this moment.'

'Don't do that – you'll end up in prison.' She met his angry gaze with a smile. 'Your aunt is wonderful, Rob. I turned up on her doorstep and she took me in and treated me like a daughter.'

'I don't know where I would be if she hadn't taken me in as a child.'

'The cottage felt like a happy home.' Judy hesitated. She could see that he was still tense and there was no point in going over the same subject again and again. 'How is the building going on? Is there much progress?'

'It's coming along splendidly. The cellars weren't touched by the fire, so it's been easy to lay the foundations for the main part of the building, and that will be completed first. I want to move in as soon as possible, and then it will be time to start on the west wing. I've got fifty able men working long hours to make sure it happens.'

'I can't wait to see it,' Judy said wistfully. 'I hate being laid up like an invalid.'

'It's a lovely day, although it's a bit chilly. If you wrap up warm I could take you in my chaise, and you could see the progress for yourself.' He gave her a searching look. 'Unless you're too tired after your ordeal.'

'I've got a sprained ankle, that's all. I wish everyone would stop treating me as if I were an invalid.'

'I'll check with Hilda first, of course. She might have other ideas, but I think the fresh air will do you good.'

'So do I,' Judy said eagerly.

'If your mother doesn't object I'll ask Nate to bring the chaise round to the front.' Rob hesitated in the doorway. 'I can't tell you how relieved I am to see you relatively unhurt, Judy. I was out of my mind with worry.' He left the room abruptly.

Judy's heart was pounding as she struggled to her feet, but an agonising spasm in her ankle wiped all thoughts from her mind and she uttered a yelp of pain just as Molly appeared in the doorway.

'What are you doing, Judy? You're supposed to be resting.'

'Rob is going to take me to Creek Manor to see the foundations for the new house.'

'Is that wise? Ma won't like it.'

'I don't care. I really want to go. Will you fetch my cape, bonnet and gloves from my room, please?'

Molly pursed her lips. 'I don't know, Judy. What if you catch a chill?'

'I won't. Please get my things.'

'All right, but I'm not taking the blame if you die of lung fever.' Molly tossed her head and flounced out of the room.

It was a pleasant drive to Creek Manor and Judy's spirits rose. Rob seemed relaxed and they chatted about mundane things, mostly to do with his plans for the new house. When they approached the entrance to the estate Judy was quick to notice that the gatehouse seemed to be occupied. The front garden had been tended and a column of smoke curled up from the chimney. The tall wrought-iron gates had been newly painted, but they had been left open and

Rob drove up the avenue, reining in the horse on the carriage sweep. Even though there was great deal of activity at the site, Judy was shocked to see the huge gap where once a fine mansion had stood.

Rob gave her a sideways glance. 'You haven't been here since the fire?'

She shook her head. 'No. There seemed little point. All my memories of living here had quite literally gone up in smoke. It would have broken my heart.'

'You really mean that, don't you?'

'Yes, I do. I was only nine years old when Daisy brought me and my family to Little Creek, and I thought that the old house was a palace. It really was when compared to the hovel we occupied in Green Dragon Yard. I was overwhelmed at first, but Cook was kind to me and so were the rest of the servants. I'd say I had a very happy childhood, especially when I was allowed to study with Jack. Then everything changed and not for the good.'

'But you survived and took over the Crooked Billet, building it into a thriving business. That takes courage, Judy.'

'It was dire necessity, Rob. Courage didn't come into it.' She turned her head to look at him. 'You could have claimed your inheritance when the old squire died. Why didn't you come forward then?'

'My mother passed away when I was very young, and it wasn't until I reached sixteen that Aunt Adeline told me the truth about my father. Until that time I thought I was a Dorning, and I was

411

content to leave it that way. Then I inherited a fortune from a distant relative, so I didn't need the money.'

'What changed your mind?' Judy asked gently.

'It was only when I realised that Jay would have been as bad a master and landlord as our father that I knew I had to shoulder my responsibilities. It was then that I set about obtaining the documents to back up my claim.'

'The old house might still be standing if you'd stepped in sooner,' Judy said thoughtfully. 'Things would have been so different.'

'Maybe the curse of Creek Manor went up in flames.' Rob smiled ruefully. 'This is a fresh start, Judy. A whole new chapter in the history of the estate.'

'Will you live here when the house is built?'

'Of course, and I have a plan for the estate that I think you will like.'

'Really? What is it?'

'Ah! That would be telling. It's to be a surprise.'

Chapter Twenty-Three

Rob's enthusiastic description of his future home made Judy smile, but she could not share his passion for the project. Despite being asked for her opinion on various aspects of the formal rooms, she felt oddly deflated. After all, the new Creek Manor had nothing to do with her. It was not as if she and her family were going to be living there as they had in the old days. The former manor house had been her home for more than half her life, and now it was gone.

'Of course, it's difficult to imagine how it will look when the walls go up,' Rob said guardedly. 'But I'm thinking of hiring more workmen in order to get the main wing erected before the end of the summer.'

'I'm sure it will be wonderful.' Judy tried to sound enthusiastic.

Rob gave her a sideways glance. 'I have something that might be of more interest to you.' He flicked the reins and urged the horse to a walk, heading towards the stables.

'Where are we going?'

'Wait and see.' He gave her a mischievous smile. He drew the horse to a halt outside the tack room, where he alighted and lifted Judy to the ground. 'Lean on me. It isn't far to walk.'

He led her into the tack room, which had been turned into an office for the surveyor and the site manager. Plans of the new house were pinned to the wall and a draughtsman's table had been set up in the middle of the room.

'It all looks very impressive,' Judy said dutifully.

Rob pulled up a chair. 'Sit down and I'll show you something that you might find more interesting. Your mother's cottage was burned down by Faulkner. I plan to replace it with this.' He opened a large portfolio and held up the contents for her to see.

Judy gazed at the architect's drawing of the prettiest house she had ever seen. 'It's beautiful, but this is a grand house. We lived in a small cottage.'

'I'm glad you approve.' He showed her the plans for the ground floor. 'You see, there will be a square entrance hall with a staircase rising in an elegant curve to the first floor. There are two reception rooms with elegant fireplaces and large windows to give the maximum amount of light. There's a smaller parlour and a large kitchen with a cast-iron range, and a sink complete with a water pump.'

Judy's eyes widened. 'How Ma would love that.

Just think, she'd never have to go outside in the cold and dark to fetch water. How wonderful.'

Rob laughed. 'I didn't think I ever see anyone excited about a sink with a pump.'

'Perhaps you've never had to traipse through rain and snow to fetch water, Rob Dorning, but I have and so has Ma. I can tell you, this would be luxury.'

Rob pointed to the plan for the first floor. 'There are four bedrooms on this floor,' Rob said proudly. 'And three attic room for servants, or,' he added, chuckling, 'as a nursery.'

Judy studied the plan, frowning. 'What does that mean?'

'It's what they call a water closet. It's an indoor privy or lavatory. All the best homes have them nowadays, and next to it is the bathroom.'

Judy stared at him in amazement. 'This house has special rooms for the privy and the tin bath?'

'I can't promise that there will be running water, although that's my plan eventually. But one day all homes will have such amazing facilities.'

'How modern and very clever. But I'll believe it when I see it.'

Rob laughed and their hands touched as he went to fold up the plans. Judy withdrew hers quickly, suddenly conscious of his nearness, and she moved away. 'Thank you for showing this to me. It looks wonderful.'

'I wanted you to share the excitement I feel for

this project, Judy. Unfortunately I have to go to London on business tomorrow, which will take me away for a while.'

'Has it to do with Jay?'

'No. There's nothing he can do other than to make a nuisance of himself, and I think he might have realised that by now. He might be my half-brother, but I'm hoping he'll go back to Australia, and that will the last we'll hear from him.'

'I do hope so,' Judy said fervently.

Rob proffered his arm. 'I think it's time I took you home. You've probably had enough for one day, but there is one more place I want to show you, if your ankle isn't too painful.'

'I'm enjoying myself so much I'd almost forgotten about it,' Judy said truthfully.

'Sharing this with you makes the whole project seem even more worthwhile.' Rob tucked her hand in the crook of his arm and they made their way slowly to the chaise. He lifted her onto the seat and climbed up beside her.

'Where are we going now?' Judy asked as he urged the horse to a brisk walk.

'The gatekeeper's cottage. I've had it redecorated and modernised, but I have no idea at all when it comes to furnishings and curtains and suchlike. I need your help, Judy.'

'In what way?'

'I've seen what you did to the old inn, and I doubt if you had two pennies to rub together.'

She laughed. 'You're right. We had other people's cast-offs, but we managed.'

'This time you can spend what you like, within reason. I'd like it to be furnished comfortably but with style – just the sort of place where I might take my bride, if I were to be married.'

'You're to be wed?'

'Yes, one day, when the time is right.'

She shot him a sideways glance. 'You proposed to me once, do you remember?'

'How could I forget? You and I almost shared a room at the Charing Cross Hotel.'

'So you do remember, although of course it was said in jest.'

'Perhaps, but it wouldn't have been practical then.' He flicked the reins. 'Trot on.'

Judy studied his profile as he concentrated on guiding the horse towards the gatehouse. His high forehead, straight nose and firm jaw marked him out as a determined man; someone who would not allow anything to get in his way when he had set his mind on something – but what about his heart? She was still mulling this question over when they arrived at the gatehouse.

'I thought that someone was living here,' Judy said as Rob ushered her into the hallway.

'No, I've had fires lit every day to make sure the place is free from damp.' Rob opened the door to his right. 'This is the parlour. You can see it's quite small, so the furniture needs to be commensurate with its size. The same goes for the other rooms.'

Judy leaned on his arm as they entered the kitchen, which was larger. Upstairs there were two reasonable size bedrooms and one not much larger than a boxroom.

'What do you think?' Rob asked when they returned to the kitchen.

'Why are you going to all this trouble for a house that you will probably never set foot in?'

'I know the value of home. Why shouldn't a gatekeeper have as much comfort as the lord of the manor? I'll expect the man and his wife to be on duty whenever they're needed, so the least I can do is to provide good accommodation for them.'

Judy had a sudden vision of Adeline Dorning's cosy parlour and she nodded. 'You're right.'

'So you'll do it?'

'Of course I will. What woman could resist the opportunity to spend someone else's money? But seriously, Rob, I'll make it really nice, but I won't bankrupt you.'

'I trust you implicitly. Just think about it as if you were furnishing your own home.'

She smiled. 'I don't know whether that will ever happen, but I will, of course.'

'You're looking a bit pale. I'm afraid I've kept you out too long. Have you seen enough?'

Judy nodded. 'Yes, I think so, and I can always ride over if I need to take any measurements. I suppose you want me to include curtains and carpets as well.'

'You see why I need your expert touch. I had completely forgotten things like that. I'll take you home, but I've just remembered I need to see the site manager, McArthur, before I go. Do you mind a quick detour?'

'Of course not. I'll sit in the chaise while you speak to him.'

McArthur was not at the building site, but one of the workmen said he had seen the manager walking back to the stables. They drove past him, but McArthur was deep in conversation with some of the workmen and Rob agreed to wait for him outside the tack room.

Judy had said little during the short drive. As he drew the horse to a halt Rob turned to her with a quizzical smile. 'A penny for them?'

'I was thinking that I know so little about you. What did you do before your relative left you a fortune? How did you make your living?'

'Didn't my aunt tell you? She usually regales anyone who will listen with stories about my heroic past, all from her vivid imagination, of course.'

'So what did you do? You must be a bit older than Jay, although you look younger.'

'Thank you. I thought you might see me as an old man.'

'Of course not. How old are you?'

'A straight question – I'm thirty-five, nearly thirty-six. A great deal older than you.'

'I'm twenty, nearly twenty-one. Age doesn't count if you get on well with someone, but you still haven't answered my question, Rob. How did you earn a living?'

'It may surprise you to learn that I studied medicine, and when I qualified I joined the army medical service. I spent six years in India and I left the service two years ago when I received my inheritance. Since then I've been trying to decide what to do with the rest of my life.'

'You're a doctor?' Judy stared at him in amazement. 'How could you give that up when you could do so much good in the world?'

'I've never been in general practice, and I've only worked in army hospitals.'

'But you outbid Dr Godfrey and his associates. Did you know they intended to build a large hospital in place of the old manor house?'

'Yes, I knew, but the estate meant more to me at the time, and I suppose I wanted to find my place in the world.'

'So now you know who you are, why don't you use your father's name?'

'To be honest I haven't given it much thought, although I think it might hurt my aunt if I were to change my surname now.'

'But you're happy to take on the estate in spite of the fact that you're ashamed of being a Tattersall.'

'I'm ashamed of the way that man treated my mother,' Rob said slowly. 'But the Dornings are equally notorious. Respect has to be earned, and I'm prepared to work hard to prove myself worthy of the position I now hold, and perhaps to redress some of the wrongs my father and Jay have done to the village.'

'But you gave up your career in medicine to become lord of the manor. That seems a terrible waste of your abilities.'

'I'm a man, not a saint. I'm sorry if I disappoint you.'

She turned her head away. 'I've no right to criticise you. Forget what I said.'

'There's McArthur now.' Rob leaped to the ground. 'I'll only be a few minutes. Are you sure you don't mind waiting?'

'No, I'll be quite all right.'

'Thank you. You're a woman in a million.' Rob strode off to join McArthur in the tack room.

'Judy.' The sound of her younger brother's voice made Judy turn her head and she saw Pip racing across the cobbled yard. He held the horse's reins, grinning up at Judy. 'Are you better? Nate said you was half dead when you came home, but you look fine to me. Trust him to exaggerate.'

'I've sprained my ankle, but otherwise I'm perfectly well.' Judy leaned closer, lowering her voice. 'What are you doing here? Why aren't you at Colneyhurst?'

'Rob's given me a job. I'm the head groom, at

least that's what I am until the new house is completed.'

'I thought you were happy at Colneyhurst, Pip.'

'I was, but it's not the same without Nate. Anyway, Rob came to see me and explained that the stables needed someone to look after the horses while the workmen are here, so I jumped at the chance to come home.'

'But it isn't our home now.'

'It will be. Don't tell me you wouldn't love to come back to Creek Manor, and Ma and Nate, too. Maybe not Molly because she's sweet on Jack Fox, or perhaps I shouldn't tell you that?' Pip coloured up and looked away, biting his lip.

'Jack and I are just friends, and if Molly is happy with him then that's wonderful, but why did you think we'll return here?'

'You'll marry Rob and be mistress of Creek Manor.'

'Who told you that?' Judy demanded angrily.

Pip dropped his gaze, staring down at his booted feet. 'I dunno, Judy. Anyone can see that he likes you.'

'And I like him, but that doesn't make a romance. I hope you haven't mentioned this to Ma or Nate.'

He shuffled his feet. 'It was Nate who first mentioned it.'

'I'll have a few words to say to our brother when I get home.' Judy glanced over his shoulder. 'Don't say anything else. Rob's coming back.'

He came towards them with an apologetic smile. 'I'm so sorry, Judy. McArthur has come up with a problem. I need to stay and sort it out.'

'Of course you must. I don't mind waiting.'

'I wouldn't hear of it. Pip will drive you home,' Rob said hastily. 'I'll make it up to you, I promise.' He turned to Pip. 'See that your sister gets home safely, and come straight back.'

Pip tipped his cap. 'Yes, sir.' He climbed onto the driver's seat. 'Has Ma made cheese and onion pie today, Judy?'

She smiled. 'As a matter of fact I think she did. It smelled delicious.'

'Walk on.' Pip flicked the reins. 'That's one thing I miss here. Ma's cooking. It would be good if you did decide to move back to the manor house when it's ready.'

'It's a long way off,' Judy said evasively. 'Never mind me. Tell me about yourself. I haven't seen you for ages.' She settled back against the squabs, resisting the temptation to look over her shoulder; she was certain that Rob was watching them until they were out of sight. She listened to her brother's chatter all the way home, only hearing half of what he had to say. Her ankle ached and she closed her eyes, allowing Pip to ramble on until they arrived back at the Crooked Billet.

Molly took one look at Judy as Pip helped her into the taproom, and she shook her head. 'Go and sit down by the fire in the parlour, Judy. You look awful.'

Judy managed a weak smile. 'Thank you for those words of encouragement, Molly.'

'Well, you do.' Molly glared at Pip. 'Why did you bring her home? Where's Rob?'

'Don't blame me. I just follow orders.' Pip sniffed the air. 'Cheese and onion pie. I hoped it was on the menu. Come on, Judy. Let's get you settled.'

'I can walk, Pip. I'm just a bit tired.' Judy acknowledged Eli with a nod and a smile as she limped past his table, and she made her way to the parlour, where she slumped down on a chair by the fire. She had hoped for a few minutes on her own but Molly burst into the room.

'Well? Did he propose?'

'Don't be silly. He just took me out for a breath of fresh air.'

Molly raised her eyebrows. 'Really? If you think that you're an innocent, Judy Begg. It's been obvious from the start that Rob Dorning only has eyes for you. How can you be so stupid?'

'I knew he liked me, and I like him.'

'So he did propose?'

'No, he didn't.'

'The silly fool.' Molly rolled her eyes. 'My Jack could teach him a thing or two about romance.' She clapped her hands to her mouth. 'I'm sorry, dear. That was thoughtless of me.'

'As I've told you before, Molly, I'm very fond of Jack, but not in a romantic way.'

'So how do you feel about Rob?'

'I really don't want to talk about it now. My ankle is aching and all I want is peace and quiet.'

'I have to get back to the bar, but you need to have a long think, Judy. Rob is the best catch in the county, and you'd be a fool to turn him down if he ever makes you an offer.' She left the room but poked her head round the door. 'And he loves you. If you can't see that you must be stupid.'

Later that day Rob called in at the pub, and Molly showed him into the parlour.

'I came to see how you are,' Rob said anxiously. 'Molly said you're in pain. I shouldn't have kept you out so long, Judy. I'm sorry.'

'Molly exaggerates. I'm fine now. I just need to rest the ankle.'

'I've come to collect my things. As I told you, I have urgent business in London and I might be away for some time.'

'You will be careful, won't you? I know you said that Jay can't do anything, but I don't trust him.'

Rob took her hand in his. 'You mustn't worry. Everyone here is on the alert. Should he show his face again he'll find himself in trouble with the police.'

'I'm not worried for myself,' Judy said impatiently. 'It's you who might suffer at his hands.'

'Do you care what happens to me?'

'Of course I do. How can you ask a question like that?'

Before Rob could answer Jack put his head round the door. 'Rob, you'll miss the train if you don't come right away. We're cutting it fine as it is.'

Rob straightened up. 'We'll continue this conversation when I return, Judy.'

'Hurry up. The chaise is outside and we'll only make it if you come now.'

'All right, Jack. I'm coming.' Rob hesitated in the doorway. 'I've left funds for furnishing the gatehouse with McArthur.'

'Just go, Rob. I'll see to everything.' Judy was not sure if she wanted to laugh or cry. 'Please go now.'

'Take good care of yourself, Judy.'

'You let him go!' Molly rushed into the room and stood arms akimbo. 'What's the matter with you, Judy? Did your experience with Jay turn your brain?'

'What are you talking about?' Judy asked wearily. 'Rob has business in London.'

'You should have let him know how you feel.'

'You don't know anything about it.'

'I'm not the silly flibbertigibbet you think I am. I know that you're pining for Rob and he's in love with you. I could bang your silly heads together.'

'Go away, Molly. You really are giving me a headache.'

'Thank goodness I have Jack. At least he's a sane

person.' Molly turned on her heel and swept out of the parlour.

Judy rose somewhat shakily to her feet and she went to look out of the window. Outside in the pale buttery sunshine she was just in time to see Rob tossing his valise into the chaise. He climbed nimbly onto the driver's seat and sat next to Jack, who drove away cracking the whip above the horse's head. Judy sank down on the nearest seat. What would she do if he did not return? She would have nobody to blame other than herself. But she had faced heartbreak when Jack left without a word. She had survived, although somehow it was different this time. Her ankle would heal, but what about her heart? Maybe the curse of Creek Manor lived on.

Chapter Twenty-Four

On a bright spring morning Judy asked Nate to saddle up Major, and she set off for Colneyhurst Hall. The air was crystal clear, the sky was cerulean blue and the saltings shimmered in the sunlight. Birds sang in the trees and clumps of primroses created pools of colour beneath the hedgerows. Catkins swayed and danced in the gentle breeze and the whole world seemed to be starting afresh. Major's age was beginning to tell and although he was willing enough, he plodded along like an elderly gentleman, but Judy was quite happy to let him have his head. It was a relief to be away from the hustle and bustle of the inn, where trade was now brisk, thanks to the dozens of workmen from Creek Manor who came to enjoy Hilda's excellent food and a pint or two of good ale.

When Judy finally arrived at Colneyhurst she was

shown into the drawing room where Daisy greeted her with a delighted smile. 'You'll forgive me for not rising to greet you, Judy, but as you can see I'm a little top-heavy.'

Judy hurried to her side and kissed her on the cheek. 'You look beautiful, as always. Are you keeping well?'

'Yes, I've never felt better. I was quite unwell all the time I was carrying the boys, so I'm convinced that this child will be a girl and I'll have a daughter at last. Ring the bell, there's a dear, and we'll have some refreshments.'

Judy tugged at the bell pull and went to sit in an armchair by the fire. 'I hope that Molly didn't cause you any bother by leaving so suddenly.'

'No, of course not. She was a good nursery maid but I'm sure she's happier being at home with you, and I gather she's engaged to Jack. That's a turn of events I wasn't expecting. Are you all right with it?'

'I'm very happy for them. They're well suited and it would never have worked with Jack and myself.'

'But there's something troubling you.' Daisy gave her a searching look. 'Is there anything I can do to help?'

'Yes, or rather, no. I don't know, Daisy. I'm confused.'

Daisy smiled. 'Love takes one like that. I suppose it must be Rob Dorning who's causing you all this bother.'

'Why do you say that?'

'I've lived in Little Creek for long enough not to answer that question. You know how news gets around, especially when there's a juicy piece of gossip to spread. I heard that he took you to see the building work, and that you spent some time in the gatehouse.'

'Rob asked me to furnish it for him.'

'There you are then,' Daisy said smugly. 'That's exactly how Marius managed to persuade me that he was serious. Men aren't very subtle, Judy. They find it hard to express their innermost feelings and we're supposed to read the signs, although sometimes it's almost impossible.' Daisy put her head on one side. 'But surely that's not what brought you here today, is it? What's bothering you, Judy?'

'Rob told me a little of his past. Did you know that he qualified as a doctor and he was in the army medical service?'

'Good heavens! No, I didn't know that.'

'He served six years in India, although he's never worked in general practice.'

Daisy put her head on one side, studying Judy's face. 'Is there a point to this? He obviously left the service, so maybe medicine wasn't for him after all, nor army life.'

'No, it's not that.'

'Then what's troubling you, Judy? I've only met Rob a couple of times but he seems like an excellent fellow.'

'He knew that Dr Godfrey was trying to buy

Creek Manor in order to build a fine new hospital, but Rob was determined to have the estate for himself.' Judy stared down at her hands clasped tightly on her lap. Why it mattered so deeply was beyond her, but it still made her feel angry.

'Marius knows the story better than I do, but it seems that Rob should have inherited the estate in the first place, and he's simply buying back what's rightfully his. Jay must be furious.'

'He is, and he's caused no end of trouble. I suppose you know that he tried to blackmail Rob into selling by abducting me.'

'Yes, my dear. I'm so sorry. Jay can be so charming, as I know to my cost. On the other hand, he has a despicable side to his character, which I didn't see until after we'd been married for some months.'

'I'm afraid there's something of the old squire in both brothers.'

'So that's the problem.' Daisy shook her head, smiling. 'You're afraid that Rob will turn out like his father.'

'I suppose I am. I think Rob wanted the estate at any cost. He didn't care that Dr Godfrey wanted to do something that would benefit everyone round here.'

'Are you upset because Ben Godfrey failed to get his way, or is it because Rob didn't tell you everything from the start?'

Judy looked up, staring at Daisy in surprise. 'You think I'm being difficult?'

'No, Judy. But no one is perfect. I think you need to remember that Ben Godfrey might have started out with high ideals, but he misused the money entrusted to him by the people he had persuaded to back his scheme. That was not entirely altruistic, and Rob was only taking back what was rightfully his. I don't think that makes him the villain of the piece.'

'Ben was sorry for mishandling the finances, Daisy. He's working for nothing in the East End to help the poor and needy.'

Daisy raised a delicate eyebrow. 'That's all very fine, but shouldn't he be paying back the people he swindled out of their money? It's all very well acting like a hero, but there are honest people whom he's cheated.'

'I suppose so. I hadn't thought about it like that.'

'Similarly, why should Rob Dorning give up what was his birthright in order to satisfy the whim of others? Ben could have chosen another site for his hospital, had he been in earnest.'

'You think I'm being too hard on Rob?'

'I didn't say that, Judy. But perhaps you could try to look at it from his point of view. His family are a bad lot on both sides, or so it seems. Maybe he feels he needs to atone by taking over the estate and running it well. Don't forget he owns half the cottages in the village – the ones that both you and I spent so much time attempting to bring up to a high standard.'

'I might have misjudged him. Perhaps I was a little carried away by Dr Godfrey's plans.'

Daisy looked up at the sound of someone knocking on the door. 'Come in.' She smiled and acknowledged the young housemaid. 'Tea for two, please, Florrie. And cake. I have a sudden craving for Cook's ginger cake, if my sons haven't eaten it all.'

'Yes'm.' Florrie grinned and hurried from the room.

'My daughter likes sweet things,' Daisy said, patting her rounded belly. 'I was more into savoury food with each of the boys, although I did once eat a whole trifle when I was expecting Timothy.' She sat back against the satin cushions. 'Give Rob a chance, Judy. That's all I'm saying, and don't put Ben Godfrey on a pedestal.'

'I'm afraid I was offhand with Rob. I owe him an apology and I'll tell him so, when I see him again – if he decides to come back. I've made a mess of things, Daisy.'

'If he loves you nothing will stop him from returning, and you obviously care a great deal more for him than you realise or you wouldn't be fretting now.' Daisy poured the tea and handed a cup to Judy. 'Now drink your tea and keep me company in having a slice of ginger cake. Tea and cake always makes things look better.'

Judy's conversation with Daisy had given her plenty to think about as she rode home. Daisy was the one person with whom she had something in common: they had both loved a Tattersall. It had not worked out for Daisy, but now Judy was seeing both Rob and Ben Godfrey in a different light. She had hero-worshipped Dr Godfrey since they first met at the London Hospital, and she had been unwilling to admit that her idol could have done anything wrong. Now it was up to her to make amends and she knew exactly what she must do. She encouraged Major to walk a little faster, and she turned his head in the direction of the village, where she paid the ferryman to take her across the water to the Creek Manor estate.

Pip was delighted to see her. 'You're in luck, Judy. Mr McArthur is in the tack room – I mean he's in his office. He trusts me to do his errands, so I know exactly what's going on.'

Judy smiled indulgently. It was good to see her younger brother so involved and enthusiastic about his job. 'That is fortunate. I was afraid I'd have difficulty finding him.'

'Go and knock on the door,' Pip said importantly. 'He's not a bad chap, just so long as you keep on the right side of him.'

'Thank you. I'll bear that in mind.' Judy handed the reins to her brother and she set off across the cobbled yard. She knocked and entered without waiting for his response. 'Good morning, Mr McArthur.' She held out her hand. 'I'm Judy Begg, we met a few days ago.'

He rose hastily to his feet. When she had seen him in the distance she had been impressed by his smart clothes and his tall stature, but without the benefit of his top hat he seemed to be much smaller, and a shiny bald pate made him look like a middle-aged baby. She stifled a sudden urge to giggle.

'What can I do for you, Miss Begg?'

'Mr Dorning asked me to choose the furnishings for the gatehouse, and I believe you hold the funds, sir.'

His stern expression relaxed into an attempt at a smile. 'Ah, yes. He did mention it.'

'Do you know when he'll return?'

'No, miss, I'm afraid I don't, although I'm not expecting him soon. I believe he had business in London that might take some time.'

'Then I'd better get started. May I have the key so that I can have a better idea of what's needed?'

'Of course, miss. Would you like me to accompany you?'

'I grew up in the old manor house, Mr McArthur. There isn't an inch of the estate that I don't know, but thank you anyway.' Judy waited while he fished around in a drawer to find the right keys.

'One for the front door and one for the back door.'

'Thank you. By the way, how shall I manage when it comes to payment? Shall I set up an account at the shops in question?'

'That would be the best way. Mr Dorning didn't

put a limit on spending, so I leave it to your good judgement.'

Judy smiled. 'Thank you, Mr McArthur. I'll bear that in mind.'

Judy set about the task methodically. Using a yard-stick borrowed from the office, she noted down the dimensions of the rooms in a notebook that McArthur had given her. She spent so much time working from room to room that everything else went out of her mind, and it was late afternoon by the time she arrived back at the Crooked Billet.

Molly and Hilda exchanged meaningful glances when Judy told them where she had been and what she was doing at Creek Manor, but she ignored their none-too-subtle attempts to make her admit that her feelings for Rob had undergone any change. She spent the evening drawing diagrams of each room and writing lists of what was needed to obtain a modicum of comfort. Hilda brought her a cup of cocoa and said 'Good night', but Judy was immersed in her task and by the time she raised the cup to her lips, the cocoa was cold.

Molly looked in on her way to bed. 'You're not still doing that, are you?'

'I've just about done all I can for this evening. Is the bar closed?'

'Yes, it is, and Jack has already gone to his room. It's past midnight.'

Judy rubbed her eyes and yawned. 'I'm going to

bed, but tomorrow I'm going to get the train to Colchester, and I intend to fill the gatehouse with furniture that he'll love.'

'I think you ought to choose things that you love, and he will love them too.'

'How do you know that?' Judy demanded, stifling a yawn.

'Trust me, Judy. I think I know a bit more about men than you do. If it comes to that, I have excellent taste. Daisy taught me how a lady should live and so I ought to come with you, if only to make sure that you don't waste Rob's money.'

'That's rich, coming from you, Molly. Jack will have his work cut out to keep you in the style you became accustomed to at Colneyhurst, even if you were a servant there.'

Molly tossed her head. 'I was more a paid companion to Daisy, as well as looking after the little ones. She gave me nice clothes and even little pieces of jewellery.'

'That's what I mean,' Judy said tiredly. 'But come tomorrow if you want to. I could do with a second opinion.'

For the next three weeks Judy spent most of her time visiting furnishing warehouses or attending the local sale room, accompanied by Molly. McArthur has taken pity on them and had given them the loan of a much more reliable horse, and a chaise that had been left in the coach house. Judy was used to handling the reins by now, and it was a pleasure for her to have the freedom of the road, with the spring sunshine turning the countryside green again. If the seller could not deliver, it was Pip who collected the items in the old farm cart, and Judy spent many hours arranging furniture and laying down carpet squares and brightly coloured rugs.

Gradually and almost imperceptibly the house became a welcoming home. Miss Creedy had been put in charge of making the curtains, and the ground-floor rooms were almost completely furnished. There had been some delay in waiting for beds to be delivered by the carter, but eventually they came, and the gatehouse was ready for occupation. Judy had taken Molly's advice and had furnished it to her taste. There were some old chairs and tables, purchased at sales, but these fitted in well with the newer pieces bought in Colchester. The fabric that Miss Creedy's nimble fingers had made into curtains was Judy's personal choice, but now it was all put together she was beginning to have her doubts. If Rob hated what she had done it would be a terrible disappointment, as well as a profligate waste of money. She had done her best to keep within a self-imposed budget, but she was unused to spending large sums, and she had had some sleepless nights when it came to adding up the total cost.

But at last the gatehouse was fully furnished. Judy stepped back to gaze critically at her work in the front parlour. All it needed now was a fire burning brightly in the grate, and a few vases of spring flowers. With a picture or two on the walls, and the welcoming smell of baking bread, it would be a home that would make anyone proud. She had done all she could, but there was always some small improvement that might come to mind and would bring her back to the house yet again. She put on her bonnet and gloves and picked up her shawl. It was time to return home, although she was not really needed at the inn. Molly and Jack had more or less taken over everything, except the preparation of food, which had always been Hilda's domain, and Judy found herself demoted to the position of general help. The gatehouse had given her something to do that had given her a purpose as well as pleasure.

She sighed as she let herself out into the balmy spring afternoon, but she hesitated as she was about to climb onto the driver's seat of the chaise. In the distance she could hear the sound of men's voices chanting, or were they singing? This far off it was hard to tell, and she was curious. The horse that McArthur had loaned her was young and eager to be off and needed only a word from Judy to trot on at a brisk rate, even though it was uphill to the building site.

'Whoa, Skipper.' She reined him in as they approached a small crowd of workmen, who had apparently put down their tools to sing hymns. Judy stood up in the footwell and sat down again abruptly when she saw who was conducting the unlikely choir.

Jay was dressed in black from head to foot and he was conducting the hymn with more energy than expertise. Judy waited until the singing came to an end, and the workmen bowed their heads while Jay recited a prayer.

'Go in peace, brothers,' he said grandly, and the crowd dispersed, leaving Jay to step down from the wooden crate on which he had been standing.

'Judy.' He walked towards her, arms outstretched.

She stared at him in astonishment. 'What are you doing here, and why are you dressed like that?'

'I don't blame you for being sceptical, Judy. I know I've been a bad man, but I've seen the error of my ways, and I've repented. I've put my past well and truly behind me and I'm continuing the good work that my stepfather started.'

Judy stared at him in amazement. 'But he was a fake and a bully.'

'He repented, as have I.'

'And now you're a preacher?'

'A lay preacher, Judy. I'm still studying, but I've had the call, and I'm a reformed character.'

'You're going to go round telling people how to behave?'

He smiled. 'I know it sounds unlikely, but I'm not the man I was. God has spoken to me and I have listened.'

'How did this happen?' Judy asked suspiciously.

'You treated me abominably the last time I saw you.'

'I know I did, and I'm sorry. I was determined to get the estate back at any cost, and I went up to London to seek legal advice, but the solicitor was not encouraging. I was furious and I walked until I could go no further. I found myself standing in a graveyard surrounded by headstones and marble statues, and I saw myself for the sorry fellow I am.'

Judy was not convinced. 'Don't tell me you had an epiphany.'

'I remembered Lemuel, the man I thought of as my father for the first part of my life. He was a brute, and I saw myself growing like him and the old squire. I seem to have inherited their worst traits, and believe it or not, I was ashamed.'

'If you say so, Jay.'

'I don't blame you for being cynical, Judy. I know it's hard to believe, but I went into the church and that's how it all began. I am now training to be a lay preacher, which I will continue when I return to Australia.'

'But it's little more than a month since you held me captive.'

'A man can change, Judy.'

'Does Jack know about this?'

'Not yet, but I will visit the inn tomorrow and tell him the good news.'

'But you're not planning to stay in Little Creek?'

'Don't worry, Judy. I intend to sail back to

Australia and take the message from God with me
to the outback. My brother can come with me, if
he so wishes.'

'And you've given up any claim on the estate?'

'From now on I intend to live a simple life – money
means nothing to me. God bless you, Judy.' Jay was
about to walk away but Judy called him back.

'Wait a minute, Jay. Where are you staying?'

'Don't worry about me. As I said, I'll call at the
inn tomorrow morning.' He strolled off in the direction of the stables.

Judy sank back on the seat, watching him until
he disappeared from view. She picked up the reins.
'Walk on, Skipper.' She must get home quickly and
warn Jack that his brother had returned. Try as she
might, she could not believe that Jay was a reformed
character. This must be one of his tricks.

Jay had gone. He had sailed on the *Lazy Jane* with
the family there to wave him off, or more accurately
to make sure that he really had boarded the vessel
and was leaving the country.

'Good riddance. That's what I say.' Hilda took
off her bonnet and laid it on the bar counter. 'I
wouldn't have believed it if I hadn't seen it with my
own eyes, and him prancing around and pretending
to be a minister. Heaven help the people of New
South Wales, that's all I can say.'

Jack went behind the bar and filled a tankard with
ale. He raised it in a toast. 'Well, I say good luck to

my brother. I hope he's sincere, but even if he gets tired of being a preacher, at least he's gone home to his wife. Aimee won't stand for his nonsense. She's a strong woman and he's in awe of her.'

'I'm just glad he's gone,' Judy said firmly. 'Now we can all get on with our lives.'

'He treated you so badly.' Molly shrugged off her mantle. 'I agree with Ma. He'll get his comeuppance one way or another. Anyway, I'm gasping for a cup of tea and something to eat, and then I'm off to see Miss Creedy for a fitting for my wedding gown. Are you coming with me, Judy?'

'I really should give Ma a hand to prepare the meals for tonight.' Judy glanced at her mother. 'Is there much to do?'

'No, dear. I can manage. You go with Molly.' Hilda started towards the kitchen, but she hesitated. 'You ought to have a new gown, too, Judy.'

'It's not my wedding, Ma. I have a perfectly good Sunday best, and the new bonnet Rob bought me in London.' Judy linked arms with her sister. 'A cup of tea sounds like a very good idea. Then we'll set off for the village.'

It was one of those late April days when the sun shone brightly as if to fool people into venturing outside without their umbrellas. Judy passed the time of day with Miss Creedy, but she did not go into the cottage with Molly. It was not that Judy was envious of her younger sister's happiness, far from it, she could not have been more delighted to have Jack as a brother-in-law. But the excitement of the wedding preparations only served to remind her that she had not heard from Rob, who had been gone for several weeks. She blamed herself for his long absence. Things might have been different had she given him the slightest encouragement, but it was the old fear of rejection that had made her hold back. She tried to convince herself that she did not care, but she knew that the fault was hers and hers alone.

Judy set off for the village shop with the list of items that their mother had given her. After a brief chat with George Keyes, who was always eager to serve up gossip with the customer's purchases, she left the shop. With the fickleness of the weather, the sky had clouded over and an April shower caused her to run for cover in the railway station. She was sheltering in the ticket hall when the London train arrived, letting off a burst of steam, and through the vaporous cloud she saw a familiar figure striding along the platform. Her heart missed a beat and she had to stop herself from rushing towards him as Rob approached the barrier and handed in his ticket.

Chapter Twenty-Five

Rob's expression lightened when he saw her and he greeted her with a smile that took her breath away.

'Judy, how did you know I was on this train?'

She shook her head. 'I didn't. I was sheltering from the rain.'

He put his valise down and wrapped her in a hug. 'I don't care who sees us. I've missed you.'

'You have?'

'Of course, but I couldn't come home sooner.'

'I suppose you were busy.'

'I've been fully occupied. Just wait until I tell you my news.'

'I have something to tell you, too.' She glanced over his shoulder as another figure emerged from the rapidly dispersing steam. 'Dr Godfrey.'

Rob smiled. 'He's part of my surprise, and Dr Marshall is following close behind.'

Judy looked from one to the other. 'I don't understand.'

'It's good to see you again, Judy.' Ben Godfrey shook her hand. 'You're looking radiant, and I think I can guess why.' He shot a sideways glance at Rob.

'I don't have to ask how you are, Judy.' Toby Marshall kissed her on both cheeks. 'Minnie sends her love. She knew I'd be seeing you, although I wasn't expecting you to meet us.'

'It was a shower,' Rob said, slipping Judy's hand through the crook of his arm. 'Nick should be here with the carriage, and we'll go straight to Creek Hall.' He met Judy's curious gaze with a smile. 'You ought to come with us, Judy. This concerns you as well.'

'Why? What's going on? Why are you all here?'

'Wait and see.' Rob guided her out onto the station forecourt where the Marshalls' carriage had just arrived. 'There's room for all of us.' He took the basket of groceries from Judy's hand and lifted her into the vehicle, despite her protests.

'Steady on, old chap,' Toby said, chuckling. 'People will think we're kidnapping her.'

'Maybe, but I don't care. Judy is a part of what we've been discussing, and she deserves to be in on our plans from the very beginning.' Rob placed the basket on Judy's lap. 'Don't worry, I'll see you home safely.'

Judy felt the warmth of his body as he sat down beside her and she did not move away. It was so long since they had been this close and it was good to be with him again. She felt completely at ease, although she was bursting with curiosity as to why he had brought the two doctors down from London. She did not have long to wait. When they arrived at Creek Hall and the greetings were over, Nick showed them into the drawing room and closed the doors.

Judy looked from one to the other, her curiosity well and truly aroused. 'I wish someone would tell me what's going on.'

'You're about to find out.' Rob rose to his feet. 'I have with me the deeds to land that I've donated for the site of a new general hospital.'

Judy stared at him in amazement. 'You've given away some of your estate.'

'Don't look so surprised. I must confess that I didn't have that purpose in mind when I purchased it, but you made me stop and think about my motives, which I have to admit were purely selfish.'

'Understandably, old chap,' Nick said firmly. 'You should have inherited the estate in the first place. I for one will be more than grateful to have this house back as a family home, and the village and surrounding area will have a modern hospital.'

'It's a most worthy cause.' Toby nodded emphatically. 'I will divide my time between Creek Manor and Harley Street. I've talked it over with Minnie and she's thrilled at the prospect. I know that both she and the girls will benefit from living in the countryside.'

'Will you move here permanently?' Judy asked eagerly. 'I'd love to see Minnie and the girls more often, and Daisy will be delighted.'

'City living isn't for my wife, and I'd like to see more of my sister and her family.' Toby turned to Ben Godfrey. 'You're quite keen to leave London as well, aren't you?'

'The hospital was my dream in the first place.' Ben gave Judy an apologetic smile. 'But I went about it the wrong way, and for that I'm truly sorry. I've been working at night covering several of the east London hospitals, and I've paid back most of the money I misused, so you see I'm not such a bad fellow, Judy.'

'I never thought you were,' Judy said hastily. 'But how will you fund this project? And will it be for private patients only?'

'I've been working with several charitable institutions.' Rob produced a leather document case and took out a sheaf of papers. 'They are prepared to donate funds for the erection and running of the hospital, and I've applied for charitable status, so we can raise money in our own right. Those who can pay will have a private wing and that will help to support the wards for those who cannot.'

'There's only one flaw in that proposal,' Toby said, frowning. 'None of us will have the time to chase donors for money. The four of us will be fully occupied with running the hospital.'

Judy glanced at Rob and, as if reading her

thoughts, he gave her an encouraging smile. 'I haven't any experience of that sort of thing, but I'd be more than willing to try.' She leaped to her feet. 'I would love to have the opportunity to do something really worthwhile, and I believe in the project heart and soul. I'm sure I could persuade wealthy people to part with their money for such a good cause.'

There was a moment of silence and she could see that all, with the exception of Rob, had been taken by surprise.

'I could do it,' she reiterated boldly. 'I was lucky enough to have a good education. Jack was lazy and didn't want to learn and so I was allowed to share lessons with him, and it brought out his competitive spirit. He didn't want to be beaten by a girl, let alone a servant. Besides which, I'm not really needed at the inn now that Molly and Jack have virtually taken over. I want to be part of your plans because I believe in what you're doing.' She sank down on her chair, waiting for someone to speak.

'If you're serious, Judy, I can give you a list of people who might be interested in donating,' Toby said slowly. 'I'm on several committees in London, and Minnie is a keen fund-raiser. I'm sure she would be only too pleased to help you. She's always complaining that she has too little to occupy her mind.'

'That would be wonderful,' Judy said enthusiastically. 'I'm a quick learner.'

'I propose that we accept Judy's offer of help,' Rob said firmly.

'I second that.' Ben Godfrey stood up. 'I can vouch for Judy's passionate interest in the welfare of the sick, especially those who are living in poverty. She accompanied me to Sarah Holden's clinic in Limehouse. She saw sights that no well-brought-up young lady should see, and she didn't bat an eyelid. I think Judy Begg would be an excellent ambassador for Creek Manor Hospital.'

'I agree wholeheartedly,' Toby said, smiling.

'As do I.' Nick reached for the bell pull at his side and gave it a tug. 'I suggest we raise a toast to the success of our project, and to the health of our newest member of the team, Miss Judith Begg.'

Minutes later, flushed from sipping sherry at such an early hour in the morning, Judy left the men to discuss their next move, and she went to the kitchen where she hoped she might find Dove.

Mrs Bee was, as usual, up to her elbows in flour as she energetically kneaded a large batch of bread dough, and Dove was seated at the table poring over an account book. She looked up and closed the ledger with a sigh.

'I really hate bookkeeping,' she said crossly. 'I'm sorry, Judy. That wasn't the way to greet a friend.'

'I should think not,' Mrs Bee added, sniffing. 'Take a seat, dear, and Flossie will make us all a nice cup of tea.'

'Thank you.' Judy sat down next to Dove. 'I suppose you both know all about the new hospital?'

Dove nodded. 'Of course. Nick doesn't keep secrets from me, and if he did attempt to do so I have ways of finding out.'

'That's true enough.' Mrs Bee chuckled and punched the dough into submission.

'So what did they decide?' Dove flexed her ink-stained fingers. 'Are they going to find someone else to take over the bookkeeping? I do hope so.'

'Well, it might be me,' Judy said warily. 'I'm quite good at figures, and I've been keeping the accounts at the inn. Anyway, I'm going to try my hand at fund-raising, but I'll have help from Mrs Marshall. I still can't quite believe that I've got a chance to prove myself.'

'Why not?' Dove gave her a hug. 'You deserve to be recognised as the intelligent woman you are, Judy. Linnet and I have often said that your talents were wasted. I think it's wonderful.'

'You don't mind that I have been offered the job?' Judy asked anxiously. 'I mean you've been working alongside your husband for the past ten years, and you've had three children in the meantime.'

Dove smiled and patted her belly. 'And the fourth is on the way, Judy. I haven't got the time or the energy to take on such a responsible position, but I think you'll be a huge success in raising money for the hospital. You were always behind Ben when it was his pet project.'

451

'And Mrs Neville needs to rest more.' Mrs Bee gave Dove meaningful look. 'Not that she takes much notice of me, but you can help by taking on the bookkeeping. You're a clever woman, Judy. You can do it.'

'I'll try my best, that's all I can say. Congratulations, by the way, Dove. It seems to be the year for new babies and weddings. I've just left Molly at Miss Creedy's, being fitted for her wedding gown.'

'I dare say you'll be next, Judy.' Mrs Bee placed the dough back in the large bowl and covered it with a damp cloth. 'I'll leave this to prove and I'll put the kettle on.'

'I can't stay,' Judy said hastily. 'Rob has promised to drive me home and we'll pick up Molly on the way.'

'You could do worse, Judy,' Dove said with a mischievous smile. 'Rob Dorning is a very presentable man and he's wealthy, too. A great catch.'

Judy stood up, hoping that neither of them had seen the blush rise to her cheeks. 'Ours is a purely business arrangement.'

'If you say so, Judy.' Dove closed the ledger with a sigh. 'I can't do any more today. The figures keep swimming about and muddling themselves up. At least I won't have this bother when the hospital is transferred to the new building. It can't come soon enough for me.'

'I really must go now.' Judy leaned over to kiss

Dove's pale cheek. 'You mustn't work too hard. I'll do anything I can to help.'

'Thank you, Judy. That would be most kind. Maybe you could spare one morning a week to come and sort the books out for me?'

'Of course. It would be a pleasure.' Judy picked up her basket. 'Goodbye for now. I'll see you soon.'

As he had promised, Rob drove Judy and Molly home. He carried the groceries to the kitchen where he laid the basket on the table.

Hilda wiped her hands on her apron. 'We thought you'd gone away for good, Rob Dorning.'

'Ma!' Judy shot her a warning glance. 'I never said such a thing.'

'Well, that's how it looked.' Hilda tossed her head. 'Are you playing fast and loose with my girl's affections, Mr Dorning? It seems to be a habit of the Tattersall menfolk.'

'That's enough, Ma,' Judy said angrily.

Rob threw back his head and laughed. 'Your mother is being honest, Judy. I appreciate candour, and in answer to your question, Mrs Begg, I am not playing fast and loose, as you put it. My intentions as far as Judy is concerned are strictly honourable.'

'It's a business arrangement, Ma,' Judy said hastily. 'I'm going to raise funds to keep the new hospital, and you'll never guess who's involved.'

Hilda shrugged. 'I don't suppose I will.'

'Dr Marshall and his family are moving down

from London and so is Dr Godfrey. They'll be working together with Dr Neville and Rob, who's given them part of the Creek Manor estate so that they can build a fine new hospital.'

'Well, I never!'

'Perhaps you'd like to come with Judy and me, Mrs Begg. I'll show you the parcel of land that I've donated, and maybe you'd like to take a look at the plans for the house I'm going to build where your cottage once stood.'

'I can't go gallivanting around the countryside at this time of the day.' Hilda encompassed the kitchen with a sweep of her arms. 'Can't you see I'm busy? The workmen will be here at any minute demanding their bread and cheese and bowls of soup.' She put her head on one side. 'But of course Judy can go with you. I can manage on my own.'

Judy was tempted to stay and help her mother, but she was eager to show Rob the fully furnished gatehouse. 'Are you sure, Ma? I do have something I want to show Rob.'

'Yes, go away. Shoo!' Hilda flapped her apron at them.

'Thank you, Mrs Begg.' Rob held out his hand to Judy. 'I don't know what surprise you have in store for me, but I'm eager to find out.'

Judy's heart was thudding against her tightly laced stays as Rob entered the house. She held her breath as he stepped into the front parlour and she crossed her fingers, hoping that his first impression was a favourable one. He gazed round, saying nothing, and her heart sank.

'You don't like it? I tried not to spend too much money in case . . .'

He turned to her with a beaming smile. 'It's perfect, Judy. You've done wonders, and in such a short time.'

'Just wait until you see the rest of the rooms.' Judy tried not to look too relieved, but she felt light-headed with delight. All her worries about spending too much or the fact that his taste might differ from hers were fading as she led him from room to room. They ended up in the kitchen where the sunlight streamed through the window.

'Well?' Judy said eagerly. 'Are you satisfied?'

'Words can't express my feelings, Judy. You've turned a perfectly good house into a wonderful home. I had thought I might live here until the main wing of the house is finished, and I was planning on asking Aunt Adeline if she would like to move in with me.'

'I'm not sure she'd want to leave her cottage. She seemed to be very happy there.' Judy turned to look out of the window. The trees that lined the avenue were bursting into leaf and there was a good view of the work in progress on the building site.

'You don't think that's a good idea?' Rob said softly.

'It's your decision. The house and everything in it belongs to you.'

'Not quite everything.'

There was something in the tone of his voice that made her turn to look at him, and the expression on his handsome features brought a blush to her cheeks. 'So who will have the house?' she asked, covering her confusion with a confident smile. 'You've gone to a lot of trouble for the new gatekeeper.'

'As a matter of fact I thought that you and your mother might like to live here, and if you're going to work for the charity that seems even more suitable. I think Aunt Adeline might be better suited to having accommodation in the east wing when it's built.'

'I don't think we could afford the rent on this place,' Judy said dully.

'It would be rent free, of course. Consider it part of your wages. We'll depend upon you to keep us going.'

'Yes, of course. Thank you.' She shot him a look beneath her lashes. 'But where will you live? The inn is fully booked, thanks to your men.'

'The coachman's house is vacant at the moment. I'll drive myself for now or Pip can fill in until such time as I need the barouche. I'm more interested in getting the manor house rebuilt than in my own comfort. What do you say, Judy?'

'I'll think about it,' she said evasively.

'You'll talk it over with Mrs Begg?'

'Yes, I will, but I'm not sure she'll want to leave

the Crooked Billet. Anyway, I think we'd best be getting back. Unless you want me to start working for you immediately?'

'No, of course not. We'll have to have a few meetings to consider the best way to go about things. You won't be on your own, Judy. I'll be there to help and support you. It's work I wouldn't want to trust to anyone but you.'

'You mean he didn't propose to you?' Molly said, throwing up her hands. 'What a fool that man is.'

'I wasn't expecting anything of the sort.' Torn between annoyance and amusement at her sister's reaction to her news about the gatehouse, Judy brushed Molly's hair into a sleek chignon.

'Of course you were.' Molly twisted round on the dressing table stool, giving Judy a stern look. 'When a man asks a young woman to furnish his house for him it can only mean one thing. What did you say to put him off?'

'Nothing. I told you I wasn't expecting him to propose, and it's the gatehouse, not his home. There's nothing romantic going on between us.'

'If you think that, you're either blind or stupid.' Molly rose to her feet, shaking the creases out of her skirt. 'Look at me. I knew exactly when Jack was going to pop the question, and I made sure he did.' She fluttered her eyelashes and made a *moue*.

'You are a spoilt brat,' Judy said, chuckling.

'I know I am, and it always works for me.' Molly headed for the doorway. 'Think about it, Judy. Give the poor man a chance.' She left Judy staring into her dressing table mirror with a puzzled frown. All her old insecurities had risen to the surface and she was still Judy Begg, the kitchen maid who aspired to higher things but had been deserted, not quite at the altar, when Jack had chosen to accompany his brother to Australia. If Rob had genuine feelings for her he would have made them clear by now. As it was, he merely wanted someone he could trust to raise much-needed money for the hospital, which just happened to be a project they both held dear. She had accepted the challenge and she would prove to them all that she was more than capable of taking on such a responsible job.

Judy picked up the brush and smoothed her unruly curls into a suitably neat style before going downstairs to help her mother in the kitchen. She had not had time to discuss Rob's offer of the house as a part of her wages, but that made it in effect a tied cottage; it put her in the invidious position of being his tenant and not a colleague.

'What's up with you?' Hilda demanded, pausing as she plated up a dish of pie and mash. 'I thought you'd be delighted to be offered such an important position. Molly told me all about it while you were out with Rob.'

'Yes, I am, of course, Ma.'

'Then why the long face?'

'It's a lot to think about, and there's something else. He's offered us the gatehouse.'

Hilda almost dropped the jug of gravy she held in her hand. 'He wants us to rent the new house?'

'No, Ma. We'd live there free of charge in return for my work raising money for the new hospital. It would be part of my wages.'

'Take this through to the bar, please. Then hurry back and tell me everything.'

Judy took the food to Molly, who sashayed over to a table where a group of workmen were having their supper. Judy left her sister to her task of charming the customers and she returned to the kitchen, prepared for a barrage of questions.

'Now sit down for a moment and tell me exactly what he said.'

Judy knew by her mother's tone of voice that it was useless to argue, and she sank down on the nearest chair, but before she could think of something suitable that would satisfy her mother, there was a loud knock at the back door and it burst open to admit Rob.

'Mrs Begg,' Rob said without any preamble, 'I'm a clumsy fellow when it comes to talking about my deepest feelings, and believe me when I say that I've never done this sort of thing before.'

Hilda stared at him open-mouthed. 'Good heavens, Mr Dorning. What can it be that's brought you out so late in the evening?'

'As Judy has no father to ask, I think it's only

proper if I put it to you first, Mrs Begg. I want to ask your daughter for her hand in marriage, but I need your permission to do so.'

Hilda took a swipe at him with the dishcloth she was holding. 'You stupid man. Of course you have my permission. What a pair you are.' Hilda pointed a finger at Judy. 'Stop gawping and take your young gentleman to the parlour.'

'Ma, I'm not ten years old,' Judy protested, but one look at Rob was enough to convince her that he would go down on one knee in the kitchen if she did not obey her mother. 'Come with me, Rob. It's the only way to silence my mother.'

He followed her into the parlour and she closed the door, leaning against it for support. Her knees had suddenly turned to jelly and her heart was beating so fast that she was breathless.

'Judy, I love you.' Rob seized her by the hand. 'I've always loved you, but I have the double curse of the Dornings and the Tattersalls in my blood. You deserve a much better man than I, but I've loved you from the start and nothing is more important to me than your happiness.'

'But just this afternoon you made everything seem like a business proposition, and yet you come here this evening and tell me you love me.'

He drew her closer, holding her gaze. 'I know, but I didn't want to say anything when we were alone in the house. It would have put you in a difficult position. If you say no I'll have to accept your decision, but I won't give up easily. You and I were made for each other, Judy.'

She met his intense gaze with a tremulous smile. 'I feel that, too.'

'I was going to propose to you when we were in London, but the peasouper got in the way. I love you, and I hate every minute that I'm away from you. I want us to be together for ever.'

She slid her arms around his neck. 'I love you, too, Rob. I really do.'

He kissed her long and with growing fervour, releasing her only to draw a breath. 'Does that mean you will marry me?'

'Yes, Rob. I will, with all my heart.'

He kissed her again. 'I didn't expect you to do so much to the house, but you've made it into a beautiful home. We could live there until the main wing of Creek Manor is completed, if you agree.'

'I do.'

'So there's nothing to prevent us getting married very soon. I don't want to risk losing you.'

Judy laid her head against his shoulder with a sigh, all her doubts dissipating like morning mist. 'A summer wedding would be wonderful.'

Chapter Twenty-Six

The double wedding was Molly's idea. The church was booked for 17 June, Thursday being a relatively quiet day in the pub, although, as Hilda said, most of the customers would be attending the wedding breakfast, even if they could not fit into the church itself.

With less than two months to go until the big day, Judy was kept fully occupied with the preparations. Rob had wanted to take her up to London to buy a new outfit for the wedding, but Judy insisted that if she were to arrive in a gown created by a fashionable London designer, it would be unfair to Molly. Miss Creedy had made Ma's wedding outfit, and if it was good enough for Ma, it was perfectly acceptable to Judy herself. Rob backed down with good grace. However, his offer to hold the wedding reception in the grounds of Creek Manor was eagerly accepted. He planned to hire marquees and the entertainment, although he was tantalisingly secretive when Judy asked for more details.

Hilda was determined to organise the wedding breakfast, and she enlisted the help of Nell Pearce and Ida Ralston, as well as some of the servants from the old manor house, who were all eager to help. Judy did not want her mother to undertake such a lot of work, but she knew it was useless to argue. Molly's contribution was to choose the colour scheme for the floral arrangements and she designed the bridesmaids' frocks. Minnie's twin girls, Lottie and Evie, were to attend both brides, with Henry and Edward Walters acting as pageboys. Dove's five-year-old daughter was to be a flower girl, under the watchful eye of her cousin, nine-year-old Michael, Linnet and Elliot's son. Judy had reservations about having so many young children let loose in church, but Molly was adamant that it could be done, and that the little ones would behave perfectly.

Not only did Judy have the arrangements for the double wedding to organise, but she also had the enjoyable task of getting the gatehouse ready for occupation. Rob admitted that he had hoped that it would be their first home when he asked Judy to furnish it for him, adding hastily that it was only until the construction of the main house was completed. Judy was delighted: she had put so much of herself into choosing the furniture, fabrics and the little touches that turned a house into a home.

The pub was busy these days, mainly with the builders, who liked to relax in the evenings over a pint of ale. Daytime trade had picked up, due to Hilda's reputation as a good home cook having spread by word of mouth. Altogether the days flew by, but when things became too hectic at home, Judy asked Nate to tack up the chestnut mare that Rob had bought for her. The ride to Creek Manor was delightful at this time of year, and Judy was able to spend an hour or two putting up pictures or re-arranging the furniture. At other times she rode to Crouch, where Adeline was always delighted to see her. Sometimes Rob accompanied her to his aunt's cottage, although, quite often, he had to attend meetings in London to finalise the plans for the new hospital, and on these occasions he stayed with Toby in Harley Street. Minnie and the children had moved into a rented house on the edge of Little Creek, and Toby planned to buy a property as soon as a suitable place came on the market.

The afternoons Judy spent in Adeline's cosy parlour provided a welcome relief from the demands of working and trying to organise a large double wedding. Adeline did not need much encouragement to tell Judy of Rob's exploits as a mischievous child, and an adventurous adolescent. Judy treasured these quiet afternoons in the cottage, and she found it easy to understand why there was such a deep bond between Rob and his aunt.

Altogether it was an exciting time and the bad

experiences in the past were fading into a vague memory. Judy was looking to the future with confidence, and for the first time in her life she knew she had found her place in the world. She was marrying the man she loved, but more than that, they were to be equal partners in making decisions regarding the estate, and ensuring the smooth running of the new hospital. Rob had been elected senior medical officer, working with Ben Godfrey and Nick Neville. Toby would be the visiting physician, and other specialists were being recruited. Plans for the new hospital had been drawn up and finalised, and it was a question now of finding enough workmen to start building.

Then there was the eternal question of finance. Judy was only too well aware that she did not have the experience or the contacts when it came to fund-raising, and she formed a committee with Minnie, Dove, Daisy and Eleanora Marshall, with occasional support from Grace Peabody and Marjorie Harker. United, they were an indomitable group of women, each with her own ideas on how to raise money for the new hospital. However, as the weeks went by there was one topic uppermost in their minds – the summer wedding. Little Creek had never seen anything like it, and invitations had gone out to everyone who lived in the village and the surrounding farms.

Judy had made sure that Seth Trundle and his parents had been invited. Their kindness after the accident in near blizzard conditions last winter was something Judy would never forget, and an invitation to the wedding was the least she could do. Mr McArthur was also on the guest list, and Judy and Rob had talked over the possibility of inviting the workmen, who lived in a semi-permanent camp on the site. In the end it was Hilda who suggested that there should be a separate marquee for the builders, where all were welcome, and that included any itinerant farm labourers. The double wedding was to be a celebration enjoyed by everyone in Little Creek, and one that Judy hoped would lay the curse of Creek Manor to rest for ever.

On the day of the wedding Judy was up even earlier than usual. As she stoked the fire in the range it was hard to believe that this was the last time she would make breakfast in the pub kitchen. Her life was about to change even more than it had during the last few weeks. By midday she would become Mrs Robert Winters Tattersall of Creek Manor, but she was not going to be a lady of leisure. She had a purpose in life now, apart from being a wife and eventually, she hoped, a mother.

She filled the kettle and put it on the hob. The mundane task of making tea soothed a sudden attack of nerves. Hilda was a stickler for tradition and she had sent Rob and Jack to spend the night at Colneyhurst Hall. She had impressed upon both bridegrooms that they were to wait at the church, and on no account would either of them be allowed to see their brides before the ceremony. Even if Rob had disagreed with Hilda, she was backed up by his aunt. Adeline had stayed the night at the inn, and Judy laid an extra place at the breakfast table, before taking the tray of tea upstairs.

Hilda was already up and getting dressed, but Adeline was still asleep when Judy took her a cup of tea.

'That's the best night's sleep I've had in weeks,' Adeline said, yawning. 'This is a very comfortable bed, Judy, dear.'

'This was Rob's room, Aunt Adeline. I hope he's slept well, too.'

Adeline straightened her nightcap and sat up to take the cup and saucer from Judy. 'I'm sure he was made most welcome at Colneyhurst. I've only met Mrs Walters once, but she seems a delightful young woman.'

'Daisy is one of the best,' Judy said earnestly. 'I'm so lucky to have such good friends.'

'You're a good girl, my dear. If I'd hand-picked a wife for my dear boy I would have chosen you.'

Judy felt the blood rush to her cheeks at this unexpected compliment. 'Thank you. I'll try to live up to your good opinion of me, Aunt Adeline.'

'Never mind me, dear. Hadn't you better get some breakfast? I know it's early but you want plenty of time to get dressed. I can't wait to see your gown.'

'You're right. I'd better give Molly a call. I can't

believe she's slept this long.' Judy took the last cup of tea to her sister's room, knocked and entered to find Molly sitting on the bed, sobbing. 'What's the matter?' Judy put the cup and saucer on the dressing table. 'Why are you crying?'

'Look at me, Judy. I can't face Jack like this. I look hideous.' Red-eyed and frantic, Molly grabbed her sister by the arm, drawing her closer.

'What's wrong? You look fine to me.'

Molly pointed to a tiny red spot on the tip of her nose. 'It must be a boil. I can't get married looking such a fright.'

Judy looked closer. She was tempted to laugh, but she could see that Molly's distress was genuine. 'It's a tiny spot. No one will notice.'

'Yes, they will. It's getting bigger by the minute, Judy. I can feel it throbbing. Are you sure it isn't a boil?'

Judy looked closer. 'It's definitely not a boil.' She reached for the teacup. 'Stop crying because you're making your eyes red and puffy. Drink your tea.'

Molly drank thirstily and handed the cup back to Judy. She sniffed and patted her eyes with a damp hanky. 'I'll have to wear the veil during the reception. I can't be seen like this.'

'Don't be silly. A touch of face powder will conceal the spot, and no one, least of all Jack, will notice. Come downstairs and have some breakfast. I don't want you spoiling my entrance in church by fainting from lack of nourishment.'

'Don't be silly,' Molly said, giggling. 'I couldn't eat a thing.'

'You'd better, or you'll have to put up with nagging from Ma and Aunt Adeline.'

'Oh! All right.' Molly sighed and swung her legs over the side of the bed. 'Hand me my wrap, Judy. I'll try to eat something and then I want you to cover my spot before you start on my hair. You're the only one who knows exactly how I want to wear it.'

'Yes, of course I will, but only if you come downstairs now. I have to get myself ready, too.'

As if by some miracle, both brides were ready on time. Judy had just helped Molly downstairs, holding up her long train, when the first carriage arrived, driven by Pip, who looked slightly uncomfortable in his Sunday best. Molly had chosen him to give her away and Nate was to do the honours for Judy. Seated beside Pip on the box of a barouche on loan from Colneyhurst was his friend Davey, who was wearing a footman's uniform that was slightly too large. However, this did not seem to bother him and he sprang down to assist Molly into the carriage, followed by Hilda. He might still be a stable boy, but he was obviously taking his temporary promotion very seriously, and he climbed up to resume his seat next to Pip. They left just as Nate drove up in the Creek Manor barouche, which was festooned with greenery and trails of pink roses. Seated beside him was none other than James, the former footman at Creek Manor. He leaped agilely to the ground, opened the door and put down the steps.

'Thank you, James.' Judy smiled. 'It's good to see you again.'

'Thank you, Miss Begg.' He assisted her into the carriage, followed by Adeline.

'Drive on, Nate.' Judy sat back, clutching her posy of pink roses. She glanced at Adeline, who was staring curiously at James as he resumed his seat next to Nate. 'James was footman at Creek Manor when I first arrived there, Aunt Adeline.'

'You seem to know him well, Judy. Most people seem to treat their servants with total disdain.'

'It wasn't like that at Creek Manor. We were like a family, with the usual upsets and dramas, but they were all put aside in times of trouble.'

'You'll know how to run your household when the new manor house rises from the ashes.' Adeline relaxed against the squabs. 'Are you feeling nervous, Judy?'

'A little, but Rob will be waiting for me at the altar. When he takes my hand in his I know everything will be all right.'

Adeline unfurled her sunshade. 'It's a beautiful day. I'm so happy for both of you, dear.'

'You do know that Rob wants you to come and live with us when the house is finished, don't you, Aunt Adeline?'

'He has mentioned it, Judy. But I told him that I'm too old and set in my ways to leave my little cottage. All my happy memories are there.'

'But you would make new ones at Creek Manor. I'd really love it if you would agree. Rob has plans for a lovely house where our old cottage once stood. I know you'd be very comfortable there.'

'We'll see, Judy. I'm not making any promises, and I imagine it will be some years before it's completed. The manor house and the hospital must come first.'

'Yes, of course,' Judy said mildly. 'But don't dismiss the idea without giving it a lot of thought. It would be wonderful to have you living closer to us.'

'I will think about it, my dear. I promise.'

They arrived at the church just as Molly was alighting from her carriage. Minnie and Dove were trying to control the small bridesmaids and the over-excited page boys, but five-year-old Victoria was having a tantrum. Nick emerged from the church to scoop his daughter up in his arms. He spoke sternly to his sons, who had been sparring with two of the Walters boys and Michael Massey. All five small boys calmed down, looking shamefaced, and Nick turned his attention to Michael.

'Do you want me to tell your father that I caught you playing with Henry and Edward when you should have been keeping an eye on your little sister?'

Michael hung his head, blushing to the roots of his hair, but by this time Judy had managed to get her lengthy train safely to the ground, and she hurried to the rescue. 'It's all right, Nick. I'm sure

Michael was doing his best. Anyway, we're here now so we'd better go in.'

'Oh, no!' Molly cried, clasping her hand to her lips. 'Who's playing the organ, Nick? Don't tell me it's Lavender Creedy.'

'It can't be,' Judy murmured. 'It was supposed to be Constable Fowler.'

Nick pulled a face. 'I'm afraid he was called out to an emergency. Miss Creedy gallantly stepped into the breach.'

Judy smothered a sigh. 'Oh, well. Things can only get better after this.'

'Who will walk you down the aisle?' Adeline asked anxiously.

Judy held her hand out to Nate. 'Nate is going to give me away.'

'And Pip is doing the honours for me,' Molly said, chuckling. 'Our brothers have their uses, Aunt Adeline.'

'They do indeed.' Adeline held her hand out to Nick. 'Let me take Vicky. I'll see that she behaves herself. You go and sit with your wife, Doctor.'

He smiled and placed Vicky in Adeline's arms. 'You be good, young lady, or Miss Dorning will tell me and you won't have any cake.' Nick gave the girls an encouraging smile as he retreated into the church.

'That sounds like someone killing a cat.' Molly covered her ears as Miss Creedy's discordant playing could be heard through the open door.

'Let's get this over,' Pip said gloomily. 'I hate wearing this stiff collar. I feel as though I'm choking.'

Nate nudged his brother in the ribs. 'Shut up. This is their day. I'm proud of my sisters.'

'So am I,' Pip added hastily. 'You both look beautiful – like princesses. But please can we go in now?'

Judy smoothed the bodice of her ivory satin gown, fingering a waterfall of Valenciennes lace. Lavender Creedy had done both of them proud when it came to their beautiful wedding gowns – it was just a pity that her talents did not extend to playing the church organ well. Judy smiled ruefully and leaned over to kiss her brother on the cheek. 'I'm ready. What about you, Molly?'

'Does the spot on my nose look awfully red?'

'Yes,' Pip said before Judy had a chance to speak. 'It looks like a boil. Your nose is twice the size it is normally.'

Judy was about to slap him when Adeline stepped in. 'Now then, young man. That's enough of that.' She turned to Molly. 'He's teasing you, dear. No one will notice anything, least of all Jack.' She took Victoria by the hand. 'I'll hold the door open and you go in first, Judy, and then Molly. We'll be right behind you.'

They entered the church to an enthusiastic rendering of Wagner's 'Wedding March', and the packed congregation shuffled to their feet. As Judy processed up the aisle, leaning gently on Nate's arm, she was dimly aware of the smiling faces on either side, and she was barely conscious of Miss Creedy's ill-fated attempts to hit the right notes. All Judy could see was Rob, standing at the altar, waiting for her.

He turned his head to look at her, and enveloped her in a smile that sent her pulse racing and filled her heart with joy.

They emerged from the church to a riotous welcome from those gathered outside, and a shower of rose petals and rice. The festive atmosphere prevailed from the moment the carriages drew to a halt in the grounds of Creek Manor. Clutching her husband's arm, Judy gazed round in astonishment as a fire-eater blew flames into the air, and tumblers in brightly coloured costumes performed amazing acrobatic feats. Music from a Dutch organ filled the grounds with its cheerful sound, and in the distance Judy could see a merry-go-round. A tightrope had been set up close to the lake and a man wearing tights and a loose-fitting white shirt appeared to be walking on the water. Small dogs wearing frilly collars and tiny pointed hats were dancing on their hind legs with a woman, who was scantily clad like a ballet dancer. Judy glanced over her shoulder, hoping that Grace Peabody was otherwise occupied and did not spot the performer's state of undress.

'You arranged all this,' Judy said softly. 'It's wonderful, Rob.'

'It's nothing less than you deserve, my love.' Rob led her past a juggler and a man on stilts. 'I told you that this will be a party to remember. I hope it will bring the whole village together, and the sins of my father will be forgiven, if not forgotten.'

'What he did has nothing to do with you,' Judy said firmly.

'We're going to start afresh and I intend to make up for his criminal neglect by being a fair landlord.'

Judy squeezed his fingers. 'I'm sure you will, and I'll help you. I know the estate so well, and all the tenants.' She glanced over her shoulder as the rest of the guests arrived in droves. There were gasps of surprise and cries of delight from the children as clowns mingled with the crowd, handing out toffees and sugared almonds. Already there were sounds of merriment coming from the beer tent, which was set apart from the two marquees, allowing the workmen to enjoy themselves without offending the more staid guests.

Molly rushed over to join them, dragging Jack by the hand. 'Isn't it wonderful?' she cried excitedly. 'You are so clever, Rob. Judy told me you had a surprise for us, and this is amazing.'

Jack shook Rob's hand. 'It certainly is. I wouldn't have thought of such a thing.'

'This is only the start,' Rob said, smiling. 'The wedding breakfast is set out in the marquee on the left, and in the other one there will be dancing and entertainment all day and well into the night.'

'We really ought to receive our guests,' Judy said urgently. She could see Eleanora and Sidney Marshall waiting at the entrance of the marquee with the vicar and his wife. 'Come along, Rob. You, too, Molly and Jack. It's your day as well.'

Molly heaved a sigh and rolled her eyes. 'It's supposed to be fun. Do I have to, Judy?'

'Yes, you do. You're a married woman now, and it's only polite.'

'Quite right, dear.' Hilda joined them, accompanied by Adeline.

'Don't worry, Molly. What they really want is to sample the drinks and make sure they're first in the queue for food.' Adeline smiled and winked. 'Come on, Hilda, we're being left behind.'

'We can't have that.' Hilda started off towards the growing crowd of hungry guests. 'Come on, girls. Do your duty or you'll have a riot on your hands.'

The wedding breakfast was a huge success. Nell Pearce and Ida Ralston had supervised the preparation and the serving of the excellent food, and Molesworth had organised the wine, cider, ale and a fruit cup that was heady with sugar and spice, and spiked with brandy. Outside the sun shone until late evening, when hundreds of lanterns were lit and flaming cressets illuminated the lake. The tables were cleared away and the professional musicians, booked by Rob, played music for dancing.

Daisy and Marius left early, having said fond goodbyes to the newlyweds. Dove and Nick left soon after, as did Linnet and Elliot. The children, all of whom had behaved very well, were exhausted, as were their parents, but the rest of the guests remained to enjoy every last minute of the celebration.

Seth Trundle seemed to have made a hit with Sukey, the Marshalls' maidservant, who had moved with them from London. Pip and Nate had no difficulty in finding dancing partners, and Judy could see that her brothers were having a wonderful time. Eleanora and Sidney were still chatting with Hilda, Adeline and Ben Godfrey, while the rest of the guests either danced dreamily to the strains of a Viennese waltz, or sat quietly chatting and drinking wine.

Old Eli had drunk so much ale in the workmen's tent that he had fallen asleep under one of the tables, and Colonel Catchpole was flirting outrageously with Marjorie Harker, her husband being away with his regiment. However, this did not seem to be going down well with her daughter, Charity, who had married Will Johnson. Mrs Johnson, Charity's mother-in-law, was too busy chatting to Clem Guppy's mother to take much notice, until Charity rushed up to the colonel and began to berate him. Judy was dancing with Rob and she saw the drama beginning to unfold, but before she could intervene Mrs Johnson took matters in her own hands and abandoned Clara Guppy. She seized her daughter-in-law by the arm and marched her back to Will, who was stupidly drunk and about to pass out. Farmer Johnson took control and went to fetch the horse and farm cart. The Johnson family were rounded up and departed clinging drunkenly to the sides of the vehicle, with Charity still protesting loudly. Marjorie Harker and Colonel Catchpole were seen to wander arm in arm towards the spinney, but they were both adults and Judy decided that it was none of her business.

'I think it's time we left, too,' Jack said, slipping his arm around Molly's tiny waist. 'We've done our duty, and now it's time for us.'

Molly laid her head on his shoulder. 'It's a lovely night for a moonlit drive. I want it to go on for ever.'

Jack beckoned to Pip and Nate, who at this moment were dancing with two of the scantily clad circus performers. 'Time to go home, boys.'

Pip looked as though he was about to argue, but Nate nudged him in the ribs. 'We'll get the carriage, Jack. We won't be long.' He turned to Judy and gave her a hug. 'Good night, Mrs Tattersall.'

Judy leaned against Rob. 'You're the first person to call me by my new title, Nate. Thank you. You'd better say good night to the young tightrope artist. She looks a bit forlorn.'

'It's time we left them all to their own devices, my love,' Rob said in a low voice. 'Shall we go home?'

Judy smiled and nodded. Those were the sweetest words she had ever heard. Arm in arm they walked slowly down the avenue to the gatehouse. Rob unlocked the door and, lifting Judy in his arms, he carried her across the threshold.

'This is our happy ending, my darling,' he said tenderly as he set her on her feet.

Judy stood on tiptoe to kiss him. 'No, Rob. This is the start of a great adventure.'

Turn the page for a sneak peek at
Dilly's next book,

Rag-and-Bone
Christmas

Chapter One

Paradise Row, Pentonville, London. December 1865.

Snow was falling fast, but even before it floated to the ground its pristine whiteness was tainted by pollution from the black lead works, and soot from the factory chimneys. The thunderous sounds from the iron foundry, situated a little further along Old St Pancras Road, added to the general hubbub, and steam engines roared in and out of King's Cross railway station.

Away from all this, as though in a different world, it was quiet and peaceful inside the stable, and comparatively warm. Sally Suggs worked tirelessly to keep the stalls spotlessly clean, and the two animals stabled there were fed only the best hay, with plenty of fresh water to drink. Pa always teased Sally, saying it was because she had been born in the stable that she had such an affinity with horses, but she was convinced that she had inherited her talent as a horse-woman from her late mother. Emily Tranter had been a famous equestrienne, who had delighted audiences at Astley's Amphitheatre until she met and fell in love with young Edward Suggs, the rag-and-bone man.

'Ain't you done here yet, girl?' Ted hobbled in from the yard and took off his cap, sending a dusting of snow onto the floor.

'Nearly finished, Pa. Then I'll go to the shop and get us something for our supper.'

'It'll be dark soon, love. You know I don't like you walking out on your own at night, and it's snowing harder than ever.'

Sally turned to him with a chuckle. 'Pa, I'm nearly twenty. I'm not a little girl any longer.'

'You are to me, my duck. You always will be, and I ain't as fit and healthy as I used to be. My old pins ache something chronic, especially when it's bitter cold like this.'

'You should be in the parlour sitting by the fire,' Sally said severely. 'You've done your bit for today. I won't be long, I promise.' She reached up to pat Flower's sleek neck as the horse nuzzled her shoulder.

'You'd bring that blooming animal upstairs if she could manage them.' Ted grumbled but his grey eyes were twinkling. 'You wrap up warm if you're going out,' he added as he opened the door that led to a narrow flight of stairs. His heavy footsteps echoed round the stable, and then there was silence.

'I would stay with you all night, Flower,' Sally said, kissing the horse's soft muzzle. 'But I have Pa to look after as well as you.'

Flower whickered gently as if in reply, and with a last loving pat, Sally turned her attention to Boney, the heavy old horse who had pulled their cart through the London streets for the last fifteen years. He was still eager to work, but age was catching up on him and sometimes his joints were stiff, causing him to lumber over the cobblestones as if each step caused him pain. Sally had tried all manner of remedies, including poultices and doses of celery seeds, but in reality she knew that Boney's working days were numbered, and in a year or two he ought to be put out to pasture – the alternative was the knacker's yard, and that was unthinkable. Her dream would be a country cottage where her father could enjoy a long retirement, and Boney could end his days in peace.

Sally finished her work in the stable and went outside to make sure that the gates were locked and bolted. Although the items in the yard had been discarded by the former owners they still had a market value, and there were always those who preferred to steal rather than earn their living by honest toil. She hurried back to the warmth of the stable and extinguished the candles. Fires were all too common in places such as this, and everything had to be kept out of reach of the horses. A lamp left burning might easily be overturned by a frisky horse, and the whole place would go up in flames.

Sally gave Flower a last affectionate pat before slipping on her well-worn tweed jacket, and tucking her hair into one of her father's old caps. Fashion had little or no place in Paradise Row, especially when working in the scrap yard or the stable. Ever practical, Sally wore a pair of patched breeches that she had come across in one of the sacks, and a pair of lace-up boots that had also seen better days. She picked up a wicker basket and let herself out into the street, locking the door behind her. A cold wind sent wisps of hay, rotting cabbage leaves and scraps of paper scudding down the road, adding sharp teeth to the swirling snow, and she pulled up her collar, wrapping her arms around her thin body.

Sally made her way to the grocer's shop on the corner. Old man Jarvis was behind the counter as usual, and his gloomy expression seemed to have been painted indelibly on his wrinkled features. His bald patch gleamed in the lamplight as did the tip of his red nose. Sally had always suspected that he kept a bottle of spirits hidden beneath the counter, taking a nip or two when he thought no one was watching. The smell of gin hung in the cloud above his head, mingling with the aroma of roast coffee beans and the sawdust that was scattered over the bare floorboards.

Sally purchased a loaf of bread and two meat pies.

'Will that be all?' Jarvis demanded testily. 'Got some fresh eggs brought in from a farm today. You won't get none tastier than these.'

Sally hesitated. Pa was always partial to a boiled egg for his breakfast and that justified the extra expenditure. 'I'll take two, please.'

Jarvis wrapped the eggs in a page torn from yesterday's copy of *The Times* and placed them in Sally's basket. 'That'll be elevenpence ha'penny.'

Sally placed a shilling on the counter and waited for the ha'penny change. It was the last of money that Pa had given her from the profit he made selling the last lot of rags to Rags Roper, the cloth merchant. She put the halfpenny in her purse.

'Good evening, Mr Jarvis.'

'Good evening, Miss Suggs.'

She left the shop and pulled her cap down over her forehead in an attempt to shield her eyes from the driving snow. The horse-drawn traffic rumbled past and the clock on the St Pancras Church was booming out the hour. It was no wonder she failed to hear the approaching footsteps. She cannoned into the man who was struggling to open his umbrella, and the force of the encounter sent her purchases flying out of the basket onto the snowy pavement.

'Look where you're going!' Sally cried angrily. 'That's my supper lying on the ground.'

'You barged into me, you stupid boy.' The man lowered his umbrella, staring at her in the flickering light of the street lamp. 'Oh, I'm sorry, miss. Are you hurt?'

'No,' Sally said reluctantly. 'But the eggs are

smashed and the pies are covered in slush. That's our supper you've ruined and my pa will be furious.' She tilted her head back to glare at the man, who was dressed like a country gentleman, which was decidedly out of place in this part of London. He was younger than she had supposed, and his rugged features were creased in a worried frown.

'I am truly sorry.' He held out his hand. 'I was also at fault. You must allow me to reimburse you for the groceries.'

Sally looked down at the shattered eggs and even if she had wanted to rescue the pies, she was too late. Two half-feral dogs sprang from nowhere and pounced on the food, growling ferociously as they vanished into the shadows with their bounty. She had eaten very little that day and the temptation to accept his offer was overwhelming.

'Thank you,' she said reluctantly. 'It cost me elevenpence ha'penny.'

He put his hand in his pocket and took out a handful of small change. 'Here's a shilling, with my apologies.'

She took the halfpenny from her purse and exchanged it for the shiny silver coin. 'Normally I wouldn't accept,' she said gruffly. 'But as it happens I'm a bit short of the readies at the moment, so thanks again.' She turned away in case he changed his mind and she hurried back to the shop to repeat her order to a surprised Mr Jarvis.

*　　*　　*

'You've taken your time.' Ted looked up from the crumpled newspaper he had been attempting to read by the light of a candle stub and the glow from the coal fire. 'I'm starving. What kept you?'

Sally placed her basket on the table and unpacked the contents. 'I had a slight mishap on the way home from old Jarvis's shop, so I had to go back and get two more pies and a couple of eggs.' She took out a small cob loaf. 'And he must have felt sorry for me because he threw in the bread for nuppence.'

'It's probably stale then. Frank Jarvis never gives anything away, the old skinflint.' Ted smoothed the creased newspaper, peering short-sightedly at the print. 'One day I'll make enough money to buy a paper every day, instead of reading what other folks have thrown out.'

'Yes, that would be nice, Pa.' Sally took off her sodden jacket and cap, shaking out her long, dark hair.

Ted eyed her curiously. 'You still haven't told me what happened between here and Jarvis's shop.'

'It was snowing so hard that we didn't see each other until it was too late and he nearly knocked me over – well, to be fair I wasn't looking either. Anyway, the food went flying and landed on the pavement, and then, to cap it all, a couple of stray dogs wolfed the pies.'

'But you wasn't hurt, love?'

'Only my pride, Pa. And the fellow paid up, so I went back to the shop and we have supper after all.'

'You was lucky to meet a gentleman, that's all I can say. There's many who wouldn't be so generous.'

Sally took two plates from the dresser that her father had constructed from an old chest of drawers and some wooden shelving. 'Here you are. Enjoy the pie and I'll put the kettle on.'

'You're a good girl, Sal. I don't know what I'd do without you.'

She smiled and placed the kettle on the trivet in front of the fire. 'You'll never have to find out, Pa. We're a team, you and me, not forgetting Boney and Flower, of course.'

'Sit down and eat your supper.' Ted shifted uneasily in his chair. 'I think you'll have to take the cart out on your own tomorrow, love. My joints are playing up something terrible tonight. I doubt if I'll be able to get downstairs in the morning, let alone do me rounds.'

'It won't be the first time, Pa. I know the route like the back of my hand.'

'Just leave the heaviest things for Finn Kelly. He'll love that,' Ted added grudgingly. 'He's always trying to get one up on me.'

'Don't worry. I can handle Kelly. He won't get the better of me. That's a promise.'

Look out for
Dilly's next book

Rag-and-Bone
Christmas

Coming
Autumn 2020